Close to the Bone

Also by Jake Lamar

The Last Integrationist

Bourgeois Blues

Close

to the

Bone

A NOVEL

Jake Lamar

 Crown Publishers, Inc. New York

Copyright © 1998 by Jake Lamar

Published by Crown Publishers, Inc., 201 East 50th Street, New York, New York 10022. Member of the Crown Publishing Group.

Random House, Inc. New York, Toronto, London, Sydney, Auckland
www.randomhouse.com

CROWN and colophon are trademarks of Crown Publishers, Inc.

Printed in the United States of America

Design by Leonard Henderson

Library of Congress Cataloging-in-Publication Data
Lamar, Jake.
    Close to the bone / Jake Lamar.—1st ed.
        p. cm.
    I. Title.
    PS3562.A4216C56 1999
    813'.54—dc21   98-21773
                                    CIP

ISBN 0-517-70407-2

10 9 8 7 6 5 4 3 2 1

First Edition

For Dorli

Love is never any better than the lover. Wicked people love wickedly, violent people love violently, weak people love weakly, stupid people love stupidly, but the love of a free man is never safe.

—Toni Morrison,
The Bluest Eye

1

Amandla

1

"What is a black man?"

It was Dr. Emmett Mercy who posed the question. He sat in a warped folding chair in the basement of a Presbyterian church on the Upper West Side of Manhattan. When he entered the church a half hour earlier, at six thirty-five on this Thursday evening in September 1994, the sky over Broadway was a metallic gray; the air was dense and muggy but a fierce wind was kicking up. A hellacious storm seemed in the offing. The spartan, wood-paneled room in the basement was empty when Dr. Mercy arrived, but rancid with the smell of stale coffee, the telltale sign that a meeting of Alcoholics Anonymous had recently taken place there. Dr. Mercy expected only five participants in tonight's workshop. He set up six folding chairs in a circle in the center of the room and, on a nearby table, arranged five hardcover copies of his book, *Blactualization: Everyday Strategies for Reconnecting with Your Authentic African American Self.* He paused for a moment to admire his portrait on the book jacket, relishing the image he projected in his somber three-piece suit, a gold watch chain glittering against the black vest, his starched white shirt and black tie, his thick forest of black hair combed straight back, bushy sideburns extending to his jaw, light brown eyes staring righteously behind round-lensed, gold-framed spectacles. Change the photo from full-color to sepia, Dr. Mercy mused, and it could have been taken in the late nineteenth century. Without making a conscious effort, Dr. Mercy, over the years, had come to resemble a figure from the time of Douglass or Du Bois.

"What *is* a black man?"

Dr. Mercy repeated his question, putting a dramatic emphasis on that second word, slowly turning his head around the small circle of black men, looking each participant in the eye. It was five minutes after seven. Dr. Mercy was pleased that all five men taking part in tonight's Amandla workshop had arrived on time, at seven o'clock sharp. After some initial chitchat—it turned out that two of the brothers at tonight's meeting had gone to college together but had not seen each other in eight years—Dr. Mercy had the men stand up, join hands, and recite the pledge he had composed: "We gather here tonight as strong black brothers, imbued with the wisdom of our ancestors, nourished by the love of our sisters, determined to protect our progeny. We meet in the spirit of togetherness, redemption, and empowerment. Amandla." Dr. Mercy loved the sound of the six men saying that word—the Xhosa word for "power," the first word that Nelson Mandela uttered to his followers after his release from prison in South Africa four years earlier—in unison. It sounded like "Amen," only more musical. The word conveyed a sense of purpose, the purpose that Dr. Mercy advertised in his literature for the Amandla workshops: "To help African American males resolve their conflicts, banish their bad habits, redeem their relationships, reclaim their unique African American identity, and gain a new sense of personal power. Black men empowering black men. That is the essence of Amandla."

Once the pledge was over, the men took their seats and Dr. Emmett Mercy posed his question. Then he posed it again and looked closely at his small audience, silently taking the measure of each participant:

There was Byron Jenks, evidently known to one and all as "Tiny," though, at five foot six, he didn't strike Dr. Mercy as being all that short. This was Tiny's second Amandla workshop and he stared raptly at Dr. Mercy, giving the group leader the absolute concentration he craved.

Sitting to the right of Tiny Jenks was Chester Beer; solid, stolid Chester, a deacon at Dr. Mercy's church in Hallisbury, New York. Chester Beer, wise-eyed and balding, a sixtyish widower whose ample girth only enhanced his natural air of gravitas, had attended all five of the previous Amandla workshops but had hardly said a word in any of them. Sometimes Dr. Mercy thought Chester came to the meetings just for the company.

To the right of Chester was the man who Dr. Mercy knew instinctively would be tonight's problem participant: Walker Du Pree, a light-skinned brother with reddish-brown dreadlocks and a smattering of freckles across his nose and cheeks. Everything about Walker, from the way he sat slumped in his folding chair—black-jeaned legs stretched out in front of him, crossed at the ankles—to the quizzical expression on his face—eyebrows arched, mouth smirking slightly—radiated insolence. Dr. Mercy would have to be on his guard with this character.

Next to Walker was Jojo Harrison, another first-timer, a middle-aged brother with a shaved head and glasses so heavily tinted that they were almost shades. He sat with his arms crossed in the leather jacket he had inexplicably decided to wear on this hot, late-summer night and that he declined to remove even though there was no air-conditioning in the church basement. His neutral expression seemed to be a scowl. Jojo would be a tough customer, though probably less tricky than Walker.

Finally, there was Hal Hardaway. The brother was casually *GQ*
in his linen suit and silk tie, a sleek briefcase propped beside his folding chair. Hal held his hands, palms pressed tightly together, as if in
prayer, to his lips, middle fingertips touching his nose. There was a
look of agitation on his face that Dr. Mercy did not know how to
interpret. As far as Dr. Mercy was concerned, Hal was tonight's guest
of honor. Tiny Jenks had phoned Emmett the night before to say that
he was bringing a friend, "a thirty-year-old senior vice president at
Burnish Enterprises," to the Amandla workshop. "The brother's in a
personal crisis," Tiny had said. Dr. Emmett Mercy was prepared to
help. He also knew that a connection at Burnish Enterprises—one of
the most successful black-owned businesses in America—could be,
well, advantageous to his cause.

Only five participants tonight. The lowest turnout yet. But Dr.
Mercy knew it wasn't the size of an audience that mattered most.
What mattered was who, precisely, you were addressing. And, inso-
far as conducting a workshop was a performance, Dr. Mercy was
determined, on this Thursday night in September 1994, to put on a
good show. Having twice posed the essential question, he was ready
to elaborate.

"A receptacle of this society's hate and fear? Is that all he is? Or
is he a valiant warrior? Or a victim? Who defines it? Who decides?
And by what standards?" Dr. Mercy's voice was firm, sonorous. He
had used this opening before and knew how effective it could be.
"How do we begin to discern the inextricably intertwined threads of
image and reality? How do we, in our own lives, reconcile the issues
that our blackness and our maleness confront us with on a daily
basis? How can you know the authentic you in a world that refuses
to acknowledge you as you truly are?" Dr. Emmett Mercy knew he
had everyone's attention now. Walker Du Pree was no longer smirking. The scowl had almost, but not quite, disappeared from Jojo Har-

rison's face. Dr. Mercy turned and gazed at Hal Hardaway. "I'm askin' *you*," he said, thrusting a forefinger at the expensively dressed and pensive young brother. "What is a black man?"

Hal took his hands away from his lips, cleared his throat, and in a tone that suggested both bewilderment and annoyance, said, "I don't understand the question."

*   *   *

When had Hal Hardaway's troubles started? Sometimes Hal dated the beginning of his psychic crisis to January 1, 1994, when, after only twenty-four hours of cohabitation, his relationship with Corky Winterset had already started to go awry. A few days later, the commercials for the Martin Luther King Jr. Day sales began airing. The campaign had been Hal's idea. "I have a dream," radio listeners heard Dr. King intone. "Today," an announcer quickly added, in a voice almost indistinguishable from Dr. King's, "the dream lives on— with Burnish Hair Care Products!" The King sound-alike then told listeners about the various pomades, relaxers, conditioners, and dyes, all available at half-price, in honor of the slain leader. The campaign was a huge success, but Hal felt sickened by it, sickened by himself.

Yet when he tried to trace the real origin of his malaise, he arrived at a later date. It was the morning of June 14, 1994, when he learned that one of his boyhood heroes, one of America's most prominent and admired black role models, O.J. Simpson, was the prime suspect in a grisly double murder. That summer, as the nation slavered over every detail of the fatal knifing of O.J.'s blond ex-wife and the waiter whose body had been found hacked up beside hers, Hal sank deeper and deeper into depression. He was losing touch with some of his best friends in New York, people who, only a year earlier, he had hung out with regularly. Nobody seemed to have time for him anymore. Hal knew that some of them resented the fact that he was now living with a white woman. And he resented their resentment—even as his relationship with Corky deteriorated. Meanwhile, his boss and mentor, Godfrey Burnish, who had once treated Hal like a possible successor, turned coolish on him, deliberately leaving him out of important meetings and decisions.

Soon, the true weirdness, the weirdness in Hal's head, began. He would hear bits of Negro spirituals in his dreams, scraps of slave songs he hadn't heard in years. He would wake up, unable to recall the shards of lyrics but realizing that all the songs were about death. About death and how good it was gonna be. About how you just couldn't wait to get to heaven. How heaven would provide all the peace denied you in this life of toil and violence and despair. In vivid flashes of daydream, Hal would see walls in front of him, huge structures like the Berlin Wall or the Great Wall of China, and imagine that a laser beam was shooting out of his forehead and sizzling, then destroying the walls, blasting them into heaps of rubble. He imagined himself careening crazily—going in the wrong direction—down a hectic one-way street, and a sentence kept running through his mind: "You're a car without a driver. . . . You're a car without a driver. . . . You're a car without a driver. . . ." He saw himself standing in some smoky, barren landscape, maniacally firing a machine gun and screaming his lungs out. A morbidity grew within him.

*   *   *

"I'm not trying to disrespect you, Dr. Mercy," Hal Hardaway said at the Amandla workshop in September 1994, when he thought he had reached the nadir of what was proving to be a miserable year. "I honestly don't understand the question. And I haven't read your book, so I can't comment on it. People tell me it's good, but I just don't feel like I need a manual on how to be black. I've been black my whole life. All my best friends are black. I work in a black company. Every girlfriend I've ever had, except one, has been black. I know blackness. I don't need to be in a workshop to find out what it is."

"Then why are you here?" Dr. Mercy asked.

Hal smiled shyly. "Tiny made me come."

*　　*　　*

"The bitch is ugly."

Hal Hardaway was baffled by people who underestimated the dominance of the visual. How could anyone doubt that sight was the most important of the senses? Certain things, certain people, were pleasing to the eye; others were not. Hal did not believe in innate, unchanging, or universal standards of beauty or ugliness. What looked right and what did not differed from one society to another. And in the society that Hal knew, a black man and a white woman, or a white man and a black woman, walking down the street holding hands was an eye-catcher. Whether or not the sight was pleasing depended on the individual, but whatever one's feelings, an interracial couple was a notable sight, something that the average American eye registered as unusual visual data. Hal had never borne any hostility toward white people. There were countless white women he found attractive, and he had flirted with white girls all his life. But he never considered asking one out on a date. Because whenever Hal spotted an interracial couple walking down the street, he always felt the same little shiver. It just didn't *look* right.

Hal saw not only with his own eyes but with the eyes of other people. His first five girlfriends—Miranda, Cassandra, Diandra, and Alexandra back at Craven University, and Dahlia in New York— were the sort of women he looked right with. He considered them

consensus beauties, the sort of women who even the most idiosyn-
cratic beholder would have to say were—on a purely aesthetic level—
pleasing to the eye. Hal relished the little thrill, the contact high, of
being with a beautiful woman in a public place. During his years with
Dahlia, he knew they were an arresting vision: the leggy and volup-
tuous sister with the milk-chocolate skin, silky fine, close-cut hair,
and mile-high cheekbones walking hand in hand with the well-built,
suavely handsome brother. Hal saw himself with Dahlia in the way
he believed strangers saw them. They just looked right together.

When a stranger looked at Hal and Dahlia walking down the
street together, hand in hand, she could assume she knew why they
were a couple: because Dahlia was a beautiful black woman. That
same stranger, when looking at Hal and Corky walking down the
street together, hand in hand, would also assume she knew why they
were a couple: because Corky was white. But Hal was not drawn to
Corky *because* of her whiteness; he was drawn to her *in spite* of it.
Hal did not stop seeing with other people's eyes when he fell in love
with Corky. He just stopped caring about the stares of strangers. And
the more in love with Corky Hal was, the less he cared, the less he
even noticed other people's eyes on them. Conversely, as his love for
Corky waned, so his awareness of the eyes of strangers increased.
With any of his previous girlfriends, Hal could look at them and
know why he was with them. But often he would look at Corky and
think, Why you? Of all the women I could fall in love with, why am
I with *you?* It was not for the reason that the stranger on the street
would assume. He knew that. And it surprised him. Because, before
he fell in love with Corky, he would, upon seeing a man like himself
with a woman like Corky, have made the same assumption as the
stranger. But knowing that he was not in love with Corky because she
was white and knowing that he was not in love with her because she
was a consensus beauty—because she was certainly not that—Hal

could not come up with any rationale for his relationship with Corky. He was unfathomably in love with her.

"The bitch is ugly."

Yolanda Yancy, vice president in charge of media coordination, was Hal Hardaway's immediate deputy at Burnish Enterprises. She was young, ambitious, and competent. But, somehow, she had not yet mastered the company's new phone system. One morning in June, Yolanda was on another line when Hal called to ask her a question about *Esteem* magazine newsstand sales. She said she would call him right back, then pushed a button on her console, returning to her conversation in progress and believing that she had dispatched Hal. But her boss had not had time to hang up on his end before he heard Yolanda say, "Speak of the devil."

"That was him?" Hal heard another woman ask.

"Mm-hm," Yolanda hummed affirmatively.

"And you saw him with this woman?"

"Last night. At Delusio's."

This was the seafood restaurant in Tribeca where Hal and Corky had dined the night before. Hal stayed on the line, trying not to breathe.

"And?" Yolanda's friend asked.

"The bitch is ugly."

Hal was flabbergasted. Corky? Ugly?

"Anyway, lemme go deal with this fool," Yolanda said. "I'll tell you all about it at lunch."

How, Hal wondered, feeling almost dazed as he hung up the phone, could anybody consider Corky ugly? Okay, so she wasn't a supermodel. Her looks might not appeal to everybody. But just about anybody, looking at her objectively, would have to concede that Corky was, at the very least, cute. Depending on your tastes, you might very well call her pretty. To some eyes, Corky might be considered average-looking, not especially attractive, maybe even plain. But ugly? *Ugly.* Wasn't Yolanda pushing it a bit? Or maybe she was speaking for a lot of strangers? Was it possible that most people eyeing Corky as she walked down the street, hand in hand, with Hal, or dined with him in a restaurant, would think she was ugly?

"You're so pretty," Hal said as he lay naked with Corky, staring into her eyes. It was one of their first nights together. Hal had already come but was still semihard, throbbing languidly inside her, Corky rhythmically tightening, then relaxing her muscles, giving Hal the delicious sensation of having his body sucked into hers.

"I have a monkey face," Corky sighed. "That's what my mother used to call me: Monkey Face."

"Aw, she just meant you were cute."

"No," Corky said, her voice turning serious, "she didn't. My mother thought my sister was beautiful. She thought I looked like a monkey."

Staring closely, his face only inches from hers, Hal noticed how wide-set Corky's blue eyes were, how her eyebrows were distinctly darker than her light brown hair and how a few faint strands nearly joined them above her nose, a nose that had a slightly puggy, pert little upturn to it. "I think you're beautiful," Hal whispered.

Corky squeezed her muscles tighter. Hal pulsated in her wetness. "My mother," Corky said, her breath quickening, "said my shoulders were too broad and my breasts too small and my ass too big."

"I love your shoulders and your breasts and your ass."

"My sister has good hair." Corky's hips moved faster. "My mother says I have bad hair."

"Damn," Hal moaned, "you people obsess on that, too?"

"My hair is too thin and wispy." Corky's hands gripped Hal's buttocks, pushing him deeper inside her. "When it gets too long, it looks like straw in the wind." Corky was gasping between words.

"That's—uhn!—what—ahh!—my mo—my uhn!—my mother—oh!—says."

"I love your hair."

"Do you?"

"I love your face."

"Oh God."

"I think you're beautiful."

"Aiiiiiiiiieeeeeeeee!" Corky was lost in a scream as her orgasm erupted.

The memory of that moment made Mr. Bone swell with affection and pride as Hal sat in his office at Burnish Enterprises that June morning. The telephone rang, disrupting his erotic reverie. It was Yolanda Yancy, returning his call. She gave him the numbers on *Esteem* newsstand sales, speaking in a crisply professional tone. A year earlier, Hal had enjoyed a joshing, harmlessly flirtatious relationship with his deputy. But, gradually, Yolanda had become more formal, almost stilted, with him. After Yolanda imparted her information, Hal hung up without saying "Thank you" or "Good-bye."

* * *

"I'm tired of being the national scapegoat!" Hal Hardaway exploded. Though Hal had seemed reluctant to participate in the Amandla workshop that night in September, Dr. Emmett Mercy gently but persistently pressed him. While the other workshop participants—Tiny Jenks, Chester Beer, Walker Du Pree, and Jojo Harrison—stared at him, Hal launched into a tirade: "Is that the sort of thing you're lookin' for me to say? 'Cause that's what I feel. I'm fucking sick and tired of black men serving as America's designated scapegoat! Some white guy can't get a job or get into the school he wants to go to, who does he blame? A black man! White women are scared to walk the streets after dark, who do they blame? Black men! And if a sister can't find a date, or a husband, that's the fault of black men, too! Who are the main figures in the scandals of the nineties? Clarence Thomas, Mike Tyson, Michael Jackson, O.J. Simpson!"

"The four horsemen of the racial apocalypse," Walker said dryly.

Hal ignored the comment. He was speaking rapidly now, the words tumbling out of him. "And look at what the subject is in each of those cases. Thomas—sexual harassment. Tyson—date rape. Jackson—child-molesting. O.J.—jealousy and wife-beating. It's all about sex! It's all about black men and their dicks! And the people love it! The American public can't get enough of it!" Hal stopped short, suddenly self-conscious as he noticed how intently the other men were staring at him.

"Please," Dr. Mercy said, "continue."

"Um, no," Hal said, flustered. "That's all. That's all I wanted to say. Somebody else talk now."

"So hook me up. I'm free this Saturday."

Pauline eyed Walker carefully, as if trying to visualize him with one of her friends. "I'm trying to think of who's the most whitish."

"Would you stop it with this whitish crap, please?"

"I could set you up with Sadie," Pauline said absently, as if she were talking only to herself.

"Sadie?" The name sounded curiously old-fashioned to Walker, making him think of corsets and hoop skirts.

"She's pretty dark, though."

"The blacker the better. What's her phone number?"

"Hey, you're gonna take all the joy out of matchmaking for me. I'll call Sadie and see if I can arrange something for Saturday night. This is kind of short notice. She might be busy."

Pauline, however, knew that Sadie was free. The two of them had been discussing Walker for weeks. Pauline could tell that when she mentioned Sadie's name to Walker, it did not ring a bell. But Sadie Broom remembered Walker Du Pree very well. How could she not? He had been one of Hal Hardaway's roommates.

*   *   *

As soon as he saw Sadie enter the bar, Walker remembered her, remembered seeing her around the Craven campus. What he had not remembered was how pretty she was. Could she really have been this good-looking the last time he saw her, seven years earlier? Sadie Broom had the exact same features, the same rich, dark complexion, the same extraordinary tangle of black hair that swirled to her shoul-ders in lush tendrils—how Walker longed to grab two greedy hand-f her hair, feel it crinkle between his fingers—and the same soft,

Her demeanor was just as Walker remembered it: perky. here Walker discovered a poignance in Sadie: While she rily at the bar, her eyes—which slanted downward, ever so slightly, at the corners—looked as if they were on the verge of tears. Maybe this was the beauty Walker saw in Sadie, the beauty that had escaped his notice back at Craven U.: the exquisite tension between Sadie's upbeat manner and her crying eyes. Or maybe it was that Sadie had somehow grown into her looks. Perhaps some women reached their apex of physical attractiveness at nineteen and others, like Sadie, peaked later. Or maybe Walker, over the years, had developed a different way of seeing.

Sitting at the bar, Sadie and Walker had a good laugh over Pauline's little subterfuge, setting up two people who already (sort of) knew each other on a blind date. (Sadie did not reveal that she had been Pauline's knowing coconspirator.) They exchanged information on Hal Hardaway, who, at Craven, had been one of their few mutual friends. Neither had seen him since college. They had both heard through the grapevine that Hal had given up his fledgling acting career and enrolled at Craven Law School. Walker had heard about Hal's two failed attempts at passing the bar exam—something Sadie had not known. Sadie knew that Hal was now working at Burnish Enterprises—something Walker had not known. They joked about the New York dating scene and complained good-naturedly about their jobs. As they left the bar and headed for an Italian restaurant they both knew and liked, Walker felt uncharacteristically optimistic. Maybe, at last, he had found a soul mate.

*   *   *

"I have trouble trusting black men."

By the time Sadie made that pronouncement, Walker was in hoping to make it to the end of their date without having a nast frontation. From the moment they arrived at the Italian re they disagreed on practically everything.

Walker raved about a film he had just seen, *The Crying Game.* "You *liked* that movie?" Sadie asked incredulously.

Sadie was thrilled by the week-old Clinton presidency, saying that it heralded a new beginning for liberal politics in America. Walker told Sadie he thought Bill Clinton was a spineless weasel and he'd had to hold his nose when he voted for him.

Walker spoke of his fondness for rap music. Sadie hated it.

Sadie was sick of New York. Walker couldn't imagine living anyplace else.

Some of Sadie's best friends at Craven U. had been people Walker couldn't stand, and though Sadie was only passingly familiar with most of Walker's college buddies, she'd had bad impressions of almost every one of them.

When the subject turned to social responsibility, Sadie said, "I don't know how any black person could buy drugs when you consider how the drug trade has destroyed our communities." Walker did not tell her that he had smoked a pipeful of marijuana before their date.

"I think everything happens for a reason," Sadie said.

"Really?" Walker said. "I don't think anything happens for a reason."

They were sitting in sullen silence by the time dessert arrived. Walker was perplexed by how quickly the good rapport between them had deteriorated. Searching for a subject they could avoid clashing over, Walker asked Sadie about her family life. "My father abandoned us when I was twelve," Sadie said.

"That must have been rough," Walker said sympathetically.

"He took off with a younger woman."

"Damn. That must have been especially hard on your mother."

"Of course. Black women have it tough enough already. When your husband leaves you for something that's supposed to be superior to you, it's devastating."

"Oh. Was your father's mistress white?"

"Nobody could really figure that out. I always thought she was a black person trying to pass."

"Did your parents' breakup affect the way you view relationships?"

"Not really. . . . Except that . . . I have trouble trusting black men."

Walker immediately turned and waved to the waiter. "Check, please."

*　　*　　*

Beware the single young woman who displays pictures of other people's children. There is a covetousness there. This is what Walker had come to believe. So he got the willies when, sitting in Sadie's living room, he noticed, on bookshelves, on the fireplace mantel, on the coffee table, photos of newborns, toddlers, and kindergartners, the progeny of Sadie's friends and cousins. At first Walker had been startled when Sadie suggested he come up to her apartment for a drink, but then he figured that since their date had been a disaster, Sadie merely wanted to make a final rapprochement. Just so that the evening could end on a conciliatory note. Just so there would be no hard feelings. Just so Pauline wouldn't feel too bad about having set them up. Walker decided to have one quick drink, to keep the conversation light, and to get the hell out of Sadie's apartment before they started grating on each other's nerves again. "Cute kids," Walker said, pointing to the sun-dappled portrait of grinning twins that rested on the side table by Sadie's couch.

"Those are my cousin Tina's boys," Sadie said wistfully. "What a couple of rascals. I love 'em to death. I don't think I could do what Tina did, though."

"What? Give birth to twins?"

"No. Marry a white guy. Tina's husband is Jewish."

Walker tried to stay calm. The last thing he wanted was an alter-cation. "You don't approve?"

"It's not that I don't approve. It's just that I want to have black children."

"You don't consider Tina's kids black?"

"Not exactly." Sadie paused, searching for the right words. Walker downed the last of his cognac. He was ready to get the hell out of there. "I don't want to sound like a bigot," Sadie continued, "because I'm not. I've had relationships with two white guys since college. But when I would think about possibly having children with those guys, I just thought . . . I just thought I couldn't do it. I don't think I would feel as close to my children if they were half-white."

"So even though the babies would come out of *your* body, you would feel less love for them if they had a white father." Walker could hear the rising anger in his voice.

"I didn't say less love."

"Now, lemme get this straight. You say you have trouble trusting black men but you'll only have children with a black man."

"With a black man I could trust."

"Do you think you have a trusting nature?"

Sadie gave Walker a look he found completely unreadable and said, "Yes." Then she pounced.

All the tension between them exploded in bed and Walker, in mid-intercourse, marveled for the forty-eighth time at how you could never be sure, never absolutely certain, before the fact, of how a par-ticular woman would make love. Walker, at dinner, had guessed Sadie would be a somewhat passive lover, the type of woman who held back, who didn't throw herself into sex with abandon. But Sadie Broom was a lover of ecstatic wantonness, a take-charge partner who Walker could tell savored the human body in detail, relishing every sensation, all the sounds and smells of sex. When they came together at exactly the same moment, Sadie was staring straight into Walker's eyes. Her gaze was riveted to his, her soft, sad eyes filled with a ferocious affection. Walker sensed something profoundly strong in Sadie's gaze, a feeling he knew was reflected back to her. It was as if they were each seeing into the other—a feeling of the deepest recognition.

*   *   *

"I hope I'm not jumping the gun by saying this," Walker said to Sadie as they sat in a booth in her favorite diner on the morning after their first night together, "but I always tell women right away that I'm not interested in getting married, that I don't particularly want to have children, that this is not a goal of mine, nothing I've ever desired, at least not since the age of about twelve. *I don't want to get married.* I always tell women this. And they never believe me."

"That's because they think they'll change you," Sadie said.

"Yes. But they shouldn't. They should believe me."

"Well," Sadie sighed. A slim, self-confident smile crept across her face, and Walker could see her not believing him. "People come into your life for a reason."

Walker let out a low groan and laid his head on the Formica-top table. Winter morning sunlight crashed through the window and glinted on the silverware that rested an inch from Walker's nose. "Aw, shit."

Sadie rubbed his neck, a bit too roughly. "Don't be silly."

"You don't believe me. I can see you not believing me."

"Oh, just relax, you. Nobody's rushing anything."

It was the arrogance of it that always amazed Walker. How could they always be so sure of themselves, so absolutely certain that they would make you want what they wanted, even when you told them, flat out, right off the bat, that you didn't want it?

"I was always honest with you," Walker would say nearly two years later, during their breakup. "I always told you the truth."

"Just because you told me the truth doesn't mean I have to like it!" Sadie would snap.

But Walker wasn't asking her to like it. Just to hear it, to take it into account. There was a failure of imagination on Sadie's part, an inability to believe that Walker's reluctance could possibly match her wanting—such a powerful and consuming thing was the wanting. The sheer force of her wanting was so great, Sadie assumed it would wear down the reluctance of a wishy-washy mere male.

*   *   *

During his first year with Sadie, Walker came to understand, in an almost physical way, the idea of halfheartedness. Because it was only when compared to his feeling for Sadie that Walker realized all his previous relationships—none of which had lasted more than a few months—had been halfhearted. With Sadie, Walker's heart actually felt full. It was this sensation of full-heartedness that, to Walker, defined being in love. The sensation would begin to fade after that first year, and when that happened, Walker imagined he could feel the fullness of his heart diminishing, like a balloon that someone was slowly letting the air out of. Yet even when Walker's heart had been most full, even when he was most in love with Sadie, he did not want to marry her. Over the years, his feeling about marriage—and children, since, in Walker's mind, the two always went together—had evolved from distaste to fear to something that had now taken on the power of primal superstition.

Sadie did not confront Walker's terror of marriage; she ignored it.

After all, she and Walker disagreed on so many things, Sadie had learned to pay no attention to her boyfriend's opinions when they differed from hers. That, in any event, was her approach during their first year together. But around the time of their first anniversary, in January 1994, Sadie realized she would have to change her tactics. Both Sadie's mother, Lorraine, and her therapist, Dr. Littlejohn, said that Walker suffered from the Peter Pan syndrome, a typically male reluctance to grow up. Sadie was advised to take a harder line with Walker. She started urging him to look for a better job. He was a talented graphic designer, yet he'd spent seven years in the same rut, in the layout department at the *Downtown Clarion*, an alternative weekly newspaper. Sadie suggested, on a more or less daily basis, that Walker pursue employment in advertising. She also began to criticize, more aggressively than before, Walker's recreational pot-smoking. She tried to get him to keep more regular hours, to stop hanging out late at night with other Peter Pans. Every Sunday, she thrust the real-estate section of *The New York Times* at him. Sadie let Walker know that it was time they moved in together. She thought they should rent—or even buy—an apartment in Brooklyn Heights or Park Slope, the two most upscale neighborhoods in Brooklyn. That was what all the young couples she knew were doing. "We're both going to turn thirty this year," Sadie reminded Walker, repeatedly. "It's time to get serious about life." By May, Sadie believed she had made excellent progress with Walker. After four months of persistently pressuring him to change his ways, Sadie thought Walker was ready to become the mature and responsible man she knew he could be. What Sadie did not realize was that, over those four months, Walker had fallen out of love with her.

One night, Sadie and Walker sat in a crowded sports bar on the Upper West Side, watching a basketball game. Sadie had never been much of a fan, but the Knicks were in the Eastern Conference finals and had a good chance of winning the championship. Walker was unusually quiet as he munched his peanuts and sipped his beer. At halftime, Sadie asked if he was all right. Walker leaned forward and spoke in the edgy, earnest tone of someone revealing a deep, dark secret. "Do you ever just feel like . . . an alien?"

Sadie took a quick glance around the sports bar and noticed that she and Walker were the only black people in the place. "Sure," Sadie said. "Anytime I'm surrounded by a bunch of white folks like this." She laughed.

Walker did not crack a smile. "I'm not talking about a racial thing. I'm talking about feeling disconnected. All the time. From all people. I'm talking about looking at the way human beings organize their lives and thinking, Jesus Christ, I just don't get it. I am just not with the program. And I don't know how to *get* with the program. It's like feeling you're from another fucking planet. And feeling this way *all the time*." Walker paused. "Do you know what I'm talking about?" he asked beseechingly.

Sadie recommended professional counseling.

*   *   *

Walker did not object to therapy in principle. He just didn't feel like doing it. But in the past few years he had begun to feel actual peer pressure to see a shrink. Most of his white and many of his black friends were doing it. It was starting to seem like part of a ritualized trajectory for a lot of young couples he knew: go into therapy, get an apartment together in Park Slope or Brooklyn Heights, get married, have a kid. As soon as she started seeing Dr. Littlejohn, Sadie became a proselytizer of the talking cure. Walker told her that he might be interested in it—someday, but not now. Sadie seemed to think that Walker's reluctance to move in with her constituted a psychological dysfunction. Walker said she might very well be right—but he still wasn't interested in therapy right now. Sadie told him his aversion to therapy was due to "fear and ignorance." Walker told Sadie that she simply liked having authority figures in her life and Dr. Littlejohn was just another older person she enjoyed obeying. He, on the other hand, was inherently skeptical about anyone in a position of authority. Sadie looked at Walker in the same way his aunt Agnes had looked at him when he was a teenager and told her he did not believe in God. It was a look that said, "You pathetic fool. Will you never see the light?" Eventually, Sadie began to press for "couples therapy." This struck Walker as particularly absurd: a paid mediator explaining two lovers to each other. It was really like hiring a parent, wasn't it? Like having your mom or dad step in to settle a dispute between you and a sibling. Or perhaps it was like hiring an interpreter, someone allegedly fluent in the languages of both male and female. But if a couple communicated so poorly that they needed a translator, what were they doing together anyway? Walker saw couples therapists as eerie ghosts of future arbitrators, like divorce lawyers.

*   *   *

It is common for adults to lament their unhappy childhoods, but their misery tends to be retrospective. As children, they may actually have been quite content. Only as miserable adults do they decide that they must have been miserable children. Walker Du Pree, however, hated his childhood while he was experiencing it. He hated doing all the things kids have to do, all the song-singing, game-playing, and nap-taking. He found most other children ridiculous and wanted desperately to be a grown-up. Yet from about the age of five, he regarded most grown-ups with suspicion. Not that he thought they were sinister. It was just that you couldn't really trust them. Grown-ups were full of unreliable information and dubious advice.

"Are you having a happy childhood?"

At the most unexpected moments—while they were standing in the frozen-foods section of the supermarket or sitting in the Laundromat or when Walker was lying on his bed reading a book—Gina Du Pree would grab her son by both shoulders and, in a tone that begged for an affirmative response, pose the question. Little Walker invariably felt compelled to lie: "Yes, Mom." "Sure, Mom." "Of course, Mom."

"Am I a good mom to you?"

"You're the best mom in the world," Walker would answer. Because he felt it was his duty to say so.

"It's not easy, you know." Once he had reassured her, Gina always let Walker know how difficult it was raising him. "I have to do everything myself. Bringing up a child is rough for *two* parents. But when you have to function all alone, like I have to, it's twice as hard. You understand I'm doing the best I can, don't you?"

"I understand, Mom."

"Good." Then Gina would usually give her son an ardent hug. "You're my favorite little boy," she would say. Walker knew his mother meant well, but he always considered that a hollow compliment. He was, after all, Gina's only child. Why *wouldn't* he be her favorite little boy?

Walker knew that his mother worked for Planned Parenthood, but it wasn't until he was nine or ten that he understood what Planned Parenthood was. Walker began to realize that Gina Du Pree's parenthood had been anything but planned. As a boy Walker felt— not consciously, but on a more painful, subterranean level—that Gina wanted to help young women avoid the same mistake she had made, the mistake being Walker.

"I've had to make a lot of sacrifices for you," Gina would always tell her son, before adding, sweetly, unconvincingly, "and every one has been worth it."

Most weekday mornings, after Walker had peed and brushed his teeth but before he got dressed for school, Gina would call him into her bedroom for "snuggle time." Walker, still wearing his pajamas, would curl up with Gina in her bed. His mother would hold him tight, caressing him and sighing. Walker loved the smell of his mother during snuggle time. In her bed, Gina had a smell that she did not have out of it. And Gina's naked body felt so deliciously soft and squishy, a way it never felt when Walker hugged her when she was all dressed up. Snuggle time usually lasted about ten minutes. Then Gina would get up and make them breakfast.

Gina never sat down with Walker to explain the "facts of life." Instead, realizing that her son preferred books to the company of other children, she gave him, on his ninth birthday, a four-volume collection, specially created for youngsters, called *The Human Cycle Library*. Whenever Walker had a question about sexuality that Gina did not wish to answer, she referred him to *The Human Cycle Library*.

Until Walker was twelve, he and Gina did almost all domestic chores together. Then, one day, as they returned from the Laundromat, Gina said, "Was that semen that I found in your sheets?"

Thanks to *The Human Cycle Library*, Walker knew that it was. He had, in fact, been anticipating his first wet dream for months. "Yes," he said, trying to conceal his pride. Gina just nodded.

After that, there was no more snuggle time. Gina began to divide the chores between them. She stopped asking Walker if he was having a happy childhood. In a sense, Walker and Gina went their separate ways. Walker started having girlfriends. And Gina, for the first time in Walker's life, started having boyfriends. Walker would never tell anyone about snuggle time. But he would always remember those mornings he spent in his mother's arms as the only regular occasions in his childhood when he was anything but unhappy.

*   *   *

He was a beautiful runner, a gliding, loping, deerlike runner who, to Walker's nine-year-old eyes, was instantly distinguishable from those other players who just seemed to barrel ahead with the ball, moving a few yards upfield before they disappeared in a pile of other bulky, helmeted bodies. Walker's uncle Fred was always coming by to watch football games with him, and though Walker had little interest in sports of any kind, he watched the games to make Uncle Fred feel good, knowing that his mother's brother was doing this out of some peculiarly masculine sense of duty and kindness since Walker didn't have a father around to do things like watch football games with him. So Walker and Uncle Fred would sit on the couch while Gina made a big Sunday dinner—she always made a big dinner on those Sundays when Fred came to her home in Harrowside, Brooklyn, a working-class and thoroughly integrated neighborhood where blacks, Jews, Italians, Irish, Greek, Chinese, and Puerto Ricans lived in peaceful, if wary, coexistence—watching the Jets or the Giants and whatever team they were playing against, or some other game with two teams from some other part of the country, Uncle Fred guzzling beer and shouting at the TV, his exhortations and triumphant yelps sounding so similar to his outbursts of disgust or disappointment that Walker often had trouble telling which team—the good guys or the bad guys—was winning. Once in a while, Uncle Fred would try to explain a rule of the game to Walker, but usually he acted as if Walker was already knowledgeable about football, and since Walker didn't even know what to ask, and was not all that interested in learning the details anyway, he just nodded along and took his cues from Uncle Fred, cheering for the good guys and heckling the bad guys—when, that is, he could tell the difference between his uncle's cheers and his heckles. Walker rarely had a sense of individual players. Whether they were black or white, playing offense or defense, all these men seemed pretty much the same to him. Except for that beautiful runner, who moved with fluid grace, eluding tacklers as if they were immobile lumps on the field, dodging, spinning, looking almost as if he were sailing through the air, like Spiderman swinging on his webropes, whirling around skyscrapers in Walker's favorite cartoon show. Whether in a game or a snippet of highlight film, Walker could always pick number 32 of the Buffalo Bills from out of the crowd. And he had that delightful name that any nine-year-old could love: O.J. . . . Juice!

Years later, Walker would have few memories of his father, but perhaps the brightest was of a Sunday afternoon when he was nine and Christian was visiting New York. Walker sat beside his father in Christian's Volkswagen. He could never remember where it was they were driving to or from. But he remembered they were listening to a football game on the car radio: the New York Jets vs. the Buffalo Bills. Maybe Gina had told Christian that his son liked football. Certainly Christian did not seem to Walker to be a fan, a true fan, the way his uncle Fred was. But Christian listened intently to the game as he drove and Walker paid close attention, too. They were not rooting for the Jets or against the Bills that Sunday afternoon in December 1973. They were rooting for O.J. Simpson. As snow cascaded on the New York City area, Juice, at Shea Stadium in Queens, was attempting to break the single-season rushing record. And Walker, who a week earlier did not even know what "rushing" meant, understood the significance of this event. Christian and Walker cheered when O.J. broke the record. But the game was not over. Play after play, it seemed, O.J. kept running with the ball. Christian's tiny car, with hot air blowing from the vents on the dashboard, warming Walker's face, was filled with exhilaration. Walker had never seen his father so animated. As the game was coming to a

close, after O.J. had broken the two-thousand-yard barrier—"Two
thousand yards," Christian said, shaking his head in awe, *"in a single season,"* practically whispering the last four words, giving each
syllable a gravity that made Walker recognize the magnificence of
this achievement—Christian and Walker were stuck in a traffic jam,
somewhere in Manhattan. Even though the Jets had lost the game,
all the drivers began honking their horns in celebration at the final
gun. Christian cheered and honked his horn, too. Everybody loved
O.J. And Walker felt privileged to be sharing this special moment in
history with his dad.

*   *   *

The funny thing was that Walker Du Pree had always associated his
father with snow. One of his earliest memories was of waddling
around in a cumbersome snowsuit, tumbling again and again but
bouncing back up after he hit the snow, feeling as if the cold air was
pinching his face as he tried to help, but mainly watched, his father
build a snowman. Christian Severance's head and most of his face
were covered in hair. Bushy brown hair dropped like a curtain just
above his bright blue eyes; his bright pink lips poked through the
coarse jungle of his beard. (Christian Severance was a hippie—that
was what Uncle Fred always said.) Walker, who couldn't have been
much older than three, was amazed that his father wore no gloves; he
was mesmerized by the sight of Christian's blunt-fingered hands turning scarlet as they scooped and clutched and molded huge chunks of
snow. Then there was that day when O.J. Simpson broke the rushing
record and Walker and his father sat in Christian's Volkswagen as
snow fell on New York. And that Sunday afternoon when Walker
was twelve and his father took him to a fancy Manhattan restaurant
for brunch and the management had to lend Christian—still a hairy

hippie in January 1977—a necktie, since all men dining in the place were required to wear one. Walker seemed to look at his father through different eyes that day. Maybe it was because he hadn't seen him in a couple of years. Or maybe it was because Walker, in his pubescence, was becoming even more critical. But at this Sunday brunch, Walker began to regard his father with a sentiment more harsh than the usual skepticism he felt toward adults. It happened when Christian described, in loving detail, his favorite pastime: ice-camping. His voice filled with emotion, Christian told his son how he relished journeying alone into deserted, frozen terrain with just a few days' provisions in his backpack. Without even a *tent:* As the sun went down, Christian explained, he would unfurl his sleeping bag in the snow, strip down to his thermal underwear, and tuck himself in for the night as the wind howled around him. He would awake with the first light, strap on the backpack, and go marching alone again, across the frigid snowscape. Christian's eyes misted over and he said that he only felt truly at peace, only felt "close to God," when he was alone ice-camping. Walker said nothing. This was when he began to consider his father a fool.

Finally, there was Christmas in Vermont, in 1982, during Walker's freshman year at Craven University, the last time he would ever see his father and the first and only time he would meet other members of the Severance family. Snow again. Walker remembered standing alone on the porch, after everyone else had gone to bed, as a blizzard kicked up. Watching the snow swirling furiously in the icy night air, Walker knew he would never be invited back to the Severance country house. He also knew he didn't want to be.

Snow. Always snow.

So after absorbing the series of shocks dealt by the Severance family attorney, who called him at his Greenwich Village apartment early one evening in June 1994 to tell him that his father had died, that the funeral to which he had not been invited had taken place three months earlier, that Christian had named him in his will, that the will had been contested by an unnamed family member but that he would inherit the full amount that had been bequeathed to him, Walker, as he hung up the phone, could not help but laugh over the way his father's life had ended: Christian Severance had frozen to death, alone, near a mountaintop in Alaska. He had almost reached the summit of Mount Connerie when, for some reason, he stopped climbing. Walker imagined his father, wielding picks and axes, scaling sheer, icy walls of mountain rock, maybe even reciting Rudyard Kipling to himself:

If you can force your heart and nerve and sinew
To serve your turn long after they are gone . . .

Walker envisioned Christian, fatigued, collapsing in the snow, struggling to sit up. Walker saw snowflakes clinging to Christian's beard—though he knew his father no longer had a beard, that the last time he saw him, that awful Christmas in '82, his father was clean-shaven and wore his hair fashionably short—then clustering, encrusting, turning the brown bush white. Walker could see his father's teeth through the frosted beard, locked in a grimace-smile as Christian exulted perversely in his consummate solitude, his closeness to God, murmuring Kipling through his clenched teeth:

. . . And so hold on when there is nothing in you
Except the Will which says to them: "Hold on!"

This was the image that sent Walker into convulsions of laughter. He was still laughing when Sadie arrived at his apartment later that night, the guffaws exploding violently from him, like sobs.

*   *   *

Before she learned of his death, Sadie knew that Walker's father was a high-school teacher in Boston. She knew that Walker's father and mother had never been married but that Walker's father had been good about child-support payments. She knew that Walker had seen his father only a handful of times and that he did not like talking about him. Sadie believed that she and Walker had both been abandoned by their fathers. She believed that this common trauma was what drew them together. They were spiritually bound by a particular kind of hurt. Despite all the differences between them, they understood each other on the most intimate level. Because their family experience had been so similar.

Then Sadie found out Walker's recently deceased father had been white. She felt utterly betrayed.

Walker insisted that his father's race had not been important.

"If it wasn't important, why did you hide it from me?" Sadie fumed.

"I didn't hide it," Walker said. "The subject just never came up."

"Because I assumed he was black!"

"That's not my fault."

"But you let me assume it!"

"How do I know what you assume?"

"Don't play innocent with me, Walker! You let me assume something that you knew wasn't true. That's the same thing as lying."

"No it's not."

"You should have told me."

"Why?"

"Because it changes everything."

"How?"

"Because you're not really black."

"Do you know how ridiculous what you just said is?"

"I mean, of course you're black." Sadie paused and eyed Walker suspiciously. "I just think it's very weird that you never told me. We've been together a year and a half. You should have told me."

Walker could see that now Sadie believed she had found the key to him, the flaw that explained everything. Ah-ha! No wonder he didn't live in the black dorm at Craven U. or join the black fraternity. Ah-so! No wonder Walker had dated so many white women. Ha! Now, Sadie would conclude, she had discovered the source of her boyfriend's alienation. It all came down to race! It was Walker's racial confusion, his inability to locate his Black Identity, Sadie deduced, that prevented him from committing to her. No wonder he feared marriage and parenthood. He couldn't decide if he was black or white.

"I'm black!" Walker protested. "I consider myself black. Everyone I've ever known has considered me black. I barely knew my father. The only family I've ever really known has been black. There is no confusion."

Sadie ignored Walker's protestations. She knew she had found the key, the problem that needed to be solved.

*   *   *

Two months after he received his inheritance, Walker had quit his job, given half the money to his mother (who had not been included in Christian Severance's will), donated another fifty thousand dollars to charities Gina Du Pree considered worthy, and, so far as Sadie could tell, was spending his days alone in his apartment, getting stoned and drawing. One evening, Sadie went to Walker's place, sat him down on the couch, and told him it was time for serious decision-making. He had to figure out what he wanted to do with all this money. Sadie reminded Walker that she was a successful management consultant, a graduate of the Wharton School of Business. She could give him sound advice. She spoke of mutual funds and money market accounts. She suggested that real estate was the best investment, that maybe it was time for him to think seriously about buying an apartment. "Anyway, these are just some ideas," Sadie said reasonably. "I want to know what *you* want to do."

"You know what I really want to do?" Walker said. "I want to draw Paul Robeson."

"Pardon?"

"Paul Robeson. I want to draw Paul Robeson."

"You mean the 'Ol' Man River' guy?"

"Hah!" Walker barked. "That's all most people know about Paul Robeson. That he sang 'Ol' Man River'!"

"I know about Paul Robeson," Sadie snapped.

"Paul Robeson was an extraordinary individual," Walker continued passionately. "I mean extraordinary. He was a great singer—you know that—but he was also a great actor. He was valedictorian of his class at Rutgers *and* the star of the football team. He went to Columbia Law School—in *1915*! Paul Robeson was a genius!" Walker was talking rapidly now, angrily. "And America destroyed him. Because he started to speak out. He became a threat to the white people who had thought he was just a nice Negro man. He was too intelligent, too charismatic. He saw and said too much. So he was destroyed. 'Cause that's what they do to strong black men in America. They destroy you!"

Sadie had never heard Walker talk like this. She tried to regain control of the conversation. "Okay, Walk, but how are you going to *draw* Paul Robeson? Isn't he dead?"

"I'm gonna draw his life. I want to create a biography in drawings."

"What, like a Classic Comics version of the Paul Robeson story?"

"No," Walker said coldly. "Not like Classic Comics."

"What then? Something like that *Maus* guy? Something artsy? I'm just trying to understand what it is you have in mind."

"I want to draw Paul Robeson and I want to travel."

"But, Walker, honey, don't you want to do something *serious* with your money?"

"Yes."

"What?"

"Spend it." Walker rose from the couch. "I'm gonna make dinner now. You're welcome to stay if you like."

Alone in the kitchen, chopping vegetables, Walker thought of how often his father had come into his life as money. Back in Harrowside, whenever things were tight, Gina would say, "I hope we get a check from Boston soon." Walker knew that "Boston" meant his father. Every once in a while, Gina would take Walker out to a restaurant for dinner. When the bill arrived, she would invariably wince, then say, "What the hell. We got a check from Boston today." Checks from Boston financed Walker's Craven education and paid for his first trip to Europe after graduation. Now Walker had received the last check from Boston he would ever get. And he had a feeling about the money that he knew Sadie would never understand. Walker felt like the money was dirty. Contaminated. All he wanted to do was get rid of it. As quickly, and as pleasurably, as he could.

While Walker chopped vegetables in the kitchen, Sadie slipped into his bedroom and took a good look around. Drawings of Paul Robeson—depicted at different ages, in different poses, from different angles—were strewn about the room, taped to the walls. A fat biography of Robeson rested on Walker's desk. Walker had torn out the book's photos and tacked them to his bulletin board. The bedroom reeked of incense. Walker, Sadie thought, must have been smoking dope around the clock, compulsively killing his brain cells under the forbidding stares of a multitude of Paul Robesons. Sadie was so mad at Walker right now. And she had to stop herself from crying. The boy was obviously in need of help.

*   *   *

One night in September, three months after Walker had received his inheritance, Sadie Broom handed her boyfriend a glossy flyer advertising some sort of black male support group. "You won't see a shrink," Sadie said. "You won't even do couples therapy. At least you could try this."

"Dr. Emmett Mercy!" Walker hooted. "You gotta be kidding!"

"He talks about all the issues you've been struggling with."

"Is this one of those Reverend Ike characters?"

"He's written a book and I've heard it's pretty good. Maybe you should read it."

"I'll wait for the infomercial to come out."

"Please, Walk. Please."

Hearing the pain in Sadie's voice, Walker felt guilty. She was sincerely trying to help him. She was, in fact, trying to salvage their relationship. But Walker knew it was already over. So maybe he would go to this Amandla workshop. He could stand to make this one last concession to Sadie.

"Okay," Walker said. "I'll check it out. But if this Dr. Mercy is wearing a pompadour and a sequined suit, I'm outta there."

3

I don't know if I could say specifically, in just a few words, what a black man *is*," Tiny Jenks said in answer to Dr. Emmett Mercy's question at the Amandla workshop. "But I can say this about black people in general: We are a forgiving people. An extremely forgiving people. I mean, just to endure as a black person in this country, you have to forgive so much. You have to forgive American history. You have to forgive white people for their constant stupidity and insensitivity. You have to forgive other black people for the crazy, self-destructive things they do. You have to forgive yourself for your ambivalence. You *have* to forgive. Just to make it through this life without killing somebody. White people always say, 'Black people are so *angry*!' Like they're surprised. I say, 'Damn right we're angry. You'd be angry, too, if you had to forgive so much every goddamned day.' "

* * *

All through her teens and into her early twenties, Deirdre Watson played a game with her sister, Carla, called "Who Has the Better Deal?" Deirdre and Carla would sit in a park, on a bench in a mall, or in a fast-food restaurant and, scrutinizing the couples who passed before them, try to determine which member of each pair, based on looks alone, had gotten the better deal.

"Her," Deirdre would say as she and Carla considered a pudgy young woman holding hands with a well-proportioned young man.

"Him," Carla would decide as she and her sister regarded a pock-marked, middle-aged man with his arm around a trim, pert blonde.

"Even," Deirdre would rule as they checked out two lovers who were equally unattractive.

The Watson sisters didn't play that game anymore, but every once in a while, when she went out with her husband, Deirdre would imagine herself and Carla as teenagers, examining a couple like Deirdre and Tiny. And Deirdre would always feel a twinge of guilt over her youthful cruelty. Because she knew that judging who had the better deal between herself and Tiny would have been a no-brainer.

Deirdre knew what first attracted her to Tiny Jenks: It was his Boy Jesus voice. The night they met, at a dinner party hosted by mutual friends in the summer of 1992, Deirdre listened raptly as Tiny talked about his job at Marjorie Earl Hospital. In his ethereal voice—the same voice, Deirdre thought, that child actors playing the young Jesus Christ in corny religious movies always had—Tiny told of an eight-year-old in his ward with cerebral palsy who, that day, for the first time, walked on her crutches from one end of a long corridor to another, all by herself. Just as Deirdre's eyes were misting over from the poignance of the little girl's triumph—actually, from the tenderness and pride with which Tiny told the story—Tiny launched into a harangue about the insane and inhuman bureaucracy at the hospital. Now his heavenly lilt was laced with stridency, with righteous indignation. It would not be accurate to say that Deirdre swooned listening to Tiny—but she did feel charmed, touched, and a bit light-headed, all at the same time, by the voice that was, at once, mellifluous and angry. Deirdre felt that Tiny's character was shining through his voice. Despite her enchantment, Deirdre was slightly vexed that she felt drawn to someone who reminded her of the Boy Jesus. Deirdre had always been skeptical about Christianity. Astrology was her religion.

At the close of the dinner party, Deirdre handed Tiny Jenks her business card. Tiny, cardless, scribbled his phone number on a napkin. "Could you also write down your birthday?" Deirdre asked. "And the city where you were born? And your exact time of birth? If you know it." Tiny laughed and gave her the information. As soon as she got back to her apartment, Deirdre fed Tiny's coordinates into the astrology program in her computer. With the punch of a key, Tiny's birth chart appeared on the screen, colorful planets arranged around a zodiac. Deirdre immediately liked what she saw. Then she called up her own birth chart and superimposed it over Tiny's. When she saw the dance of planets that resulted, the mélange of conjunctions and squares and oppositions, of sextiles and trines and quincunxial aspects formed by the celestial bodies in her chart and Tiny's, she knew why she had felt such a profound affection for him at dinner. Deirdre was so happy she began to cry. She had found her soul mate.

Deirdre knew what she and her sister, Carla, would have said about Tiny back when they were teenagers. They would have made fun of his "dark little peanut head." They would have mocked his shortness and his crossed eyes. But at the age of thirty-two, Deirdre found herself powerfully attracted to Tiny. After Carla met Tiny for the first time, she did not comment on his looks. She simply said to her sister, "That man really loves you." That was all she had to say. Because by the time they had both reached their thirties, Carla and Deirdre knew what it was like to be wounded by men who, if they had loved them at all, had never loved them enough. No one had ever appreciated Deirdre the way Tiny did. He even loved her little quirks and habits. He did not wish to change her in any way. "This man really loves me," Deirdre would sometimes whisper to herself. "He really loves *me*." The Watson sisters were old enough to know that when it came to deals, Deirdre had hit the jackpot.

In their early days together, one of Tiny's physical features did present a slight dilemma for Deirdre. She was never certain, when staring at her lover, which of his eyes to gaze into. While one of Tiny's eyes returned her level gaze, the other always seemed to be trying to look at the tip of his nose. Deirdre always tried to focus on the eye that seemed to be focusing on her, but, inevitably, her attention would be drawn to the queer eye. One morning over breakfast, Tiny and Deirdre talked about the merits and the inconveniences of contact lenses, which they both wore. "My vision's actually not so bad," Tiny said. "Even though one of my eyes is not perfectly aligned with the other."

"Yeah, I know," Deirdre said.

"You *know*?" Tiny sounded alarmed.

"Well, I've noticed."

"You mean you can tell?"

Tiny was so sweet in his innocence that Deirdre wanted to laugh and take him into her arms. She knew better, though. "It's not obvious," Deirdre said casually. "You have to look very, very closely to notice it at all. I just happen to stare into your eyes a lot, baby."

Tiny beamed. And Deirdre wondered: Does anyone see, ever really *see*, themselves as other people see them?

*   *   *

Tiny Jenks and Deirdre Watson had the impenetrable aura of a young and happy couple around them. Without trying to, they made other people feel like insignificant outsiders. Tiny and Deirdre, one year after their wedding, were constantly sharing whispers, winks, and inside jokes; billing and cooing and making references that only they would understand. Ordinarily, such behavior annoyed Hal Hardaway. But on this September night as he sat across the table from Tiny and Deirdre, watching them crack up over some allusion one of them had made to something the other had said a week earlier, utterly banished from their sphere, Hal felt sentimental, nostalgic. There was an empty chair at Tiny and Deirdre's table that night, reserved for Corky, who had called Hal at six o'clock to say she would not be able to make it to his friends' place for dinner since her boss—the judge—needed her to work late. Such cancellations were becoming more frequent. Hal tried not to complain. On those nights when Corky knew she would be free, Hal rearranged his schedule so he and his girlfriend would be able to spend more time together.

At Tiny and Deirdre's place, after the lasagna was finished, Hal watched his host and hostess unself-consciously nuzzling each other. He remembered how, back in their early days together, he and Corky used to curl up in one of the booths of their favorite ice cream shop and spoon Häagen-Dazs into each other's mouth, so absorbed in their intimacy that Hal was oblivious to the stares aimed at them. Hal and Corky rarely went to that ice cream shop anymore. And they no longer shared the intimate absorption of a young and happy couple. Watching Tiny and Deirdre giggle, Hal felt overcome by a sense of loss. How he envied Tiny and Deirdre. Suddenly Hal's vision went blurry. Tears stung his eyes.

"Hal," Deirdre said, her voice squeaking with surprise. "You're crying."

Tiny and Deirdre had popped out of their bubble of intimacy and were now staring fearfully at Hal. "You all right, bro'?" Tiny asked.

"Yeah," Hal said, pressing the fleshy part of the palm of his left hand against each eye, trying to staunch the flow before tears began rolling humiliatingly down his cheeks, "I'm okay." He failed to block a sniffle. "I'm okay. It's just like I told you earlier, Deirdre, I haven't been myself. I haven't felt like myself in a long time."

Deirdre gave Hal a knowing and sympathetic smile. When Hal arrived at their apartment in the Fort Greene section of Brooklyn that evening, Tiny had not yet gotten home from the hospital where he worked. Deirdre was there, though, sipping a rum and Coke and reading a book as fat as a dictionary. Deirdre made a sour face when Hal told her Corky wouldn't be showing up. Deirdre had never said anything negative about Hal's girlfriend. Unlike most of the black couples Hal had socialized with for years, Tiny and Deirdre did not quietly withdraw after learning that their friend was living with a white woman. Tiny and Deirdre had met Corky twice and had, ostensibly, gotten along well with her. But every once in a while Hal would catch Deirdre grimacing slightly—for the secret entertainment of Tiny—literally behind Corky's back. Or raising an eyebrow and shooting Tiny a bemused look when Corky used a word like "gross" or "neat." Deirdre wasn't brazen about it. Her nasty little facial expressions were just barely unsubtle enough for Hal to catch.

"Oh, well," Deirdre sighed upon hearing the news of Corky's cancellation that night. "That'll just leave more lasagna for us." She made a joke about getting fat and mixed Hal a rum and Coke. Hal sat down and noticed the title of the thick book Deirdre had been reading: *The American Ephemeris for the 20th Century.* Thumbing through the book, Hal saw that it was a series of calendrical charts, showing the position of all the known planets of the solar system during each day from January 1, 1900, to December 31, 2000. Deirdre, he remembered, was obsessed with astrology. "So—how ya been, Hal?" Deirdre asked, handing him his drink. Her tone sounded excessively concerned, as if Deirdre had been worried about him.

"Oh, you know," Hal said automatically, "samo, samo." He

took a sip of his drink, then, without thinking about what he was saying, answered again, this time responding more to Deirdre's fretful tone. "Actually, to be honest with you, I'm not so good."

"What's the matter?"

"I don't know. It's hard to put my finger on. I just feel . . . agitated . . . distracted. I don't feel like myself. Whoever the fuck *he* is."

"How long have you felt this way?"

"I've been aware of this, I don't know, agitation, for a few months. Since June maybe. But when I really think about it, I've been feeling strange for a year. Maybe longer."

Deirdre nodded solemnly. "That makes perfect sense. You turned twenty-nine last year, thirty this year. Right?"

"Right."

"You're having your Saturn return. It happens to everyone around that age. Why do you think everybody's life changes around twenty-nine or thirty? It takes Saturn that long to return to the position it was in the day you were born. Everybody's life sort of starts over with their Saturn return. You start to become your real self. Depending on exactly where Saturn is in your birth chart and its aspects to other planets, a Saturn return can be a traumatic event." Deirdre's tone was as matter-of-fact as it was sympathetic. She spoke as if she was saying something everyone should know. Deirdre did not show the slightest hint of apology—that "Well, you know, this is all kinda foolish, but it's fun to talk about anyway" attitude—that so many people displayed when discussing astrology. Deirdre spoke with the casual conviction of a serious believer. "And that's not even to mention the Uranus-Neptune conjunction."

"Say what?" Hal chuckled.

"Uranus and Neptune, two of the big outer planets have been conjunct—passing at the same degree in the heavens. They were exactly conjunct for most of 1993 and a lot of this year. Right now, they're only about two degrees apart, so we're all still feeling the effects of the conjunction."

"Meaning what?"

"Sudden changes. And a whole lotta shit coming up to the surface. Neptune, you see, is the planet of the murky depths, that which is hidden. Fantasy, intuition, imagination. Uranus is the planet of revolution, freedom, chaos. Uranus and Neptune have been doing this cosmic dance since the end of 1988, in the sign of Capricorn. Capricorn: the sign of structure. That's why for the past five or six years, the whole structure of the world has been changing. Along with the structure of everyone's life. You don't know your exact time of birth, do you?"

Deirdre had asked Hal this before. "Naw, it's not on my birth certificate and my mom was totally drugged out. All she knows is it was sometime between nine and twelve on the morning of—"

"I remember the date," Deirdre said. "Though without a more precise time of birth, it's hard to say exactly where in your chart the action is taking place. But have no doubt, Hal, that you really are changing. Somewhere, deep inside you, a revolution is going on. It's happening to everyone. Whether we want it to or not. No one can escape the effect of the Uranus-Neptune conjunction."

Fortunately, Tiny walked in the door at that moment and they all started talking about something else. Hal liked Deirdre. He just thought she was a little bit crazy.

But Deirdre Watson was certainly the best thing that had ever happened to Tiny Jenks. Hal's father and Tiny's had been best friends at college. Though the Hardaways lived just outside Philadelphia and the Jenkses in New York, the families kept in close touch and Hal grew up thinking of the three Jenks kids as cousins. Byron was the runt of the litter. He won his nickname when he was born several weeks premature, weighing in at just under six pounds. Always the shortest boy in his class, and saddled with a high, girlish voice, Tiny endured years of relentless teasing with perfect serenity. Hal considered Tiny the kindest person he knew. All through high school, Tiny couldn't get a date. Plenty of girls liked Tiny—but none wanted to go out with him. He fared better at college, where, during his freshman and sophomore years, his height shot up from five to five and a half feet. His girlfriends, at college and through most of his twenties, tended to be white and, like Tiny—who was noticeably cross-eyed— a bit odd-looking, with crooked noses or ungainly physiques. Hal had always figured his buddy couldn't do any better. Tiny's women were always the first to break off the romances. The brother, sweet as could be, was just unlucky in love. Hal thought of Tiny as someone who would remain a bachelor for years to come.

Then, seemingly out of nowhere, along came Deirdre Watson— who was not only a sister, but a damn good-looking one, too. And tall: at least five foot seven. And accomplished: She made a comfortable living selling computers. Hal imagined that any number of eligible black men would be interested in Deirdre. Yet she chose Tiny. From what Hal could tell, Deirdre had actually been the aggressor, setting her sights on Tiny and pursuing him until he was hers. Hal knew that there were plenty of short, cross-eyed men in the world who bedded and wedded fine women. But, ordinarily, such short, cross-eyed men had a lot of money. Tiny Jenks, who worked as a physical therapist with injured and disabled children, earned a paltry salary. Hal could only think that Deirdre had fallen in love with Tiny's kindness.

Deirdre's love transformed Tiny. In the two years they had been together, Tiny had become far more confident and opinionated. Hal had even noticed a touch of vanity in his old friend. For the first time in his life, Tiny acted like someone who considered himself good-looking. Since his wedding in the summer of 1993, Tiny also began to consider himself wise. Now that he had "settled down," he sagely advised all his single friends to do the same. Tiny seemed to think that, through his marriage to Deirdre, he had achieved some kind of enlightenment, discovered some precious secret that eluded his more ignorant and immature friends. Hal often winced at Tiny's newfound condescension.

Yet sitting across the table from Tiny and Deirdre now as they gently nuzzled each other, surrounded by their impenetrable aura of affection and happiness, Hal thought that maybe his friend really had discovered the meaning of life. Hal looked at the empty chair at the dinner table, the place that had been saved for Corky, and wondered if he would ever learn what Tiny already knew.

"Hey, bro'," Hal heard Tiny say in his soft falsetto, "it's gonna be all right."

Hal had been unable to stop his tears. Embarrassed, he sat hunched over the remnants of his lasagna, elbows propped on the table, face buried in his hands, shoulders shaking with each muffled sob. When he looked up again, he saw only Tiny at the table. He figured that Deirdre had slipped into the next room. "I'm really sorry, man," Hal said. "I don't know what the fuck is wrong with me."

"It's Corky, isn't it?" Tiny said.

The tears had stopped. Hal was beginning to compose himself. "It's so hard to figure out, man. 'Cause it's nothing obvious. It's all just below the surface. But something's wrong. I don't even know how to talk about it. All I know is I'm really in pain over this, Tiny. I feel like I'm in pain all the time."

"Is Corky the source of your pain?"

Hal groped for the right words. "I know she doesn't mean to hurt me. She hurts you the way a child hurts you. She doesn't know. She can't acknowledge that she's doing it. But you try to make her see. You tell her, not in so many words, 'Hey, honey, when you say or do that, you're hurting me. So please don't hurt me.' But she keeps on doing it and you keep saying, 'Please stop hurting me. Please stop hurting me. Please stop hurting me.' And her response is: 'I'm not hurting you.' Finally, you're crying out, 'Please stop hurting me!' And then she says you're being abusive. I mean, how can you get through to a person like that?"

"You can't," Tiny said abruptly, with a certainty that startled Hal. Tiny fixed Hal with his cross-eyed stare. "Only Jesus could bring sight to the blind. And look what happened to him."

They both smiled. Hal wanted to tell Tiny about the bizarre dreams and visions he'd been having for the past couple of months, but he already felt too vulnerable. "I really love Corky. I really do. I want things to work out with her. But I don't know anymore. Corky says she doesn't believe in marriage." Hal could feel the tears coming again. Not since childhood had he wept in front of another person. He was ashamed at showing such weakness. Especially since he was not crying over a death or an illness or a financial catastrophe. He was only crying over a woman. Yet in spite of his shame, Hal was grateful he could cry in front of Tiny. If anybody could sympathize with him, it was Tiny. Tiny, who had been hurt by so many women— most of them white. Tiny, who fairly oozed compassion; who spent all his working hours tending to the crippled. Tiny, Hal had thought many times, was the kindest person he knew. "Hey, man," Hal said, wiping his face with a napkin, "I'm really sorry about this. Thank you so much for listening to me."

"You know," Tiny said as he continued to hold Hal in his cross-eyed stare, "I've never thought you and Corky would last." Tiny's voice was colder than Hal had ever heard it. "Your backgrounds are just so different."

Hal was too stunned to respond. Tiny's tone was smug, scolding. And that word he used: *backgrounds*. Did he mean that because Corky was white and Hal was black their relationship was doomed? The chastising little emphasis Tiny had put on the word, as if he—

who had dated white girls almost exclusively for years—was daring to criticize Hal for loving someone of a different *background*. But Tiny was now in a position to pull a blacker-than-thou on Hal because Tiny, in the end, after all his white girlfriends, had done the right thing and married a sister. So: Tiny had never thought Hal and Corky's relationship would last—because their *backgrounds* were so different. Tiny simply assumed that Hal and Corky's problems were racial. But what if their problems had nothing to do with their *backgrounds* at all? What if Hal told him that? Would Tiny believe him?

Tiny rose from the table, grabbed a book from a nearby shelf, and handed the slender volume to Hal. " 'Blactualization'?" Hal said. "Is that a word?"

"You haven't heard of Dr. Emmett Mercy?" Tiny said, seeming to scold Hal yet again. "You should know about this brother. I'll lend you the book."

"What is it exactly?"

"Observations. Aphorisms. Parables. Folk wisdom. Stories from his personal experience. His philosophy. It's deep stuff. If you're open to it."

"I'll check it out," Hal said unconvincingly.

"He holds these workshops. There's one Thursday night. I'd like you to go with me."

Hal set the book down on the table. "Not interested."

"Hal," Tiny said, "when you say 'Please stop hurting me,' do you ever wonder if it's yourself you're talking to?"

*   *   *

It was Chester Beer's turn to answer Dr. Mercy's query at the Amandla workshop. A big, slow-moving man, Chester shifted his weight on the folding chair. "There was a night—oh, this musta been

just before the end of the war, I was still a boy and my mother and
me had just moved up to New York, to Harlem. And one time, my
grandmother came to stay with us. She had never been out of the
state of Alabama before. Man, she loved New York. One night we all
went to Carnegie Hall. Don't ask me how my mother afforded it. She
musta been saving up. We went to see Paul Robeson. I remember
watching my mother and my grandmother watch Paul Robeson
sing—the rapture in their faces. I remember Robeson. So . . . powerful. The majesty that man had onstage. After the show we went to the
Automat on Fifty-seventh Street. And my grandmother couldn't
believe it. Sandwiches poppin' outta glass cases. You didn't see that
in Alabama in the forties. Grandma just couldn't stop marvelin' at
the Automat. And Mama couldn't stop laughin' at Grandma's astonishment. And I sat there, eatin' my sandwich and just lovin' being
with these two women. And I was thinking of Robeson. My daddy
had disappeared when I was a baby. And y'all have to remember this
was the days before everybody was talkin' about black pride and
Black Power. But watching Paul Robeson on that stage that night, I
felt pride. And I felt power. That black man gave me a gift that night.
Later on, sittin' in the Automat with my mother and my grandmother, I thought I knew what it felt like to be a man."

Dr. Mercy felt a lump in his throat. At other meetings, when he
had asked him the question, Chester Beer had responded tersely but
sincerely, "A black man is strength" or "A black man is endurance."
Dr. Mercy was beginning to think that Chester's ideal image of the
black man was John Henry, dying with the hammer in his hand. But
tonight, the wise-eyed deacon had responded with a moving story
from his personal experience. Dr. Mercy considered this an important
breakthrough. Now he hoped that Chester's openness would inspire
the other men in the workshop. "Thank you, Chester," Dr. Mercy
said softly. He turned to the last man in the circle, Jojo Harrison, who

continued to scowl in his heavily tinted glasses, arms folded across his chest. He had still not taken off his leather jacket, and his smooth, dark pate was starting to glisten with sweat. "Jojo," Dr. Mercy said, "what is a black man?"

Still scowling, Jojo said: "Pass."

4

Do you know what Ronald Reagan calls Nancy? Have you ever heard this? His nickname for her? Do you know what the President of the United States calls his wife in private?"

Hal Hardaway, groggy and hungover, wondered why his roommate was always coming up with these strange questions and theories and little bits of trivia.

"No," Hal croaked.

"Mommy!" Walker Du Pree yelped. "Ronald Reagan calls his wife Mommy! That's his pet name for her. Do you realize what this means?"

Hal spat into the sink. "No."

"When they're having sex and Ronnie has an orgasm, he cries out 'Mommy!' Can you imagine? This guy's coming inside his wife and screaming 'Mommy!' Isn't that *sick*? Mommy? Do me, Mommy?"

Hal and Walker stood side by side, each before his own sink and mirror in a long row of sinks and mirrors in the communal men's bathroom on the second floor of Mould Hall, a massive, industrial-looking freshman dormitory on the north campus of Craven University in Craven, Delaware. Hal and Walker had been roommates for one week, assigned to a suite with two other freshmen, Bill and Bob (white guys). Hal and Walker shared one of the two bedrooms in the suite, Hal in the bottom bunk, Walker in the top. Hal thought Walker was all right—he just never stopped talking.

"What are the implications of that?" Walker asked urgently.

Hal, leaning forward, feeling a bit wobbly on this Saturday morning, hands gripping the edges of the sink, unleashed a deep, gurgly belch that brought back the tart and fruity flavor of all those Napalm Surprises he'd sucked down the night before at the Deer Hunter, a seedy bar and favorite Craven townies' hangout where he'd gone with other members of the freshman football squad. When Hal looked up and peered into the mirror, he felt almost blinded by the whiteness of the Mould Hall bathroom: the white tile walls, the slick white curtains hanging in the shower stalls behind him, the hot white fluorescent lights overhead. He cocked his head and, looking into the mirror to the left of his, saw the reflection of Walker. His roomie was a wiry, high yellow brother with a rusty brown, uneven Afro that, as far as Hal was concerned, needed to be cut off. Walker had intense, black button eyes, a blondish, peach-fuzzy mustache, and a hyped-up way of talking that Hal didn't mind most of the time but which he was not at all in the mood for this morning. Hal could see Walker staring back at him in the mirror, a quirky glint in his eye. Walker had his toothbrush raised, but he was too busy yammering to bring it to his mouth, and Hall suddenly became annoyed by the sight of the pristine dollop of minty green gel resting uselessly on the white bristles. "Can you imagine?" Walker whispered gravely. "Mommy? . . . What the fuck is going on with this guy?"

"Aw, shut up and brush your teeth," Hal groaned.

Walker smiled, brushed for a while, spat into the sink. "What do *you* like to call women?"

Hal, ignoring the question, turned and headed toward one of the shower stalls. But Walker already knew the answer. Hal was the first man he had ever met who always, unfailingly, referred to women as bitches.

*   *   *

Most people are the stars of their own life movies. You may be the love interest in someone else's ongoing autobiopic, the villain in another's, a mere walk-on or extra in countless other unfolding epics. But when it comes to your own life as cinema, you are the indisputable lead—top billing. In Sadie Broom's personal movie, however, Sadie Broom was always the sidekick. It had started early in her childhood, most of which Sadie spent tagging behind her beautiful, charismatic, always-popular sister, Victoria, who was four years older. Not that Sadie was unattractive, uninteresting, or unpopular. Let's just say she was no Victoria. While many a sibling would have resented Victoria, Sadie revered her sister. And when it came to playmates and school chums, Sadie befriended girls like Victoria—the charming, conventionally pretty girls who seemed to glide through life with a golden spotlight trained on them. The Victorias of the world were the stars of Sadie Broom's movie. And Sadie was their faithful sidekick, the dependable best buddy, the wisecracking foil who would neither steal the show nor end up with the male lead.

By the time she entered Craven University in September 1982, Sadie Broom had unabashedly embraced and cultivated her supporting role. During Freshman Week, it was easy for Sadie to pick out the black women who would be the stars of the class. She immediately won over the four most radiant beauties, the serious divas of the Class of '86: Miranda, Cassandra, Diandra, and Alexandra. Sadie wasn't glamorous enough to feel competitive with them or insecure enough to feel threatened by them. Each of the serious divas felt a special sisterly bond with Sadie. She seemed to be the only woman who could really understand their problems, all those dilemmas that came with being gorgeous and sought after, the sort of problems that did not inspire much sympathy from most other women. Sadie was the sort of pal the Mirandas, Cassandras, Diandras, and Alexandras of this life invariably praised as a "good listener." And when the Mirandas and Cassandras and Diandras and Alexandras talked about a sidekick like Sadie, they always described her as having a "great personality." They loved playing matchmaker for their sidekick and would try to interest men in her by raving about her "great personality." They would never understand that few descriptions could extinguish the interest of a potential boyfriend as instantly as those two words, since "great personality" was almost always a euphemism for "ugly." But Sadie was not ugly. And she really did have a great personality. It was during her years at Craven University that Sadie Broom slowly became aware of an emotion just below the surface of her indefatigable good humor, her patience and reliability, an emotion no one would ever suspect resided in such a sweet-natured sidekick: a deep and pitiless rage.

There was, to be sure, an element of self-interest in Sadie's friendship with the serious divas. Sadie's mother had found her future husband at college. And Sadie's grandmother had found her future husband at college. Sadie had grown up with the idea that finding a future husband was one of the basic features of the college experience. Since the serious divas would presumably attract the most desirable black men at Craven University, Sadie, by inhabiting the divas' sphere, might capture some male attention for herself.

It didn't work out that way. The sort of men who were interested in the divas were not the sort of men who were attracted to sidekicks. The serious divas thought they were doing Sadie a favor when they hooked her up with men they themselves would never even consider dating, young brothers who were not deterred by their describing Sadie as having a "great personality." They were nerds and ne'er-dowells, nice Negroes whom Sadie usually found tedious. She dated them anyway. They were, in short, male sidekicks. But what Sadie wanted was a hero, a dashing male lead, a man whom—once she married him—she could make the star of her life movie.

To Sadie's eyes, Hal Hardaway was a star of name-above-the-title caliber. He was what Sadie's mother, Lorraine, would call a "pretty nigger"—one of those smooth-featured, caramel-colored, delicious-looking black men. Harry Belafonte, Billy Dee Williams, and Billy Eckstine were in the Pretty Nigger Hall of Fame. Julian Bond and Cassius Clay: They had been two of Lorraine Broom's favorite pretty niggers. As the prettiest nigger in the freshman class, Hal Hardaway seemed destined to go out with one of the serious divas. Eventually, he would go out with all four of them, in almost clockwork progression. Miranda was Hal's girlfriend freshman year. He took up with Cassandra in the fall of sophomore year, started dating Diandra at the beginning of junior year, and capped his Craven career with Alexandra, his senior sweetheart. Thanks to the divas, Sadie would learn every intimate detail about Hal Hardaway, from how he liked his eggs (sunny side up) to how well he performed cunnilingus (by all four reports, very well indeed). By the fall of senior year, Hal had finally figured out that Sadie was the best friend of all his college girl-friends and he began confiding in her himself, asking her sage advice on the mysterious ways of women. Sadie would talk to Hal for hours, indulging his petty male angst, all the while burning for this man, and burning mad, furious at him for not being attracted to her. It wasn't, Sadie thought, that Hal was actively *not* attracted to her. It was just that he seemed to regard her as a buddy, a sexless sidekick.

*   *   *

"I'm telling you," Walker said adamantly as his baked ziti grew cold, "Rocky loses! In the first *Rocky* movie, he *loses* the fight."

"Bullshit," Hal said as he wolfed down another forkful of the revolting dinner. "Rocky Balboa always wins."

"In *Rocky II* and *III* he wins, but not in *Rocky I*. That's what makes it a superior film. Don't you remember the last thing you hear in the movie, right before the closing credits?"

"Yo, Adrienne, I love you!" Hal said in a dead-on impersonation of Sylvester Stallone.

"No! The last thing you hear is the voice of the emcee saying, 'The winner, and still heavyweight champion of the world—Apollo Creed!' "

"Damn, would you look at those bitches," Hal sighed.

"That's the whole point of the first *Rocky*. Nobility in defeat. That's why it's such a good movie. The other two are just about winning. That's why they suck. Don't you—"

"Walker, my man, I'm trying to change the subject here. Would you please cut the film analysis and check out these two magnificent bitches?"

Walker turned around in his chair, and through the crowd of tray-toting students in the freshman dining hall, the meandering swarm of anxious teenagers looking around the cavernous cafeteria on their tenth night of college, trying to seem as if they knew where they were going as they searched the tables desperately for a familiar face, anyone they could sit with to avoid the ignominy of eating alone, he spotted Miranda and Cassandra—or was it Diandra and Alexandra?—striding confidently to an unoccupied table, knowing—Walker could see the certain knowledge in their faces—that as soon as they sat down, the table would rapidly fill up with admirers. "Yeah, they're pretty cute," Walker said, "but not as cute as they think they are."

Hal, finished with the main course, took a lusty bite out of a pinkish apple and talked as he chewed. "I'm goin' after Miranda, bro'. I've targeted her."

"Bon courage."

"What's that mean?"

"It's French for 'You ain't got a prayer, motherfucker.' "

Hal bit another huge chunk out of the apple. "You just watch me, Walker. The bitch is *mine*. You oughta go after Cassandra."

"Too rich for my blood."

"Go for it, man. Eye of the tiger. You shoulda hung out longer at Psi Delta Zed the other night. Cassandra mentioned you after you left."

"She did?" Walker bleated. Psi Delta Zed was the big black fraternity on the Craven campus. Hal had taken Walker to a party there, and after sitting alone in a corner for two hours listening to groups of young men engaged in competing chants—"Eighty-three rocks the house!" countered by "Eighty-four rocks the house!" followed by "Eighty-five rocks the house!" which was quickly opposed by "Eighty-six rocks the house!" and back again—and drinking lukewarm beer, Walker quietly slipped away. Psi Delta Zed was chockablock with gorgeous women that night, but Walker had been too bashful to talk to any of them. That Cassandra had noticed him at all was an unexpected thrill, but knowing it was uncool to show his excitement, he switched to a blasé tone. "What did she say?"

Hal smirked as he continued to chew his apple. "She said she'd seen you around campus and you didn't seem very . . . *friendly*." Somehow, Hal managed to load the word with racial innuendo.

Walker winced. "Story of my life. Black people are always suspicious of me. I think it's the way I talk. I sound white, whatever the fuck that means."

"Are you uncomfortable around black people?"

"I'm equally ill at ease with all kinds of people."

"You shoulda stayed. They broke out some excellent coke later."

"Really? I've never done it before."

"You've *never* done coke?" Hal said, straining the incredulity a bit, Walker thought.

"Naw, man. I've never even smoked a joint. Look, at Harrowside High, there were only three types of guys: jocks, hoodlums, and nerds. The jocks got all the girls, the hoodlums did all the drugs, and the nerds got into good colleges. I was a nerd."

"You don't know what you've been missin', bro'."

"What, are you a cokehead or something?"

"Fuck no! I've never paid for it. But I'll do it if it's around. Where I went to high school, it was just considered a rite of passage." Hal took a gulp of milk from a little red carton. "Actually, I've only done it a few times. So don't be runnin' around tellin' people I'm a coke-head or some shit like that."

"Your secret's safe with me."

"Gotta watch my rep."

"What for?"

"Yo, man, I'm gonna run for office someday. I don't need no skeletons rattlin' around in my closets. Gotta think ahead."

"Are you serious? What, do you wanna be the first black President of the United States?"

"Fuck the presidency. I wanna be a senator. That's the best job. Maximum power with minimal responsibility. Executive positions suck. I want to legislate. I wanna be a lawmaker!"

"Good God, you've got it all figured out, don't you?"

"Damn straight." Hal downed the last of his milk, then crushed the carton into a jagged ball. There were three other unopened cartons lined up neatly on his tray beside three square and spongy yellow slices of cake topped with thick white frosting. "Gotta plan ahead. After college, three years of law school, then I'll probably return to Philly, take a job in a law firm, but just for a few years while I make the right contacts. My parents are already plugged into the Democratic Party establishment there. I figure I pay my dues for a few years, then in 1994, I run for Congress. After three terms, I get elected to the Senate in the year 2000. I'll be thirty-six then. After that, who knows? Maybe Senate majority leader. If the circumstances are right, I wouldn't rule out a run for the presidency. I'll have to wait and see."

Walker found Hal's game plan highly implausible. But, at the same time, he was so awed by the scale of his roommate's ambition, he didn't dare laugh. Part of Walker believed that people who talked this way were precisely the sort who wound up running the world. Even though he knew Hal thought he was a flake, Walker was fascinated by his roommate. Hal was from a Philadelphia suburb where virtually everyone was wealthy and black. He spoke of black youth groups, black country clubs, black debutante balls. Hal's father ran a black real-estate agency; his mother taught at a black public high school (though Hal had attended a predominantly white, private high school). Hal had been one of those well-rounded, most-likely-to-succeed types: good student, editor of the yearbook, three-letter athlete in football, basketball, and track. Hal told Walker the first day they met that the world was divided into two groups: winners and losers. It was obvious which category Hal belonged to. But Walker was beginning to notice that Hal was careful not to put himself in situations where he might run too high a risk of losing. For instance, Hal had played quarterback on his high-school football team, but he had tried out for wide receiver on the Craven freshman football squad since only two quarterbacks would be selected, while there were four open spots for wide receivers. By consistently hedging his bets, Hal could always emerge a winner.

"Goddamn," Walker said. "I'm still trying to figure out what I'm gonna major in."

Hal gobbled up one of the spongy cakes in two bites and continued to talk with his mouth full. "Economics or poli sci for me. Something that looks good on a law school application." He took a long, thirsty swig of milk, wiped his mouth with the back of his hand. "You really don't know what you're gonna major in?"

"I'm thinking about fine arts."

"What! What the fuck are you gonna do with a fine-arts degree?"

"Beats me. But drawing is what I like to do most."

"Yo, Walk, man, repeat after me: Would you like fries with that?"

"Would you like fries with that?"

"Good. Practice that line. 'Cause if you major in fine arts, that's what you're gonna be sayin' for the rest of your life."

*   *   *

It was during Freshman Week at Craven University that Walker Du Pree encountered, en masse, for the first time in his life, the sort of Americans he had, for the most part, seen only in movies and on television: white Anglo-Saxon Protestants. Growing up in Brooklyn, attending Harrowside High, Walker had known plenty of white people, but the white people he'd known were Jews, Italians, Irish, Greeks. They were white, but they were always something else as well; they were ethnic. Not that the WASPs lacked ethnicity—how could they? It was more that the WASPs Walker saw on the Craven campus seemed like generic Americans; no more or less American— as far as Walker was concerned—than he or his friends, but somehow more *prosaically* American. Of course, there were WASPs in New York, but they seemed to get lost in the crowd, churned up in the city's ethnic swirl. There may have even been a few WASPs at Har- rowside High, but if there were, they probably seemed more Irish or Jewish or Italian or Greek than WASPy. And they certainly didn't look or dress like the Craven U. WASPs, a large majority of whom seemed quite affluent: big, raw-boned people in khaki shorts and crisp striped or pastel shirts with button-down collars; pointy-nosed girls in plaid, pleated skirts with matching ribbons in their hair. Walker finally grasped the meaning of a term he'd heard before but had never quite understood: "well scrubbed." These Craven preppies, who, by and large, seemed very pleasant and unassuming, were all exceedingly, sparklingly well scrubbed.

(Walker, at this point in time, had never even contemplated his father's ethnicity. To Walker, his father was simply a hippie.)

Standing beside a dripping keg of weak, foamy beer in the humid air of a gymnasium at yet another of the freshman mixers Craven U. had scheduled that week, Walker noticed the young woman's name tag before he'd really noticed her, noticed how cute she was with her glossy auburn hair and freckles. But it was that name, written in a loopy hand, in orange Magic Marker on a white patch adhesively stuck on the faded purple Lacoste "alligator" shirt, just above her right breast, which, though small, had a tantalizingly supple upturn to it, that caught Walker's attention. And, as she drew closer to him, Walker, squinting to make out the full name in the dim light of the gymnasium, said aloud: "Corky Winterset."

"Hiya!" the extremely healthy-looking girl said merrily, glancing at the name tag in front of her and adding, "Walker Du Pree."

"Corky," Walker said pensively. "Cor-ky. Corky? My God, where do you people come up with these names?"

"What do you mean?" Corky asked, startled.

"I mean, Corky, Buffy, Marky, Bucky. These WASP nicknames, they're really weird."

Corky eyed Walker searchingly. She seemed to be trying to figure out whether his teasing was playful or hostile. Walker was not entirely sure himself. Finally, she just laughed. "Oh, yeah?"

"Yeah. You know, I had my Craven alumni interview with a guy named Skip. This is a grown man I'm talking about. The guy was pushing fifty. And he goes by *Skip*?"

"Hey, gimme a break. We wouldn't have such weird nicknames if we didn't have such awful real names. That guy Skip is probably named Mumford Whittier Wentworth. If your name was Mumford, wouldn't you rather be called Skip?"

"Point taken. So what's your excuse, Corky?"

"You mean my first name? Enid."

"Ouch."

"I rest my case."

"What's your middle name?"

"Eleanor."

"That's a little better."

"But still . . ."

"Yeah, you're right. Stick with Corky."

"Thanks for your permission. But, you know, you shouldn't confuse me with those snotty, East Coast WASPs. I'm from the heartland."

"Where?"

"Lincoln, Nebraska."

"Oh no! Land of the corn people!"

Corky cocked her head, pursed her lips, and gave Walker a long, appraising look. Walker was suddenly afraid that he'd offended her. He was about to apologize when Corky smiled and said, "You must be from New York."

Three hours, four parties, and several large plastic cupfuls of weak and foamy keg beer later, Walker and Corky found themselves squished side by side, legs touching, on a tattered brown leather sofa in Myriad, continuing the conversation they'd started in the gym, but having to talk loudly now, even though their faces were separated by only a few inches, to be heard over the ear-shattering punk rock that reverberated through the room. Myriad was a rambling white clapboard house populated by Craven upperclassmen who prided themselves on their eccentricity and eclecticism. These were young men—women were welcome in Myriad but none chose to live there (except unofficially if they spent a lot of time with boyfriends who were members of the house)—who shunned fraternities, dabbled in theater and the arts, wore earrings and ponytails, T-shirts and ripped jeans, worshiped Bruce Springsteen, smoked a lot of grass, and spent their weekends playing Ultimate Frisbee. There were plenty of WASPs in Myriad, but they were cool WASPs, the kind who wouldn't be caught dead in a pair of khakis. While the name Myriad was meant to evoke breadth and diversity, the striking thing about the house was how similar most of the men who lived there seemed. The true oddball in the house was Anthony, a tall, anorexically thin junior with a punky buzz cut, clad in black and sporting a nose ring (a relatively unusual sight in Delaware in 1982), who was jumping madly around the crowded living room, as if he were on a pogo stick, and screaming along with the song that blared on the stereo: "I'm so booooored with the U.S.A.—but what can I dooooooooo?"

Corky was talking about field hockey. "I'd really like to make the team here. I loved playing in high school. But the girls here are so serious about it. Now I think I just want to make the team out of pride, but I don't actually want to play on the team when they all seem like such a bunch of jerks."

"Field hockey!" Walker chuckled. "Never saw that in Brooklyn. What's the other sport all the preps play? Lacrosse! I was walking across the quad my first day here and saw all these white people wielding big sticks. You field hockey and lacrosse players!"

"You're really funny," Corky said. She was beginning to sound a bit drunk. "I've never heard anybody talk about white people before. Like we're some kind of tribe. The white people."

"I can tell you why you've never heard anybody talk about white people before."

"Why?"

"Because you probably don't know any people who aren't white people."

"That's not true!" Corky grinned. "I know you."

It was almost three o'clock when Walker escorted Corky to Grimm Hall, the drab and blocky freshman dorm on Craven's south campus. Walker knew he wasn't going to get laid that night. And though he was wildly attracted to Corky, he didn't mind. He sensed that she liked him, too. He felt that since they'd met in the gym, he and Corky had really focused on each other. No matter where they went that night, no matter who else was around them, Walker and Corky seemed to inhabit their own zone of privacy. And while they had not discussed anything so substantial, Walker felt an easy intimacy with Corky. He was eighteen and often felt delirious with turbulent energy. But talking with Corky, Walker had gradually felt overcome by an emotion he could not quite define—a sort of tranquillity.

They stood, face-to-face, in front of Grimm Hall. "Well," Corky said, scrunching up her face, then saying the words in an uncertain tone, seeming to mock the banality of the expression, conveying that she did not know what else to say but that this tired old pleasantry could not possibly capture her feeling at this moment, "it was . . . *nice* meeting you?"

"Yeah," Walker said, feeling his body leaning forward, almost unconsciously, his eyes slowly closing, his lips slowly parting.

Corky suddenly sprang forward and, lips tightly puckered, gave Walker a quick, thoroughly unerotic peck on his slightly open mouth. "Night," she said breezily, then disappeared into Grimm Hall.

Walker began the mile-long trek back to Mould Hall, on north campus, where he would climb into his narrow top bunk and, for the first of many nights, dream of Corky Winterset.

*   *   *

"What about that one?" Hal asked, resisting the urge to point.

"Too fat," Walker said.

"Fat? That ain't fat, man. That's cash butter."

"Cash butter?"

"Damn right. All the bitches you like look like they're starvin'. You oughta go out with some Cambodian boat people."

There was a tiny terrace outside the sitting-room window of the suite that Hal and Walker shared with the two white freshmen, Bill and Bob, in Mould Hall. On this, their third Saturday at college, they had wedged a couple of folding chairs into the cramped little concrete space that constituted a balcony, sat down, each with a can of beer in hand, and rated the young women who walked and biked along the crisscrossing paths of Craven's quadrangle, laid out before them, two floors below.

"Check out this sister," Hal said. "Striped shirt. Walking toward the administration building." Hal tried to remember her name. She was another member of the Class of '86. Sandy, Sally, something like that.

Walker waggled his head from side to side. "She's all right."

"Too black for you, huh?"

Walker sucked his teeth in annoyance. "It ain't like dat," he said, affecting the sort of black Brooklyn street accent that was not his natural tone of voice but one he could speak in at will. "I likes all de ladies."

"Uh-huh," Hal said skeptically. In the half hour they had been sitting on the terrace, casing the quad, Walker had responded with ho-hum indifference to every sister Hal had zeroed in on. Meanwhile, the women Walker called to Hal's attention were almost all white, and as far as Hal was concerned, none of them, on a scale of one to ten, rated better than a six. "So, whatcha doin' tonight?"

"Got a date with Corky Winterset," Walker replied.

"No shit. Miss Omaha chic."

"One: She's not from Omaha, she's from Lincoln. Two: She isn't chic."

"Aw, but she's got style—for a white bitch." Hal guffawed.

"Yeah, she's not skinny and she's got a big butt. You like that sorta thing."

"Well, yo, check it out, there's a party tonight at Phi Alpha Smegma."

"The football frat?"

"Some call it that. This is a party you have to be invited to—unless you're a good-lookin' bitch. But you can come as my guest. If it looks like you ain't gonna get any play from the Omaha chic—which I'm sure you're not—come by Smegma. Just mention my name at the door."

"How about her?" Walker said, as if he had not even heard the invitation, nodding his head toward another pale and skinny girl whom Hal would never even have noticed.

"God-*damn*, Walk! Don't you have any standards?"

"I think she has a real interesting quality," Walker said, sounding perplexed by Hal's objection.

"Depends on what you're interested in."

"I've always had eccentric fancies. My favorite Charlie's Angel was Kate Jackson."

"You're fuckin' weird, man."

Walker shrugged. "Well, you know what they say: There's no accounting for taste."

*   *   *

The day after not showing up for their date, Corky ran into Walker at the library and apologized profusely. Walker was sure she had a very good excuse, but he was too pissed off to really hear what it was.

Corky said they should get together again soon. Walker said, Yeah, sure. Though he would occasionally see her around campus and wave hello, Walker did not have another conversation with Corky until two years later when they wound up in the same life drawing class. They usually sat side by side that semester, scrutinizing the same naked subjects and trying to replicate them on paper. After class, they would often go out for coffee and talk. And talk. And talk. Walker always felt the same easy intimacy he had felt with Corky the first night they met. Every time they were together talking, lost in conversation, he felt as if everyone around them had dematerialized. That year, Corky was going out with Jim Munger, a friendly prep Walker knew from one of his English classes. Walker and Corky talked in general terms about love, sex, and affection, never naming names when it came to speaking from specific romantic experience.

One Sunday afternoon, in the fall of their senior year, Walker phoned Corky on the spur of the moment and asked her if she wanted to have an adventure. Corky said, Why not? She was living off-campus, sharing a house with four other women. Walker arrived at her place with a small parcel of pot brownies, freshly baked by one of his housemates at Myriad. Sitting on enormous beanbags in Corky's room, getting high on narcotic pastry, Walker noticed a black-and-white photo tacked on a cluttered billboard. "Wow," he said, rising to take a closer look at the picture of the great man, resplendent in long robes, a sword hanging from his belt. "This is Paul Robeson in *Othello*."

"Yeah," Corky said. "I saw that picture in a book and really liked it, so I made a copy."

"Do you know anything about him?"

"Wasn't he a Communist or something?"

"Oh, yeah. But mainly Paul Robeson was a bad motherfucker."

Corky suddenly looked stricken. "Really?" she gasped.

Walker laughed. "I mean that as the highest of compliments."

"Oh," Corky said, and after a moment, she laughed, too.

Walker took Corky to see a play that Sunday afternoon in 1985, a student production of *A Raisin in the Sun,* featuring a friend of Walker's. Midway through the second act, Walker took Corky's hand in his. Corky did not want to withdraw, but she didn't want to encourage Walker either, so instead of squeezing Walker's hand, she left her fingers lax between his. She enjoyed the play, and after the final curtain call, Corky and Walker went backstage to congratulate Walker's friend Hal, who had played the male lead. Corky thought Hal was talented enough to be a professional actor. Certainly, he was good-looking enough.

Walker and Corky had dinner at a Chinese restaurant; afterward, he walked her to her house. He remembered the night three years earlier, when she dispatched him with a quick peck in front of Grimm Hall. This time, Walker pulled Corky toward him and kissed her full on the mouth. At first Walker felt resistance. But slowly, slowly, Corky began to relax. Then, just as it seemed she was about to give in to the kiss, to truly kiss Walker back, she pulled away. "I'm sorry," Corky said. She started to blush. "I'm really sorry. I can't. I really like you. But not in that way. You understand, don't you?"

"Yeah."

"I hope you do. Because I wouldn't want anything to affect our friendship."

"Don't worry about the friendship," Walker said. Corky smiled, feeling reassured. Walker turned and headed back to Myriad. As far as he was concerned, there was no more friendship to worry about.

*   *   *

Back when Sadie Broom was a sophomore, one of her friends in Craven's senior class told her that the final month of college was a time of sudden couplings, a period when young men and women who had known each other for years but had never had sex together decided to satisfy their curiosity, to sleep with people they might never have the chance to sleep with again. Those last weeks before graduation created a bedroom window of opportunity, and the fact that you and your lover might go in separate directions forever made the encounters all the more exciting. That, in any event, was how Sadie's friend made it sound. But by her final week at Craven U. in May 1986, Sadie—lonesome and boyfriendless for all of her senior year, angry with herself for having failed to find her future husband after four long years of college—wasn't even thinking about getting laid. All she wanted was to get the hell out of Craven, Delaware. College had been a washout. She was looking to the future, to a month of traveling in Europe (paid for by her otherwise good-for-nothing father), to another month of hanging out with her mom, back home, in Washington, D.C., and finally, to her move to New York, where she would start her job at Tanzer & Mur Consultants. As she put the past four years and her failed search for a fiancé behind her, a distant deadline was taking shape in her mind: By this day in 1996, by the time of her tenth Craven class reunion, she would, at the very least, be engaged, if not already married. On this Monday night, at ten o'clock, sitting amid the half-packed boxes and pieces of clothing and luggage scattered about the small off-campus apartment she shared with her cat, Aretha, Sadie felt a peculiar new confidence stirring within her. She decided that her sidekick days were over. No more supporting roles for Sadie Broom! From now on she was going to be the star of her life movie. Anybody who didn't like it should just get out of the way—or risk being fired from the set!

The doorbell rang. It was Hal Hardaway. She had seen a lot of Hal this last year of college, though she had stopped lusting after him sometime around Christmas when she realized that, for Hal, she was a bizarre anomaly: a woman who was actually a friend. She gathered that it was precisely because he could talk to her, could share his intimate feelings with her in a way he never did with the women he slept with, that he did not want to sleep with Sadie. He was too close to her to want to make love to her. That, anyway, was what Sadie thought. There was also the fact that, until very recently, Hal had been seeing Sadie's good friend Alexandra. Still, it was just so obvious to Sadie that, temperamentally, Hal belonged with her.

I might like you better if we slept together . . .

During the first semester of senior year, in the fall of 1985, when Hal started opening up to Sadie, the line from the horny Romeo Void dance tune often ran through her head. The singer was a woman.

I might like you better if we slept together . . .

She knew if she could make love to Hal just once, he would be hers forever. He needed to see that physically they could be just as compatible as they were emotionally.

But there's something in your eyes that says maybe that's never . . .

Sadie knew she was a good-looking woman. Of course, she had her days when she thought she looked like shit. She had her common worries about diets and cosmetics and the clothes that enhanced her body's gifts and concealed its flaws—as she saw them—but she never doubted her basic physical attractiveness. There was nothing about Sadie, however, that was glamorous. And it was glamour Hal wanted in a woman: that touch of Whitney Houston; that dash of Vanessa Williams. Sadie would never have that quality. She would never look like a girl you would see in a music video, and she was glad of it. By Christmas, when she realized that Hal would never be attracted to her because she looked too much like a real woman and too little like the women on MTV, when she recognized the shallowness of Hal's laws of attraction, she did not stop liking Hal, but she did stop lusting after him. She stopped being angered by Hal's attitude toward her. In fact, she was somewhat tickled by it. She could tell that Hal was both astonished by and proud of his bond with her. She was his friend, but not his girlfriend. She was a woman he spent a great deal of time with, but he wasn't sleeping with her. Incredible.

Never say neveeeeeeeeeer . . .

But on this Monday night, as soon as she saw Hal standing in her doorway, Sadie felt an erotic rush. She did not believe Hal had come to her apartment to have sex with her. But she felt certain they were going to have sex. The carnal frisson between them that night was unmistakable. At first they fell into their usual pattern, sitting side by side on Sadie's couch, sipping beers, talking about Hal's problems with Alexandra. The eight-month-old romance was coming to an end. To the dismay of lover, friends, and family, Hal had decided to abandon his plans for law school—had declined even to take the entrance exam—and pursue an acting career. His starring role in a Craven production of *A Raisin in the Sun* the previous November had convinced him that the theater was his true calling. After graduation, he would move to New York, get a cheap apartment, a job waiting tables, and start going to auditions. Alexandra thought Hal had taken leave of his senses. She did not think he was a particularly good actor and eventually told him so. Though they were not engaged, Alexandra, who was, herself, headed for law school, told Hal there was no way she would ever marry a struggling actor.

"She's forced the issue," Hal told Sadie as they sat amid her boxes and baggage, their bodies not touching, but the vaguely itchy titillation between them growing. "It's Alexandra or acting. That's the way she wants it. I have to choose acting."

"You gotta do whatever's going to make you happy," Sadie said sensibly. She thought Hall had some promise as an actor, but she seriously doubted he had the tenacity to persevere in a field so fraught with rejection, disappointment, and petty humiliations. Sadie figured Hal would try acting for a year or two, then return to his senses and get his ass into law school. "Obviously, this is something you need to do. I say go for it."

"You know, Sadie, I want to thank you for always being so supportive. I'm really gonna miss you."

Yes, Sadie thought, it's going to happen. It's going to happen tonight. Right now. "I'm gonna miss you, too," she said softly.

Hal leaned toward her. She slowly parted her lips. And from that moment, everything was awkward. As they kissed, their teeth kept colliding. They couldn't seem to get their mouths properly merged, as teeth clacked together, tongues darted about like nervous goldfish. They craned their necks, readjusted the position of their heads, bumped noses. Sadie found herself sliding backward on the couch, Hal slumping toward her. Their top rows of teeth knocked together again and Hal inadvertently bit Sadie's tongue. "Ow!" she yelped. "Sorry," he muttered. Hal was lying on top of her now. Was it Sadie's imagination, or did his gestures seem oddly tentative? He grabbed her breast, squeezed it, massaged it a little, then pulled his hand away. Sadie could feel Hal's cock harden against her pelvis. (They were both wearing blue jeans.) When she slowly began to grind her crotch against his, the erection seemed to fade. Then it came back. Then faded again. She stroked his back, his butt, his hair—but passionlessly. What the hell was wrong? They looked into each other's eyes, but Hal became instantly embarrassed and buried his face in her neck. She felt his tongue slide into her ear and, at the same time, he moaned too loudly, the sound piercing Sadie's eardrum. "Ow!" she yelped again. "Sorry," he muttered. Oh, this was all wrong. Sadie had heard for years that Hal was a fantastic lover. And Sadie considered herself a passionate woman, easily aroused, her body unusually sensitive, responsive, to a man's touch. As Hal continued to wriggle atop her, clumsily slipping a hand beneath her shirt and licking her neck, Sadie could only think he considered her ugly. She simply wasn't glamorous enough to excite Hal Hardaway. As they continued their tepid fondling, Sadie could feel herself and Hal growing more self-conscious. "Hey," Sadie said gently. "I don't think this is such a good night for me. I'm really tired and sort of headachy. I think I'm getting my period. So maybe we shouldn't. Is that all right with you?"

Hal was, if anything, relieved. Every other time he had kissed a woman, it had been with a feeling of raw desire. But when he leaned over to kiss Sadie, what he'd felt was an almost painful tenderness, a tenderness he found inexplicable, so different was it from the fervor he'd felt with every other woman he had ever kissed. And as he and Sadie began to make out, Hal felt overwhelmed by dread. He did not know what had made him start this, and now he was afraid he wouldn't be able to go through with it. Mr. Bone had never let him down before, but on this night, he didn't seem up to the task. For the first time in his sexual life, Hal felt that his emotions had overruled his body. Dread was weakening Mr. Bone. But what was the source of the dread? It was, Hal would realize as he left Sadie's apartment and trudged back to his fraternity house, a feeling of almost incestuous intimacy. Kissing Sadie Broom was like kissing his little sister.

Sadie went to bed alone and dejected that night. Hal also went to bed alone that night, feeling at once exhausted and rattled, as if he had just tricked fate, avoided something dangerous and inexorable. Hal and Sadie saw each other a few more times that week, never alone, always at big graduation parties. They were both moving to New York and they vowed to keep in touch. But, of course, they didn't.

5

A rotting head of lettuce led to the end of Hal Hardaway's acting career. In June 1987, Hal had survived a full year as a typical struggling New York thespian. He spent his days going to auditions and his nights waiting tables. Most of the time, he felt intoxicated with a sense of adventure. He met Dahlia Burnish at his second "cattle call." She was ten months older than Hal and had been trying to make it as an actress for five years. Dahlia had decided not to enroll at Vassar College after she won a place in the chorus of a short-lived black Broadway musical. Though Dahlia had yet to win another role, she was devoted to acting. Her unshakable dedication inspired Hal, perhaps because he knew he did not possess it himself. And his relationship with Dahlia—who was so beautiful, so hungry for success onstage—was essential to the romance of Hal's life as an "actor."

Then, one night, Hal and Dahlia went to Freddy Vinson's place for dinner. Hal had met Freddy only once before, but he had tremendous admiration for the veteran black performer. Freddy was known as an actor's actor. He had never been a star, but he'd never sold out (that is, gone to Hollywood) either. Over a twenty-year career, he'd worked with the Negro Ensemble Company and the Black Theater Collective and had won rave reviews for his "searing" portrayals of supporting characters in earnest plays by dignified Afro-American authors. Hal felt honored when Freddy invited him and Dahlia into his home—until he saw what a drab and shabby home it was, a two-bedroom apartment in a run-down building on Staten Island, sparsely furnished with tattered armchairs, ancient dressers with drawers missing, a black-and-white TV with an uncoiled wire hanger in place of an antenna. Freddy's wife seemed zomboid with depression and his two daughters, aged eight and ten, bickered incessantly. As Hal and Dahlia and the Vinsons gathered around the lopsided kitchen table, Freddy talked of how he was praying to get a part—not in the latest August Wilson drama, but in a Burger King commercial. *"That's* where the money is," Freddy said. "You get a piece of change every time they air the commercial."

Freddy's wife pulled a ragged head of lettuce from the refrigerator. Regarding its lank, brown leaves, she apologized to Hal and Dahlia, saying there wouldn't be any salad with dinner tonight. "Hey!" Freddy protested. "That's good food there!" Mrs. Vinson said the lettuce was too old. Freddy grew more adamant. "You crazy? We just bought that lettuce. Don't be throwin' away good food!" So the salad was served. As Hal forced himself to swallow the soggy, withered strips of brown lettuce, he contemplated the fact that in the world of black New York stage actors, Freddy Vinson was considered a success. Suddenly, Hal felt a surge of prideful indignation. There was no way in hell *his* future children were going to eat spoilt leafy greens! That was when Hal decided it was time to apply to law school.

*   *   *

There was one major obstacle standing between Hal and law school: the LSATs. Hal's fear of the law school entrance exam had been partly responsible for his decision to pursue an acting career. During his senior year at Craven, around the same time he won the lead role in a production of *A Raisin in the Sun,* Hal took one look at an LSAT practice book and felt like crying. For much of his life, he had considered law school an inevitability, but now, confronted with the prospect of another major, standardized test, Hal was prepared to toss aside his long-standing ambitions and chase Broadway stardom. Had it not been theater, Hal probably would have found some other field of endeavor—*any* other field of endeavor—that did not require the taking of a standardized test. Hal knew that once he sat down to fill in those tiny circles with his sharpened No. 2 pencil, he would, as he so often had on such exams, freeze. His vision would go out of focus. The questions would not make any sense. He would read them over and over again until the words seemed to float off the page. He would stare at the floating, incomprehensible words. Then he would be struck by a vertiginous sense of dread. He would feel as if he were falling into the exam, plummeting amid the floating words. Finally, he would fill in one of the tiny circles. His choice was often random.

Back when he was a public school student in Pemberton, the Philadelphia suburb where he had grown up, Hal actually enjoyed taking standardized tests. He was always the first student in the classroom to finish such an exam, and after he was done, he would sit with his hands folded on his desk and sneak glances at the other students as they struggled to fill in all the tiny circles before the teacher announced that time was up. Hal always scored higher than anyone else. When Hal was in the sixth grade, his parents decided he should apply to one of Pennsylvania's most exclusive private schools. Naturally, to be accepted at the Seward Rodson School, one had to pass a difficult, standardized test. So, on a brilliant Saturday morning in November 1975, eleven-year-old Hal sat in the backseat of his dad's Oldsmobile. Hal's dad was behind the steering wheel; Hal's mom sat beside him in the passenger seat, reading a map and giving directions.

They were on their way to the Seward Rodson School, where Hal was to take the entrance exam. While Dad and Mom seemed a bit nervous, Hal felt perfectly calm, almost serene. He figured the Seward Rodson exam would be just like all the other standardized tests he'd taken: a piece of cake.

The exam was scheduled to begin at ten. Just five minutes before the hour, the Hardaways arrived at an imposing, ivy-covered house in Rodson, Pennsylvania. The building looked closed. Hal's dad got out of the car, rang the building's doorbell. No answer. He walked all around the building. The place appeared empty. Finally, Hal's dad approached a man raking leaves on the far side of the lawn that surrounded the house. When Hal's dad returned to the car, his face seemed to have been transformed; it looked as if he was wearing a mask of fury. "It's the wrong fucking building," Hal's dad snarled at Hal's mom. "We're in the wrong fucking town!" It turned out that this house in Rodson was the *old* Seward Rodson School, and, for the past ten years, had been used solely for administration. The *new* Seward Rodson School was located in the neighboring town of Seward, Pennsylvania. It would take at least half an hour to get there. Flustered, Hal's mom started fumbling through papers, brochures, and maps, trying to explain how she could have made such a mistake. "You stupid, fucking bitch!" Hal's dad exploded. Suddenly, he flung out his arm and, with the back of his hand, smashed Hal's mom in the face. The impact of his knuckles on her cheek sounded like a small firecracker. The violent *pop* made Hal jump in his seat. Hal's dad started driving while Hal's mom sat quietly weeping and dabbing a tissue at the blood that trickled from her mouth.

Hal was numb with shock. His parents often snapped at each other, sometimes even shouted at each other, but he had never seen one of them hit the other. Except for on television, Hal had never seen one grown-up hit another. Hal felt as if he could no longer think straight. The violence replayed itself over and over in his mind's eye.

He kept seeing his dad's hand flying quickly through the confined space of the Oldsmobile. He kept hearing the horrible *pop* of knuckles against flesh and bone. For the next forty minutes, Hal's dad muttered under his breath while driving; Hal's mom kept sniffling as she stared at the map; and Hal sat dumbstruck in the backseat.

They arrived at the new Seward Rodson School. By the time the Hardaways found the classroom where the exam was being held, it was ten forty-five. The pleasant-looking white lady who was administering the test greeted them outside the classroom and explained that she had waited fifteen minutes for Hal but finally had to begin. Hal entered the classroom and saw a sea of little heads bent over sheafs of paper. All the children were busily coloring in tiny circles with sharpened No. 2 pencils. Hal took his seat and stared at the exam on the desk in front of him. The questions did not seem to make any sense. The words slowly floated off the page. Hal felt nauseated. He felt like crying. He kept seeing his dad's big hand flying in the air, kept hearing the *pop* as it smashed into his mom's face. Fighting back tears, he slowly, slowly filled in the tiny circles. At one-fifteen, the other students turned in their exams and left the classroom. The pleasant-looking white lady told Hal he had another half hour. Hal flipped through the sheaf of papers in front of him and saw a multitude of tiny circles still waiting to be shaded by his pencil. With fifteen minutes left, Hal stopped even reading the questions. He simply colored in the circles in such a way that they created a zigzagging pattern that snaked through the final pages of the exam. When he met his parents outside, he told them he thought he'd done well. Because he knew that was what they wanted him to say.

Hal was accepted at the Seward Rodson School. Only in his sophomore year did his dad tell him he had received a very low score on the entrance exam. Hal's dad said he made a personal appeal to the people who ran the school, flaunting Hal's high scores on other standardized tests and his perfect grade point average at the public school in Pemberton. This, Hal's dad said, was why Hal had gotten into Seward Rodson. Over the years, Hal would hear his dad boast about how he had forced Seward Rodson to accept his son after he had "choked" on the entrance exam. Naturally, Hal's dad did not mention that Hal had to take the test less than an hour after watching him smash his wife in the face. And Hal would never bring it up himself. So far as he knew, his dad never hit his mom again. The Hardaways' marriage, in fact, seemed far more stable and happy than most. By the time he was sixteen, Hal had blotted the scene in the Oldsmobile from his mind. But whenever he took another standardized test, he felt the same way he felt during the Seward Rodson exam. He had no conscious memory of the burst of violence he had witnessed. Still, the pain of seeing that violence returned to haunt him every time he sat down to fill in tiny circles on an exam.

While Hal earned very good grades at Seward Rodson, his SAT scores were abysmal. He decided against applying to the most ferociously competitive American colleges and set his sights on the less famous but highly respected Craven U. Hal's parents expected great things from him. Everybody did. Politics seemed an obvious choice for someone with Hal's intelligence, charm, and good looks. And a law degree was a traditional stepping-stone in the careers of most American politicians. Then, in his senior year, Hal got bit by the proverbial acting bug. He also felt as if he were being bitten—*mauled* might be the more accurate word—by the Doberman pinscher that was his terror of the LSATs.

* * *

In this life, there are winners and losers. That was what Hal's dad always told him. Hal, of course, had been raised to think of himself as a winner. When, in May 1991, he graduated from Craven Law School, he had never felt so victorious. His LSAT score had been pathetic, but thanks to his excellent scholastic record as an undergraduate, Craven U. was willing to admit him to its small graduate program in legal studies. Once again, Hal received sterling grades in his classes, and by the spring of his last year at Craven Law, he had won a spot at the New York firm of Ayton Schenker Harmon & Thicke. The job would start in September. Hal was so thrilled by his success in law school, so impressed with himself for getting the job at Ayton Schenker (starting salary: seventy thousand dollars), that he hardly gave any thought to the hurdle awaiting him in August: the New York State bar exam. Even though it was another standardized test, Hal had convinced himself that passing the bar would be a mere formality. Hal studied hard that summer and, after the two-day bar exam, felt confident that he'd done well. He started the job at Ayton Schenker. He loved getting dressed in his suit and tie every morning. The other associates and partners at the firm—almost all of whom were white—treated him with the utmost respect. At Ayton Schenker, Hal felt he was in his element—a winner among winners.

Then, in November, he learned that he had failed the bar exam.

"Don't worry about it," Dahlia Burnish told him. "John-John Kennedy failed the bar two or three times and he still got to keep his job at the District Attorney's office."

"Yeah," Hal said, "but he's John-John Kennedy. If I fuck up again, Ayton Schenker's gonna say, 'So long, black boy.' "

"So don't fuck up again," Dahlia said reasonably.

Hal had never told Dahlia, had never told anyone, about his test phobia. Dahlia had encouraged him to apply to law school, and during the three years he spent back in Craven, Delaware, they managed to see each other at least every other weekend. By the time Hal started at Ayton Schenker, his girlfriend had won a part on a popular daytime soap opera. Though her character only appeared every five or six episodes, Dahlia was assiduously making a name for herself. With Hal earning so much money at the law firm, they were discussing buying an apartment, in Park Slope or Brooklyn Heights. Hal and Dahlia had been together for five years. He was twenty-seven. She was twenty-eight. Marriage was the logical next step.

But now, with his failure on the bar exam, the presumed trajectory of Hal Hardaway's life had been thrown out of whack. His two years as an aspiring actor could be considered a slight detour, a hiatus, a youthful lark. But failing the bar exam was something altogether different. Something more akin to a derailment. Everyone at Ayton Schenker told him not to worry about it. Plenty of lawyers had flunked the bar on their first try, they said. They assured him that he would pass it next time. But their assurance only made him more anxious. Hal felt that some of the partners, despite their professed faith in his success next time around, looked askance at him. And he knew what was running through their minds: "affirmative action case." If Hal failed the bar a second time—he was scheduled to take the test again in March—he would validate his colleagues' worst notions about black people. But, more significantly, a second failure would change Hal's estimation of himself. If he flunked again, Hal would be the sort of person he had always disdained. He would be the thing he least wanted to be. Hal would be a loser.

*   *   *

When, in June 1992, Hal learned that he had failed the bar exam for a second time, he went to bed—for a week. He would rise for the occasional meal and shower, but mainly he slept. It was as if the blow of a second failure had knocked him unconscious for the better part of seven days. He called in sick at work, knowing that once Ayton Schenker found out he'd flunked, he wouldn't have a job anyway. How could the firm allow him to practice law when he was not, officially, a lawyer? As word of Hal's disgrace spread, friends and family left messages of condolence on his answering machine. Dahlia spent two nights with him that week and Hal could tell that her feelings toward him had changed. They didn't make love. Dahlia didn't even seem to want to touch him, sleeping right on the edge of her side of the bed, gently pushing him away when he drew near.

Finally Hal emerged from his hibernation. He got up one morning, put on his suit and tie, and went into the Ayton Schenker office to submit his resignation. That night, Dahlia made a suggestion: "Maybe you should see my uncle Godfrey."

Hal had met Godfrey Burnish at a couple of Dahlia's family functions, but he had known of the tycoon—one of the wealthiest black people in America—since his childhood. Like most African Americans he knew, Hal had grown up using Burnish Hair Care Products. His parents and grandparents had subscriptions to Burnish's *Esteem* magazine, a monthly chronicle of the achievements of black Americans, but Hal tended to read the journal only when he was waiting for a haircut: Stacks of *Esteem* could be found in virtually every black barbershop in the country. He knew a bit of the Horatio Algeresque legend of Godfrey Burnish, had heard of the future millionaire's impoverished childhood in Mississippi. He vaguely remembered a story about young Godfrey and a friend who had allegedly made disrespectful comments to a white woman. Godfrey's friend, it was said, had been lynched while Godfrey somehow managed to escape the white mob, hopped a train north, and, with only one dollar in his pocket, arrived in Harlem. The eighteen-year-old Godfrey got a job sweeping up tufts of hair in a barbershop, then wowed customers with his own formula for a fragrant pomade. A bad back kept him out of service in World War II. When his boss went off to fight in Europe, Godfrey took over the barbershop and began selling his unique pomade. By 1950, Burnish Hair Care Products dominated the Negro market. Two years later, Godfrey started *Esteem* magazine and Burnish Enterprises was born.

Godfrey Burnish was the older brother of Dahlia's late grandfather Albert. After the war, Albert went to New York to serve as his brother's right-hand man. Dahlia's father, Albert, Jr., did not work for the family company. Neither did anyone in Dahlia's generation of Burnishes. And Godfrey—whose sexuality was a subject of much whispered speculation in black bourgeois circles—never married or produced an heir. Dahlia knew that her uncle was a compulsive mentor, always looking for new young protégés to groom. She also knew that he had been impressed by her boyfriend—Hal was the sort of promising young man who always impressed his elders. So she set up a meeting.

"I don't know why you'd want to be a lawyer, anyway," Godfrey Burnish said as Hal, still feeling shellshocked a week after he'd resigned from Ayton Schenker Harmon & Thicke, sat in the old man's palatial office. "Frankly, I regard lawyers as the hired help. I just pay them to do my dirty work. Lawyers don't call the shots. They just take orders. They facilitate. *I'm* the big kahuna. No mere lawyer ever gets to be the big kahuna. Don't you want to be the big kahuna, son?"

"Um, yeah, I guess."

"Speak up, youngblood!"

"Yes, sir!" Hal fairly shouted.

"Yes what?"

"Yes, I'd like to be the big kahuna."

"Good! 'Cause I don't know much, youngblood, but I can recognize potential. And you've got lots of it. You'll start work tomorrow. Be in my office at eight o'clock sharp."

*   *   *

After six months of working at Burnish Enterprises, Hal Hardaway felt like a winner again. Godfrey Burnish had personally tutored Hal in all aspects of the business. As Special Deputy to the Founder, his initial title, Hal, a complete novice, wielded authority over top executives who had been with the company for years. A less artful diplomat would have incurred voluminous resentment from his colleagues. But Hal was so charming, and so obviously good at whatever job he took on at B.E., that his coworkers seemed happy to defer to him. He had a particular knack for the media operations. Hal effortlessly came up with snappy ideas for stories for *Esteem,* as well as for WBUR, the company's radio station, and BAIT, Burnish Arts and Information Television. Before he knew it, he was attending some of the most glamorous functions in New York, hobnobbing with the city's black elite.

And he owed it all to Dahlia, his beautiful, charismatic Dahlia. The irony was that she was not in New York to share it with him. He had only been at B.E. two weeks when Dahlia was chosen for a part in a sitcom about a group of black fashion models. The show was supposed to take place in New York, but was filmed in Los Angeles. Hal and Dahlia had maintained a long-distance relationship when he was at law school, but back then, the distance was only between Manhattan and Craven, Delaware. And they both had more flexible schedules. "Don't worry, baby," Dahlia said just before she moved to L.A. "Lots of couples do the bicoastal thang." Six months later, Hal had visited Dahlia in L.A. four times. But Dahlia's shooting schedule had not allowed her to come to New York at all.

During those lonely months in New York, Hal realized just how much he needed a special woman in his life. Since hooking up with Miranda early in his freshman year at Craven, Hal had never gone more than two weeks without a steady girlfriend. Separated from Dahlia by three thousand miles, Hal found that it was not just sex or companionship that he missed. It was something else, something more essential to his nature. Hal, you will remember, often saw himself through other people's eyes. Thus, the adoring gaze of a lover had become a necessity for him. Hal took great pride in being a good boyfriend. He showered his girlfriends with candy and flowers. He never forgot a birthday or an anniversary. The women loved him for it. And Hal loved seeing his reflection in their loving eyes.

Another of Hal's qualities that he believed made him a good boyfriend was his absolute refusal to fight with any of his girlfriends. Each of his Craven U. lovers had, at one time or another, tried to quarrel with him, but Hal, with a tension-deflating joke, an appeasing hug, a quick apology, or capitulation to the woman's will, always managed to avoid a confrontation. Hence, Miranda, Cassandra, Diandra, and Alexandra were each shocked when Hal abruptly ended their romances. None of them had seen the breakup coming. Because Hal was always so agreeable. But once he had decided a relationship was over, it was decidedly over. There was no chance of winning him back. And while each woman was wounded by Hal, none of them could stay angry with him for very long. Because Hal had been such a good boyfriend.

In all his years with Dahlia, Hal had never once argued with her. Early on, he let her know he would rather end the relationship than have a fight. Dahlia attributed this to Hal's ineffable sweetness. The truth, however, was that Hal was terrified of losing his temper. Hal thought of his temper as a nuclear arsenal. He had never unleashed it. He didn't dare. Because if he ever did, the result might be total destruction.

Fortunately, Dahlia had never provoked him. That was one reason why Hal felt they were made for each other. By January 1993, they had been together six and a half years. Yes, the last six months, with Hal in New York and Dahlia in L.A., had been rough. Sure, they'd only seen each other four times. But Hal felt confident that either Dahlia's TV show would be canceled and she would return to

New York or Godfrey Burnish, wanting the best for his niece, would transfer Hal to B.E.'s Los Angeles office. Hal just had to be patient.

But the desire to marry and start a family was swelling inside him. Hal had been a good son, a good student, a good boyfriend, and was now, at B.E., proving himself a good executive. He was ready to be a good husband and father. He was eager to see himself through the worshiping eyes of his children. And what beautiful children they would be! With the combination of his genes and Dahlia's, how could their kids not be gorgeous? The vision was beginning to cohere: Hal would succeed Uncle Godfrey as chairman of Burnish Enterprises and, with the admiring eyes of millions of African Americans on them, he and Dahlia would create a magnificent black dynasty.

Then, late one night, Dahlia called from L.A. to say she was breaking up with Hal. She had fallen in love with someone else. Hal lost it.

"How could you do this to me?" he screamed into the phone. "After everything we've been through together! After everything I've done for you!" The words were exploding from him, beyond his control. "You betrayed me! How could you do this? After I've been so faithful to you! Do you know how many women throw themselves at me? Every day! And I have never—never!—thought of cheating on you!" If Dahlia was yelling back at him, if she was responding at all, Hal did not hear it. He was enveloped by his own shouting. "Don't you ever, *ever*, call me again!"

Hal slammed down the phone, ripped the cord from the wall, and set about drinking himself into a stupor. When he awoke the next morning, fully clothed, on his living-room floor, feeling as if his tongue were coated with paste and nails had been hammered into his skull, Hal was, at once, ashamed and relieved. Ashamed because, for the first time, he had lost his temper with a woman; relieved because losing his temper had not been as harmful as he had feared. Though he had yelled at Dahlia, he had not used a single curse word. He had not called her a bitch or a ho or any other derogatory name. He had lashed out—but he had not unleashed the full, devastating force of his nuclear arsenal.

*   *   *

"I know you," Hal heard a chirpy white-girl voice say. He turned around to find her standing just six inches away from him in the jam-packed ballroom. He recognized her immediately. "You're the actor," Corky Winterset said.

"And you're the Omaha chic," Hal replied.

"The what?"

"The Omaha chic. That's what we used to call you."

"But I'm not from Omaha. I'm from Lincoln."

"So what? I'm not an actor."

At that, they both broke into drunken giggles. Hal didn't know why, but he felt extremely happy to see his old college classmate.

Ten days had passed since Dahlia Burnish broke up with Hal over the telephone. For ten days, Hal had lived with his festering anger. Dahlia had sent Hal two letters during that time, but he had tossed both in the trash without even opening them. He was afraid that if he read the letters, he would feel compelled to call Dahlia and unleash his nuclear arsenal. And this he did not want to do. So he kept his rage to himself. He continued to work closely with Godfrey Burnish, but told the founder nothing. He and the founder had never discussed Dahlia before and Hal decided that this was not the time to start. Still, he couldn't help but wonder if Godfrey Burnish had heard, through the family grapevine, what had happened. Even if he had, he wouldn't show it. Hal knew the founder well enough to know that. So Hal and the founder, on the morning of January 20, 1993, talked only of politics as they and a dozen other top executives boarded the Burnish Enterprises company jet and flew down to Washington for the inauguration of Bill Clinton. Only Godfrey Burnish was invited to the White House ball that night, but there were other parties all over town and Hal, with a flash of his credentials, could get into many of the most exclusive affairs.

How could she do this to me? How could she do this to me?

Even as he party-hopped around Washington, Hal's rage at Dahlia festered. Many a man in his situation would want nothing more than to get laid, to gain some sort of psychic revenge through a meaningless fuck. But Hal wasn't wired that way. He'd never had, nor had he ever sought, a one-night stand. Ten days after the breakup, Hal was not seeking a mere carnal replacement for Dahlia. He was looking for a wife. She would have to be at least as beautiful—or as much of a consensus beauty—as Dahlia. And, of course, she would have to be black. On the night of Bill Clinton's first inauguration, Hal flirted with every good-looking sister he met at every party he attended. Yet at two in the morning, at his umpteenth Democratic bash, Hal found himself sitting on a chaise lounge, in the corner of a crowded ballroom, drinking glass after glass of champagne, and immersed in giddy conversation with—of all people—Corky Winterset.

"At first I didn't like Clinton," Hal said. "I just couldn't identify with him. Then I thought, Well, if I were a member of Clinton's generation, what would I be like? Probably I'd be an overweight draft-dodger with a bad marriage. So in the end I found I could identify with the guy after all."

Corky laughed. "God, that sounded just like something Walker would say."

"How is the old Walk Man?"

"I was about to ask you the same question."

Hal was surprised. "Aren't you in touch with him?"

"I haven't seen Walker since we graduated from Craven."

"You're kidding. Neither have I."

"Gee. And I thought you two were good friends," Corky said, her voice suddenly turning a bit sad. "And I guess you thought he and I were still good friends."

Hal shrugged. "I guess we both thought wrong."

Corky took a long, melancholy sip of champagne. "You know, the older I get, the more things I find I was wrong about. Is that happening to you, too?"

Not wishing to contemplate the question, Hal changed the subject. "So—what have you been doing since college?"

Corky told Hal about the three years she spent bouncing around the world, trying to sell freelance articles to travel magazines. "Then I turned twenty-five and decided it was time to become a serious person." So she enrolled in law school, at Georgetown University. She was now in her final year, but was not at all sure that she wanted to practice law.

Hal, putting on a "been there, done that" tone of voice, told Corky that he'd worked at a law firm for a year, but quit. "Lawyers don't call the shots," he said sagely. "They just take orders. They facilitate." Hal saw no reason to mention that he'd never passed the bar exam.

Corky said she had just learned that she had won a two-year clerkship with a judge in Brooklyn. "A woman judge," she said proudly. "I hear she's an ass-kicking lesbian feminist. I'm really psyched!" The clerkship would begin the next year, in January '94. "Which means," Corky said, "that as of right now, I still have three years before I have to decide what I really want to do with my life." Hal asked her what she would be if she could be anything she wanted. Corky was silent for a long moment, then said, in a way that Hal found deeply, inexplicably poignant: "I want to be a serious person. Whatever I do, I just don't want to be a lightweight. I want to be serious."

At three o'clock, Corky said she should go home. The man who had brought her to this party was, she said, a gay lawyer, active in Democratic politics. Hours earlier, she had seen him disappear with a handsome younger man. "So I guess I've lost my ride. It's okay. I only live about six blocks away, near Dupont Circle." Hal offered to walk her home. "No," Corky said, "you probably have to get up early to catch a plane." Hal said he wouldn't be flying back to New York until the afternoon. Corky brightened at the news. "Well, if you really don't mind walking me . . ."

The night was clear, crisp, unusually warm for mid-winter. Hal and Corky talked about politics, about how glad they were that twelve years of Republican rule had finally come to a close. They arrived at Corky's apartment building. "So," she said, "did you really call me the Omaha chic?"

"Yeah," Hal said bashfully. "Yeah, I did."

They stood on the sidewalk, staring into each other's eyes and, for several seconds, not saying a word. Hal thought of how Corky had greeted him at the party—"You're the actor"—and realized why he had felt such a sudden affection for her. Though they had barely known each other at Craven U., Corky was a connection to Hal's past; she reminded him of an earlier, perhaps even a better, self. Hal could still remember the excitement of performing in *A Raisin in the Sun,* could still remember the passion he brought to the role of Walter Lee, Lorraine Hansberry's complicated hero. He knew he would never act again. In his two years of going to auditions in New York, no director had ever even called him back for a second look. Thus, his star turn during his senior year at Craven had been his first and last taste of glory on the stage. Yet it was this performance that Corky remembered him for. She would never know how much that touched Hal.

"Would you like to come upstairs?" Corky asked. "I don't have any alcohol, but I could make you a cup of herbal tea."

The next thing Hal knew, he and Corky were kissing—or, more accurately, Corky was kissing *him*, unabashedly, right there on the sidewalk. Hal had always thought that preppy white girls would be boring in bed; that they would just sort of lie there and make the man do all the work. But he could tell by the way Corky kissed him, by the way her mouth devoured his, that, once again, he had thought wrong.

*   *   *

Break it down. Break it down. Break it all down.

Throughout 1993, Hal kept his relationship with Corky a secret. During the first half of the year, she would visit him in New York or he would fly down to D.C. for weekends of tumultuous lovemaking. There was something thrillingly illicit, almost subversive, about their romance. Hal continued to excel at Burnish Enterprises. He wrote a conciliatory letter to Dahlia and she thanked him for his forgiveness. Corky graduated from Georgetown, easily passed the bar exam, and in September went to South America for a three-month trek through the jungle. Hal could not remember when, precisely, he and Corky decided to move in together. Somehow, it was simply understood that once she returned to the States, they would get an apartment together in Brooklyn.

Break it down. Break it down. Break it all down.

Hal felt as if he was changing in ways he could not quite comprehend. But he did not fret over the changes. He didn't even think about them very much. He was being driven by mysterious forces. Day after day, the words ran through his mind, almost as if they were being whispered to him by a voice not his own, a voice urging him to topple the entire structure of his life.

Break it down. Break it down. Break it all *down.*

Later, much later, Hal would wonder if the voice he heard inside his head had been urging him toward true love or self-destruction.

*   *   *

On December 31, 1993, Hal Hardaway and Corky Winterset moved into a brownstone apartment on President Street in Park Slope. Hal wanted to be transparent before Corky. He wanted her not just to see him—to truly *see* him—but to see *through* him. He believed that Corky desired the same kind of transparency. Lying in bed on their first night of cohabitation, Corky, for no apparent reason, began telling Hal about her years as a violin "quasi-prodigy." She loved playing, she said. She even loved practice. She thought of it as magical: putting lovely sounds in the air. It never felt like work. Any time she played the violin, she was having fun. Corky felt that way from the time she was six till the summer she turned fourteen.

"It was the same summer my parents got divorced," Corky said. "They sent me to this elite music camp. And I thought I was pretty hot shit. But so did all the thirty other kids in the violin section. And we were. You have to understand that we were all really, *really* good musicians. Then one day they brought this little girl from Japan to the camp. They sent us all to the big auditorium to hear her play. This little girl—and I mean *really* little, like *maybe* three feet high—this girl, Tsunami, ended thirty violin careers that day. It wasn't just that she was more technically proficient than any of us. I mean, technically, she blew us all away. But what killed you was the beauty of her playing. There was wit and joy and heartbreak in it."

"Tsunami," Hal said. "I think I've heard of this girl."

"Oh, she's hugely famous now. But I'm talking about fifteen years ago. Nobody had heard of her yet. She'd just gotten off the plane from Tokyo and come to our music camp to destroy us. I'm not kidding. She wiped out thirty careers that day. Until that day, I *loved* playing the violin. I thought that in another year or two I might be playing in serious concert halls. But after I got home from camp that summer, I never picked up the violin again. I was only fourteen years old and this whole part of my life ended. Forever."

Hal thought he understood the subtext of Corky's story. In just a few days, she would begin her two-year clerkship with Judge Judith Proctor. She was understandably anxious. What if she didn't measure up? What if she wasn't as good as the other clerks? What if law led to the same disillusionment, the same disappointment in her-self, she had experienced with the violin? Hal detected a sorrow, a deep hurt, in Corky's voice as she told her violin story. As they lay in bed, their naked bodies entwined, Hal caressing her hair as she stroked his chest, he felt a bittersweet intimacy. He wanted to share with Corky his own fears and failures. He told her that he had twice flunked the bar. But he went further, confessing his test phobia, revealing the shame and self-doubt it had caused him. He went all the way to the source, telling Corky about the morning of the Seward Rodson entrance exam, piecing together the sequence of events, truly remembering each detail for the first time in years, as he recounted seeing his dad hit his mom in the car. He spoke of the crushing depression he felt after his second bar exam disaster, when he knew he would have to resign from Ayton Schenker Harmon & Thicke, when he felt like an embarrassment to every black attorney who had ever struggled to succeed in a white law firm. But he wanted Corky to know that a strong person could come back from defeat. Today his career was thriving, and by working at Burnish Enterprises, he was doing more to help the black community than he could ever have done working at Ayton Schenker. "I know you must be nervous about starting work on Monday," Hal said tenderly. "But you have to have faith that no matter what the judge throws at you, you'll be able to handle it." Hal paused. "Right?" Corky did not respond. "Hey," Hal said, "don't you believe me?"

"Your father *hit* your mother?" Corky asked incredulously.

Hal was taken aback. "Um . . . yeah . . ."

"Was it a slap," Corky said, "or a punch?"

"He hit her with the back of his hand."

"Jesus Christ."

"Look, my dad hitting my mom is not the point of the story."

"Did he hit her often?"

"No. That was the only time he ever hit her."

"Do you know that for a fact?"

"Look, Corky, my parents have been married for thirty-three years. They've had their ups and downs, but they're a very happy couple." Hal's voice was firm but not angry. Corky merely had a mistaken impression. Hal wanted to correct it. "I just don't want you to think my father is some kind of wife-beater or something. He's not."

"You shouldn't diminish violence against women, Hal."

"I'm not diminishing it. But it's not the point of the story. Look, you told me about Tsunami and what she did to your violin playing, how it had a big impact on you. I'm telling you about a similar event, my choking on the Seward Rodson test and how it affected me."

But Hal had misinterpreted the subtext of Corky's story. As far as Corky was concerned, the tale of her abandonment of the violin was really about her parents' divorce. She stopped playing just as her parents stopped being married. Tonight was her first night living with Hal. She was scared. She knew how brutally love could end.

*   *   *

Hal lived his life with Corky under constant suspicion of machismo. When during their first weekend in the Park Slope apartment he wanted to watch one of the college bowl games, Corky accused him of being "a macho man." If Hal stayed out late with friends, Corky said he was "insensitive." If he worked late at the office on a night when Corky arrived home early, she said he was giving his job a higher priority than their relationship. Sometimes Corky would raise her voice to Hal. If Hal raised his voice to her, she said he was being "abusive." None of the things that Hal felt made him a good boyfriend—his thoughtful little gestures, his candy and flowers— seemed to matter to Corky. When Hal suggested they spend more time together, Corky accused him of being unsupportive of her career, of trying to turn her into a "housewife."

What Hal found most frustrating was that all his past girlfriends had praised him for *not* being macho. From Miranda to Dahlia, they had all told him what an unusually sensitive man he was. So why did Corky feel differently? Why did she seem to think that Hal was always looking to oppress her with his maleness? Hal decided it was because of the story he had told her on their first night of cohabitation, when he desired utter transparency with his lover and so revealed his test phobia. Yet the only detail of the story that seemed to register with Corky was the fact that Hal's dad had hit Hal's mom. Corky would occasionally refer to Hal's "history of family violence." Hal would point out—as he had on their first night in the apartment—that his dad had hit his mom only once, that their thirty-three years of marriage had been notably stable and content. In April the Hardaways came up from Philadelphia to spend a weekend with Hal and Corky. To Hal's delight, everyone got along famously. The weekend seemed to assuage any doubts Corky may have had about his parents. Yet she continued to hold Hal in suspicion, talking about her need to resist his unconscious attempts to "disempower" her. Hal began to feel that Corky's suspicion had nothing to do with his actions. It seemed to have nothing to do with *him* at all, but, rather, to be based on some *idea* of him. And so Hal developed an unspoken suspicion of his own: that Corky was wary of him because he was black.

Hal thought that such a suspicion, the notion that his white girl-friend harbored racist assumptions, should make him angry. But it did not anger him—it hurt him. He considered trying to talk to Corky about it but decided that would only cause more problems. Hadn't it been his desire to talk, to "communicate," to be transparent before the woman he loved, that started this nonsense? And there was always the possibility that if they did discuss it, Hal would lose his temper. By June, he had quarreled many times with Corky, but he had never become genuinely angry. And he had not even come close to unleashing his nuclear arsenal. He wanted Corky to appreciate the fact that he had never gone ballistic on anyone. But he knew that talking about his rage, however dormant it was, would only fuel Corky's suspicion of him. So he didn't talk about it. Hal now aspired to the opposite of transparency. He made himself as opaque with Corky as he could. Total openness, Hal decided, was neither possible nor desirable.

But, damn, he loved Corky. He just flat out loved her. *Break it down.* He would do whatever was necessary to make their relationship work. If it meant censoring himself, being extra careful about what he said and did so that she could not misconstrue his words or behavior, so be it. *Break it down.* Besides, maybe he did have a few macho tendencies. He would work on squelching them. And perhaps Corky did hold a few unconsciously racist sentiments. She was, Hal had discovered, generally obtuse on the whole subject of race. Hal would show her, by his example, how wrong certain stereotypes were. *Break it all down.*

One morning, in the sixth month of their cohabitation, as Hal and Corky dressed for work, a television newscaster reported the murder of Nicole Brown Simpson and the man who would forever after be referred to as her "friend," Ronald Goldman. Hal and Corky stood frozen before the television. A clip of O.J. Simpson appeared on the screen. "The former football star," as the newscaster identified him, was being led away from his home in handcuffs. Corky took one look at O.J.'s face and said: "He did it."

*   *   *

By the time Hal reached his teens, everybody in America knew who O.J. Simpson was. If they didn't know him from the football field, they knew him from those TV commercials: sharp and classy in his three-piece suit, briefcase in hand, running with that gorgeous stride through an airport terminal, rushing now not to pick up yardage but to pick up his Hertz Rent-a-Car, as folks standing and watching in wonder, including a white-haired little old lady, shouted joyously, "Go, O.J., go!" Once, during his senior year of high school, in the fall of 1981, seventeen-year-old Hal, rushing to catch a plane to go to a college interview in Boston, wearing a three-piece suit and carrying a knapsack, was running through Philadelphia airport, and as he passed another black guy, the brother called out, "Go, O.J., go!" Hal laughed so hard, he almost broke his stride. But he also felt strangely proud, thinking, Hey, I must look *good!*

After O.J. retired from playing, he could still be seen near football fields, microphone in hand, commenting from the sidelines. Hal watched O.J. in bad movies about cops and astronauts, and the Hall of Famer was always popping up in new Hertz commercials. Now O.J. was teamed with Arnold Palmer in the ads. Arnold Palmer, the whitest of heroes in the whitest of sports: golf. Like O.J., Arnie had that pleasant, open, TV-friendly quality, that American niceness. O.J. was no longer a larger-than-life superman. He had, in a way, become something more transcendant than that. He was part of that constant television family. Without really knowing anything about him, every-body felt they knew him.

On January 2, 1989, Hal was riding the train back to Craven Law School after the Christmas break. Flipping through the newspaper, he spotted a short item that made him gasp. In California, on New Year's Eve, O.J. Simpson's wife had made a frantic call to the police. When the cops arrived at the estate, O.J.'s wife was outside, cowering half-naked in the bushes, her face freshly bruised. Hal felt sickened. One thought leapt to the front of his mind: I hope she isn't white.

*   *   *

The photographs could have been labeled BEFORE and AFTER but they weren't. There was the earlier black-and-white shot of O.J. Simpson and his first wife—his black wife—Marguerite and their two children. Marguerite was a good-looking woman, no doubt about it. Kids as cute as could be. But O.J., who, unless he was running with a football, was always photographed with a winning smile on his face, looked absolutely miserable. He stared at the ground, his mouth twisted in a thin frown. Then there was the other picture, a color shot taken some years later, of O.J. with his second wife, his arm wrapped around Nicole's waist, her golden hair falling to meet her burgeoning cleavage. And O.J. was beaming—he looked as if he was about to burst with happiness. It hurt Hal, it almost caused him actual physical pain, that O.J. looked so miserable in the first photo and so happy in the second.

Most images of O.J. hurt Hal in the summer of 1994: the image of O.J., tight-lipped, glowering, as the police led him away for his initial questioning; the image of O.J., in surrender, after the bizarre freeway chase, standing in the courtroom, his eyes rolling horribly up into his head; and the mug shot. Hal could barely even stand to look at the mug shot, at O.J.'s utterly expressionless face, the chilling absence of affect in his gaze.

Hal remembered when he was six years old and his mother told him Grandpa was coming to visit and Hal raced to the door when his grandfather arrived, knowing that Grandpa would swoop him up in his arms and twirl him in the air and then give him a chocolate Tootsie Roll Pop. But Grandpa stood motionless in the doorway. He didn't smile. He didn't offer candy. He didn't seem even to recognize Hal. Hal's mom took Grandpa to the guest room. The next day, as Hal walked past the guest room, he saw his grandfather through the open door, sitting on the edge of the sofa bed, staring up at the ceiling, wearing only an undershirt and boxer shorts. Grandpa kept massaging his bare thighs and knees and moaning, "Oh, Lord, yes, Lord, Lordy Lord. Oh, Lord." Grandpa would stay with the Hardaways for a week before they put him in a nursing home. But that day, when he watched his grandfather rubbing his bare legs, praying to the ceiling, oblivious to everything around him, lost in his senility, Hal thought: Grandpa's become somebody else.

That was the same feeling Hal had when he looked at O.J.'s mug shot. O.J. had become somebody else. A man who had been so comfortably familiar had suddenly, grotesquely, transmogrified into a dead-eyed stranger.

*   *   *

Hal had always found something vaguely disconcerting about Godfrey Burnish's appearance, but he could never figure out exactly what it was until this day in September 1994 as he sat in his boss's office for the first time in three months and realized that the seventy-five-year-old founder of Burnish Enterprises had a head like a baby's. He had a bald, bulbous pate that looked tender and ripe, almost squishy, and not much of a neck at all, with delicate, perfectly white strands of hair that looped around his ears—tiny ears they were, resembling snail shells—and wisped in little curlicues around the back of his creamy brown babyhead. Godfrey Burnish was a stocky, ebullient man whose energy and enthusiasm made him seem at least twenty years younger than his age. Only his clothes, his wardrobe of 1950s-style boxy brown and blue suits, which he always wore with little twin peaks of white handkerchief poking from the breast pocket, marked him as an old man.

"So what's on your mind, youngblood?" Godfrey Burnish asked.

The founder's forty-second-floor office had white carpeting, a white desk, white chairs, and white couches. With its bright overhead lights, Godfrey Burnish's office had a celestial feeling about it. For a moment, Hal spaced out, imagining that he and the founder were floating above the clouds.

"Cat got your tongue?" the old man asked.

Hal had requested the meeting two days earlier but had not been able to decide on a specific agenda. He considered the emotional approach: *How come you've been freezing me out for three months, Mr. Burnish? Is it because you heard I'm living with a white girl now? Your niece Dahlia broke up with* me, *you know, not the other way around!* But now that he was actually sitting before the founder, Hal decided it was best to avoid the personal and stick to business.

"Well, sir," Hal said, pausing to clear his throat. "It's about *Esteem* . . . and its coverage of . . . certain issues." Hal knew that the founder knew what he meant by "certain issues." Since the butchered corpses of Nicole Brown Simpson and Ron Goldman had been discovered three months earlier, both BAIT and WBUR had covered the story extensively, but *Esteem* magazine had not published a single word about O.J. Simpson and the double murder charge he faced.

Every time an article on the case had been planned, the founder—
who had edited the magazine himself for its first twenty years, before
his other responsibilities at the company became too consuming—
vetoed the piece. "The trial will be starting soon," Hal continued,
"and the editors feel that they're ignoring what is maybe the biggest
story of the decade. They think our readers might be wondering why
Esteem publishes nothing on the one subject everyone in America is
talking about. So, um, what I think they'd like to do is to publish
something that would be totally unbiased, of course, and written in
the best possible taste, keeping in mind that *Esteem* is a family magazine—"

"Heh heh heh heh heh . . ." Hal was interrupted by Godfrey Burnish's soft chuckling. "Heh heh heh . . . Ah, youngblood . . ." The
founder rose and walked around his desk, his hands in the pockets of
his cigar-colored suit, his face impishly animated. He stood in front
of Hal, leaning back on the desk, smiling and shaking his tiny babyhead. "You know, you put me in mind of my trip to Ghana last year.
I went and visited a fortress where they used to keep and trade slaves
before shippin' 'em off. I went down into the dungeons, the airless
caves where our ancestors were crammed together like animals. I was
among other African Americans, and when we emerged from the
caves, my fellow tourists wept. Lord, how they cried. One brother
was bawlin' his eyes out. But you know what, youngblood? I wasn't
sheddin' no tears. I had a great big grin on my face. I was grinnin' my
ass off! I had to stop myself from laughin' out loud with joy! Do you
know why, youngblood? Do you wanna know why? Because I came
out of those dungeons, out of that pit of cruelty, and I thought, We
black Americans are some *bad motherfuckers.*"

Godfrey Burnish uttered the last two words in a tone of awe. "We
are the baddest people on the planet. *On the planet.* Our ancestors,
yours and mine, survived imprisonment in those caves, then survived

the middle passage—and keep in mind, that trip across the ocean, chained in the hull of a ship for months, killed off half the Africans that left the motherland. But not our direct ancestors, yours and mine. They survived! And their children, and their children's children, and generations more of our ancestors survived the atrocity of slavery. And then what? The Civil War ends and in the next one hundred and twenty-nine years, a *mere* one hundred and twenty-nine years— from the year my granddaddy was born to today—we have become the most impressive ethnic group in the world!"

Hal laughed and Godfrey Burnish suddenly lunged forward, thrusting a chubby forefinger in his face. "You think I'm jivin' you, youngblood?" the founder barked. "You think I'm jivin'? I ain't jivin'! Who is the most respected public figure in America today? Colin Powell! Who's the first American novelist to win a Nobel Prize in twenty years? Toni Morrison! The most exciting movie director? Spike Lee! What is the world's most beloved music? Jazz—which we invented! This is not even to mention the blues! Gospel! Rock and roll! Rap! All across the globe people listen to and try to imitate *our* music. What's the most popular sport in the world?"

"Soccer," Hal said.

"Bullshit! It's basketball! You go walk the streets of London, of Paris, of Jerusalem, what do you see the kids wearin'? That red-and-black Chicago Bulls jersey, number twenty-three. Michael Jordan, an African American, is the most famous person in the world. Go to Rome, to Rio, to Tokyo, to Capetown! What do you see? These kids in their baseball caps and baggy pants, tryin' to look like *our* youth! Put it all together, youngblood. We have given, are giving, the world its living culture of today. The world loves what we stylize. And this is just one hundred and twenty-nine years, one hundred thirty-one if you want to date it from the Emancipation Proclamation, since our people have been free. After two hundred fifty years of slavery, we have, in a little more than one and a quarter centuries, become the cultural leaders of the world! The rest of humanity takes its cue from *us!* And I haven't even mentioned all the scientists and great legal minds, all the scholars and political and business leaders we've pro-duced—while fighting for true citizenship *the whole time*! And that was why I just had to smile when I walked out of those slave caves. I was just so damn proud, youngblood. 'Cause we are the baddest people in the history of mankind."

"I agree with you," Hal said politely, "but there are still a lot of problems."

"What sorta problems?"

"Well, one third of all black Americans still live in poverty."

"One third!" Godfrey Burnish boomed. "Do you realize what you're sayin', youngblood? A mere one hundred twenty-nine years after slavery, *only one third* of our people live in poverty. That means *two thirds* of us are doin' all right! We're not even talkin' about the glass bein' half full or half empty. The glass is two thirds full and you're *complainin'* 'cause it's one third empty!"

"All right," Hal said. "Since things in general are going well for black people, you could say that *Esteem,* which mainly publishes pos-itive articles, can afford to write about someone, someone who was as much of a role model as the other people you mentioned, a famous black man, who is now accused of killing a white woman and—"

"HAVE YOU EVER BEEN CHASED BY A LYNCH MOB?"

Godfrey Burnish was suddenly in Hal's face, screaming. The fea-tures of his babyhead were furiously contorted, making the founder look like a deranged elf. Hal was so startled he couldn't respond before the founder shrieked again:

"HAVE YOU EVER BEEN CHASED BY A LYNCH MOB?"

"Can't say I have."

"*I* HAVE!" Hal watched a fleck of spittle fly from the back of

Godfrey Burnish's throat and felt it hit his cheek. "In Pustulana, Mississippi—in 1937!" The founder lowered his voice a notch but was still yelling. "Do you know who the mayor of Pustulana, Mississippi, is today?"

"Can't say I do."

"A black man," the founder said triumphantly. He stood up straight, took a moment to compose himself, then returned to his seat behind the desk. Hal knew there was no point in saying anything, so he remained silent. "Ah, youngblood, don't you see? This is the best time. The 1990s are the best time in the entire history of civilization, and we are living in the best country ever in which to be black. You should be rejoicin', son, singin' hallelujah. I've seen so much in my seventy-five years—I just want to spread the good news. Black people don't need *Esteem* magazine to give 'em drama and trauma. They can get that in plenty of other places. So there will be nothing about this case published in *Esteem*. Not so long as I'm drawing breath." Godfrey Burnish paused for several seconds, then said, "Besides, I've known O.J. since he was at U.S.C." The founder stared steadily at Hal. "O.J. didn't kill them people." Godfrey Burnish looked at his watch. "Now . . . is there anything else?"

"No, sir."

"You may go." Hal rose and was reaching for the door when the founder said, "Cheer up, youngblood. You will go very far in this company . . . if you just learn how to think."

6

Dr. Emmett Mercy wanted to be a designated interlocutor, one of the elite corps of black pundits who were paid money—sometimes *long* money—to tell white people what to think about black people. He knew that as a designated interlocutor, one's first duty was to put white readers at ease. Your tone must at all times be pleasant and reasonable. You must convey that America's racial situation was serious but not dire. Express a nostalgia for the civil disobedience and social protest of yesteryear but point out that such measures are no longer necessary or constructive. Affirmative action was essential in the 1970s, back when Emmett was applying to college and graduate school, but by the 1990s had pretty much served its function. "Mend it, don't end it": That would be the motto of the clever designated interlocutor. Your purpose was not to provoke, to criticize, or to question. Reassurance was your task. Most white Americans, in their hearts, yearned for racial healing, for fairness: As a designated interlocutor, it behooved you to remind white people of their basic decency. There was no racial dilemma so impervious that it could not be managed by reasonable people. You call on the President to create blue-ribbon commissions of experts to study various social problems connected to race. You hope that you will be appointed to some of those blue-ribbon commissions. "Racism *still* exists," you coura-geously tell your audiences. You know that most white folks think they wiped it out back in the sixties. It was up to you, the designated interlocutor, to remind your audiences that not all white people were as enlightened as they were. Sadly, racism still existed. But you had to reassure the people who had designated you interlocutor that someday soon it wouldn't.

Dr. Emmett Mercy realized he was still a long way from becom-ing a designated interlocutor. But he knew the protocol. When he was tapped, he would be ready. In the meantime, and as a necessary phase in the journey that was his life, he had to win the hearts and minds of black people.

*   *   *

"I'm a hoodlum in remission. You know what I'm sayin'?" Outside the uncomfortably warm, stale-smelling Presbyterian church base-ment, on this Thursday night in September 1994, a hard rain battered Manhattan. Inside, at the Amandla workshop, Dr. Emmett Mercy was telling a version of his life's journey. "I'm a recovering gangsta. Like a lotta young brothers, I didn't have a father figure at home. I looked for surrogate daddies in the streets. I thought my homeys could father me. Then I knew I had to father my own self. That's when my ass got drafted. And over there in 'Nam was the only time I felt a brotherhood with the white man. The white fellas in my com-pany—I'm talkin' about the grunts, not the officers—they were my brothers. Then, in April, 'sixty-eight, over Vietnam radio, I'll never forget it, Charlie said, in English: 'Attention, black man. In America, they have murdered your King. Your fight is not here against the yel-low man. Your fight is back home.' And I knew they got that right. I recognized that no matter how tight I mighta been with the fellas in my company, no white man could ever really be my brother."

Dr. Mercy knew he was rambling, but he couldn't help himself. The stories he told were in his book, *Blactualization: Everyday Strategies for Reconnecting with Your Authentic African American Self*. He tried to tell them as he told them in the book, but in conversation the stories never had the flow and coherence of the words on the page. As he could hear himself rambling from one disjointed anecdote to another, his thoughts became scattered. He began to lose a sense of exactly what it was he had set out to say. He kept talking anyway. "You see, we're living through the Great Reeducation. Things we thought we knew, stuff our grandparents knew and tried to teach us, we have to learn again. See, what's happened in America over the last thirty, forty years is things that shoulda never been brought together *were* brought together. And now we have to relearn how to separate those things that by their very nature are meant to be separate. Y'all might not wanta face it, but integration was the problem. That's what led to the breakdown of our communities. That's what has cut us off from our history, from our truest, most authentic selves. Integration deafened us to the folk wisdom of our ancestors. It's time to regain what we lost!"

Dr. Mercy knew he had an important message to bring to people. He had known it from a young age. It took him a long time to find the proper vehicle for his mesage. After the army and college, he spent six months trying to write a novel. Most days he could not concentrate long enough to produce a word. On those days when he did write, he was never satisfied with the result. He finally gave up when he recognized that the Novel was not an authentic African American form of expression. The Sermon, on the other hand, was. Emmett enrolled in divinity school, but unable to complete his dissertation—his thesis was that God, especially the Old Testament God, was demonstrably black—he gave up his idea of becoming a preacher. Emmett realized there was a new religion in America and its name was therapy. He enrolled in New York University's graduate program in psychology. Once again, he failed to earn a doctorate when he found it impossible to complete a dissertation. This time around, Dr. Mercy's subject was the psychological phenomenon of cathexis, that is, the investment of emotional and/or mental energy in a person, object, or idea. A person could cathect his mother. One could cathect an heirloom, like the gold watch chain—not the watch, just the chain—that Emmett's mother had given him. Mark David Chapman cathected John Lennon; he cathected him to death. It was Emmett Mercy's thesis that America had cathected race. America was a roiling cauldron of racial cathexis. Emmett could see that. He could talk about it. But he could never get his ideas on paper. (Or even on the computer screen.) Emmett ultimately recognized that conventional therapy—created by white people for white people—was irrelevant to the lives of African Americans. He took a job as a school administrator in Hallisbury, an hour northwest of New York City. Hallisbury was an almost all-black suburb that had once been upper middle class and was now struggling not to become lower middle class. Though he was not, technically speaking, a Ph.D., he had come close twice, so he had no qualms about signing his name or always introducing himself as Dr. Emmett Mercy. When he moved to Hallisbury in 1986, Dr. Emmett Mercy was thirty-seven years old. He felt he had not yet accomplished anything. He had not even married or had children. He was absolutely convinced that he had an important message to deliver. All he needed was someone to articulate it for him.

"You see, my generation of brothers, we paved the way for y'all." At the Amandla workshop, Dr. Mercy focused on Hal Hardaway— who was, like Tiny Jenks and Walker Du Pree, fifteen years his junior—as he spoke. "Back in the sixties and seventies, when the real battles were bein' fought, it was us who paid the price. Y'all get to reap the benefits. Now, I ain't dissin' you young brothers. I ain't mad atchya. I'm jus sayin' y'all might have something to learn from my generation. We might have something to teach you about responsibili*tee*. 'Cause one of the problems with brothers in y'all's situation is that you haven't faced enough adversi*tee*." Dr. Mercy was speaking loudly now, unable to keep the anger out of his voice. How could he help but resent young black men like Hal and Tiny and Walker, these bourgeois buppies who had never suffered, never sacrificed, and never learned? They were just fifteen years younger than he was, but given the advantages, the opportunities, all the privileges that had simply been handed to them, they might as well have been born in another space-time dimension. Soon these arrogant and coddled neo-Negroes would be publishing books, teaching at universities, expressing their vision of the Afro-American experience. Much as he wanted to, Dr. Emmett Mercy knew there was little he could do to stop them. But he *could* try to tell them what to think. "I don't care how educated you are," Dr. Mercy said, still addressing Hal more than the others. "It don't matter how much money you make or how prominent you are in your profession. You cannot escape the ineluctable modalities of racial consciousness."

Looking at Hal Hardaway, it occurred to Dr. Mercy that the clean-cut young brother in the expensive suit was precisely the sort of man his mother would have wanted him to be. Hell, Hal even worked at Burnish Enterprises! Where would Lady Mercy have been without B.E. in her life? She used Burnish Hair Care Products to get her already fine, light brown hair even straighter and lighter. She applied thick coats of Burnish creams to her face to get her already yellow skin as light as possible. Lady Mercy—though folks suspected she had given herself a siddity nickname, "Lady" was, in fact, what it said on her birth certificate—was even a devoted subscriber to *Esteem* magazine. Living in Impediment, Ohio, in the days before she purchased her first television, Lady Mercy pored over every issue of *Esteem,* her window to the rarefied world of Dorothy Dandridge and

Lena Horne. Lady was even prettier than Lena Horne—people told her that all the time. Lady Mercy was known as the prettiest girl on the black side of town. Once, on an errand to the hardware store, ten-year-old Emmett overheard two old men talking about his mother. "Lady Mercy so pretty, I bet she don't even shit," one old man said to the other. "And if she do, I bet it don't stink!"

No black man was good enough for Lady Mercy to marry—not even Emmett's father, a soldier stationed in Germany. "I don't need no nigga tellin' me what to do," Lady Mercy liked to say when Emmett would ask her why she and his father weren't together. There were plenty of black men in Impediment who were interested in Lady. "I ain't studyin' none of 'em," Lady said. She always made time, however, for Dr. Winkler, a pediatrician from the white side of town who had a habit of showing up, at any time of night, on Lady's doorstep. If Dr. Winkler was around for breakfast, he always gave Emmett a dollar. Hush money.

"So black and ugly." This was Lady Mercy's most damning insult. If some man in town had bothered her, Lady, when recounting the incident to Emmett, would always describe her harasser as being "so black and ugly." The other salesgirls at Impediment's colored department store, Lady maintained, were jealous of her because they were "so black and ugly." Lady always told her honey-toned son how glad she was that he wasn't any darker. *And* Emmett had "hazel" eyes. Whenever Lady saw him with darker playmates, she would ask Emmett why he was hanging around with children who were "so black and ugly." In the mid-sixties, as darker and darker models began to appear in the pages of *Esteem* magazine, Lady Mercy would stare at the photos and shake her head in dismay. "Soooooo black," she would say, before pausing and adding, with a shudder of revulsion, "and *ugly.*"

One of the great regrets of Dr. Emmett Mercy's life was that his mother had not lived long enough to see him marry exactly the sort of woman she despised.

*   *   *

Forty minutes into the Amandla workshop, Dr. Mercy was pleased. Tiny Jenks had the floor, and in that voice of his that was both delicate and sharp, like a glass scalpel, he spoke of gratitude, of how every black man owed a debt of gratitude to every black woman. "Since I've been married," he said, "I've understood that better." Dr. Mercy felt there was good sharing going on. Tiny had gotten the ball rolling earlier when he picked up on Emmett's theme of personal responsibility. Walker Du Pree then opened up, talking about how his fear of responsibility prevented him from marrying his girlfriend, a wonderful black woman. Chester Beer, after his earlier, surprising openness when reminiscing about his mother and grandmother and seeing Paul Robeson at Carnegie Hall and dining at the Automat, had reverted to his usual workshop mode: attentive but silent. Jojo Harrison, scowling in his leather jacket and heavily tinted glasses, had barely moved, let alone spoken. And Hal Hardaway, Dr. Mercy sensed, was beginning to crack. After saying, straight up, that the woman he lived with was white, Hal then talked about problems of communication, about things unsaid, words misinterpreted. But he steadfastly refused to acknowledge his real dilemma, the one Dr. Mercy could hear in his voice, see in his face: Hal was thinking about marrying outside the race, and it was tearing him apart.

"You know," Dr. Mercy said sternly, "sometimes we reject our truest selves in the search for some ideal. We run after some prize, something society tells us we should want. And in chasing after this phantasm, this bauble, we are really running away from ourselves. Look at Brother O.J. Here is a man who was destroyed by white women just as surely as some of our brothers are destroyed by liquor and crack! Didn't y'all see what it said in *Newsweek*? O.J. was *addicted* to white women! 'Cause he was tryin' to run away from his blackness. That's what brothers do, you see. Y'all know what I'm sayin'. 'Cause you've all seen it. A black man who hates being black. Who secretly hates himself because he's black. So what does he do? He gets involved with a white woman."

"What about Charlie Parker?" Walker said.

"Huh?" Dr. Mercy was startled by the interruption.

"Bird had a white wife. Do you think he was trying to escape his blackness?"

"Well, now, I'd—"

"What about Richard Wright? He had a white wife. Jimi Hendrix had white lovers. So did Paul Robeson. Did they all secretly hate being black? What about Harry Belafonte? There's a man who's done more to help black people in this country than you could ever hope to do, Dr. Mercy. He has a white wife. Does that make him a traitor to the race?"

"What about Sidney Poitier?" Chester joined in. "He's a proud black man with a white wife."

"Yeah," Hal said, perking up. "And what about Miles Davis with Juliet Greco? Are you gonna tell us *Miles* had an inferiority complex?"

"Henry Ossawa Tanner was married to a white woman," Chester said.

"Thelonious Monk had a white mistress," Hal added.

Emmett felt as if he was losing control of the session. Finally, someone jumped to his defense. "None of those examples refute what Dr. Mercy is saying," Tiny Jenks declared.

"Oh no?" Walker shot back in his obnoxious white-boy accent. "Well, I'd like to know what it is you meant by adversity, Dr. Mercy?"

Emmett felt that Walker was openly challenging him. He was ready to strike back. "I mean that character is built by adversity. Those of you who have not faced enough adversity will, therefore, be of weak character."

"Define adversity," Walker said.

"Not havin' enough to *eat* is adversity," Dr. Mercy fumed. "Bein' so po' you don't even know if your ass is gonna be out on the street *tomorrow*. That's adver*sitee*!"

"Then by that standard, all poor people are of sterling character. Have you found this to be true, Dr. Mercy?"

Before Emmett could respond, Hal piped up again. "Do you think that just because someone has economic security they don't have any pain?"

"I didn't say that," Dr. Mercy protested.

"Or do you think that material problems," Hal continued, "make all other problems insignificant by comparison?"

"Yes!"

"What about an incest survivor?" Walker asked. "You could be a rich girl, but let's say your father sexually abused you on a regular basis when you were a child. It doesn't matter how much money you have. You could still be in a lot of pain as an adult."

"Well, what I would say to you," Dr. Mercy retorted, "is that black America is the abused child of the American family!"

"All I know," Tiny said in his delicately sharp voice, "is that everybody in this life, at one time or another, has to eat shit. Don't matter how high and mighty you are, there will always be somebody, maybe somebody you love, who will be eager to teach you humility. Everybody has to eat shit. Sometimes I think life is just one big shit casserole. And we all gotta have a slice."

"*Bon appetit!*" Walker said.

For the first time, Dr. Emmett Mercy had lost his grip on an Amandla workshop. "Okay, okay," he said nervously, "let's think about what Brother Tiny just said." Struggling to find the right words, Emmett felt like someone trying to take hold of handfuls of smoke. "You see, what it all leads back to is what I said before, you know what I'm sayin'? I said it before and I'll say it again: You cannot escape the ineluctable modalities of racial consciousness."

"Ineluctable modalities?" Jojo Harrison said. This was the longest string of syllables the scowling man with the shaved head and the dark glasses had put together all night. The other men in the workshop were startled, not only by the fact that Jojo had spoken, but by the way he sounded. Jojo had a voice like a blunt instrument. "Nigga, what the fuck is you talkin' about?"

Dr. Mercy was flustered. "Well, now, Brother Jojo, listen here—"

"You listen to me, nigga!" Jojo boomed. "You is one jiveass turkey!"

"Excuse me," Tiny said politely, "but could I ask that we not address each other as nigger?"

"Say what, nigga?" Jojo yelled at Tiny. "You know what your problem is, little man?" Jojo rose from his folding chair and stood in the center of the circle. Dr. Mercy considered this a very aggressive gesture. "You just afraid of black women!" Jojo said, pointing at Tiny. "Well, *I'm* not! I'm sick a them damn crows! Your wife tell you you should be grateful? Sheeeeeeet. You oughta smack some sense into that bitch!"

"Hey now, hey now," Dr. Mercy interjected. "We do not advocate violence against our sisters here. Now, Brother Jojo, please sit down, I—"

"And you!" Jojo said, turning and pointing at Hal. "What the fuck you so scared of? You wanna fuck a white bitch, go fuck a white bitch! You ain't gots to feel *bad* about it. What the fuck you whinin' about, nigga? I tellya, I fucked many a white bitch in my day!"

At this, Walker Du Pree burst into laughter. Hal simply stared at

Jojo, who stood over him, a finger thrust in his face. Chester Beer stared at the floor, as if he hoped that Jojo would, if ignored, disappear. Tiny looked at Dr. Mercy, his eyes pleading with the workshop leader to do something. Dr. Mercy could not think straight. He was furious at Jojo, but he was even angrier at Walker, who had started all this conflict and now seemed to think it was funny.

"Oooooooh, yeah," Jojo continued. "I've fucked lotsa them white bitches. A white bitch'll do shit a sister would *never* do. I had a white bitch used to like to lick my asshole. And damn if it didn't feel *good!*"

Walker was now laughing like a hyena.

"Whatchoo squealin' at, yellow nigga? You sho looks like a faggot to me with them braids. You like to take it up the ass, don'tcha, yellow nigga?"

"We're not here to insult our gay brothers," Emmett said meekly.

"Yeah, you laughin'," Jojo jeered at Walker, " 'cause you know it's the truth."

"That's enough now," Chester Beer said, looking directly at Jojo. "You take that shit outta here, man."

"And you!" Jojo said, whirling on Chester. "You is one sorry, country-ass nigga! Impressed by a damn Automat? They shoulda never let yo ignorant ass outta Alabama!"

"Brother Jojo," Emmett said, "I'm gonna have to ask you to leave."

"Shut the fuck up, jiveass turkey! You ain't done nothin' but talk shit all night. Yo, I was in 'Nam, too, and I wasn't shootin' *nothin'* but white boys! Niggas would go out on patrol with them crackers and just niggas come back alive. You know why? 'Cause we was shootin' 'em honkies in the back! You damn right. Niggas be sayin' *Blam*! That's another one of you muthafuckas we ain't gonna haveta worry about when we get back home."

"Are you through?" Dr. Mercy said. He stared evenly at Jojo. He had relocated his nerve. His voice was firm and sonorous again.

"Say what, jiveass turkey?"

"Are you through?"

Jojo Harrison paused, seemed to take a moment to collect himself. "Naw," Jojo said flatly. "I got one more thing to say. You wanna know what a black man is? You wanna know what a black *man* is?"

"Yes."

Jojo grabbed his crotch, squeezed hard. "You lookin' at it." With that, Jojo Harrison turned around and stalked out of the church basement.

*   *   *

Dr. Mercy tried to resume the session after Jojo's exit, but he soon realized that the atmosphere had been irrevocably poisoned. He spoke words of reconciliation, but none of the remaining brothers in the Amandla workshop seemed to be concentrating. Dr. Mercy glanced at his watch. The session was scheduled to run for another half hour, until eight-thirty. But Dr. Mercy knew it was pointless to continue. He had lost them. He handed Hal and Walker, Amandla first-timers, forms on which to write their addresses and telephone numbers. While Hal filled out the form, Walker folded his up and stuffed it in his pocket. Dr. Mercy offered copies of his book, at half the cover price, but no one was buying. Out in the street, the rain had stopped. Standing in front of the church, the men exchanged handshakes and awkward good-byes. Dr. Mercy offered to drive Chester Beer home. They were silent all the way to Hallisbury. Dr. Mercy did not know what, exactly, was on Chester's mind and he was too upset to say what he was thinking: that the Amandla workshop had alienated Hal Hardaway, someone who might have been a valuable asset in helping Emmett get his important message out.

After dropping Chester off at his home in the "old town" section of Hallisbury, Dr. Mercy drove east to the more isolated, affluent area of the suburb. One year earlier, Emmett and his wife, LaTonya, had lived near Chester in old town. Then royalties from the paperback edition of *Blactualization* began to kick in. Dr. Mercy was introduced to the lucrative lecture circuit. Now he was about to start work on his second book, a book that he hoped would have a broader appeal; a tome that would catapult him from the black self-help literary ghetto into the ranks of designated interlocutors; a masterpiece that would do nothing less than define the future of the black race in America. He would call it *The Destiny of Our People*. It would be a monumental undertaking, but he was prepared to face the challenge. As a writer and thinker, he had, at last, found his voice. In fact, he had married it.

LaTonya, LaTonya, LaTonya; Lord, how he loved his kinky-haired, broad-nosed, full-lipped, big-titted, bountifully buttocked, dark brown beauty. He had fallen in love the minute he saw her, six years earlier. It was Chester Beer who had found LaTonya, wandering in the street, on the run-down edge of old town, and brought her to the Hallisbury homeless shelter. Chester wondered if she was a crack addict or a prostitute. LaTonya was a mess when Emmett first laid eyes on her, curled up on a cot, staring straight ahead at nothing, refusing to speak. But Emmett could feel her spirit. There was loveliness and intelligence, grace and fire in this sister. He knew as he watched LaTonya, oblivious to him, shivering slightly under the threadbare blanket, that he and this broken woman, who radiated a power that only he could see, were fated to be together. Before he had said a word to LaTonya, Emmett knew he would marry her—and the bony clatter he imagined he heard was the sound of Lady Mercy twirling in her grave.

With love and kindness and the maximum daily dosage of extremely potent antipsychotic medication, Emmett saved LaTonya's life. And LaTonya had repaid him in the most miraculous way. It began as a simple favor. In 1990, a year after they had married, LaTonya offered to transcribe Emmett's tapes. She had seen them lying around the apartment in old town Hallisbury, boxes and boxes of audiocassettes, filled with the rambling thoughts of Emmett Mercy, the oral notes on his two abandoned dissertations, and later attempts at philosophical essays. Emmett told her the tapes were gibberish. LaTonya said she didn't care.

When Emmett read LaTonya's typed version of one box of his tapes, he could not believe he was reading his own ideas, his own experience. And, in fact, he wasn't. It was LaTonya's version of his ideas and experiences, rendered in prose that was shapely and nimble. Playing back the audiocassettes, Emmett was astonished by what LaTonya had done with his vague memories, his convoluted anecdotes and inarticulate musings. LaTonya had gone and written a book.

Of course, it was *his* book, *Blactualization.* LaTonya may have done the actual writing, but she was working from Dr. Emmett Mercy's raw material. It was Dr. Emmett Mercy who signed the book contract; his name and photo that appeared on the book jacket; and his fame that bought them their big new house in the bougiest quarter of black suburbia. And though it was LaTonya who would do the day-to-day typing on *The Destiny of Our People,* it was Dr. Mercy who would meet with publishers as the author of the work. Dr. Mercy believed he was crossing over from the marketplace of ideas to the marketplace of the personality. That was why he hoped Hal Hardaway had not been upset by the breakdown of the Amandla workshop that night. An article by or about Dr. Mercy in *Esteem* magazine, an appearance on WBUR Radio or Burnish Arts and Information Television could be extremely useful in helping Emmett get his important message out. Such exposure in the media might even lead someday to the realization of Dr. Mercy's newest ambition: hosting his very own TV talk show.

As he pulled into the driveway of his big new house, Emmett thought of how lucky he was to have LaTonya for a wife. He knew that even once he became a full-blown celebrity, a famous designated interlocutor, LaTonya would keep him grounded. Emmett was even considering putting LaTonya's name on his next book. Not as coauthor, though. *"The Destiny of Our People* by Dr. Emmett Mercy" and then, in much smaller type, "As Told to LaTonya Mercy": That was what he envisioned on his next book jacket. He was sure LaTonya would appreciate such a magnanimous gesture. LaTonya, LaTonya, LaTonya. Dr. Emmett Mercy knew that, along with his growing fame, would come temptations. It was already starting to happen: gorgeous sisters coming up to him after one of his lectures, thanking him for his wisdom, gazing at him with admiration and desire in their eyes, handing him their telephone numbers. Dr. Mercy had not yet given in to temptation. He knew that someday he might. But if he did, it would be only for carnal pleasure. No one could take the place of LaTonya. She would always be his Number One Woman. Dr. Mercy decided that if and when he did give in to temptation, he would keep it secret from LaTonya. He also felt confident that if LaTonya did find out, she would understand. And forgive.

Walking into his big new house, tired and glum, Emmett looked forward to holding LaTonya in his arms, nuzzling his nose in the dark abundance of her breasts, reveling in the sweet solace she gave him. LaTonya was in the kitchen, warming up Emmett's dinner. She wore a kente-patterned bathrobe and fuzzy slippers. A red-and-white bandana was tied around her head. After a comforting hug and a kiss, Emmett sat down at the kitchen table and told his wife how tonight's Amandla workshop had gone all wrong. He talked about Jojo Harrison and his negative vibrations. He blamed himself for losing control of the conversation. And he talked about the young executive from Burnish Enterprises whom he had so desperately wanted to impress. LaTonya listened attentively to her husband as she filled his plate with mashed potatoes and peas and two thick pork chops smothered in onions and gravy.

"This brother from B.E.," Emmett said, "he could have any black woman he wanted. He's got looks, brains, money. And yet he's all hung up on some white chick."

"Tccch." LaTonya sucked her teeth in irritation. "Some people just have to do everything the hard way."

"Funny you should say that."

"What?" LaTonya turned from the stove and walked toward the table, carrying Emmett's steaming plate of food.

"This brother from B.E.—his name is Hal Hardaway—"

Midway between the stove and the table, LaTonya Mercy abruptly stopped, her body going rigid. As she froze in the center of the kitchen, the plate dropped from her hand. There was an explosion of gravy, of flying peas and ceramic shards, as the plate shattered on the white linoleum floor.

The demon had taken control.

7

Hal's testicles ached so agonizingly he couldn't walk straight. Crouched in a sort of bowlegged stagger, he made his way toward Smegma House, his eyes squinting from the pain in his semen-gorged balls. Three o'clock in the morning and the party at the football frat was reaching a frenzied crescendo. Hal could hear the howls of thick-necked athletes and the guitars of Lynyrd Skynyrd when he was still three blocks away. Hal had not expected to show up at Smegma. He had expected that, by three A.M., he would be in bed with Miranda. Hal had planned it all so meticulously. First he took Miranda to see a romantic movie, *An Officer and a Gentleman*. Then he treated her to a candlelight dinner. By the time they left the Italian restaurant, arm in arm, Hal was certain he would have sex with Miranda that night. They went to a big party at Harambe, the dorm where most black upperclassmen lived. At two o'clock they were slow-dancing, Miranda sensuously rubbing her pelvis against Mr. Bone. Half an hour later, Hal and Miranda were kissing feverishly outside her dorm, Plimsoll Hall. As Miranda fumbled for her key, Hal's main worry was that he would prematurely ejaculate. Miranda was so gorgeous and he was so hot for her, he didn't know if he'd be able to control Mr. Bone.

"Thanks for a great night," Miranda said as she swung open the door.

"Hey," Hal said, trying not to become alarmed, "the night is just beginning."

"I'm sorry, Hal, I have to get up for choir tomorrow morning."

"You're not serious!"

"Call me tomorrow." Miranda closed the door on Hal.

That was the start of his testicular torture. As he stumbled toward Smegma House, it occurred to Hal that after Miranda's rejection, he should have gone straight back to his dorm and jerked off—if only to end the excruciation. But he didn't want to return to Mould Hall at two-thirty or three. Because if Walker was there in the room, or returned later, it would be obvious that Hal had not gotten laid that night. The uncool roommate he had so impressed with his bravado might then guess the secret, Hal's private disgrace: At age eighteen, near the end of his first month of college, Hal Hardaway was still a virgin.

Walking into the pandemonium of Smegma House, Hal slipped in a puddle of beer and nearly fell. Through the dense crowd, he spotted someone emptying a bottle of grain alcohol into a half-empty punch bowl. Hal headed in that direction. Angry, horny, and feeling like a chump, a loser, Hal was determined to get seriously drunk. After several hours of drinking already, he was well on his way to oblivion. He quickly downed two glasses of punch and was starting on a third when he heard a quiet woman's voice slice through the cacophony around him: "Where have you been? I've been waiting for you."

Hal turned and saw Tony Dawson staring intensely at him.

"What about *her?*" Hal had said to Walker ten hours earlier as they sat on the Mould Hall terrace scoping out the quad. Hal pointed to Tony Dawson, who was walking along a path a hundred yards away. She noticed Hal pointing at her and waved. Hal smiled and waved back. "Too black for you, eh?"

"Nooooo," Walker said.

"Too, quote unquote, fat?"

"Wrong again. Too crazy. Look in her eyes. Tony is in my Spanish class. She's got a crazy person's eyes."

Only then did Hal realize what he had always found slightly unsettling about Tony Dawson. "She does have kind of a weird stare."

"Most crazy people have it," Walker said authoritatively. "Actually, it's more like an absence. When you look into their eyes, something is missing. You know how most of us have this little switch in our mind that tells us, 'Hey, don't do that crazy thing you're thinking about doing'? Crazy people don't have that mechanism. You can see that absence in their eyes."

At Smegma House, standing face-to-face with Tony, Hal knew exactly what Walker meant. "I was worried you might not show up," Tony Dawson said. Tony rarely said anything at all, and when she did speak it was always in this soft, virtually expressionless voice.

"Worried?" Hal said with a nervous laugh. "You shouldn't worry about me, Tony." Hal gulped down the rest of his punch, then refilled his glass. He felt a bit wobbly, but at least the pain in his balls was receding. "So is this a good party?"

"It's okay," Tony said, continuing to concentrate on Hal, as if she were reading a text that was written on his face. Tony Dawson was an assistant manager on the football team, a miserable job from what Hal could see. Tony and the other two assistant managers were called on to fetch towels and Gatorade, to pick up scattered pieces of equipment, and to keep schedules and log books up to date. Members of a football team's managerial staff were usually nerdy, out-of-shape guys who could never have made the squad as players but loved the sport and wanted to get to hang around jocks. Tony Dawson was the only woman, and the only black person, on the Craven football team's managerial staff. Hal did not consider Tony pretty. But she had enormous tits and a behind that was the quintessence of cash butter. Like all the other guys on the team, Hal flirted with Tony during football practice and made lewd comments about her in the locker room. He definitely did not want to be her boyfriend. Miranda was the only woman Hal had on his mind. But the way Tony Dawson was always staring at him, concentrating on him, made Hal think that maybe she had a crush on him. Now, standing six inches away from him at the Smegma party, staring crazily, Tony, in her soft monotone, asked, "Do you wanna dance?"

"Sorry," Hal said. "All I wanna do right now is pee."

Uncertain on his feet, moving cautiously through the crowd toward the nearest bathroom, Hal feared he might pass out. As he stood over the toilet, eyes closed, he felt as if he were floating. He heard his stream of urine splashing into the smelly bowl of water and let out a long, satisfying "Aaaaaaaaah . . ." He slammed down the lid and flushed the toilet. When he opened the bathroom door, Tony Dawson was standing outside. "Your turn," Hal said. As he started to walk out of the bathroom, Tony blocked his path. "Excuse me," Hal said. Tony grabbed Hal by the shoulders and pushed him back into the bathroom. She then followed him inside, closing and locking the door behind her. "Aw, shit," Hal said. "What are you doing, Tony?"

"Don't you want me?" Tony asked in her bland, uninflected voice.

"I'm really out of it right now, Tony, I—"

"I can give you what you want. I know what you want. I can give it to you. I want to give it to you." Tony moved toward Hal. She pressed her breasts against his chest. "Don't you like me?" She started to unzip his fly, groped for his cock.

"Yo, yo, Tony," Hal said, trying as gently as he could to push her away.

"Don't you like me?"

"Yes, I like you."

"Then let me give you what you want."

Now Hal felt as if he were wrestling with Tony in the small, confined space of the bathroom, twisting his body, pushing her away as she tried to get a firmer grip on him. "Don't you like me?" Tony kept saying. "Don't you like me?"

"Goddamn it!" Hal finally yelled. "Back off!"

Tony's arms suddenly dropped to her sides. She took a step backward, looking stunned. All her energy seemed to have instantly disappeared. She plopped down on the closed toilet seat. Tony no longer stared at Hal. Her gaze was focused on the dirty white tiles of the bathroom floor. Hal worried that he had hurt her feelings.

"Hey," Hal said, looking down at Tony's bowed head, feeling more and more woozy in his drunkenness. "I'm really sorry. It's just that, you know, I like somebody else." Tony mumbled something Hal did not understand. "Hey, Tony . . . Hey."

"You think I'm ugly," Tony said.

"No, I don't."

"You think I'm ugly," Tony said again, still staring at the floor.

"That's not true. That's not true at all."

"You think I look like a monkey."

"What?" Hal was flabbergasted. "Tony," he said deliberately, "I do not think that. I would *never* think that." Hal paused. "Tony?"

"Leave me alone."

"Hey, Tony, I think you're really nice." Hal leaned down to get closer to her.

"Get away from me."

"I just want to say—"

"GET THE FUCK AWAY FROM ME!" Tony exploded.

Hal jumped back. Without saying another word, he left the bathroom and closed the door behind him. He made a beeline for the
punch bowl, poured himself another glass, and gulped it down.

*   *   *

"Strip pokeeeeeer!"

Hal had not realized he'd fallen asleep until Duane Kordo's
maniacal scream jolted him awake. Hal found himself slumped on a
couch. He looked at his watch: four-thirty. He glanced around the
room. The Smegma party had thinned out. There were several couples slow-dancing to a ballad Hal did not recognize. Surrounding the
slow-dancing couples were the dregs of the party, horny men and
lonely young women, drifting around the room and warily eyeing one
another. Hal noticed that he was the only black person left at the
party. It was time to go home. Rubbing his eyes as he rose from the
couch, Hal heard Duane Kordo holler again.

"Strip poker! In the pool room!"

Kordo strode across the dance floor, brandishing a deck of cards.
Four other freshmen—Hal knew them only by their last names:
Loomis, Wilson, Carmichael, and McBride—hovered around Kordo
like fawning suitors. Duane Kordo was the rookie sensation of the
Craven team, a punishing steamroller of a fullback, a former high-
school star out of prime football country—Monongahela, Pennsylvania—who had been recruited by the top powers of the NCAA before
busting up his knee at the start of his senior year. Failing to win a
Division I scholarship, Duane Kordo wound up at Craven U. Even
with a surgically repaired but still iffy knee, Kordo dominated the
competition in Craven's league. Here, after all, was a guy who could
have been—and might still be—an NFL prospect, playing with and
against guys who knew that a good seat in the season tickets holders'

section was as close as they were ever likely to get to the pro game. All of Duane Kordo's teammates—including Hal Hardaway—were in awe of him. Now Kordo was right in Hal's face, yelling.

"Strip poker! The chicks are down in the pool room! Be there, dude!"

Kordo was a massive person, with a large, blocky head, a blond crew cut, and eyes that were swimming-pool blue. Staring into Duane Kordo's eyes, Hal saw it, that quality of which Walker had spoken, the absence in a crazy person's eyes.

"I'm goin' home, man," Hal said.

"Pussy!" Duane Kordo yelled in Hal's face. He turned and, entourage of lesser football players in trail, headed for the staircase to the basement.

* * *

Hal was not sure where he was. His eyes were closed, his body was moving, though just barely, his feet shuffling on the sticky wood floor. He slowly became conscious of the body entwined with—if not propping up—his. Hal opened his eyes and saw that he was dancing with a girl with teased blond hair and thick, flourlike makeup that was starting to flake. She didn't look like a Craven student. Probably a townie. Hal did not know how he had wound up dancing with her. Before he arrived at Craven U. Hal had never been drunk in his life. At college he seemed to be shit-faced every other night. But never like tonight. He could not remember things that had happened only minutes earlier. Or he forgot them and then they came rushing back like long-lost memories. It was happening right now. He remembered being in the room in the Smegma House basement that contained a pool table. The room was decorated in a nautical mode, with heavy ropes and nets hanging from the wood-paneled walls. There were rickety model ships and embalmed fish embedded in wooden plaques scattered about the low-ceilinged den. A metal door was open, revealing Smegma's backyard. And sitting around a green felt card table were Duane Kordo and his entourage of Loomis, Wilson, Carmichael, and McBride. There was only one other person—the only woman—at the table: Tony Dawson.

"Yo, Hal!" Duane yelled. "Come on down, dude! Tony's the shittiest poker player you ever saw. She loses the next hand—"

"And it's off with the shirt!" Loomis shouted.

The guys all started hooting and pumping their fists. Hal looked at Tony but she did not look back. She stared at the cards in her hand, the crazy absence in her eyes, an inscrutable little half-smile on her face.

Now slow-dancing with the white townie, Hal could not remember when he had gone down to the pool room. Or why. Or when or why he had returned upstairs. He sort of remembered this girl with her teased blond hair and cakey makeup approaching him. "Did anybody ever tell you you look just like O.J. Simpson?" she squealed.

Now the white townie was saying good-bye to Hal. "My ride is leaving. You should get some sleep."

Hal smiled and waved. He went back down to the pool room.

"Brown Sugar" was blasting on the pool room's stereo. Loomis, Wilson, Carmichael, and McBride were taking the room apart, knocking paintings of stormy seascapes off the walls, tearing down the heavy ropes and fishnets. Duane Kordo was dancing furiously around the room, miming a microphone and drowning out Mick Jagger as he shrieked, "Aaaaaaaaaw, brown sugar! How come ya dance so good, yeah!" Kordo contorted his face and gyrated his hips. Dancing beside him was Tony Dawson, wearing only a bright white bra and matching panties. "Just like a black girl should, yeah!" Duane Kordo wailed.

Tony Dawson danced with her eyes only half open. She did not look at Hal. She did not really look at anyone. She spun around, her large breasts bouncing rhythmically to the music. It occurred to Hal that he might be dreaming. There was a sense of unreality about the scene before him. Maybe it was going to be a wet dream. Watching Tony dance, Hal could feel Mr. Bone go rigid. But Hal was also afraid. He had the feeling, much more acute in dreams than it usually is in waking life, that absolutely anything could happen. He had the sense, again with a dreamlike acuity, that something terrible was about to happen and there was nothing he could do to stop it.

Then Hal thought he heard Tony Dawson say, in her quiet, toneless voice: "You wanna tie me up?"

Kordo's boys were now dancing around Tony, wrapping her in the rope and fishnet. "Yeeeeeee-hah!" Duane Kordo yelled into his imaginary microphone.

The next thing Hal knew, he was alone in the room, leaning against the pool table, trying to remain upright. A grating Rod Stewart song was playing on the stereo. Where had everybody gone? Hal felt a breeze waft in through the open metal door. He staggered outside, into the vast backyard of Smegma House. In the early-morning darkness, Hal saw Duane Kordo dancing around a tall tree, unfurling a long expanse of rope as he circled the oak three times. Tony Dawson had her back against the tree. The heavy rope that had decorated the walls of the pool room hung loosely around her body. Loomis, Wilson, Carmichael, and McBride stood nearby, hooting and clapping and pumping their fists. Hal stood behind them, mesmerized. Tony was looking straight at him. He was a good twenty yards away, but her crazy gaze pierced the darkness.

"Woooooo-hoooo!" one of Kordo's cronies shouted. "Brown shugah!"

Duane began unbuckling his belt.

"Go for it, dude!" one of the cronies yelled.

At that moment, Hal worried for Tony's safety. He took a step forward, thinking he should intervene, try to stop what was about to happen, was already happening. He heard Kordo unzip his fly. Hal was about to do something—but then he saw Tony Dawson smile. She had barely moved. She just stood there, her back pressed against the tree, the whiteness of her bra and panties shining against her dark brown skin, cutting through the darkness of the early morning, heavy ropes and strands of fishnet hanging loosely around her. Was Hal mistaken or was Tony Dawson actually smiling? "Help," Tony said in her soft, uninflected voice. "Help," she said again. But because she did not move and because she seemed to have that little smile on her face, everyone—everyone, that is, except Hal—just laughed. "Help," Tony said again quietly, without moving an inch.

"Brown shugah!" somebody yelled again.

Hal stood frozen on the moist grass of the Smegma House backyard. He did not know if he wanted to leave, to intervene, or to fuck Tony himself. So he simply watched. Duane Kordo was rubbing his body against Tony's. He was grunting and fumbling with her panties as she rested motionless against the tree, crazy eyes staring straight ahead. Kordo's jeans were halfway down his hairy white butt. He was writhing and grunting, but Hal could not tell if he was actually fucking Tony or just dry-humping her. Loomis, Wilson, Carmichael, and McBride were no longer hooting and clapping. Like Hal, they simply stared in fascination. Kordo's hips were bucking wildly now and he was grunting and gasping so loudly, so theatrically, that Hal thought for sure he was just play-acting. And Tony Dawson, who now had her eyes closed and her mouth slightly open but who still did not move or make a sound, must have been, Hal thought, playacting, too, pretending to be a damsel in distress, tied to a tree and letting out meek little bleats of "Help, help." Yes, this was just frat house fun and games. This was college, right? Finally, Duane Kordo stopped his grunting and writhing. He slowly stepped away from Tony. None of the six young men standing on the lawn said anything. There was no music coming through the open door of the pool room: The Rod Stewart song had ended a minute earlier. All Hal heard was the faint chirping of crickets.

Then came the sound; not a cry or a sob or a scream. Tony Dawson was moaning. Or rather, she let out one long moan, a wrenching ululation that seemed to come from someplace deep inside her. As the long, horrific moan echoed through the backyard, Tony Dawson slowly crumpled to the ground and curled up on the moist grass. Hal could feel himself backing away. He turned and walked quickly across the backyard. Now he was on a sidewalk. He could still hear Tony Dawson moaning. But he was walking, walking very fast, away from the scene of the crime.

2

Cathexis

8

Ah, yes, the Stinky Skunk Spud, that glorious alliterative moniker that seemed to radiate from the flimsy printed menu—a menu!—that the proprietor handed to Walker Du Pree, standing out from the other selections, the varieties of Thai stick and Moroccan hash; that Stinky Skunk Spud, so sublimely smelly that Walker's head jerked back when he opened the small plastic Ziploc bag that contained two grams of the stuff—bright, glow-in-the-dark green it was, traffic-light emerald with almost indiscernible red threads running through it, not a single seed in the packet, of course—practically knocking him off the fake cowhide-covered stool he'd mounted at the bar of the Great Dane coffee shop, an Amsterdam institution. He sprinkled some of the marijuana on the glossy wood counter. The fragrance of it, at once peppery and sweet, filled his nostrils. Walker had always hated joints. After twelve years of smoking grass regularly, he had never learned how to roll a decent one. He pulled out the cheap metal pipe he'd bought and stuffed the bowl. He raised the pipe to his lips. Ignition. Inhalation. Ooooooh, so smooth. And tasty green. He closed his mouth and swallowed, felt the smoke fill his lungs. Exhaled. He savored that herbal flavor on his tongue. Now came the real test. Yes, the shit was as iridescent and as fragrant as could be. And though he could never remember how to convert grams to ounces, he'd just bought two grams of this Stinky Skunk Spud for twenty-five Dutch gilders, which, at the current rate of exchange, was roughly twelve U.S. dollars, and he knew he had more than two dime bags of dope in this plastic sack, and besides, what used to be known as a dime bag cost you twenty bucks in New York these days anyway, so . . . wait a minute. Walker paused and stared into space. What had he just been thinking? Right. Would it get him stoned? Well, he had to laugh, because he knew he already was. Walker took another hit. He felt tingly fingers, at least twenty of them, massaging the inside of his scalp. He felt that dreamy elevation. Getting high. What an apt expression it was. Walker felt lightsome and omniscient. This is what he had come for. And, it occurred to him, this particular exaltation was, in fact, what he lived for.

Walker took a look around the Great Dane. Two guys in black leather jackets, with short haircuts and pale, dour faces, sat at the bar. One guy was sipping tea, the other rolling a joint. The Dane was a dark and oaky place. The television above the bar was tuned to MTV Europe, the volume turned all the way down. A black French rap band—Walker recognized them but couldn't remember the name—its members dressed like Compton homeboys in baseball caps and baggy jackets, gesticulated extravagantly, violently, silently. U2 was playing on the Great Dane's sound system. Walker turned around and checked out the couple sitting at the small table behind him. The girl had stringy brown hair and wore a yellowish thermal undershirt that matched her skin tone. She was nodding slowly to the music and smoking a cigarette. The guy had a ponytail and a goatee and stared vacantly at nothing. A sizable chunk of hashish rested beside the ashtray. Walker smiled. This was all like some weird dream he might have. Here he was, sitting in a public place, getting totally fucked up—and so was everyone around him! Pothead paradise.

"Hullo," the girl behind the counter said brightly. She had a round, open face with deep dimples and a spiky haircut.

"Oh, hi," Walker said, feeling spaced out and goofy. She wanted to take his order for food and/or beverage. Yes. Different from the little drug podium at the back of the Great Dane, that lectern-type stand where Walker had gone to buy his Stinky Skunk. Glancing toward the drug podium, Walker saw a tall, thin man in a suit, tie, and trenchcoat, a man with a briefcase—he could have been a lawyer or a banker—a perfect Dutch yuppie, make a purchase. The yuppie slipped the dope in his coat pocket and walked briskly out of the Great Dane. Walker turned back to the open-faced barmaid. He looked at the blackboard behind her, scanned the selection of herbal teas, coffee, cappuccino, soft drinks. The only liquor available was Amstel and Heineken, on tap. This made perfect sense to Walker. Drunk and stoned could be an unpleasant combination. Whereas a good caffeine-marijuana buzz made one feel deliciously serene and alert. His eye caught a display of pastries behind a glass case. "All righty," Walker said, "I'll have a cup of coffee and, uh, is that chocolate cake in the window there?"

"It's chocolate hash cake," the spiky-haired girl said gaily.

"Really?" Walker beamed. "Gimme a slice of that."

The cake was chocolatey enough, but it had a dense, slightly gummy texture. Walker chewed contentedly, staring into the big wall mirror behind the bar.

Fortified by his narcotic dessert, Walker stepped out into the shadowy afternoon. The atmosphere of gloom was one of the things he loved best about Amsterdam in November: the low brick buildings, in varying shades of gray, black, and deep red, the always-gray sky, the black water in the canals that snaked all through the city, the gritty, often rain-slicked cobblestones. The murkiness of the place offered a satisfying contrast to his drug-induced levity as Walker Du

Pree strolled down the street—he was on Oudezijds Voorburgwal, which, like just about all the streets in Amsterdam, the Nieuwendijks and Reguliersbreestraats and Uilenburgergrachts and Oosterdokskades, he didn't even bother trying to pronounce, simply recognizing the jumble of characters and associating them with certain landmarks to get his bearings, but not even saying the names in his head—with a jaunty little bounce to his gait. He walked across a short bridge that stretched over a canal, turned onto another unpronounceable street, and wandered into the heart of the red-light district, a world of narrow, twisting, neon-bathed alleys where the sex shop windows displayed not only huge pink and brown dildos, leather masks, nipple clamps, inflatable dolls with O-shaped mouths, and photos of men fucking women and men fucking men and women fucking women, but, to Walker's endless disgust and fascination, pictures of women fucking animals: a German shepherd lying on his back, a distracted, somehow forlorn expression on his face, as a grinning, very pink-skinned woman sat astride him, the dog's penis disappearing into her vagina; a lank-haired woman with a drawn, junkie's face, her open mouth poised over the thin red dick of a goat, the long scarlet member looking almost like a particularly bright licorice stick as it protruded from a nest of gray fur.

Walker turned down one of the streets where prostitutes were displayed behind glass doors like lunch specials at an Automat. Behind each door, there in plain sight, was a woman wearing nothing but lacy panties and a brassiere, or perhaps a slip or a bikini. Sometimes they simply sat on chairs, in narrow rooms bathed in purple light, and stared out at the street, looking supremely bored. Other hookers stood preening behind the glass doors, smiling lasciviously, trying to make eye contact with you. Most of them were pretty skanky-looking, but once in a while Walker would spot a stunner, usually an Indonesian woman with long, jet-black hair and unblemished, dusky skin. But he walked quickly past the human display cases. There were always pimps lurking about, coming up to any man who paused too long, trying to make a deal, lure you inside. Horny and lonely as he was, Walker could not bring himself to pay for sex. Not to mention the risk of incurable disease. He assumed all the hookers had their clients use condoms. Still, the idea of paying a woman, even a beautiful Indonesian woman, fifty gilders to suck him off through a latex sack did not appeal to Walker. Then why did he always quicken his pace, even as he cast furtive glances the women's way, when he walked through one of the prostitute rows? Because there was always that modicum of temptation, that what-the-hell impulse of curiosity that had to be squelched.

Better simply to buy a porno magazine, go back to his room in the Hotel Elyssia, smoke another bowl of Skunk, and jerk off. Walker ducked into the nearest sex shop and perused the vast selection of hardcore fare. It was repugnant stuff, of course, demeaning to women, no doubt about that, but also, in its self-conscious vileness, an abasement of men, a gruesome presentation of what men were capable of. But Walker was in the mood for a good crawl through the slime of sexual degradation—as long as it was only in a magazine. He picked up a publication with the evocative title *Plaster My Face with Cum*. Here was real truth in advertising, as the magazine consisted of one-hundred-plus pages of photos of penises shooting gooey projectiles, splattering semen all over the cheeks and chins and lolling tongues of an international mélange of women—black, Asian, Latino, Scandinavian. . . . Most of the photos featured captions in four languages: Dutch, German, French, and English. English English, that is, as opposed to American English: "I chatted up Nigel at the disco. I wondered if he'd have enough wads in his ball bag to satisfy me. But after giving me the shag of my life, he treated me to a spunky shower!" or "It takes two blokes to keep me in shape. And I can't wait to get a mouthful of that energy-giving protein. That's all the vitamins I need, lads!" Walker paid fifteen gilders for *Plaster My Face with Cum* and headed back to his hotel in Amsterdam Centrum.

Working your way through the streets near Amsterdam's main train station was always a challenge when you were stoned. In addition to the cars, you had to worry about all these people on bicycles—and all sorts of people, even little old ladies, rode bikes in Holland. Traffic in the bike lanes did not follow the red, green, and yellow lights, which seemed to flash in bizarrely rapid succession, for cars and trams, those huge streetcars that zoomed along deep metal grooves carved into the street. There was a wild, crisscrossing network of tram paths near Centraal Station and the trams moved with alarming speed. So, stepping off the sidewalk and into the bike lane, you had to watch out for the speeding cyclists, who had tinkly little bells on their handlebars to warn you, then scurry across the street for the nanosecond when the light was green, looking both ways for the cars that might suddenly be coming at you and keeping an eye out for charging trams, which, given the internecine tangle of tram paths, might be coming from any direction. The trams had big clanging warning bells, which you had to be careful to distinguish from the little tinkly warning bells on the bicycles.

Walker stood on the curb, *Plaster My Face with Cum* in a brown paper bag tucked under his left arm, hands in his pockets, still enjoying his marijuana and hash cake high, waiting for the green figure of a goose-stepping man to appear in the little box across the street. He was surrounded by people striding purposefully and speaking Dutch, that queer language full of clunking consonants and ear-grating inflections. It sounded to Walker like German, only not quite as harsh. But the spectacle of so many Aryan-looking people speaking a language that sounded almost German made Walker feel strangely close to World War II. He had never felt that way in France or Italy or Spain. And he had absolutely no desire to visit Germany. He often read about dark-hued people getting beaten up in Berlin. Hell, if he wanted to get killed by a bunch of crazed white thugs, he could have just taken the subway from Manhattan to Bensonhurst—he didn't need to travel all the way to Europe for that shit. But in Amsterdam he felt as if a powerful memory of the war lingered in the atmosphere, as if—

Ding ding ding ding ding ding ding! Holy shit! Walker looked to his left and saw a dozen ruddy Dutch people zooming toward him on their bicycles. Somehow, without even realizing it, he had stepped off the curb and into the bike lane. He saw a white-haired old woman at the head of the charging pack, staring in wide, blue-eyed disbelief at his carelessness. *Ding ding ding ding ding ding ding!* The cyclists were ringing their bells madly now, trying to tell Walker to get the hell out of their way. Walker did not dare move backward, back up on the sidewalk. He was too stoned to attempt such a complicated manuever, and he suddenly imagined himself screaming in a snarl of spokes and handlebars and tumbling bodies. He leapt forward, dodging the hurtling Dutch granny by two inches, nearly losing his balance before righting himself, and in the next instant—*Clang clang clang clang!*—an enormous yellow tram was bearing down on him. *Clang clang clang clang!* Now he heard warning bells on both sides. He ran forward, feeling a rush of wind from the northbound yellow tram that passed behind him and glimpsing, to his right, a big blue southbound tram barreling toward him. Pure instinct propelled him forward. He felt the front of the blue tram graze the lace of the shoe on his right foot, which had unfurled and trailed behind him. Then, spinning around a white car that had seemingly come from out of nowhere, horn honking frantically, Walker stumbled backward onto the sidewalk, almost but not quite falling flat on his ass. His first impulse was to look down. Yes, his feet were planted firmly on the sidewalk, the undone lace of his right shoe a black squiggle against the pavement. He clutched the brown paper bag containing his porno mag in his left hand. He looked up and saw a cluster of pedestrians staring at him in blank astonishment. Walker smiled, shrugged, turned away, and strode toward the Hotel Elyssia.

It was only while sitting on the bed of his shabby, vaguely urine-scented hotel room that Walker realized how close he had come to catastrophe. He smoked another bowl of dope. As the drugs began to take effect, he noticed the copy of the *International Herald Tribune* he had bought that morning. The date caught his eye: Thursday, November 24, 1994. Oh, yeah. It was, in America, Thanksgiving Day. Walker laughed. He took a moment to consider all that he was thankful for today. He was thankful that he had not been run over by a bike, a car, or a tram. He was thankful for his Stinky Skunk Spud. And for *Plaster My Face with Cum*. But he was most thankful that there was an enormous ocean separating him from Sadie Broom, his would-be—or was it would-have-been, could-have-been, perhaps even should-have-been?—wife, back in the U.S. of A.

*   *   *

"Maaaaaah—" Walker's mouth opened involuntarily and he suddenly felt as if a family of ants were crawling wildly in his nasal passages. "Maaaaaah, aaaaaah—" He had just enough time to grab his handkerchief from his back pocket and raise it to his face. "Chwaaaaach!" It was a sneeze so explosive he felt as if he'd been punched in the solar plexus, his body jerking forward violently as a torrent of snot splattered into the hanky. Before he could catch his breath, he felt another eruption coming on. "Tchaaaaach!" That one actually made his face hurt.

"Gesundheit," the girl behind the counter said.

Walker, sitting about twenty feet away at a corner table in the Flutterbye coffee shop in Amsterdam, still holding his handkerchief to his nose, waved to indicate his thanks for her consideration. The tingling in his sinuses had already begun again and he let go another atomic sneeze. Now he was embarrassed. The hanky was soaked with mucus. He balled it up and wiped a dangling booger from his left nostril. The blond barmaid looked worried. "Excuse me," Walker muttered. They were the only two people in the Flutterbye, an airy, yellow-lighted place with hanging plants and birchwood tables and booths located on a tiny street named Haringpakkerssteeg. "Sorry," Walker said, clearing his throat. "I don't know what's—" Suddenly his face began quivering. He raised the sopping hanky to his nose and sneezed again, but this sneeze was a standard *ah-choo,* nothing like the trio of thunderous expulsions that preceded it.

"God bless you," the barmaid said in a slightly raspy, heavily accented—though Walker could not discern exactly what type of accent—voice. "But please, do not sneeze again. For your own good."

"For my own *good?*" Walker said with a laugh. "Why? Will you kick me out if I sneeze again?"

"No, no, no. It is a bad omen to sneeze five times."

"A bad omen?"

"Yes. It's a Finnish belief. One sneeze means good luck. Two means bad luck. Three is money. Four is love. But five sneeze is death."

"Yikes."

"You sneeze four times in a row now, so you must not be uncareful."

"I'll try not to be, though, you know, if you block a sneeze, everything shoots back into your head and you can have a brain hemorrhage."

"Will that kill you?"

"Possibly."

"Well, five sneeze in a row is certain death, so you must pay attention."

"I'll try, but—" Walker's nose started twitching uncontrollably. "Uh-oh." The barmaid raised a hand to her mouth. She was smiling, but at the same time looked genuinely frightened, sort of like a little kid waiting for you to lunge at her and yell *Boo!*—wanting you to scare her, but not to be too realistically scary. But Walker wasn't faking it. He really was about to sneeze. "Maaaaaah—" His mouth opened beyond his will. He held up the drenched snot-rag. And then, just as suddenly as it had come upon him, the imminent sneeze subsided. His face relaxed. He lowered the hanky and smiled. "All right," he said with a sigh.

"Only four sneeze!" The barmaid smiled broadly and now she looked positively switched on, illuminated from within. "That means love."

*   *   *

"Hey, brother man."

Walker had glimpsed, peripherally, the fedora, a blur of green felt in the corner, when he entered Kaffeteria, a coffee shop on the Leidseplein that was designed as a sort of New Wave American diner, all chrome and Formica tops with swivel-seated stools at the counter and plastic-upholstered booths, everything painted in a garish Crayola-like pastiche of colors and bathed in fluorescent light. Walker had only visited Kaffeteria once before and he'd seen the suave-looking black guy in his green felt fedora that time, too, engaged in quiet conversation with a couple of young, immoderately pierced and tattooed Dutchmen. On this occasion, a typically dreary December afternoon, Walker had just ordered a cappuccino and was getting ready to drink it at the counter when the old man, sitting in a corner booth, greeted him in a friendly rasp. Walker turned and smiled. "Hey," he said.

The old man in the fedora (elegantly wide-brimmed, it was, and tilted at a roguish angle across his brow) gestured for Walker to come over to his table. The old man wore an ocher-colored shirt, a silk, very dark green tie, and a wheat-toned jacket. Something about the hue of the old man's skin made Walker think of coffee beans. He had a neatly trimmed mustache and a little patch of hair, carefully clipped into a V-shape, beneath his lower lip. His eyes were large, watchful, and slightly rheumy. Walker sensed that the old man's stare might be unnerving to some people, but he was unfazed by it. "You're a member of my tribe," the old man rasped in a voice that would have been perfect, Walker mused, for a late-night deejay on a very cool jazz station.

"Your tribe?" Walker asked as he stood beside the booth.

"I'm talking the North American cohort of the African diaspora."

"What if I told you I'm from Ethiopia?"

"I'd say you a lyin' motherfucker." The old man emitted a short, tubercular-sounding laugh. He took a sip from the glass of fruit juice that sat on the table before him, beside a copy of a Dutch newspaper. "Our people don't walk like no purebred Africans. We just cut through the air differently. Where you from, homeboy?"

"New York City. Brooklyn."

"Which part of Brooklyn?"

"Harrowside."

"I know Harrowside," the old man said, a hint of nostalgia in his voice. "Sit down, brother man." Walker slid into the booth. "I'm from Tennessee myself. Little town called Luckett. Name's Martin Frost." He extended a hand; Walker shook it. "My friends call me Frosty. Consider yourself a friend."

"Thanks. I'm Walker Du Pree." Walker had brought along a drawing pad and a clutch of pencils. "Would you mind if I sketch you while we talk?"

"Go right ahead, brother man."

Walker flipped open his pad and got to work, starting with Frosty's magnificent hat. "So what brought you to Europe, Frosty?"

"World War Two. I arrived on D-day. Actually, it was the day after D-day. My platoon was assigned to pick up dead bodies on the beach. We're collecting bodies while the motherfuckin' Nazis are still shootin' down on us from up on the cliffs. That's the kinda work they gave to the brown-skinned regiments."

"Damn."

"The day the war ended I was about a mile outside Berlin. I was stationed there for another year."

"And what?" Walker asked, busily drawing but at the same time concentrating on what Frosty said. "You decided not to go back to the States after you were discharged?"

"I fell in love with a German girl. Ilse. We were thinking about gettin' married and movin' to the States. I told my daddy. Sent him a letter and a picture." Frosty laughed his hacking laugh again. "Can you imagine my daddy, a black man born in the nineteenth century, havin' his brown-skin boy tell him he's comin' home with his blond, blue-eyed Aryan wife to live in Luckett, Tennessee? In nineteen hundred and forty-six! My daddy wrote me back, said, 'Negro, have you lost your mind?' "

Frosty and Walker both laughed. "So what happened?" Walker asked.

"Well, I didn't know what to do. Then one day Ilse said she wanted to take me to her hometown. She was from this little village in the mountains called Habichtsburg. Middle of nowhere, man. We arrived late on a Saturday night at the farmhouse where she'd grown up. I met her two sisters who were living there. Everyone else in the family had been killed during the war. The next morning, Ilse, her two sisters, and I go to the village church. We walked in about five minutes after the service had begun. The minister was the first person to see us. He had been preaching, but as soon as he spotted me at the back of the church, he stopped cold. I mean, he just *froze,* standing up there in the pulpit, with his mouth wide open but no sound comin' out. Everyone in the church turned and stared. And this congregation—it was the whitest bunch of people I'd *ever* encountered. And I could tell from the complete shock, the awe, in their faces that they had never even *seen* a black person before. Ilse and I took our seats and the service continued, though people couldn't stop stealing peeks at me the whole time. Finally the service ended and I just wanted to get the hell outta there. I mean, these were *Germans,* man. And here I was a black man—who, for all I knew, from the way they *looked* at me, might be considered some kind of beast or demon—and having seen what these folks had done to the Jews, I didn't even want to contemplate what they might be inclined to do to a nigger! But before I could split, who should come walkin' up to me but the minister. Everybody got all quiet again. Everyone's eyes were on us. The minister shakes my hand and says, in English, 'So what brings you to our village?' Ilse told him I was her fiancé. The minister smiled and said, 'Congratulations! Welcome to Habichtsburg.' From that moment on, I was completely accepted by the people of that town. The minister married Ilse and me a couple of weeks later and I spent the next ten years in Habichtsburg. Totally embraced by the community. Think about it, brother man: Here I was, in the heart of Nazism, in a land that represented racist evil to the entire world, and my white wife and I were more accepted there than we would have been anywhere in the United States of America."

"Damn," Walker said, shaking his head as he continued drawing Frosty. "What did you do in Habichtsburg?"

"Made my money as a carpenter. And wrote my first three books."

"What sort of books?"

"Novels."

"No kidding. How many have you published?"

"Eleven."

"Eleven novels!" Walker, looking up in surprise, dropped his pencil. "I can't believe I've never heard of you."

"That's 'cause I ain't never been published in the States. I've been published in lots of countries. But not in my own."

"Jesus," Walker whispered. He pulled out another pencil and resumed drawing. "And Ilse?"

"She died. A long time ago."

"I'm sorry."

Frosty, impassive, took another sip of his fruit juice. "Since then I've lived all over Europe. I like it here."

"Guess you don't ever get homesick, huh?"

"As a matter of fact, I went back to live in the States once. Three years, in the early seventies. People told me how much the place had changed."

"Had it?"

Frosty smiled wryly. "I realized that as a genuinely independent-minded black man living in America, my fate was limited. I could allow myself to be castrated and/or lobotomized by white America, or I could allow myself to be castrated and/or lobotomized by black America. There were, of course, variations. I could allow myself to be castrated by whites and lobotomized by blacks, or vice versa. As far as I'm concerned, moving back to Europe was an act of pure self-preservation."

*   *   *

When it came to matters of social conscience, Sadie Broom was just as practical as she was in other areas of her life. She knew exactly what she was good at and how best to apply her talents in helping less fortunate members of the black community. For two hours every Monday evening, Sadie tutored an inner-city high-school kid. The subject: the Scholastic Aptitude Test. Sadie had always performed exceptionally well on standardized tests. She also considered such tests ridiculous as a measure of intelligence. To Sadie, taking standardized tests was akin to doing crossword puzzles. An inherent knack for the form helped, but it was possible to learn all sorts of little tricks to get a handle on the game. To Sadie, SAT prep courses proved that the exam was a scam. At her private high school in Washington, D.C., Sadie knew wealthy white kids whose cumulative scores improved by two hundred points or more after their parents enrolled them in expensive drill sessions. Had these kids somehow become two hundred points *smarter*? Of course not. They had just learned a few useful tricks. Sadie's parents could have afforded to send her to one of the prep courses, but there was no reason to. Sadie had the knack. What she loved about multiple-choice tests was that the correct answer was always staring you in the face. Coming up with answers to tough questions, off the top of your head, was far more difficult. But if the correct answer was laid in front of her, 8.5 times out of ten—to be exact—Sadie Broom would pick it. The trick was figuring out which answers were wrong. Sadie's objective was to teach that trick to her pupils.

Ruthlessly practical as she was, Sadie only worked with the most gifted inner-city kids. She did not want to tutor young blacks unless they were absolutely determined to go to college. She wanted to take the best students that the community service agency could send her— and make them even better. She preferred to work with young women. And she insisted on tutoring only one student at a time. In the fall of 1994, Sadie's pupil was the most brilliant she'd ever had, an enthusiastic and ambitious high-school junior from the South Bronx named Shawna Davis. By early December, Sadie felt she had developed a genuine friendship with her star student. Shawna had recently talked about becoming a management consultant—just like her tutor. Sadie felt that each time Shawna visited her apartment on the Upper West Side, the teenager gained a privileged glimpse of life's possibilities. After two hours of drills, Shawna and Sadie would often talk for another hour or two about the young woman's hopes and dreams. Sadie took a special pride in serving as Shawna's role model.

Then, at the end of a lesson in December, Shawna told Sadie she had some exciting news: "I'm pregnant!"

Sadie was flabbergasted. "But you're only sixteen!"

"I'll be seventeen by the time I have the baby."

"But what about college?"

"I'll still go to college. Mama says she'll take care of the baby while I'm in class." Shawna scrutinized Sadie's face. "You look like I just told you I have a terminal disease."

Sadie had to stop herself from crying. "But Shawna, what about your future?"

"What about it?"

"I can tell you, Shawna, it is extremely hard to be a management consultant and take care of a child."

"How do you know?"

"How do I know?"

"You don't have any children, so how do you know how hard it is?"

Sadie sighed in exasperation. "Shawna, it's just logical! You have to be logical about this!"

"I *am* being logical," Shawna said, speaking in the same serene tone she'd maintained throughout the conversation. "Mama will help me with the baby while I'm in college, and by the time I start working, my kid will be in school. And if I'm making the kind of money you make, I'll be able to afford a good nanny."

"Oh, Shawna," Sadie said with a mournful groan. She felt consumed with worry for her pupil. But Sadie also felt disappointed in herself. She felt as if she had somehow failed. Hadn't Shawna learned anything from her example? "Are you sure you want to keep this baby?"

"Yes, I'm sure." Shawna paused, then added, "Look, I don't want to be some lonely thirty-year-old with a good job and no man, wondering if I'll *ever* have a baby."

Now Sadie was wounded. She didn't know if Shawna had intended to hurt her. She had never told the teenager anything about her private life. Shawna didn't know that Walker had recently left her. Shawna probably didn't even know Sadie's age. And, at sixteen, she probably didn't imagine that someone like Sadie could be as old as *thirty.* "I guess I see your point," Sadie said gently.

They were silent for a while, then Shawna said, "You know, I saw this guy on TV, the man who's gonna be the new Speaker of the House. . . ."

"Newt Gingrich."

"Yeah, him. He thinks girls like me are dirt. He doesn't want to know that I'm a good student and that *I am going to college.* Nothing is going to stop me. But people like Gingrich think I'm gonna go through nine months of pregnancy and bring a child into this world just so I can get some measly welfare check. I know lots of teenaged girls with babies, and not one of them had a baby to get a damn welfare check!"

"Why *do* they have babies?" Sadie asked plaintively, leaning forward in her chair. "I honestly want to know. I mean, why do *you* want to have a baby?"

Shawna smiled and shook her head. "Why do *you* want to have a baby, Sadie? Why do all your yuppie girlfriends want to have babies?"

Sadie stared at Shawna but did not answer. She was stung by that word: *yuppie.*

"We want the same thing y'all want," Shawna said, sounding eminently logical. "Unconditional love . . . from an uncomplicated person."

*   *   *

Lorraine Broom had never been particularly keen on Walker Du Pree. She complained to Sadie about her boyfriend's lack of ambition, his immaturity, his bad manners. And those dreadlocks—*shyeeeeeesh!* Then Walker inherited an enormous sum of money from his father and Lorraine began to appreciate his good qualities. She generously offered Walker advice on what he should do with the money. She did not hesitate to proffer what she considered constructive criticism when he decided to give half his inheritance to his mother. By November 1994, Walker and Sadie had been together almost two years and Lorraine was growing fonder of her "future son-in-law" (as she started introducing him to friends) all the time. When, that month, he up and decided to go travel in Europe, telling Sadie to forget any marriage plans she had for them, Lorraine was not upset with Walker. She blamed Sadie. Not explicitly. But every time Sadie spoke with Lorraine about Walker, her mother's voice was filled with reproach.

One night in December, Lorraine called Sadie, ostensibly to make plans for the family get-together in D.C. at Christmas.

"So how many letters have you gotten from him?" Lorraine asked.

"Two, Mommy." Sadie felt she had to defend herself. "But he's only been gone a month."

"How many times have you written to him?"

"Twice."

"That's all?"

"I'd write him again but I don't have an address. He's traveling, Mommy."

"Don't you even know what country he's in?"

"I think he's in the Netherlands."

"You *think*?"

"Look, Mommy, I'm not gonna beg Walker to come back home. If he wants to play Junior Year Abroad, let him. I'm focused on other things."

"Are you focused on the fact that you're going to be thirty-one soon? Do I have to tell you how difficult it is to find a decent black man in this day and age?"

"Walker does not qualify as a decent black man."

"I can't believe it. You and Victoria are going to be the last of the cousins to get married and have children. Who would have thought it? *My* girls! Over thirty and not even engaged. Even your cousin Celia has two children already!"

"Yeah, but Mommy, Celia's husband is in prison."

"Well, at least she knows where she can *find* her man!" Lorraine shrieked. "That's more than I can say for *some* people!"

After she got off the phone with Lorraine, Sadie began to reconsider Dick's offer. Three weeks earlier, Sadie's boss, Dick Danvers, thought she would jump at the chance to spend a year in the Paris office of Tanzer & Mur Consultants. But Sadie had turned him down. The enchantment of Paris that people were always babbling about had somehow eluded Sadie. In addition to visiting the city for three days the summer after college, she had already taken three week-long business trips to Paris. And Sadie had never been able to see what was supposed to be so great about the place. Dick, a self-professed Francophile, told Sadie she was passing up the opportunity of a lifetime. He had no trouble convincing Melissa Gordon to accept the Paris assignment, but that morning Dick told Sadie that Melissa had just learned she was pregnant and wanted to stay in New York. "This is your last chance," Dick said.

Now, alone at home, still annoyed by her conversation with her mother, Sadie attempted to watch television—always something of a challenge for her. She tried to focus her attention on the show about the corny young white people who frolicked around Manhattan and wore slick hairdos and expensive clothes and were always hugging and promising to be "there" for one another. After five minutes, she turned off the TV. Sadie began to realize that in the month since Walker had left, she had lived in a state of disbelief. She simply could not *believe* that he had walked out on their relationship. Sadie, along with everyone else she knew, simply *assumed* that she and Walker would get married. Everything had been on course. Then Walker had to go and fuck it all up. They should have been moving in together by now. They should have been engaged. Walker should have been receiving professional counseling!

That night Sadie dreamed she was in a first-grade classroom, playing a game of musical chairs. But she was her current age in the dream and all the other players were young women she knew: family, friends, colleagues. As some goofy, childish tune played, Sadie and the other women marched in a circle, around the row of tiny school chairs. She realized that all the women in the game—except her—had recently gotten engaged, were married, or had children. Her sister, Victoria, was conspicuously absent from the group. Suddenly there was only one chair left and Sadie and a woman who appeared from out of nowhere, a woman she did not recognize—a white woman who did not resemble anyone she knew in her waking life—were the final two players, marching around the single little chair, waiting for the silly music to stop. The next thing Sadie knew, Walker was sitting in the chair. The music stopped. The white girl lunged for the chair and Sadie, in her dream, was about to burst into tears, because she knew she had lost the game.

At work the next morning, Sadie went straight to Dick's office and, without even saying hello, asked, "When is my flight?"

*   *   *

"What a weather." Eva Thule sighed as she looked out on the damp and gloom of Nieuwe Spiegelstraat. She and Walker sat in a booth in the window of Slow Hand Easy, a Jamaican coffee shop with red, black, yellow, and green decor and Bob Marley on the sound system. Walker crisply finished shuffling the playing cards and slid the neatly stacked deck across the table.

"Cut," he said.

"It's not necessary to cut every time, you know," Eva said with mock impatience, as if the task were so arduous.

"It's a custom," Walker replied. "I'm a traditionalist in many ways."

Eva squinted in concentration at the cards. She reached out warily and, with thumb and middle finger, gingerly lifted half the deck. She placed it beside the other half with delicate precision. She sank back in her seat. "Whew! That was exhausting. Before you deal, how about another joint?"

"I'm just a boy who can't say no."

"Do you want I should make?"

"You know I can't roll a joint."

"Acch, you just don't apply yourself." Eva unzipped her knapsack and spilled half its contents out on the table. Peppermints and sourballs, tightly wrapped in cellophane, skittered across the rough wood surface. "Would you like a sweetie?"

"Sure, sweetie." While Walker unwrapped a little orange rock of candy, Eva went to work with the rolling paper and marijuana. It had been two months since Walker met her at the Flutterbye, when he had come perilously close to that fifth, potentially fatal, sneeze. Since then, he'd hung out regularly with Eva and sometimes with Eva and her boyfriend, the French guy she lived with, Jean-Luc. The three of them had even spent Christmas together. At first Jean-Luc was jealous of Walker's friendship with Eva.

"These French men," Eva complained. "They think you are either married to a woman or just fucking her. They don't see that a man and a woman can be friends."

On the other hand, Jean-Luc had reason to be suspicious: Walker was, in fact, in love with his girlfriend; but only in the most idle way possible.

Walker didn't exactly miss Sadie, but he was still preoccupied with her, still turned their relationship over in his mind every day. He would walk the somber streets of Amsterdam for hours, hands stuffed in his pockets, shoulders hunched, reconstructing arguments he and Sadie had had, retracing the trajectory of their failure, sifting through the wreckage. "Thank God I didn't marry her," he would mutter hotly. "Thank God I didn't marry her. Thank God I didn't marry her."

Seeing Eva invariably calmed him. He was profoundly attracted to her, had been from the start. Most men were. Eva was one of those women who was so radiant, with her golden hair and aquamarine eyes, that you could hardly look upon her yet had to force yourself not to stare. But unlike most of the conventionally beautiful women Walker had met, Eva Thule didn't seem to *know* she was beautiful. She was anything but aloof. She managed to convey that she was approachable but not available. Not that Walker was inclined to make a move on her. He would, as was his habit, wait for the woman to initiate contact. Or at least to give him the green light, that subtle signal, usually something in the way a woman leaned toward you. Walker never got a green light from Eva. But she'd never given him a red light either. What he got from Eva was a yellow light. A constant yellow light. And, at the age of thirty, Walker finally knew better than to run a yellow light. Why risk losing Eva's friendship? Or antagonize Jean-Luc? Besides, his mind was still on Sadie. Still, whenever he spent time with Eva—and given Jean-Luc's busy schedule at the French restaurant where he waited tables, Walker and Eva were spending a lot of time together—he felt that ticking anticipation that everyone stalled at a yellow light feels. He was just waiting for that sucker to turn green.

Eva was from a land of snow. She had been born on a dairy farm in Finland. Her father was a Swede, who, after knocking up her mother, disappeared. When Eva was four, she and her mother moved to Eskilstuna, Sweden. Eva would later assume that her mother had gone there in search of her fugitive lover. She did not find him, but she did meet a sweet-natured older man, a bureaucrat in the vast Swedish welfare state, who took good care of her and her fatherless child. At eighteen, Eva left home to see the world. She bounced around Europe, working as an au pair, a waitress, a stewardess on a cruise ship. She met Jean-Luc while they were both doing scut work on an ocean liner. They decided to go to Amsterdam because neither of them had been there before. Eva had no idea how long they would stay, but she was beginning to feel like settling down somewhere. She had vague aspirations of being a painter. Walker had seen a few of her works: vibrantly colored images of flowers that, in their lush detail, were highly derivative of Georgia O'Keeffe but showed some nascent promise.

Watching Eva expertly manipulate the reefer as they sat in Slow Hand Easy, Walker thought that this twenty-four-year-old Scandinavian farm girl had a wonderful knack for hanging out. And it occurred to him that there was a specific talent to lounging, and you either had it or not. Sadie didn't know how to hang out. She always had to be *doing* something. She even watched television in a purposeful way, only watching the specific programs she wanted to watch, turning the TV on when the program began, clicking it off when the program ended. She never channel-surfed. Walker did not fault Sadie for her lack of sloth, her dedication to busy-ness. It was just another way in which they were different. Sadie could never get stoned, play gin rummy, and engage in rambling conversation while a Prince CD played on the stereo and the Cartoon Channel flickered silently on the TV screen. But Eva *loved* doing that sort of thing. Sadie detested marijuana and chastised Walker relentlessly for smoking it. Eva, on the other hand, could match Walker puff for puff.

"So tell me, Wocker," Eva said, lighting the joint and taking a long drag, "who is this O.J. Simpson?"

"*Who* is O.J. Simpson?" Walker repeated incredulously.

"This is the question."

"Where have you been the past seven months, hiding under a rock?"

"No, just not living in America. It's only the Americans who talk about him. But always I hear them in the Flutterbye talking about him."

Eva passed Walker the joint. He took a hit. "O.J. Simpson was a football player and a very nice Negro man who may or may not have carved up his ex-wife and some guy she knew."

"May or may not, you say. Do you think he did it?"

"Of course he did it."

"But why?"

"Haven't you ever wanted to kill one of your boyfriends?"

"No! Never!"

"Haven't any of them wanted to kill you?"

"Perhaps."

"There you go." Walker suddenly became irritable. "What the

fuck. I don't understand relationships anyway. I don't know anything about people. Okay? Remember that: *I don't know anything about people. I just guess.*"

"Nobody knows anything about relations."

"Sometimes I think Francis Bacon had it right."

Eva perked up. "Francis Bacon? The painter?"

"Yeah. I read an article about him where somebody said Francis Bacon had this theory that in every relationship there is the cherished and the cherisher. That you are either one or the other. Do you know that word? Cherish? To cherish."

"Yes, I understand. I don't know if I agree, however."

"Think about it. Think about the relationships you know of. Chances are one person is more in love than the other. Or maybe they're equally in love, but one person *cherishes* the other more. At the end of a relationship, who do you think is more hurt, the person who initiates the breakup or the person getting dumped?"

"The person getting dumped, of course."

"Not necessarily. I would say it is *always* the cherisher who is in the most pain. Even if the cherisher is the one ending the relationship—maybe because they could no longer stand not being cherished—it is the cherisher who will suffer more."

Eva took a thoughtful drag on the joint. "Interesting theory." She passed the grass back to Walker.

"So—in your relationship with Jean-Luc, who is the cherished and who is the cherisher?"

"Oh, we're both," Eva said instantly.

"Hah!" Walker scoffed. "Everybody in a relationship says that. 'Oh, we're both. We're both the cherished and the cherisher. Everything is equal.' "

"But this can be true. Jean-Luc and I have a very shareful relation."

"Aw, come on, Eva, I've seen you guys together. You *know* Jean-

Luc worships you. You know that. You just don't want to admit that you're the cherished. People who are the cherished are always a little bit embarrassed by it. But you shouldn't be. It's *good* to be the cherished."

"So you don't believe one person can be both?"

"I think most of us have *been* both, at one time or another, in one relationship or another. But I believe Bacon's law is that in each particular relationship you are one or the other, that the roles are defined at the get-go—"

"The get-go?" Eva asked uncertainly.

"The very beginning of the relationship. You are either the cherished or the cherisher and that's that."

"Yes, but have you seen any of Francis Bacon's paintings? He was fucked up."

"That's certainly no reason to doubt the truth of what he's saying."

"And who knows if he really said it? You tell me you read this in an article. But who knows if Francis Bacon ever really said this?"

"Well, sure, but—"

"And if he *did* say it, who knows if he really believed it? He might just be—how do you say?—talking a lot of shit."

"Yes, I suppose we've all been guilty of that."

"And what about you, Wocker? In your last relation, were you the cherished or the cherisher?"

"I'm still trying to figure that out."

Eva raised a skeptical eyebrow. The joint was now a little stub between her fingers. She took a final drag, then crushed the butt in the ashtray. "Deal the cards, Mr. Smartsy Pants."

9

It was that twilight time Hal disliked—not quite dawn, but not night either, five-thirty A.M., when the sky was a pearly blue-gray and the sporadic tittering of the birds in the trees slowly escalated. If Hal was awake at this hour, it either meant he'd had to get up too damn early or he'd stayed up too damn late. Hal walked hurriedly across campus, feeling as if his brain had shut down, not thinking about what he'd just seen happen at Smegma House, not really thinking at all. His legs carried him forward, without his conscious effort, taking him back to Mould Hall. As he entered the dormitory, he heard a car approaching. Safely inside the building, he watched, through the window of a thick metal door, a blue, white, and orange campus police car cut across the quad, heading, no doubt, for the football frat.

Entering his suite, gingerly closing and locking the door behind him, Hal saw Walker in the sitting room, slumped on the battered couch, head back, eyes closed, mouth open, the remote control in one hand, a half-empty bottle of beer in the other. The TV was on, with the sound turned all the way down, and one of those redneck preachers Hal detested was silently sputtering. A record spun round and round on the turntable, the needle suspended in the LIFT position, hovering over the vinyl. On the coffee table in front of Walker was a small mountain of marijuana, a wooden pipe, rolling papers, and other paraphernalia. With the back of his hand, Hal lightly tapped his roommate on the cheek. Irritated, Walker opened one eye. "Morning," he croaked.

"Yo, man," Hal said, "where's the Omaha chic?"

"She stood me up."

Hal barely suppressed a smile. "Damn, Walk, she didn't even call?"

Walker rubbed his eyes and scratched his rusty 'fro. "Naw, man. Corky blew me off."

Hal pointed to the grass. "I thought you didn't do drugs."

"First time. Some guys I know from Myriad came over with it. I liked it. I don't know. Pot seems to suit my personality somehow. When I got high, I felt like myself, only more so."

"Spoken like a true drug addict." Hal sat down on the couch, took the remote control from Walker, and clicked off the TV. "Man, I'm tired."

"So how was your date? Musta been pretty good if you're just walkin' in now. Don't tell me. You boned Miranda, didn't you?"

Hal was prepared to lie, to tell Walker yes, to brag about how good it had been, how he'd driven Miranda into convulsions of ecstasy. It would be only a temporary lie since he was bound to bed Miranda in the very near future—he was certain of it. But before he could start lying, the sound came back to him, that sound Tony made as she slumped to the ground, that deep, hollow moan, a guttural blast of pure pain. Hal had never heard a sound like it before, and he knew he would be unable to describe it, ever, to anyone. "Something really weird happened," Hal said.

"Don't tell me. Miranda's a transvestite. I knew it!"

"No," Hal said, thinking he should not tell this to Walker but knowing he would tell it anyway, so strong was the need to tell.

"Something else." They moved out to the cramped little terrace of their suite, and as the sky turned orange and gold, Hal told Walker what had happened at Smegma House, how he wasn't even sure of exactly what *was* happening, not sure if Tony Dawson was playing along, actually enjoying herself, not at all certain, in his drunkenness, in the darkness, if Duane Kordo was really fucking Tony or just rubbing up against her. But then Tony was crumpled on the ground, moaning. As he talked, Hal went from feeling drunk to already hungover, without the usual period of sleep that comes in between. He did not look at Walker as he spoke. He just stared out at the other redbrick dormitories and the tidy little plots of grass and crisscrossing walkways of the Craven quadrangle. And as he spoke, he began to digest the awfulness of what he had seen. And, in digesting it, Hal was able to blot the awfulness from his mind. And, as the awfulness of what had happened to Tony Dawson was blotted from his mind, the scary realization took its place: He had been a witness, perhaps even a party, to a crime. He did not put it in those words to Walker. He didn't have to. The implication was clear. "I guess," Hal said, "what I'm wondering is, what do I do now?"

"Report it," Walker said instantly. "To the dean or the police. Right?"

"Well . . . I don't know. I told you, I saw a police car on its way to Smegma. So it's already been reported."

"Yeah, but still . . ." Walker let the sentence trail off.

"Yeah," Hal said, his head beginning to throb. "Well, I'm probably going to hear from someone. The authorities. But I didn't *do* anything. You understand that, right? I didn't touch the bitch."

"I understand. But seeing as she's just been raped, you might refrain from calling her a bitch."

"But *was* it rape?" Hal asked urgently. "I mean, I don't know. She seemed . . . willing."

"On the other hand, she *was* tied to a tree."

"Yeah, but *jokingly*. She wasn't bound tight or anything! It just seemed like a game! And I didn't touch the—" Hal paused, took a moment to collect himself. "I didn't lay a finger on Tony."

"So—you'll tell that to the authorities. I mean, there were other guys there, right?"

"Right." Hal buried his face in his hands. "Fuck. This is bad, man. This is really bad."

Walker put his hand on Hal's shoulder. "Listen, if you want me to go with you to the campus police right now—"

"No." Hal shifted his shoulder slightly. Walker took his hand away. "I need to get some sleep, man. I feel like shit. I'm sure someone will be calling here for me. Right now I just need to get some sleep. That's understandable, isn't it?"

"Sure."

Hal and Walker looked into each other's eyes. Hal already regretted, as he knew he would, telling Walker the story. "Yo, man," he said quietly.

"You don't even have to say it, Hal. I'm not gonna tell anybody."

"I mean, this could be pretty serious, and I just—"

"Your secret's safe with me," Walker said in a tone that Hal found deeply reassuring.

"Okay. I'm gonna get some sleep." Hal glanced at his watch. It was almost six o'clock. "I'm sure somebody's gonna be looking for me soon. Wake me when the call comes."

*   *   *

But that Sunday the call never came. Hal spent the afternoon alone in the suite, stumbling back and forth between his bed—the narrow lower bunk where he thrashed about in sweat-soaked sheets, struggling through feverish, dream-haunted bouts of sleep, waking up every twenty to thirty minutes, wondering if he'd slept at all, but knowing that he hadn't been awake, unnerved by yet unable to remember the images in his dreams but hearing Tony Dawson's horrible moan in his head—and the toilet. He would stagger into the men's bathroom across the hall, a surge of liquid burning in his throat, burst into a stall, drop to his knees, his torso hunched over, hands gripping the porcelain, feeling as if a heavy, boot-clad foot were stomping on his gut, feeling his digestive process move rapidly in reverse as chunks of hamburger, watery, brown-toned jets of ketchup, mashed and beer-soggy bits of bread and french fry, all of it speckled with sesame seeds, splattered against the side of the bowl or splashed into the toilet water, spraying drops of vomit back into Hal's face. Eventually, the imaginary boot would be removed from Hal's gut and, still hunched over, staring into his regurgitated junk food, smelling beer and wine and punch along with that familiar, sour puke smell, Hal would find himself pleading, the words tumbling from his lips like the vomit: "Please God, please God, please God, please God, please God, please—" before another explosion of half-digested food interrupted his prayer. After a couple more rounds of spewing, praying, and flushing, Hal would return to his bed to thrash about until it was time to throw up again. By four o'clock that afternoon, the contents of Hal's stomach had been fully disgorged and he was able to sleep peacefully for the next four hours. Not once did the telephone ring.

At eight o'clock Hal awoke, took a shower, got dressed, and greeted Bill and Bob, the two white suite mates, who were studying in the sitting room. They asked if he was all right. He said he was just very hungover. He asked where Walker was. They said at the library. He asked if anyone had phoned for him. No one, he was told, had phoned at all. Hal went to Cantona's Pizzeria, cautiously chewed and swallowed two slices, returned to his room, got back into bed, and slept a deep, dreamless sleep until his alarm clock buzzed him awake at eight A.M. Walker was snoring lightly in the top bunk as Hal dressed, packed his knapsack, and slipped quietly out of the room.

Hal felt like a condemned man that Monday. He managed to conceal his dread as he went to classes, socialized at lunch, feigned surprise when he heard rumors of a rape taking place at Smegma House Saturday night. All day, Hal expected police officers to show up at one of his lectures and drag him away in handcuffs. When, at football practice, Coach Stevens announced that five freshman players had been indefinitely suspended, Hal knew it was just a matter of time before he, too, would be busted. He'd stayed away from his suite in Mould Hall all day out of fear that the dean would call. *Indefinite suspension.* The words made Hal queasy and he wondered if he might start throwing up again right there at practice. How would he ever explain this to his parents—his parents, who had given him so much, worked so hard, and sacrificed so selflessly to send him to college? How would his mother, his sweet, kind mom, who was always so proud of him, how could she ever endure the shame Hal was about to inflict on her, on their entire family? Indefinite suspension: The punishment would be scandalous enough, but the cause . . . *the cause . . .* How could the Hardaway family ever explain that their precious Hal had stood by and watched as a young black woman was tied to a tree and raped—by a white guy! As he trudged back to Mould Hall Monday night, Hal knew that an indefinite suspension would be no better than expulsion. Because, after being implicated in the rape of Tony Dawson, there was no way Hal would ever be able to show his face on the Craven campus. He would have to transfer to another, no doubt lesser, college. And there, on his *permanent record,* would be his night of shame. It would be there forever, for all to see. College administrators, law school admissions officers, potential employers, all those future voters who someday might have sent Hal Hardaway to the U.S. Senate: They would all know of his disgraceful behavior. He would never be able to justify it to them, his imagined judges, because none of them had been there, none of them would be able to understand the queer, dreamy quality of the incident at Smegma House. They would only know that Hal Hardaway was forced to leave college because he was present at a rape. At eighteen, Hal felt that his entire life was about to be irrevocably ruined.

The sitting room was clouded with marijuana smoke when Hal entered the suite. Walker, Bill, and Bob, giggly and bleary-eyed, sat around a large purple bong. It was the first time Hal had seen Walker since early Sunday morning when he'd returned from Smegma. Seeing Walker stoned, Hal wondered if maybe his roommate had been so groggy and out of it the day before that he'd forgotten everything Hal had told him. That possibility evaporated in the next instant when Walker said, casually, "Hear about the rape?"

"Yeah," Hal said, imitating Walker's nonchalant tone. "Pretty fucked up."

"Didn't you go to that party at Smegma?" Walker asked.

Bill and Bob were now staring inquisitively at Hal. What the fuck, he wondered, was Walker trying to pull here? Had this scrawny little wannabe busted him to Bill and Bob? After promising not to tell! Walker wasn't even looking at Hal—he was languidly picking seeds out of the pile of marijuana on the coffee table. As Bill and Bob, a goofy glaze in their eyes, continued to stare at him, Hal tried to stay cool and figure out why Walker had asked him the question. Was he expecting Hal to fess up, right here in front of these two white geeks? Or maybe . . . maybe Walker was cleverly offering Hal the chance to exonerate himself. Without another moment's hesitation, Hal uttered the lie he would repeat many times over the next several days: "I left the party before anything happened."

"Too bad!" Bill chortled. "You missed out on a gang bang!"

"Yeah," Hal said tonelessly. "Remember, Walk? I got in around four-thirty." Hal had moved up his time of arrival by one hour. "You were asleep on the couch. I woke you up."

"Yeah, sure," Walker said, continuing to fiddle with the dope.

"Those Neanderthals at Smegma." Hal shook his head and let out a short, hard laugh. "They're fucking crazy." He paused for a moment, then, trying not to sound anxious, asked, "Did anybody call for me?"

"Not yet," Walker said archly.

Hal bid good night to his suite mates. He had been in his bed for an hour when he heard Walker climb into the top bunk. After a few minutes, Walker whispered, "Hal? Hey, Hal . . . are you awake?" Hal did not answer. "Hey, if you want to talk . . . Hal . . . Hal?"

"I don't want to talk."

"Okay."

They lay awake in their bunk beds for another half hour, both of them silent. Only when he heard Walker's light snoring did Hal feel relaxed enough to go to sleep.

*   *   *

The dread that had eaten away at Hal for more than forty-eight hours began to dissipate when he saw Tuesday morning's *Daily Cravenite*. The front-page article mentioned only "five male freshmen, all members of the football team," and one "female freshman," also referred to as "the victim." The story did not divulge the names or the race of any of the students. That day, in one conversation after another, Hal carefully reiterated his alibi, telling people that he had attended the party, that he had seen Tony Dawson and Duane Kordo and the four other players—Loomis, Wilson, Carmichael, and

McBride—getting drunk together but that he left Smegma "before anything happened." He repeated the lie to his fellow players at Tuesday's football practice and they seemed to believe him. Wednesday's *Cravenite* announced that "the victim" had decided not to press charges against the student who had "sexually assaulted" her or the "four other freshmen who stood by watching." It would be up to the authorities at Craven University alone to determine the punishment of the football players. By the time he returned to Mould Hall after lunch, Hal was absentmindedly whistling a merry little tune, so confident was he that he had escaped the ruination he had feared. As he bounded into the sitting room of the suite, Bill handed him a message: "Please call the Dean of Students *ASAP*."

Sitting in Dean Jeremy Leach's office, Hal continued to lie his ass off, claiming that he left the party before the incident. He knew lying was risky, but looking the Dean of Students in the eye, Hal could feel himself beginning to believe his own cover story. Each time that Leach—a wimpy little guy with slicked-back blond hair who wore tortoiseshell glasses, a crisp white button-down shirt, bright red suspenders, and a blue Craven school tie—repeated that "several witnesses have placed you at the scene," Hal would grow more indignant in his denials. Sitting in Leach's office, Hal began to fully appreciate the essential fact of his situation, the sole reason why he was able to lie with impunity to Dean Leach, the one thing that might save him from ruination: Tony Dawson had not named him. Yes, "several witnesses" had named him—but not "the victim." If she had, he would have already been suspended. It was the other players who placed him at the scene of the crime. But if the black victim herself had not fingered him, and he denied being there, what, other than the word of five guilty white boys, did the administration have on him? Could the university risk punishing a black student under those circumstances? Hal didn't think so.

The more indignant Hal became, the wimpier Dean Leach got. By the end of the meeting, the dean was apologizing for having summoned Hal at all. Hal magnanimously said he didn't mind, that he was, in fact, happy for the chance to clear his name.

As he left the dean's office that Wednesday afternoon, Hal knew he had been spared. But why had Tony Dawson spared him? Because she had a crush on him? Because he was black? Or because she knew that Hal was not at fault? Yeah, Hal thought, that was it: Tony knew he was innocent. *He* hadn't sexually assaulted her; Duane Kordo had. And it was those four white boys, *not* Hal, who egged Duane on. *They* were the accomplices. Tony must have known that, given the circumstances, there was nothing Hal could have done. Hal decided that Tony must have known she was asking for it. That was why she hadn't pressed charges. And Hal had been spared. Whatever the reason, Tony had spared him.

At football practice Wednesday afternoon, coaches and players, white and black alike, gave Hal the cold shoulder. He knew they must have heard he had been there, in the Smegma House backyard. But he didn't care. Hal had been spared. That was all that mattered.

On Thursday morning the *Cravenite* reported Duane Kordo's expulsion and the one-year suspensions of Loomis, Wilson, Carmichael, and McBride. That afternoon word spread that Tony Dawson had dropped out of Craven and returned to her hometown in Michigan. Hal could hardly believe his luck. In a single day, the victim, the perpetrator, and all the other witnesses had been swept off campus. There was only one person left at Craven who knew, really *knew*, about Hal's involvement: Walker Du Pree. But Walker was not an actual witness. And besides, Walker had said nothing to Hal about the incident since Monday night. They had hardly seen each other at all that week, and when they did, Walker prattled on in his usual way, giving not a hint that he even remembered what Hal had told him early Sunday morning. After nearly a month of college, Hal still wasn't sure what to make of his roommate. But he had a hunch that Walker would keep his mouth shut. By late Thursday afternoon, Hal felt completely out of danger. Then he went to football practice.

*   *   *

The coach had to know what was going on. This was just a scrimmage between the starting team and the second-stringers. "Light tackling": That was what Coach Stevens had ordered. But as he ran upfield, following the play Coach Stevens had called for him—seven of the last ten plays had been called for him—Hal knew he was going to get hammered. His entire body hurt, but he ran obstinately upfield, cutting sharply to his right and heading—as the play required him to do—directly into heavy coverage: The three senior defensive backs crouched, poised around a patch of grass near the fifty-yard line, exactly where Hal was supposed to catch the pass. They were waiting for him. They seemed to know exactly which plays were being called for Hal. The three defensive backs—Crenshaw, Dickey, and Boggs—seemed to know the plays before Hal did. Time after time, Hal would emerge from the huddle—having received the play from the quarterback, who had received it from Coach Stevens—trot up to the line of scrimmage, and see Crenshaw, Dickey, and Boggs pointing at him and aligning themselves on the area of turf where they knew he would soon arrive, running full speed, twisting his body around, leaping into the air and stretching out his arms, reaching to grab the missile that the quarterback consistently fired too high for him. And each time he found himself in midair, either snatching the ball from the sky or watching it sail past his fingertips, Crenshaw or Dickey or Boggs or some combination of the three slammed into his body. With each play, the hits became more vicious. But Hal kept running the plays, kept charging into the coverage, determined to take the hits, to catch that damn ball and, if he caught it, to hang on to it no matter how savagely the defensive backs hurled themselves at him. He would not ask to leave the field. Even though his body felt as if it were covered, from head to toe, by a single, enormous bruise, though the turf beneath his feet seemed to undulate, shifting and sliding in earthy waves, he was, after seven plays called for him, determined to go up for that eighth pass.

In the locker room, just before Thursday's practice, other players seemed to move away from Hal when he came near them. As he was strapping on his shoulder pads, Titus Boggs, captain of the Craven defense, a black granite statue of a man, walked up to Hal and said, "Your shit is fucked up." Hal and Titus stared hard into each other's eyes. "You hear me, man? Your shit is *fucked up.*" As Titus stalked away, Hal deduced that this was meant to be the team's condemnation of him. But why should they be pissed at him? What should he have done? What would any of *them* have done in his position? Confess to a crime that the victim had not accused him of committing? Out of what? Team loyalty? He was especially annoyed that Titus Boggs, a *brother,* would condemn him for what he had done. He had considered Boggs a righteous young black man, but here the brother was, willing to side with a bunch of dumbass white football players against Hal. Well, fuck Boggs—and all the other black players, too. And Coach Stevens and the whole fucking team. Fuck 'em all. Hal could withstand their ostracism. What he did not anticipate was that they would try to kill him.

"DAAAAAARRRRRRGGGGGGHHH!" Hal was in midair, his body fully extended, arms flung out in front of him, when he heard Titus Boggs's famous war cry. Hal's head was twisted as he looked up and over his right shoulder, his gaze fixed on the spiraling bullet of a football. Peripherally, he caught a glimpse of Boggs, sailing toward him above the grass. He had seen Crenshaw, an ignorant hillbilly as far as Hal was concerned, on his left, before he took flight. Just as the football slipped through his fingers, Hal felt Boggs crash into him. Every nerve in Hal's body seemed to scream, though no sound emerged from him. He was propelled backward through the air. "YAAAAAAHEEEEEEEEE!" Crenshaw's Appalachian holler echoed in Hal's ears as a helmet rammed into his vertebrae. He felt as if his spine had snapped like a breadstick. As his body, arms flailing, twirled through the air, Hal was hit for a third time when his helmet came in contact with Dickey's shoulder. On impact, Hal's head jerked close to ninety degrees and his helmet went flying. Hal was unconscious before he hit the ground.

                    *   *   *

Luckily, Hal suffered only a minor concussion. It was lucky, of course, because the damage could have been far worse. It was also lucky because Hal got to spend three days in the Craven infirmary— right next door to where Tony Dawson stayed for two days after her sexual assault—and Miranda visited him several times each day. Here, Hal surmised, was the final element he needed in his seduction of the serious diva: pity. And it worked. The day he was released from the infirmary, Hal and Miranda lost their virginity together.

Hal's minor concussion was also lucky for the Craven football team.

"Jesus holy fuck. Jesus holy fuck. Jesus holy fuck. . . ."

These were the words, muttered fervently by Chad Dickey, that Hal heard as he came to, his face buried in the prickling grass, his mouth filled with dirt and blood, after he'd gone up for that eighth pass.

"Jesus holy fuck. Jesus holy fuck." Dickey was a pink and beefy

party boy, the sort of easygoing prep who might be considered the
"typical" Craven student. Hal had always liked Dickey, until he
started slamming him into the turf at Thursday's practice. Now, as he
opened his eyes and tried to remember where he was, Hal could hear
the abject fear in Chad Dickey's voice. "Jesus holy fuck." Then Hal
heard the only slightly less fearful voice of Coach Stevens: "Can you
feel your legs, son? Can you feel your legs?" Yes, Hal thought he
could.

Because Hal had suffered only a minor concussion, Coach
Stevens would not have to face a lawsuit. And the injury—a bad one,
to be sure, but not *too* bad—allowed Hal to quit the team with
honor, as a wounded warrior. Hal would not have to feel that the
other players forced him to quit the team because of his role in the
Tony Dawson case. Hal did not capitulate to their intimidation tactics. He did not quit the team out of fear, because he lacked guts. He
quit because he'd suffered a legitimate, but not too serious, injury.

After his release from the infirmary, Hal would spend nearly
every night of his freshman year with Miranda in her room in Plimsoll Hall. He saw Walker mainly on those occasions when he
returned to their room to pick up books and change clothes. The following year, Hal would move into Psi Delta Zed, the black frat, and
Walker would move into Myriad, the house where all the weird white
boys lived. Hal and Walker would remain friendly throughout their
years at Craven. Every few weeks, they'd go out for pizza together.
But Hal socialized almost exclusively with Craven's black community, while Walker barely socialized with the black community at all.
Hal and Walker never discussed Tony Dawson. In fact, by sophomore
year, Tony had all but disappeared from Hal's memory. Neither Tony
nor any of the football players who had been suspended returned to
Craven U. As far as Hal Hardaway was concerned, the entire incident
might never have happened at all. What remained was the subtle

sense of unease he always felt with Walker. Because Hal knew that Walker Du Pree *had* something on him.

*   *   *

Did Walker Du Pree consider Hal Hardaway a friend? Not exactly. Yet sitting beside Hal at a bar on Amsterdam Avenue after the Amandla workshop in September 1994, Walker found that the old fascination lingered and he flattered himself by thinking it might be mutual. More than eight years after they'd last seen each other, at Craven U., it occurred to Walker that Hal was someone he could have been but could not make himself become. Walker wondered if Hal felt the same way about him. Sadie once described to Walker how she regarded her sister, Victoria: "Half of her consciousness is exactly like mine. And the other half is so completely different I can't even comprehend it. Half of her is more like me than anyone else I know. But her other half is someone I can't stand." Walker had been an only child, so he could only guess that the ambiguous affinity he felt for Hal was something akin to brotherhood.

After the Amandla workshop broke up and Dr. Emmett Mercy went off with Chester Beer, it was Tiny Jenks who insisted that Hal and Walker go out for a drink together. "Y'all should get reacquainted," Tiny said. "Sure, you could exchange business cards, but you know you'll never call. The two of you are right here, right now. You should make the best of it. I'm going home. Y'all go have a drink."

Sitting elbow to elbow at the bar on Amsterdam Avenue, Hal learned that the black girlfriend Walker had mentioned but not named in the Amandla workshop was Sadie Broom and Walker learned that the white girlfriend Hal had mentioned but not named during the session was Corky Winterset. It would be impossible to say who was more shocked. Walker responded with a seizure of giddy laughter while Hal just shook his head and kept saying, "How bizarre."

Then Walker said something people often say when confronted with the uncanniness of life: "If you put this in a novel, nobody would believe it." Of course, people's actual lives are full of coincidences that seem choreographed, startling symmetries. That they respond to such fateful synchronies with comments like Walker's is a sign of how little people trust novels.

*   *   *

"So—did you ever nail the Omaha chic?" Hal asked as he sat in a booth with Walker at Cantona's Pizzeria. It was May 1986, their last week of college.

"Naw," Walker sighed. "I came close once. But you know what? Corky would never say so, but I think she's hung up about my being black."

Hal let out an obnoxious snort of a laugh. "Yeah, but you ain't really black!"

Walker briefly wondered if maybe once during the past four years he had slipped and told Hal his father was white. But he knew that was unlikely. He almost never mentioned his father at all. "Of course I'm black," Walker snapped. "I've been black my whole life."

"Yeah, yeah. But you know what I mean. You're not *really* black."

"*Really* black? Versus what? Are you getting metaphysical on me here, Hal?"

"See? That's what I'm talkin' about!"

"What?"

"What you just said. That's not something a black person would say."

"But I *am* a black person. And I just said it. So it *is* something a black person would say. How could it not be?"

"Maybe you should try fucking black women."

"I've fucked black women."

"Yeah, but you've fucked a lot more white women than black women."

"I've *met* more white women than black women."

"You could make more of an effort."

"You know what the difference between you and me is, Hal? You choose your lovers on the basis of race and I don't. Only ten percent of the female population of the United States is black. Only one in ten women on this campus is black. Therefore, if you don't choose to date black women exclusively, chances are you will sleep with far more white women."

"Have one in ten of your women been black?"

Walker paused to do a mental calculation. "Yes!" he said triumphantly. "Exactly ten percent. See? I'm color blind."

"Or maybe just blind."

*　　*　　*

"You really don't remember that conversation?" Walker said eight years later at the bar on Amsterdam Avenue. "You don't remember saying I wasn't really black?"

"Not at all," Hal said.

"You don't remember that you used to always refer to women as bitches?"

"Bullshit."

"Always."

"Always *when*?"

"Freshman year."

"Yo, Walk, I went out with Miranda Saunders freshman year. If

I'd *ever* called her a bitch, I wouldn't have lived to become a sophomore."

Walker and Hal were silent for a while. They sipped their beers, tried not to stare at each other's reflection in the huge mirror behind the bar. Walker knew that Hal and Sadie had been friends at Craven, but whenever Hal's name came up in conversation, Sadie would get all fluttery and distracted, leading Walker to wonder just how intimate the friendship had been. "So," Walker finally said, "did you ever . . . have sex with Sadie?"

"Naw," Hal said. After a second, he added: "Never wanted to." Glancing in the mirror behind the bar, Hal saw Walker's face light up with sudden anger. "Yo, Walk," Hal said quickly, "I didn't mean that the way it sounded. Sadie's great. She and I were really tight senior year."

But Walker was not angry because he thought Hal had insulted Sadie. Walker was angry because he believed Hal was insulting *him*. Hal was saying he had not slept with Sadie simply because he had not felt like it. Meanwhile, Walker had wanted urgently to sleep with Corky but never had. And who was sleeping with Corky now? Looking at Hal in the mirror, Walker said, icily, "Fuck you."

＊   ＊   ＊

Hal, Walker believed, was one of those puzzling men who loved "the thrill of the chase"; who relished courting a woman, followed a strategy of seduction, and then became bored with his conquest. Walker, on the other hand, did not like pursuit; Walker liked having. And he rarely grew bored with his conquests, since most of his sexual relationships lasted only a few hours. Until he fell in love with Sadie Broom at the age of twenty-eight, Walker's preference was for one-night stands; or relationships with women who lived in faraway cities; or with women who already had boyfriends and were mainly interested in Walker as a diversion. Since Walker was interested in having sex with as many different women as he could, he never "targeted" an object of desire, the way Hal did. For someone with a reputation as a womanizer, Walker was an extremely passive example of the breed. If he had slept with a lot of women, it was mainly because he focused on women who made it plain that they wanted to sleep with *him*. And this was a varied lot. Women of all shapes and hues and temperaments. Walker was not interested in conventional beauty. He was interested in the *click* of mutual desire. Hal—despite his obsession with tactics—was genuinely looking for love. Walker was not. Nor was he merely horny. It was the kissing and cuddling after intercourse that he always enjoyed most. Walker longed for the intimacy that came only with sex; and affection without the inevitable pain of love.

*   *   *

Walker found Hal to be a more appealing person at thirty than he had been at eighteen or twenty-one. On the one hand, Walker hated the idea of Hal being with Corky Winterset. On the other hand, Hal had spoken with obvious sensitivity about his white girlfriend at the Amandla workshop, before Walker knew the woman's identity. Maybe Hal and Corky were actually right for each other. Sitting at the bar on Amsterdam Avenue, Walker and Hal finished their beers. It was clear that neither of them wanted to order a second round. After a long silence, Hal brought up the workshop: "I've been thinking about something Dr. Mercy said. About adversity."

Walker rolled his eyes in exasperation. "I don't know where anybody gets off putting a value on somebody else's pain."

"Maybe he's right, though. Maybe we haven't faced enough adversity."

"Look, guys like Mercy are never gonna approve of guys like us.

We were born in the sixties and they're never gonna forgive us for it. All they want us to do is shut up and be grateful."

"Maybe that *is* what we should do."

"I *am* grateful," Walker said. "But I'm never gonna shut up."

They paid the bill and stepped out of the bar, then walked over to Broadway. Walker was heading uptown, to Sadie's place; Hal, on his way back to Park Slope, decided to hail a cab. "So," Walker said as Hal stood in the gutter with his arm outstretched, "are you gonna marry Corky?"

Hal seemed surprised by the question. "I don't know," he said. "Are you gonna marry Sadie?"

Walker pursed his lips and shook his head, slowly, no. "I'm leavin' this country, man."

A yellow taxi pulled up to the curb. "Give my love to Sadie," Hal said.

"Tell Corky I said hi," Walker replied.

They gave each other the Black Power handshake. As Hal slipped into the cab and closed the door behind him, Walker said, through the open window, "Do you ever think of Tony Dawson?"

"Who?" Hal asked, just as the taxi pulled away from the curb and sped down Broadway.

"Yeah," Walker said to no one, "that's what I thought."

10

Sadie hated Paris in the springtime. Sadie hated Paris in the fall. Sadie hated Paris in the winter, when it drizzled. She hated Paris in the summer, when it also always seemed to be drizzling. She hated the women in Paris, who, even if they were just running out to buy a baguette, always seemed to be trying to look chic, in their microscopic skirts and high heels. Even old ladies in Paris were always showing off their legs. What were they trying to prove? Sadie Broom was the type of woman who liked to throw a jean jacket over a T-shirt, slip into a pair of sweatpants and sneakers when she went to the grocery store. But in Paris, even if she was just doing the laundry, she felt she had to put on makeup and, if not a skirt—and, unlike the French versions, *her* skirts weren't practically obscene; they always came down to the tops of her knees—then at least a nice pair of slacks. It was a pressure that French women put on one another, just so they could be looked at by men. And all the time they pretended to be so enlightened, so liberated. Mylène, a young consultant in the Paris office of Tanzer & Mur, actually complained about the lack of male attention she'd received during a year she spent in the firm's Manhattan headquarters.

"I would ride in ze New York metro," Mylène said, "and none of ze mens would be looking at me. I zink, Am I suddenly ugly?"

"Believe me," Sadie said, "you wouldn't want men on the New York subway staring at you. They'd probably be thinking about chopping you up."

"But even in ze office, ze mens, zay seem to be afraid of ze women. Zere was no joking, no flirting."

"Well, American women realize there's a thin line between flirting and sexual harassment."

"Pwuh!" Mylène made that French sound, puffing up her cheeks, then exhaling, a noise of exasperation, usually accompanied by an arrogant shrug of the shoulders, that Sadie had come to detest. "But iz not natural."

Sadie didn't bother trying to argue with her. It was impossible to get through to these Frogwomen. Hell, you couldn't walk two blocks in Paris without seeing some billboard somewhere featuring a naked woman. Ads for perfume, shampoo, even for a home appliance store—the French equivalent of Sears—displayed bare-breasted women. Mind-boggling. Same thing on TV. What did this do to the children here? Sadie wondered. And yet French women had the nerve to consider themselves feminists! Well, Sadie thought, Simone de Beauvoir had turned out to be a doormat for Sartre, hadn't she? So what could you expect?

Sadie Broom found French eating habits revolting. Sidewalk *boucheries* were spectacles of savagery, with skinned—or often still furry—rabbits hanging upside down, ducks and pheasants—unplucked!—dangling from hooks, enormous severed pigs' heads sitting in flat pans. In a restaurant, even if you ordered a steak well done—which Sadie always did—you were likely to get a bloody, oozing slab thrust in front of you. Then there were all those thick-as-molasses sauces and desserts that threatened to send you into sugar-induced cardiac arrest, coffee so strong you could practically feel it burning away your stomach lining. And wine—always wine.

The French were the biggest alkies Sadie had ever seen. She managed to hold out for her first two weeks in Paris, then, one day at lunch hour, raced into the nearest McDonald's and almost wept with joy at her first bite into a Big Mac. Real food at last! Since then she'd become a regular at Pizza Hut, Burger King, and, best of all, Kentucky Fried Chicken. Sadie had to smile every time she walked into KFC, because the clientele, unfailingly, was just as it was back at the KFCs she frequented in the States: about ninety percent black. Try and tell Sadie Broom there was no such thing as a global black culture!

All her American colleagues in the Paris office of Tanzer & Mur teased Sadie about her love of fast food. They were all so impressed with themselves and their Francophile tastes. Everything French was superior, as far as they were concerned. One of her American expatriate coworkers—a native New Yorker who had lived in France for twenty years—even bragged one day about the murder rate in Paris. In one year, 1991 or '92, Sadie couldn't remember which, *only* ninety-eight people had been killed by violent crime in Paris, he said. Sadie said that sounded like a lot to her. The American countered that during the same year in New York City, two thousand people had been murdered. Well, Sadie sniffed, that was pretty bad, but ninety-eight murders hardly qualified Paris as safe. What if you happened to be one of those ninety-eight?

When Sadie first moved to Paris, the firm set her up in what they believed to be a highly desirable building, one of those sand-colored seven-story nineteenth-century structures with long, shuttered windows, twisting, red-carpeted staircases, and a tiny, cagelike elevator. *Classique.* Sadie loathed it. Everything about the place felt old and cold and unsafe. Anyone could bust down that rickety, wooden front door. And the door to her apartment had only two locks. After four weeks, Sadie found another apartment, one with a heavy metal door

and four locks in a twelve-story building that was all concrete and
reinforced glass, with security cameras in the lobby and elevator. Her
colleagues at the firm were mystified, but Sadie finally felt at home.
Safe.

Sadie was constantly meeting black American expats who blathered about how "free" they felt in Paris, how they could finally be
"themselves." Did they really believe there was no racism here? How
could they be so naive? But Sadie knew what they were *really* talking about. The streets of Paris were packed with interracial couples.
Everywhere you looked, you saw white men with black women,
black men with white women. It was bizarre. Sadie was sure that
white Frenchmen were just trying to live out some sick Josephine
Baker fantasy, thinking every black American woman was, at heart,
some nympho who wanted to jump around topless in a skirt made
of bananas. And black American men, of course, were practically
salivating over their white babes as they strolled arm in arm with
them down the Champs Élysées. That, Sadie knew, was what bougie
Negro expats were talking about when they boasted of how free they
were in Paris. Free to chase after skinny white bitches—*that* was
their freedom.

                    *   *   *

And another thing: Why didn't French people know how to walk
down the street? In New York or D.C., pedestrians knew how to bob
and weave, maneuvering briskly through the city's crowded streets,
aware of the people around them. You glided past slow people if you
were in a hurry or stuck to one side of the pavement if you were taking your time. Parisians, on the other hand, seemed to lack the basic
internal compasses that American city-dwellers were born with. They
meandered aimlessly, even during rush hour, drifting left and right
through crowds, like blind people without canes or Seeing Eye dogs.

Two Parisian pals would blunder mindlessly along, chatting away, blithely unaware of other pedestrians as they hogged the center of the city's insanely narrow sidewalks. French people also had a penchant for stopping abruptly and pausing—for no apparent reason—at the bottom of a flight of stairs in the metro station, causing anyone descending the steps behind them to crash into their backs or quickly twirl around them. Of course, if you did bump into an oblivious French pedestrian, which Sadie did at least once a day, he turned and snarled at you as if it was *your* fault.

Even French *pigeons* seemed to lack a sense of direction, waddling arrogantly right in front of your feet, daring you to step on them. When the filthy birds did take off, they flew straight toward your face. Sadie found herself constantly ducking as the foul urban fowl flapped their soot-covered wings inches from her nose. Once, while walking through the squalid Place de Clichy, Sadie felt something hit her upside the head with a dull thud. It felt as if she had been struck by a soccer ball. Sadie, slightly staggered by the blow, turned to see a dingy pigeon land awkwardly in the gutter, then waddle away. Nauseated, she rushed home, stripped off her clothes, jumped into the shower, and washed her hair five times in rapid succession.

At least as obnoxious as the pigeons were the dogs. The streets of Paris were full of them, wandering about like strays. How many times had ferocious-looking Rottweilers, Dobermans, and German shepherds—unleashed!—come bounding down the street toward Sadie, seemingly ready to attack, while their masters strolled absentmindedly half a block behind? And where there were dogs, there was, of course, dog shit. Walking the streets of Paris was like tiptoeing through a minefield of rancid turds. People even brought their dogs into public eateries. Once, in a café, Sadie saw a group of young Parisians cooing over a Chihuahua as it gamboled across *the top of a table.*

Another time, as Sadie and Mylène waited to be seated for din-

ner in an expensive restaurant in the trendy Marais district, the manager's dog, a fat little black poodle, flounced out into the center of the
gray stone floor, raised one of its pudgy hind legs, and pissed right in
front of the table of four well-dressed customers. As Sadie watched in
incredulous revulsion, the little black poodle flounced away again,
leaving behind an expanding pool of urine. And the four well-dressed
customers didn't even notice! They just continued eating and talking,
jabbing their forks into their chunks of meat and stuffing the food in
their mouths with Gallic gusto, hardly pausing to chew, pontificating
and gesturing extravagantly as the spreading pool of dog piss began
to reek. Finally, the aged manager bumbled by and, seeing the puddle
on the stone floor, remarked casually, "Ooo-la-la, du pipi." He disappeared, then returned with a few sheets of newspaper, which he
lackadaisically dropped on the floor. As the urine soaked through the
newspaper, the sophisticated Parisian diners remained utterly oblivious to the incident, which would have been grounds to have a simi-
larly posh Manhattan restaurant shut down by the Board of Health.
Mylène couldn't even understand why Sadie walked out of the place,
refusing to eat there.

The French were positively perverse when it came to bodily functions. During her second week in Paris, Sadie stopped by a café for a
cup of coffee, then went downstairs to the ladies' room. Entering the
coffin-sized water closet, she was startled to find no toilet, just a wet,
porcelain floor with a hole in it—a drain, she assumed, that was
missing its pockmarked, metal cover. She returned upstairs and told
the woman behind the bar that she saw only a shower in the ladies'
room. The barmaid and the cluster of male customers standing at the
counter drinking burst into contemptuous laughter. Not even waiting
for an explanation, Sadie, her face feeling hot with embarrassment
and rage, stormed out of the café. She would later learn that she had
had her first encounter with a Turkish toilet—a "squatty potty," as

one English woman at Tanzer & Mur called it. And no matter how compellingly her bladder and bowels protested, Sadie Broom would never, ever, use one of those disgusting facilities.

But even the Turkish toilets didn't sicken Sadie as much as the sight of Parisians incessantly kissing, making out, almost having sex for Christ's sake, on buses, bridges, in cafés, on street corners and park benches. Even *old* couples, gray-haired grandmas and grandpas, could be seen pawing each other in public places. One night, as she and Mylène sat in a café, Sadie watched a couple in a nearby booth as they practically licked each other's faces.

"Jesus," she hissed, "why don't they just go get a room?"

Mylène threw up her hands in exasperation. "Say-dee," she said, "you are such a typical American!"

Sadie was stunned into silence. She had been called many things in her life—but never *that*.

*   *   *

Having never read *The Diary of Anne Frank,* nor seen the movie version, Walker expected the little Jewish girl's hiding place to be a run-down hovel in some dark and remote corner of Amsterdam. So he was startled to learn that Anne Frank House was actually a quaint old office building in one of the more posh sections of town, overlooking the canals on Prinsengracht. On an unusually sunny afternoon in March 1995, Walker and Eva Thule stood in a line of about twenty people waiting to enter the sanctuary that had become a museum and one of Amsterdam's biggest tourist attractions.

"So tell me about your ex-girlfriend," Eva said.

"Sadie?"

"What is she like?"

"Sadie is a nice American girl. In fact, she is highly representative of the breed: the Nice American Girl, also known as the NAG. Every nice American girl will eventually turn out to be a nag."

"What do you mean with this word *nag?*"

"I mean a woman who is always hassling you." Walker assumed a needling, nasal voice. "Why don't you get a better job? How come you're not more like so-and-so? Where were you last night? When are you coming to bed? When are you gonna wake up? Why can't you be more supportive? Nag, nag, nag."

"I thought you said she was nice."

"She *is* nice. Everybody thinks so."

"And why, then, did you not marry with her?"

"Look, the reason why men and women get married and have children is to give them people to blame, people other than themselves, when they inevitably fuck up their lives. Everyone, if they live long enough, will rack up countless disappointments, mistakes, stupid decisions. It is simply easier to blame these on your wife, husband, or children than to take responsibility for your own wretched life. Me, I feel fully capable of fucking up my life on my own. I'm not looking for anyone else to do it for me."

"I am sorry, Wocker, but what you say is very fool-headed. People get married for love and comradeship, and the reason they have children is from a biologic imperative."

"Come again?"

"*A biologic imperative,*" Eva repeated impatiently. "All creatures exist to create themselves again, to reproduce. You should know this."

"I told you: I don't know anything about people."

"Yes, I begin to agree that you don't."

Walker was stung. He and Eva had always gotten along so well. He thought she enjoyed his acerbic observations. Now he realized he might be alienating her with his negativity. Eva and Walker fell silent as they waited to enter Anne Frank House. They both stared out at the bustling Prinsengracht, at all the purposeful Dutch people hurrying along on foot or gliding by on their bicycles. The harsh sunlight bounced off the choppy waters of the canals. It occurred to Walker that he would probably never sleep with Eva. In recent weeks, he had begun to think he stood a pretty good chance. A man like Jean-Luc, he figured, could never hold the interest of a woman like Eva. Not that there was anything necessarily wrong with Jean-Luc. It was just that, to Walker's eyes, there didn't seem to be anything particularly right with him either. Walker imagined Jean-Luc's mind to be a pleasant meadow: sunny, placid, with no action but the quiet rustle of the breeze blowing through the leaves of grass. But maybe that was precisely the sort of man Eva needed to be with. A dull, average-looking man with no ideas who worshiped her. Maybe Eva wasn't so special after all. Maybe it was only because Walker was physically attracted to her that he imagined she was clever and complicated. Maybe she was just as much of a simpleton as her boyfriend. Maybe it was Walker's fate never to get the women he really wanted, the Corky Wintersets and Eva Thules.

Walker suddenly felt someone's eyes on him. Looking to his left, he saw a fortyish Dutchman with a long, lean face and a fashionable, short haircut, rolling down the street on his bicycle. Walker glimpsed a light gray shirt and black tie peeking through the man's chic black leather jacket. The Dutchman looked like some sort of mod professional, like a TV executive or the owner of an art gallery. What was most striking, though, was the scowl, the look of bottomless disdain on his face as he glared at Walker. Just as he passed Anne Frank House, pedaling furiously, the Dutchman, still glowering at Walker, called out, "Shit goes to shit!"

The comment hit Walker like a blast of burning hot air, as if a furnace door had swung open in front of his face. Most of the people standing in line turned and looked at Walker, stunned. Walker turned and looked at Eva. He saw nothing in her face but bewilderment.

Now he glanced back down the street and his impulse was to chase after the Dutchman and smash his head open. But the racist bicyclist was already disappearing down Prinsengracht. In the next instant, Walker felt the same bewilderment he saw on Eva's face. *Shit goes to shit?* Yes, the bastard had definitely been addressing Walker—he had looked right at him. And Walker was the only black person in the line. So Walker was the first shit. And the second shit? This quaint little building where a Jewish girl and her family hid in terror until the Nazis discovered them and sent them to a concentration camp, where the little girl would die. The house was shit, then, because these Jews were, to the chicly dressed Dutch yuppie, shit. Of course, Walker had known what the man meant as soon as he said it. But now, dissecting the comment, Walker was astonished by the sheer sweep of the man's hatred. Blacks and Jews. Walker Du Pree and Anne Frank. An obscure American tourist and one of the best-known victims of racism in the twentieth century. Shit goes to shit. Walker looked at Eva again. She still seemed more baffled than anything else. Finally, not knowing what to say, Walker shook his head and whispered, "Wow."

Walker wandered through Anne Frank House in a daze. Only the ordinariness of the place registered with him. He was still mulling over the Dutchman's slur, the astounding magnitude of his racism, a racism that encompassed eras, cultures, continents. Shit goes to shit. In a short while, the tour of Anne Frank House was over. Walker and Eva were back out on the sunny sidewalk of Prinsengracht. Walker stuffed his hands into the pockets of his bomber jacket. "So," he said quietly, "what do you say we go to Slow Hand Easy and smoke a joint?"

Eva tenderly linked her arm with his. "And play rummy?" she asked with a smile.

"Yeah, that sounds like fun."

11

The demon would save her. For a long time, the period when she lived in a world of shadow, the demon had been in a comalike sleep. Later, during her years of clarity, she could feel the demon stirring, but quietly; she could just barely sense its strange energies. But now the demon was back in all its raging pain. The demon was roaring inside her. She could feel it, pushing from inside, straining against the surface of her body, the sensation of innumerable porcupine needles, sticking from within. The woman they called LaTonya hardly said a word. She just lay in bed, sweating and shivering as the demon roared, its breath burning the inside of her skin. The woman named LaTonya might disappear, just as the girl they called Tony had disappeared, plunged so deep into the world of shadow that she herself became a shadow. But the demon would not let LaTonya disappear. There was nothing for LaTonya to do. The demon had taken control. Sometimes, in the months after names began to come back—and the memories attached to the names, an explosion of names that started with Emmett saying "Hal Hardaway" in the kitchen of their big new house—the woman they call LaTonya is falling, falling through space, plummeting backward off a cliff. She just keeps falling and falling, waiting to hit the ground and shatter in pieces. Yet she knows

she will not hit the ground. Because the demon has taken over. The
demon will save her.

*   *   *

Uncle Daddy put the demon in her. The first thing she remembered
was the prickling of Uncle Daddy's whiskers on her cheek and his hot
breath with the smell that was not bad or good, only sharp and sweet
at the same time, and burned inside her nostrils. The girl they called
Tony believed that in this earliest of memories, Uncle Daddy had
lifted her affectionately from her cradle and whispered gently in her
ear. But the woman they called LaTonya knew that her earliest awareness of being alive was when Uncle Daddy put the demon in her.
Uncle Daddy would spend years putting the demon in her, when
nobody else was around. It was in the little girl's bed—little Tony's
bed—that the earliest memory took place, the scratch of stubble on
her cheek, the sweetly searing breath in her nose. And the things
Uncle Daddy whispered to the girl called Tony would come back to
the woman called LaTonya, drifting into her mind from time to time
like scraps of long-forgotten lyrics from some obscene song.

"Show me your sticky," Uncle Daddy would say. "Lemme see
your sticky. Lemme touch your sticky." The girl would lie there,
whimpering. "Hush up, now," Uncle Daddy would say. "You a ugly
little thing. But I give you love." Sometimes it hurt so much, the pressure inside, as if Uncle Daddy was trying to reach up inside her; as if
she could feel him reaching up into her stomach, into her heart, into
her throat. If she cried out, she would then find the needlelike
whiskers in her mouth. "Hush up, now. Hush up, now. I'm givin' you
love. You ugly little thing." Sometimes it hurt so much she thought
Uncle Daddy was trying to split her open. And it was when the pain
became too much that the demon would protect her. The demon that

Uncle Daddy was putting in the girl everyone called Tony would blot out her consciousness. The little girl would slip into the world of shadow while the demon subsumed the pain—and, in subsuming the pain, protected the little girl. Every time Uncle Daddy put a piece of his body inside her body, he put more of the demon in her. Each time he took a piece of his body out of her body, a little more of the demon remained inside. "Don't you tell nobody about our lovin'," Uncle Daddy would say after he had taken his body out of hers and the girl they called Tony returned from the world of shadow, still whimpering but fully conscious again. "If you tell anybody, they gonna send you where they sent your mama, and ain't nobody ever gonna see you again." Uncle Daddy would leave her bed. The demon would hide inside her, waiting to come roaring back when Uncle Daddy returned to push more and more demon through the sticky. And the little girl they called Tony lived in terror that Uncle Daddy's threat was serious, that if she told anyone about their secret, she would be sent to the place they had sent her mama, the place from which nobody seemed to return, the place called prison.

Grandy took care of the girl called Tony. "You lucky I'm around," Grandy used to tell Tony, " 'cause your mama wanted to throw you in the garbage." Tony did not understand why Grandy— the mama of Tony's mama—thought what she said was funny, but every time she said it, she laughed and laughed.

"I wanna see my mama!" Tony would sometimes cry.

"You can't see your mama," Grandy would say. "Your mama's in prison."

"Why is my mama in prison?"

"Your mama is a thief and a ho."

"I wanna see my mama!"

"Don't be tellin' me you wanna see your mama. Your mama woulda throwed you in the garbage. You ugly little thing!"

Soon Tony stopped wishing she could see her mama. Instead, she wished that her mama had done what she had wanted to do and thrown the baby Tony in the garbage. When she would see the huge green truck on the streets of Slackerton, Michigan, when she would stop and stare at the men in the green uniforms emptying trash cans into the filthy maw of the truck and hear the grinding, crunching sound of the truck devouring the garbage, Tony would think, I should be in there.

*   *   *

"We got a gorilla for sale," the children used to sing, playing off the lyrics from a popular cartoon, "Tony Gorilla for sale!" The girl called Tony would bow her head and hurry away from the kids who taunted her. "Hey, mister, how much is that gorilla in the window?" Many years later, the woman called LaTonya could still feel the hurt of the Slackerton kids' cruelty, but as an adult, what hurt the most was that all those children who had viciously compared her to an ape had been black.

"Ain't nobody ever gonna give you love like I do," Uncle Daddy used to whisper as he put the demon in her. " 'Cause you a ugly little thing." Uncle Daddy was the brother of Tony's mama. Uncle Daddy and his wife lived five miles away from Grandy in Slackerton. They had no children. Uncle Daddy used to come to Grandy's house a lot. His wife never did. Grandy gave Uncle Daddy money. Grandy owned the busiest liquor store in Slackerton and Uncle Daddy worked there. Grandy used to think Uncle Daddy stole from her. "A hard-workin' woman like me, and I got two good-for-nothin' thieves for children! They just like their good-for-nothin' father!" Tony knew what had happened to Grandy's husband. Grandy used to brag about it to her friends, how she poured a skillet full of burning hot grease

on him while he was asleep, how he leapt out of bed and ran screaming from the house, never to be seen or heard from again. "Lucky for
him, he got away," Grandy would boast, laughing, " 'cause I was
about to cut his dick off and shove it down his throat!"

It was Uncle Daddy who told the eight-year-old Tony that her
mama had died in prison. Nobody would ever tell her how. Two
years later, Uncle Daddy died after he accidentally drove his car into
a brick wall. "I've buried both my good-for-nothin' children,"
Grandy would say to her friends, with a bitter laugh.

Even after Uncle Daddy's death, the girl they called Tony was
afraid. She was no longer afraid that if she revealed their secret, she
would be sent to prison like, her mama. Now she was afraid that
Uncle Daddy had been right when he said nobody would ever love
her as he had. Because she was ugly. She belonged in the garbage. She
was Tony Gorilla. And the demon that Uncle Daddy had put inside
her was curled up and hiding, waiting for the time when it could
come roaring back.

*   *   *

"You've been sexually assaulted, haven't you?"

You don't know who you are. The girl they called Tony is dead.
The demon has gone away. And you may or may not exist. You used
to feel what Tony felt, but she is dead now and you are sitting up in
bed, in a hospital.

"Have you been sexually assaulted?"

The white lady is talking at you. She wears clunky glasses and her
brown hair is pulled back in a tight bun. So many white people talking at you. In the last weeks of her existence, the girl called Tony saw
more white people on the campus of Craven University than she had
seen in eighteen years in Slackerton, Michigan.

"You've been sexually assaulted," the white lady says.

You came to Craven U. with the girl called Tony back when you felt what she felt. The little girl called Tony always did well in her studies. She did so well, the other kids eventually stopped teasing her for being ugly. But she knew she was ugly. And she was afraid; afraid that nobody would ever love her the way Uncle Daddy had. Uncle Daddy had put the demon inside her and the demon needed loving.

"We've notified your grandmother. She's on her way here from Michigan."

The demon knew what the boys wanted. The girl called Tony would hang out with them in front of the liquor store Grandy owned. Cousin Harry ran the store at night when Grandy was home watching TV and Tony was supposed to be at the library. Cousin Harry never told on Tony. Besides, Tony wasn't doing anything bad. Tony wasn't doing anything at all. Tony was just there, hanging out with the boys in front of the liquor store. The girl called Tony almost never spoke and received excellent grades in school. It wasn't the girl called Tony the boys cared about. The boys cared only about the demon. Because the demon gave them what they wanted, the thing the girls would not give them. The boys in front of the liquor store aspired to being hoodlums, but they were still too young and awkward to threaten anybody. They drank malt liquor from brown paper bags. They got high and bragged about how bad they were. They were ridiculous, these apprentice thugs, too ridiculous for the girls they chased after to give them what they wanted. But the demon gave it to them. In the alley behind the liquor store, in the playground of Slackerton Park, in the back of a beat-up old car, the girl called Tony would slip into the world of shadow, her consciousness blotted out by the demon as the boys writhed against her. While the girl called Tony never made a sound, the demon roared in pain, the pain of loving.

"I'm going to show you some photos," the white lady with the clunky glasses and the bun is saying to you. "I need you to identify who was there when you were sexually assaulted." She points to a picture of a white boy. You recognize him. His face was right in Tony's face just before she died. You remember the way his tongue hung out of his mouth as his eyes rolled back in his head. "He was the assailant?" You nod yes. But you still do not know what happened. You know that the girl called Tony, as the white boy writhed against her body, was waiting for the demon to blot out her consciousness, to protect her. But the demon had gone away.

"What about him?" the white lady says, pointing to a photo of another white boy in a book that is full of photos of boys. At the top of the page you see: CRAVEN VARSITY FOOTBALL TEAM: 1982. "Was he also present?" the white lady says, still pointing at the photo. You nod yes. The white lady points to three more photos of white boys, and every time you nod yes. Then she points to the picture of the black boy.

The black boy's face was the last thing the girl called Tony saw before she shattered and died. The white boy was writhing against her body. The demon had inexplicably gone away. The demon was not there to protect her, to subsume the pain. As the white boy slammed his body against hers, his tongue hanging out and his eyes rolling back in his head, the girl called Tony wondered if she'd be able to endure the pain. She saw the black boy. She cried to him for help. Yes, the black boy would protect her, save her. She had already cried to him for help. But he did not move. Why wasn't the black boy helping her?

The white lady is still pointing at the picture of the black boy. "Was he also present at the scene?"

You shake your head no.

"I wanna tie you up!" the white boy had said.

"You wanna tie me up?" the girl called Tony had asked in dis-belief.

But the white boy did tie her up. The black boy wouldn't have done that to her. The black boy would have liked to help her. The demon would have given the black boy what he wanted. But the demon was gone and the girl called Tony was powerless. She cried out to the black boy for help. He just watched. Why wasn't he help-ing her?

"I'm going to ask you again," the white lady with the bun and glasses said firmly, her finger pressing down hard on the photo of the black boy. "Was this young man present at the time of your assault?"

Again you shake your head no.

The black boy wanted to help her, to protect her, to save her, to give her loving. The girl called Tony was sure of it. But the white boy continued to pound into her and the black boy did not move. The girl called Tony was looking at the black boy when she broke into a thou-sand pieces. You were the body lying on the ground. And the girl called Tony was dead.

"Are you absolutely certain that he was *not* there?" the white lady angrily asks you.

This time you nod your head yes. The white lady slams the book closed in disgust.

Grandy arrives in Craven and takes you back to Slackerton, Michigan. Grandy calls you Tony. She also calls you a slut, a tramp, a ho. "Just like your mama!" You try to tell Grandy that Tony is dead and that the demon has gone to sleep and cannot be awakened. You tell Grandy that Uncle Daddy put the demon in Tony. You tell her how Uncle Daddy touched Tony, the things he said to her. Grandy is all over you now, tearing at your hair, scratching your face. "You a lyin', ugly black ho!" Grandy rips off her shoe and beats you with it. "All the money I pay to send you to that college and you just a lyin' ho like your mama!" She beats you till the heel flies off the shoe and then keeps thrashing with the floppy piece of leather. She beats you until you disappear, consumed by shadows.

*   *   *

By September 1994, the woman they called LaTonya had enjoyed six consecutive years of clarity. She stuck to a healthy diet, she did not drink or smoke. She scrupulously took her medication every day. Once a month she met with a psychiatrist at Hallisbury General Hospital—where, for a time, she also worked as a security guard—who checked up on how the powerful drugs were affecting her body and asked questions about her mental and emotional state. The psychiatrist was always pleased and encouraged by LaTonya's progress. Sometimes he would ask the woman called LaTonya about the past, especially about the years between 1982, when she dropped out of Craven University, and 1988, when she was found wandering the streets of old town Hallisbury, alone and disoriented. The woman called LaTonya would always say she remembered nothing from those years. This was not entirely accurate. There were a few things she could recall and others she could glean about the years she spent as a shadow. She spent a long time, more than a year, living in her room in Grandy's house, never going outside. Then there was a longer period when Grandy was ill and the shadow took care of her. The woman called LaTonya could remember policemen and people dressed in white in Grandy's apartment. That must have been when Grandy died. But what happened after that?

"You were a homeless person," Emmett told her. "But nobody knows for how long. You looked like you had lived in the street for at least a couple years."

Homeless? Living in the street? Begging? The woman called

LaTonya had no recollection of such an existence. Some mornings, as she lay beside her husband, Emmett, slowly drifting from sleep to wakefulness, she would feel as if her body were moving, gliding through space, and she would believe that this was the sensation of riding on a bus, of sleeping while riding on a bus. She deduced that during her shadow years she had spent a lot of time on buses. So she knew how she had made it from Slackerton, Michigan, to Hallisbury, New York. But why had she come to Hallisbury?

"You came here to meet me," Emmett said. "God brought you to me. You knew we were supposed to be together. You just had to come and find me."

If she could not be sure exactly what had happened to her there, she did know precisely when she emerged from the world of shadow. She remembered the kindness in the man's face as he stared down at her. She was curled up on a cot. She had seen the man before. She believed that he was the one who had brought her to this place. He knelt down beside her cot. "LaTonya," the man said as he continued to stare kindly into her eyes. No one had ever called her that. Yet she knew it was her name. The kind man put his arms around her. He held her close to him and, in the enveloping warmth of his embrace, the shadow world melted away and she found herself in a world of clarity. Later she would learn that the kind man had gone through all sorts of trouble to discover her name—she carried no pieces of identification on her person. He said her name exactly as it appeared on her birth certificate, a copy of which he had just received by fax. Slowly, the kind man let go of her. He smiled and walked away. Soon LaTonya would discover his name. He was called Chester. Chester Beer.

"Chester was our angel," Emmett often said. "Chester found you so you could find me."

Once she left the homeless shelter and started taking her medication, the woman they called LaTonya felt as if her mind had been dunked in ice water. Suddenly she was *awake,* more alert and attuned to the thing they called reality than she had ever been. Chester Beer got her a room in a halfway house. He also pulled numerous strings to get her a job as a security guard at the hospital. And Chester, her angel, helped her with her application to Hallisbury Community College.

"Chester got you on your feet," Emmett liked to say. "And I swept you off your feet."

*   *   *

A year after leaving the homeless shelter, LaTonya could not believe her luck. She had a good job, she was receiving a decent education, and—it felt like a miracle—she was married. She was LaTonya Mercy now, wife of Dr. Emmett Mercy of the Hallisbury School Board. They lived together in an apartment in old town. She had fallen in love with Emmett on their first date (in fact, it was her first real "date" with anyone, the first time any male had taken her to a restaurant, or displayed to her any of the niceties of courtship). She fell in love with Emmett when he told her something no one had ever told her before. Emmett told LaTonya she was beautiful.

LaTonya took her medication every day, to ensure that she would continue to live in a world of clarity. Still, she knew the demon was alive inside her. It was sleeping, sleeping deeply. Sometimes when she had sex with Emmett she could feel the demon stir. But there was no pain. Emmett gave her loving without pain. There was no need to be protected, to slip away into shadow, to have her consciousness blotted out. She was present with Emmett when they made love, more present than she had ever been back when she was the girl they called Tony and was so eager to give the boys what they wanted. And yet there were those times when her body was fused with Emmett's and she could sense, ever so faintly, the groggy stirring of the demon. It did not frighten her.

Only once in her first six years of clarity did the demon threaten

to seize her. It was soon after she and Emmett married, in 1989. She
wanted to write to her cousin Harry, the only family she knew she
had left. She did not remember cousin Harry's address. But she
remembered the address of Grandy's liquor store in Slackerton,
Michigan, and, figuring cousin Harry had taken over the business,
wrote to him there, just to let him know that she was alive and well
and living in Hallisbury, New York, and was now called Mrs.
LaTonya Mercy. Cousin Harry quickly wrote back, thanking her for
her letter, congratulating her, saying he missed her, wishing her well.
He also sent her a fat package stuffed with correspondence that had
arrived at Grandy's house—where cousin Harry now lived—almost
all of it addressed to Grandy and some pieces of mail dating back to
1986. Aside from a few pieces of junk mail, there was only one envelope addressed to the girl named Tony Dawson. The envelope was
from Craven University, from the office of a woman with a name
LaTonya did not recognize. Inside the envelope was a small clipping
from a newspaper, a newspaper from Pittsburgh, dated May 9, 1988.
At the top of the tiny rectangle of newspaper, someone had scribbled,
in black felt-tip pen, *FYI*—which LaTonya recalled meant "for your
information." The clipping announced that an unemployed steel-
worker, aged twenty-four, had been beaten to death in a barroom
"altercation." It was only on the second reading that the name of the
dead man registered with LaTonya: Duane Kordo.

Suddenly the woman called LaTonya felt the demon raging in
pain, roaring inside her face. She quickly tore up the newspaper clipping and the envelope, and as she flushed the scraps down the toilet,
she could feel the demon retreating, slipping back into its deep, comalike sleep. The outburst of the demon had lasted only a few minutes.
And once it was over, the woman called LaTonya realized who had
sent her this news item, for her information: the woman with all the
questions, the white lady with the clunky glasses and the tight bun.

But LaTonya did not need this information. She lived in a world of clarity now. She wanted to be normal. She wanted to do what all normal people seemed able to do. She wanted to forget.

For several years, forgetting was easy. There was nothing to forgive if you were able to forget. Then, one night in September 1994, Emmett came home from an Amandla workshop and uttered the name that jolted the demon from its slumber. But just as the girl called Tony had changed into the woman called LaTonya, so had the nature of the demon been transformed. It still raged in pain, but it was no longer blind loving the demon so urgently needed. The demon roared, but it was in control. The demon possessed clarity. The demon was calling the shots. The demon would see that justice was done.

12

It was only in the late mornings, or early afternoons, just as he was waking up, that Walker would realize he was fending off a major depression. Lying in bed, disturbed by the dreams he could never quite remember, Walker would feel the malaise creeping up on him like a fever. Then he would masturbate, take a shower, and leave the hotel. He had a favorite restaurant on Ossenspookst where he would wolf down a Dutch breakfast of fried eggs and huge greasy slabs of ham while drinking coffee and reading an English-language newspaper or magazine. Then he would return to his vaguely urine-scented hotel room—he had worked out a monthly rate with the proprietor of the Elyssia—grab his drawing pad and pencils, and head for a favorite coffee shop, his depression fever now running high, taking over his body, almost, somedays, staggering him, until he got to the Great Dane or the Flutterbye or Slow Hand Easy and smoked a bowl of the antidote. He could feel his malaise evaporate as the dope entered his nervous system. Aaaaaaaaaah, the tasty green. Whatever would he do without it?

In America most people he knew had stopped getting high after college. They looked down on potheads. Yet they had no qualms about legal, socially accepted prescription drugs that served the same purpose as herb. Once, Zelda Kornblum, one of Walker's colleagues on the *Downtown Clarion,* was singing the praises of Prozac. "It's like I'm high all the time!" she exulted.

Walker laughed. "Yo, Zelda, you should try *actually* being high all the time. It's probably a lot cheaper."

Zelda looked at him as if he'd said something obscene.

Some days—and this drizzly April Monday was one of those days—the depression fever hit Walker so hard, he would lie there for hours, floating in and out of sleep, unable to drag his sorry ass out of bed. Staring at the stucco ceiling, he thought of a story Frosty had recently told him. Walker often passed by Kaffeteria, but he only went inside when he spied Frosty through the plate glass window of the coffee shop. Walker loved drawing the cranky old writer and listening to his stories. Over the years, Walker had developed a particular fondness for cranky old black men, because he knew that someday he would be one himself.

"Back in the early sixties, I was living in Paris," Frosty had told Walker. "I knew this sculptor, Christophe, and his wife, Pascale, who was a painter, and they had this cute daughter, Gabrielle, who was in her early teens. Gabrielle was always talkin' about the future, about the life she was gonna have, the sort of apartment she wanted in the Sixteenth arrondisement—where all the rich folks lived—and the sort of house she would own someday on the Côte d'Azur, the sort of man she would marry, the sort of children she would have. Man, that kid had it all mapped out. Her parents were artists, you see, and they were always struggling and you could tell Gabrielle hated it, just hated not havin' a lot of money. And when she talked about her aspirations, yes, she was talkin' about money, but it wasn't just money this kid was talkin' about. It was a whole way of life. You dig? Anyway, twenty, twenty-five years later, I'm visiting Paris and I see Gabrielle behind the wheel of a Jaguar on the Boulevard Saint Germain. She recognized me before I recognized her. She must have been about thirty-five, maybe a little older, but I could still see the teenaged girl in her face. I asked her what she was doin' and she told me she used to work for some cosmetics company but quit when she had her first kid. Her husband was a lawyer. She had an apartment on the Avenue Foch, in the Sixteenth arrondisement, and a house in Antibes, on the Côte d'Azur. And she's tellin' me all this in a very . . . *neutral* way. Finally I said, 'Gabrielle—are you happy?' She looked me in the eye and said, 'I have what I want.' And I said again, 'But are you *happy*?' And now she looked at me like I was dense or something and she said again, matter-of-fact as could be, 'I have what I want.' Shut me right the fuck up, brother man. 'Cause, you see, I'm an American, and when you're American you think bein' happy is the point. Fuck the *pursuit* of happiness. You think happiness is *owed* to you. You think happiness is a *right*. And if you ain't *happy*, you ain't shit. That's why you hear all these miserable people in the States always sayin', no matter how fucked up their lives may be, 'I'm happy!' Or complainin' that they *ain't* happy. Or ain't happy *enough*. Maybe they got everything they want, but it *still* don't make 'em happy. But, you see, for a European, or for Gabrielle, anyway, happiness was beside the point. She looked at me like she didn't even know what I was talkin' about. *Happy?* 'I have what I want.' "

Well, Walker was not happy, nor did he have what he wanted. Not that he knew what he wanted or what would make him happy. What he did have was something that most people wanted and would have made them very happy indeed: roughly half a million dollars in the bank. He could have had a million if he hadn't given half his inheritance to his mother. And *she* certainly seemed happy, sailing around the world with her boyfriend, Julius Goldstein, Harrowside's old Jewish tailor, who had fitted Walker for his very first suit. Lying in bed, Walker wondered if it was the *not* knowing that made him feel so feverish with depression. He considered getting up and immediately smoking a bowl of Stinky Skunk Spud. But if he did that before a shower and his first cup of coffee, he knew he would go right back to sleep. Maybe that was what he wanted. Just to go to sleep. Not forever, but for a few years anyway. Walker Van Winkle.

No, what he wanted right now was an orgasm. He pulled *Plaster My Face with Cum* from the nightstand drawer. Walker would never actually want to plaster a woman's face with cum. And, of the many women he'd had sex with, he couldn't think of one who would *want* to have her face plastered with cum. He was sure he could stroll over to the red-light district and pay an Indonesian prostitute to let him give her a facial. But he doubted she would enjoy it. And she'd have to clean it off afterward. And that image, of a joyless woman mopping semen off her face with a towel, would kill any pleasure Walker might get from the act. But there were no joyless women in this magazine. And no towels.

Walker was having trouble getting hard. He felt about halfway there, his dick maintaining the consistency of a hunk of boudin sausage. But the more he looked at the photos in the magazine, the more real the images of the women became, the more he thought about actually doing what the men in the pictures were doing, the softer he got. He tossed *Plaster My Face with Cum* across the room. It landed on a pile of American newspapers, "general interest" magazines, and opinion journals, most of which Walker had not bothered to read. As he continued to stroke his penis, he tried to think erotic thoughts. Sadie entered his mind. His quasi-erection began to flag more quickly. It was terrible. He and Sadie had had lusty, tender, frolic sex the whole time they were together. But ever since they'd broken up, he found it impossible to masturbate with her in mind. He drifted back through memories of past lovers. He tried to imagine sex with Eva Thule. He reconjured memorable sex scenes from movies. To no avail. Was all that dope he smoked sapping him of his precious bodily fluids? Suddenly he felt like crying, a common occurrence these days. The feeling, that is, not actual tears. And on this bleak afternoon, swaddled in sheets and blankets, alone in the shadows of his hotel room, Walker, as he had all the other times since arriving in Amsterdam, fought back the tears. He would not allow himself to cry. He felt he had no right to do it.

What, after all, would he be crying *for*? The breakup with Sadie had been painful, but it was for the best, the best thing for both of them, he was sure of that. The death of his father? Walker had never really known Christian Severance, and the last time he'd seen him, that Christmas in Vermont, he hadn't particularly liked him. So what, or who, was there really to mourn? Walker was now a wealthy man—thanks to his father's death. This was cause for tears? Of course not. Walker remembered Jojo Harrison, from the Amandla workshop, thought of how scornfully Jojo would have jeered at a black man with nearly a half million dollars lying in bed alone and crying. Crying for himself. That's all he would be crying for. So Walker choked back his tears, felt a burning in his throat, felt the depression suffusing his body now.

Obliviousness. People did not understand that obliviousness could cut just as deeply as cruelty. It must have been something about him, some quality specific to Walker Du Pree that rendered others oblivious to his pain. He felt as if he'd walked around most of his life bleeding profusely and trying to get people to notice.

"Excuse me," he'd say, "but my guts are hanging out here. Could you help me?"

"You look fine, Walker," each person would say as entrails spilled at their feet. "Now, let me tell you about *my* problems."

Obliviousness. *This* was something to cry over? Walker had never been poor. He hadn't grown up in a ghetto. He'd never suffered, never, really, materially suffered. No one else pitied him, so why should he pity himself? On the other hand, why get out of bed? This was a question Walker found himself pondering every late morning and early afternoon in Amsterdam. Why even get up? Just as he felt himself succumbing to tears, he fell back asleep.

*   *   *

Walker was surprised by Pappy Severance's invitation. In the twenty hours since Walker had arrived at the Severance country house in Vermont, the old man had barely acknowledged him. Now Pappy asked if Walker wanted to come with him to get a Christmas tree. It was the morning of December 24, 1982. Walker had wondered why the Severances did not already have a Christmas tree when he arrived. Maybe, he assumed, the family just liked waiting until the last minute. In Harrowside, Brooklyn, where he had spent his previous eighteen Yuletides, if you waited until Christmas Eve to go shopping for a tree, you were bound to get stuck with some scrubby and diseased-looking conifer. This, evidently, would not be the case in Vermont. Walker hesitated for a moment when Pappy invited him to come along. He wondered if maybe Christian or one of the other Severances had put the old man up to it. He also flinched at the idea of spending a long car ride into town with the somber patriarch of the clan. On the other hand, Walker thought it might be refreshing to escape the Severance property for a while. Maybe once they'd driven into town, Walker could slip away from Pappy and shop for a present for his mother. Trying to conceal his ambivalence, Walker answered Pappy's invitation with a hearty, "Sure! Thanks!"

Once they stepped outside, Pappy did not head for his car, but instead grabbed an axe from the pile of wood on the porch. Walker followed Pappy as he trudged through the snow behind the Severance house. They walked uphill, across a blindingly white expanse of snow, toward a forest of pine. Walker was tickled. Why *buy* a Christmas tree when you could chop one down in your own backyard? Pappy was silent as he climbed the hill, clutching the axe handle in his bare, veiny hand, the snow crunching under his heavy boots. He wore a puffy down coat and the sort of flappy hunting cap that Walker had always associated with Bugs Bunny's nemesis, Elmer Fudd. Most people would have looked as ridiculous as Elmer Fudd in such headgear, but the hunting cap suited Pappy. It occurred to Walker that such hunting caps had been designed precisely for men like Pappy Severance.

This is my grandfather: Walker could not help but feel astonished as the words ran through his mind. *I'm related to this guy.* Though he had had a full day to get used to the concept, Walker continued to look at Pappy and all the other white Anglo-Saxon Protestants staying in the rustic manse through a haze of unreality, thinking, in silent amazement: *I'm related to these people* (or, sometimes: *I can't believe I'm related to these people*).

Pappy inspected several trees, muttering to himself. He was not quite rude to Walker; not exactly. He just didn't seem to take any particular notice of him. Pappy had the sort of stern, lean face, with jagged cheekbones and a bristling white beard, that Walker associated with old photographs of New England seamen—a grizzled, whale hunter's face. "Ay-yoh," Pappy muttered when he decided on a tree to kill. A wiry man of eighty, Pappy was far stronger than he looked. He hacked away with long, even strokes of the axe. Once the chopping was done, Pappy took hold of the tip of the tree, Walker grabbed the stump, and they trudged downhill through the crunchy snow. Though they had barely said a word to each other, Walker had the feeling that this tree-chopping excursion had been Pappy's way of making friends.

*   *   *

More than twelve years later, when he was living in Amsterdam, rapidly spending the money his father had left him, Walker had trouble remembering the first names and the faces of most of his Severance relatives. But he could never forget their excruciatingly polite manner with him. He believed that most of them were doing their best. They wanted to make him feel welcome, accepted. But the strain, the effort behind their magnanimity, showed. Maybe they were each thinking: *I can't believe I'm related to this guy.* They were the same sort of pink, well-scrubbed people he'd been startled to discover when he'd entered Craven U. that fall. But these were his uncles, aunts, and cousins. His father's people.

Until that Christmas, Walker had never thought of his father as having an ethnicity. He had a race, of course. Whiteness was one of the essential facts about Christian Severance, the others being that he lived in Boston, that he worked as a high-school English teacher, that he sent Walker and his mother money, that he and Gina Du Pree had never married, and that Gina would answer no other questions about him. When Walker classified his father socially, he applied the same label his uncle Fred had always stuck on Christian Severance: "hippie." But when Walker saw the blue Volvo pull up to the entrance of Mould Hall, his freshman dormitory, and finally recognized the man behind the wheel—the clean-shaven man with the short, Brylcreemed hair, the man in the crisp white shirt, tweed jacket, and old school tie, this man who bore only the faintest resemblance to the hairy guy Walker used to call Daddy—he realized that Christian had shed his hippie image and, in the process, acquired an ethnicity. With the sense of shock people feel only when recognizing the obvious, Walker thought, My father is a WASP.

*   *   *

Nobody ever told Walker the whole story; the whole story about his mother and father. Gina Du Pree would offer only those six facts she considered essential. Uncle Fred and Aunt Agnes occasionally provided Walker with bits of information. He knew from them that his parents had met while both were working in the civil rights movement. He knew that they had attended the March on Washington together in 1963, and since he was born nine months later, Walker liked to think that he had been conceived there. He gathered that his parents had not been together very long—but he didn't know for sure. He guessed, he speculated, he fantasized about the life his parents had shared before he was born, about the life his father lived each day. When, in November of his freshman year, Christian Severance called to invite him to the family Christmas celebration, Walker was thrilled. Now, he thought, he would be able to piece together more of the story.

And by the time the Severance clan sat down to dinner on Christmas Day, this is what Walker gleaned: that the family was very rich and very uptight; that Christian, the second of three sons, had been the family fuck-up, the druggie, the dropout, the draft dodger; and that Christian now seemed eager to earn the family's favor. Perhaps that was why he had invited Walker here. Presumably, all the Severances knew that Christian had fathered a child by a black woman. Maybe it—that is to say, Walker—had been a family scandal. Maybe now Christian was trying to redeem the situation by introducing Walker to the family. Maybe that was why, from the time Christian pulled up to Mould Hall, all shorn and respectable-looking, in his blue Volvo, there was a constricted, formal air about him. Did Walker only imagine it or did his father seem burdened by a sense of obligation, of duty?

There were three outsiders among the twenty people gathered at the Severance country house: Walker; Helga, Pappy's buxom German

nurse (since Pappy seemed to be in superb health, Walker leapt to the
conclusion that the fiftyish Helga's services were less medical than
sexual), who spoke to no one but Pappy (whose first wife, the mother
of his three sons, Walker's grandmother, had died ten years earlier
and whose second wife, a much younger gold digger, Walker gleaned,
had been recently dispatched with a hefty divorce settlement); and
Lydia Rose, Christian's girlfriend, who flew up from Boston on
Christmas Eve. Lydia and Christian taught at the same high school.
She looked to be about thirty, with dark hair and eyes. Lydia was far
more at ease with Walker than the Severances were, and he estab-
lished an instant rapport with her. While Walker and Lydia spent
much of their time in Vermont sitting by the fireplace talking, Christian seemed to be avoiding them both. Observing Christian's behavior with the other male Severances, Walker grew increasingly
annoyed. His father seemed to be kissing the asses of the other men
in the family. Walker could not figure out why. Was it simply that he
wanted to get in their good graces after years of being the family
fuck-up? Or did he want something from them? Why wouldn't Christian give Walker a fraction of the attention he was lavishing on these
other people? Walker was hurt. But he did not believe his father was
trying to hurt him. Christian was just oblivious.

Walker had no clue as to the source of the Severance fortune until
Pappy said grace at Christmas dinner, calling on the Lord to bless "all
good and decent people, all creatures great and small, and all the
valuable minerals of the earth." So, that, Walker assumed, was how
the Severances made their money: They tore it out of the ground.

Lydia and Walker sat next to each other at the table, directly
across from Christian, who talked compulsively to his older brother
Ed, on his right, and his cousin Gus, on his left, occasionally addressing people who sat near Lydia and Walker on the other side of the
table, but assiduously avoiding eye contact with either his lover or his

son. Christian had been drinking since noon; his face was red and puffy as he jabbered enthusiastically about nothing, his eyes darting crazily every time he looked toward Walker or Lydia, bouncing away from their gaze.

Helga tapped a spoon against her water glass and the room fell silent. Walker noticed Pappy Severance standing at the head of the table. He assumed the old man was about to propose a toast, but instead Pappy began reciting:

> *"If you can keep your head when all about you*
> *Are losing theirs and blaming it on you,*
> *If you can trust yourself when all men doubt you,*
> *But make allowance for their doubting too . . ."*

Pappy spoke in a voice as dry as sawdust. Everyone at the table except Christian—who sat with his eyes shut tight, head bowed, arms folded across his chest—stared at the patriarch, this wiry, cold-eyed man who rarely seemed to speak at all, as he made his way, from memory, through the entire Rudyard Kipling poem.

> *"If you can fill the unforgiving minute*
> *With sixty seconds' worth of distance run . . ."*

The old man's voice had grown more passionate as he approached the closing lines. Walker began to have the creepy feeling that this was an annual tradition.

> *"Yours is the Earth and everything that's in it,*
> *And—which is more—you'll be a Man, my son!"*

Everyone at the table, except Christian, who kept his head bowed and his arms folded, applauded with pitterpat delicacy. A few people said, "Thank you, Pappy," and raised their wineglasses to him. Suddenly Christian burst into violent applause. "Bravo!" he cheered. "Bravissimo, Pappissimo! Bravo!" He stuck two fingers in his mouth and let out a piercing whistle. "Lovely interpretation, as always. Though shouldn't you say, 'Then you'll be a Man, or Woman, my son, or daughter'? We mustn't be chauvinistic."

"That will do, Christian," Ed Severance, the oldest brother, said grimly.

"Actually, let's dispense with Kipling next year. Enough of the Victorians. We're a Modern family! Why don't you recite 'Richard Cory' next Christmas?"

"Just ignore him," Ed said quietly to the table at large.

"You know that poem, don't you, Walker?" For the first time that day, Christian looked his son in the eye. "I hope they taught you *something* at that Brooklyn public school. Richard Cory—the lovely young rich man who went home one night and put a bullet through his head. Now, *that's* a poem that speaks to Severance tradition. Welcome to the family, Walker!"

"That's quite enough, Christian," Ed said.

"I'm just trying to teach *your nephew*, Ed, something about his proud family heritage. He needs to know that Severance men tend to blow their heads off. With shotguns. I'm inclined to call it Hemingwayesque. But at least Ernest had something to show for his angst. Severance men blow their heads off out of boredom. Why, Pappy here is the first Severance male to survive past seventy. But you'd never off yourself, would you, Paps? You just drive other people to commit suicide."

"Just ignore him, everyone," Ed said firmly. And, to Walker's puzzlement, most people at the table followed Ed's order.

"No one in my generation of Severance men has sucked on the old double-barrel . . . yet!"

"Stop it, Chris," Lydia said.

"I don't answer to *Chris!*" Christian snarled, glaring at his girl-friend. "Miss *Rosenbaum*. Did you know that's Lydia's real last name, Walker? Not *Rose*, as she told you, but—"

Cutting Christian off, Lydia turned to Walker and addressed him in a casual tone. "My father's name was Rosenbaum. But when he got a job at a big Wall Street law firm, they suggested he change it. This was back in the forties. That sort of thing was pretty common then."

"He changed his name!" Christian yelled. "They told him to change his name—so he did it! Can you imagine? And now Lydia's name is Rose and no one can tell she's a Jewess!"

"Assimilation," Lydia said with a smile and a shake of her head, gamely trying to make light of Christian's attack on her. "Ya gotta love it."

"But what did *I* know about blacks and Jews?" Now Christian was looking dead at Walker. "When I was growing up, I didn't meet any blacks and Jews. Do you know why? Because there *were* no blacks and Jews! They didn't exist!"

Years later, Walker would be baffled by what he felt at this moment: a harrowing sense of embarrassment; embarrassment for his father. He felt as if Christian had thrown up at the table. Or perhaps, more precisely, he felt as if Christian were spewing vomit. He felt it was compulsive regurgitation, that Christian couldn't help himself. The sickness had to come out. It could not be contained.

"You see, Walker," Christian said imploringly, "I'm a victim of racism, too. I'm a victim, too! I'm just as much a victim of racism as *you* are! Don't you see? I am just as much a victim of racism as *you* are!"

There was a long silence as Walker gave his father a level stare. Finally he said, "I really don't see how you can say that when you hardly know anything about me."

For several moments, Christian seemed unable to respond. He

simply stared at his son, his eyes turning watery. "But I'm a victim, too," he said wanly.

"Christian," Pappy said in his sawdust voice. "You are excused from the table."

Christian slowly rose from his chair and, without a word to anyone, disappeared upstairs. The enormous pool of invisible vomit that everyone could see spread inexorably across the table, spilling over the sides. Ed and the other Severances tried to pretend they didn't see it. People commented on the wonderful meal. They talked about the stock market. And the snow. But the natural course of conversation had been destroyed. Christian was gone, but no one could forget the puke he had left behind.

The next morning, Lydia drove Walker to the airport. Christian, she explained, could not rouse himself from bed. "Your father has a lot of unresolved issues in his life," she said sympathetically, inanely. It was clear that, for whatever reason, Lydia deeply loved Christian.

But Walker felt nothing for his father. He had stopped feeling anything for Christian the night before, after everyone else had gone to bed and he stood on the porch of the Severance country house, knowing that he would never see this place again, wondering if he would ever see his father again, as he stared out into the night, mesmerized by the relentless snowfall.

*   *   *

Why get up? The question was back in Walker's mind as he awoke again in his bed in the Hotel Elyssia on this Monday in April 1995. But noticing the rumble in his stomach and the darkness outside his window, Walker had a good answer to the question: He had slept the entire day away and he was starving. He took a quick shower, got dressed, and smoked a bowl of grass. He would head over to Mr.

Happy's, the ultimate pig-out bar where the menu listed burgers in two sizes: MASSIVE and NOT-SO-MASSIVE. On his way out the door, he grabbed a magazine from the unread pile, figuring it was time for an O.J. update, to read the latest about the bloody socks on the former football player's bedroom floor, the bloody glove that was found in his backyard, Nicole's poor dog howling over her butchered body, the cops' (mis)handling of vials of DNA evidence, the latest juror who had been dismissed and under what circumstances. Nobody seemed to care anymore whether O.J. did it. The relevant question had become: Could anybody prove it?

Out on the dark, blustery street, Walker saw Eva and Jean-Luc, arm in arm, moving quickly toward him but not seeing him, Eva staring at the ground, shaking her head and saying something, emphatically, in French and Jean-Luc, his anxious eyes fixed on Eva. "Hi, guys," Walker said.

They looked up, startled. Eva gave Walker her big, bright smile, kissed him once on each cheek. "Boy, it is good to see you. Jean-Luc and I are fighting. As always."

Jean-Luc looked hurt. "C'est pas vrai!"

"Yes, vrai," Eva said, focusing on Walker. "He has won a job tending bar in Antibes. He wants to be a beach bum in the South of France."

"Sounds good to me," Walker said.

"Yes!" Jean-Luc shouted, patting Walker on the shoulder.

"But I want to stay in place somewhere for a change," Eva said. "I've been traveling for six years already. I want to go to university and I would like to do it here, in Amsterdam. I speak Dutch okay. My English is improving. I don't want to work in bars and cafés my whole life."

"Why not?" Jean-Luc said. "It's a good life!"

"But it's not for me," Eva said, still seeming to address Walker more than Jean-Luc. "I don't want to live in a beach town. Not even if it is on the Côte d'Azur. I like it *here*!"

"But, Jean-Luc," Walker said, trying not to sound as hopeful as he felt, "you're on your way to Antibes?"

"I think so, yes. At the end of the month. I thought Eva would be happy to go with me."

"Wocker, you don't need to listen to us fight. So how are you? Are you going out to dinner?"

"Yeah, just thought I'd mosey on over to Mr. Happy's, read a magazine—" With that, Walker made a completely unself-conscious gesture, just a fling of the wrist, casually displaying the cover of the magazine he had been carrying, rolled up, in his left hand, a magazine he believed to be *American Century* but which he had scooped up absentmindedly from the pile of magazines by the door as he left his hotel room and which he now noticed, with sudden, sickening mortification as he held it up for Eva and Jean-Luc to see, was *Plaster My Face with Cum.*

"And are you also going to masturbate in the restaurant, Wocker?" Eva asked dryly.

*   *   *

A little more than an hour later, Walker still felt queasy with embarrassment. He and Eva and Jean-Luc had had a good laugh over his toting an obscene porno magazine—not even a relatively tame *Playboy* or a slickly produced *Penthouse,* magazines that could at least boast of publishing articles, but some of the tawdriest, most degrading sleaze Amsterdam had to offer. Yes, they had a brief, hearty laugh over it, then Eva and Jean-Luc went on their way, continuing their argument, and Walker returned to his hotel room, where he wished he could flush himself down the toilet. In lieu of that, he tossed *Plas-*

ter My Face with Cum into the wastebasket, smoked another bowl of dope, made sure it was a copy of *American Century* magazine he picked up, and, as he walked to Mr. Happy's, resigned himself to the idea that Eva would never, ever, sleep with him now. Even if Jean-Luc moved to the South of France and she was as lonely and sad and horny as Walker, never would she have sex with a man who would buy *Plaster My Face with Cum*. He sat at the bar in Mr. Happy's, for-lornly eating a heaping plateful of barbecued chicken, drinking pints of beer, and reflecting on his stupidity. The place was crowded, as usual, and filled with the cacophony of clanging, hooting, buzzing pinball machines, heavy metal music, and ongoing conversations in various languages. Walker stared at the portrait of Mr. Happy, a white-faced clown with orange dreadlocks and a sinister, red-lipped leer, that hung above the bar. Mr. Happy held an overflowing pint of beer in one hand and a burning splief in the other. Walker was mus-ing that if Mr. Happy came to life and if Walker and Mr. Happy were the only two men left in all the Netherlands, hell, in all of Europe, Eva would rather have sex with this grotesque circus clown than with a repugnant wanker like himself when he suddenly felt someone poke him in the side. It was an aggressive poke, a bony forefinger sliding between his ribs, pressuring his gut. Annoyed, Walker turned to the poker and saw a man he did not recognize at all, a thirtyish, sandy-haired man, a bit pale and on the short side, with inquisitive eyes behind thick-lensed glasses. He had a trim little mustache and wore a black turtleneck and a thick brown corduroy jacket. "Hello, mate," he said with an inscrutable little smile.

"Hi," Walker said tentatively, trying to figure out if he had ever seen this man before.

"How are you?" the man asked in an accent Walker could not identify. "Enjoy your meal?" He was still smiling mysteriously and stared at Walker as if the two of them shared some secret.

"Yes," Walker said. "I'm sorry, but do I know you?"

"I know *you*. I've seen you about."

Walker felt a tingling at the nape of his neck. He was not threatened, exactly, but he felt poised, prepared to meet some unknown danger. "Have you?"

"You're the one who likes Finnish girls." The man continued to smile and stare. His accent was beginning to sound South African to Walker's ears. Walker was less sure of the tone of his comment. Was it an observation or an accusation?

"Well," he said, "I have one friend who's half-Finnish and a girl."

"No, but I've seen you all over, with several. You were at that party at Margo's the other night."

"I don't know any Margo. And I don't know you and I don't think you know me, and what's it to you who I hang out with?"

The presumptuous man held up a palm. "Sorry, mate. Perhaps I got you confused with somebody else. A black fellow who's always with Finnish girls. You're not him. But you look just like him."

"You mean we really do all look alike?"

The man chuckled. "No offense intended, mate. I have seen you about, though. It's interesting: blacks and blondes. The contrast. The attraction. You're a lucky man. They're beautiful women."

If this was the man's idea of friendliness, it wasn't working with Walker. The presumptuous man, Walker felt, was being mock chummy, was, in fact, baiting him. "Yeah, right," Walker said. Now he locked eyes with the stranger for a long time. He remembered an anthropology course he'd taken back at Craven U., recalled something the professor once said: If two mammals stare into each other's eyes for more than nine seconds, they're either going to have sex or kill each other. Walker did not know how long he and the rib-poking, presumptuous man had stared into each other's eyes. But he certainly knew they were not going to have sex.

Finally, the presumptuous man looked away. With a nervous laugh and a wave, he said, "Well, I'll be seeing you again." Walker said nothing. The man turned and walked out of Mr. Happy's.

*   *   *

Walker and Eva were alone among the birchwood surfaces and hanging plants of the Flutterbye coffee shop, sitting on opposite sides of the counter, Eva taking only a few hits from Walker's pipe—she was, after all, on duty, and even though business was slow on this rainy afternoon, she didn't want to risk getting too spacey—as they talked about the presumptuous man in Mr. Happy's. Walker was glad to have this little tale to tell as soon as he sat down at the counter so as to avoid any reference to *Plaster My Face with Cum.*

"It was just weird is all," Walker said. "I mean, is this guy stalking us or what?"

"Nobody is stocking you, Wocker," Eva said curtly. "You smoke too much grass, it's making you paranoid. The funny thing is I know the fellow he made the reference to. It is Mbundi. Mbundi is from Togo. And he does like Finnish girls, Scandinavians in general. But you look nothing like Mbundi. He is far darker than you."

"How do you know him?"

"He comes in here all the times."

"I've never seen him." Walker paused. "Is he after you?"

"He knows I am taken. He just flirts. Most of the times, he comes in with a girl anyhow. Usually Berit. She is from Helsinki and they are both very nice."

"And this guy from Mr. Happy's, following Mbundi and me around, what's *his* deal?"

"Probably, he was just trying to be friendly."

"No, he was probably saying, 'Better watch yourself, boy. We don't like seeing your kind with our women.'"

"I doubt it very much."

"Or maybe he'd like to watch Mbundi have sex with Berit. Lots of white men fetishize black men."

"Really, Wocker, why do you make so big a deal of it? It sounds like nothing."

"Well, as we say in the States, it's a black thing, you wouldn't understand."

"You really must stop with this black thing. You are not in the States. You are not even really black, you know."

"Oh no?"

"You are *métis*. That is what the French would call you."

Now Walker was angry. "Why is there always someone trying to tell me I'm not really black?"

"But your father, he was white, yes?"

"Yes, but I barely knew my father. Maybe if I had known him, I'd feel differently. But I consider myself black. My father was white, but I am black. You can call me *métis,* mulatto, multiracial, or mongrel, but it all boils down to black! Other people can consider themselves whatever they want, I don't begrudge them that right. But as far as I'm concerned, I am black and I'm tired of people telling me I'm not!"

Eva seemed stunned by Walker's ire. "Okay," she said softly. "I didn't mean to upset you."

"Remember Anne Frank House? *That* guy certainly considered me black."

"Yes," Eva said. "Yes." They were quiet for a long time. "People can be so strange about looks. I get so tired of this," Eva said, grabbing a hunk of her yellow hair and tossing it away from her face. "And these," she said testily, pointing to her aquamarine eyes. "When I worked as an au pair in London, one day I went into a coiffure and asked to chop off my hair and dye it black. The woman in the shop tocked me out of it. But I was so tired of people liking me—

or hating me—just because of how I look. Now I accept, most of the times, my looks. Because they don't matter to me."

"But you can't escape the fact that they matter to other people. The way you look matters to Jean-Luc."

"Yes, but if he cared only for my looks, there would be no love between us. If Jean-Luc cared only for my looks, our relation would not survive."

"Is your relation going to survive?" Walker almost whispered the question. He and Eva had both, ever so gradually, leaned forward, their elbows on the counter, to the point where their foreheads were almost touching. The air between them seemed to grow dense.

"I don't know," Eva said.

Their hands rested on the counter. Walker gently moved to take Eva's right hand in his. But as he tried, slowly, delicately, to interlock his fingers with hers, Eva, just as gently, balled her hand into a loose fist. "Are you going to Antibes with him?"

"Yes. I think so."

"Are you in love with him?"

Eva leaned away from Walker. The motion was not abrupt, but she clearly wanted more space between them. "It is so mysterious. I know you, Wocker. You are one of the people who wants to figure things out. You want to know *why* two certain people fall in love. I know you look at Jean-Luc and you wonder why I am with him."

"That's not true, I—"

"Yes it is. But, as I say to you, these are mysterious things. We should not try to explain, to search for rules and formulas. How can people get so concerned with the exterior when they talk about what is so interior?"

"Love conquers all, eh?" Walker said sardonically.

"No," Eva said. "Love does not conquer. Love *defies*."

*   *   *

Why, Sadie Broom wondered as she sat beside one of the tall windows in a palatial apartment in the ritzy 7th arrondisement, had she
let Mylène drag her to this tedious excuse for a party? Sadie sat in her
chair, downing glass after glass of champagne, getting drunker and
drunker, glancing now and then at the view behind her—the Eiffel
Tower, ablaze in golden lights against a blue velvet sky, looking, to
Sadie, like a spacecraft out of Spielberg—but paying more attention
to that obscenity hanging on the wall, the huge poster encased in
glass that she alone seemed to notice. It was nearly two in the morning. The party was winding down. There were six French couples
clustered around the living room. Sadie could hear a more lively
group, which included Mylène, in the brightly lit dining room next
door. But here, in the dim blue light of the living room, each of the
six couples inhabited its own little space on various divans and, *in
each couple,* the woman silently leaned toward the man as the man
talked. These scrawny, effeminate Frenchmen prattled pompously,
tirelessly, as the women, with their gaunt, unsmiling faces, listened
raptly, like little girls being told bedtime stories. Sadie reached over
to the lukewarm bottle of champagne on the windowsill, poured herself another glass, and continued to watch, in growing disgust, the
ciphers listening to the bores. Even back at Craven U., in those days
when she considered herself a sidekick, Sadie would never just sit
mute as some man blathered in her ear. She would talk back, engage
the guy, have a *conversation,* for Christ's sake. But these grim, emaciated women just sat there, focused on the grim, emaciated men
droning on and sculpting the air with their hands. And no one at this
party but Sadie had even paused to take note of the framed poster
that you would never, ever, see in an equally "sophisticated" American home, that obscenity hanging on the wall.

Why, Sadie wondered, had she come to Paris at all? She had toured Europe after college, knew that she didn't care for the place. What the fuck was she doing here, anyway? Sitting in this opulent living room, a lone black woman, surrounded by strangers, more drunk than she had been in years, Sadie admitted to herself that she had come to France, had signed up for the stint in Tanzer & Mur's Paris office, just to spite Walker, to show him that *he* wasn't the only one who could up and leave the USA. He wasn't the only globe-trotting Negro around. Anything he could do, she could do better. She wondered what Walker was doing right now. Last she'd heard, he was still in Amsterdam. Getting stoned and fucking Dutch bitches no doubt! Sadie could feel her old, familiar anger beginning to bubble inside her. Why had Walker abandoned her like that? Didn't he realize she was the best thing that had ever happened to him? He would never find anyone, certainly no European bitch, who would love him as much as Sadie had loved him. How could he just walk out on their relationship like that, upset the plans she had so carefully laid? Now here she was, thirty-one years old, without a man, with the deadline for engagement she'd always carried in her head, her tenth class reunion at Craven, only a year away. How many times had she fantasized about returning to that grassy campus, triumphant, with a rock on her finger and a sought-after black man on her arm? How could Walker do this to her? She just wanted to hit him, wanted to scratch his skin off! But just as suddenly as the rage had taken over Sadie, it began to subside. She turned the situation over in her mind again and realized that, perhaps, she had not come to Europe as a hollow act of revenge. Maybe she had come here to reclaim her man, to track him down and bring him back where he belonged, back with her, back to America.

Sadie heard the doorbell ring, then a loud exchange of greetings, in French and English. Mylène entered the living room with the group of new arrivals, five or six people, one of them clearly an African American. "Say-dee!" Mylène said excitedly. "I like you to meet Charlie Jackson. He is like you—a black person from New York!"

"Actually, I'm from D.C.," Sadie said.

Charlie Jackson, a short, chunky brother with dreadlocks and a round, pleasant face, shook Sadie's hand. "I'm from Cleveland myself," he said, "but I spent my last three years in the States in New York."

"Oh yeah? How long you been here?"

"Ten years."

"My God, how do you stand it?"

Charlie looked at Sadie as if she'd said something incomprehensible. "I love it here."

"Tcccchh." Sadie sucked her teeth in annoyance. She noticed that Mylène and the other new arrivals had stepped back, as if to give Charlie and Sadie a chance to get acquainted, and were talking among themselves. The six French couples remained seated in their little clusters, the men prattling on, the women all ears. "So what do you do, Charlie?" Sadie asked, the question sounding almost sarcastic.

"I play guitar."

"Where, in the metro?" Sadie let out a huge, horsey laugh. She saw Mylène turn and glare at her.

"Noooooo," Charlie said slowly. "I play all over Europe, in clubs."

"And you make a living at that?"

"Yes, I do," Charlie said patiently, as if he were speaking to a slow-witted child. "Are you all right, Sadie? You seem a bit . . . out of sorts."

"Well, Charlie, you really don't know what *sort* I am, do you?"

"I'm beginning to get an idea."

Sadie glanced at the obscenity hanging on the wall, then turned back to Charlie. "You say you've lived here ten years, huh?" Charlie nodded. "Then maybe you can explain something to me." Sadie took Charlie by the arm and walked him across the living room. She pointed to the enormous poster in its glass frame. At the top of the poster were the words LIFE'S A BALL, written in big black block letters. Just below the line was a grotesque cartoon: a dark brown face, eyes bulging, flashing crooked white teeth surrounded by ruby-red lips, crowned with a black scrawl representing nappy black hair. Below the hideous face were stubby brown fingers clutching an orange basketball, but the top portion of the basketball was missing; in its place, seemingly growing out of the ball, was the red meat of a watermelon, studded with black seeds. Below the basketball, in black block letters, were the words EAT IT UP. Still pointing at the poster with one hand and grasping Charlie's arm with the other, Sadie said, "What the fuck is that?"

Charlie tittered. "That's a big nigger head eating a basketball watermelon."

"Yeah, I know," Sadie said hotly. "But what the fuck is that *about*?"

"Life's a ball, eat it up." Charlie chuckled uncertainly. "Weird."

"What the fuck *is* this shit?" Sadie fairly shouted. All conversation in the room stopped. Sadie could feel everyone's eyes on her now.

Charlie stared at Sadie, a plaintive look in his eyes. "You shouldn't look at that too long, Sadie."

"But what does it say about the people who put that on their wall?"

"Hey, Sadie, this ain't America. You're looking at it out of context. It's like those black jockey statues you see outside restaurants here. You could probably get sued for that in America. It's in a different context."

"*What* fucking context?" Sadie fumed. "That's what I want to know! I mean, anyone who would put this shit up on his wall, what does he think about us? How does he see *us,* Charlie? You and me. I wanna know what the fucking context is. What the *fuck* is this about?"

"Fuck, fuck, fuck," a French voice jeered. Sadie whirled around and saw one of the wispy male partygoers lounging on a divan, his silent, skeletal girlfriend curled up beside him. "Fucking this, fucking that. I feel like I'm in an American movie."

A peculiar sense of calm came over Sadie, a *sangfroid.* She took a couple of steps forward and stood over the Frenchman. "Actually, if this were an American movie," she said glacially as she contorted her right hand into the shape of a pistol and pointed it directly in the Frenchman's face, "I'd blow you away." As the Frenchman stared at her, aghast, Sadie threw her hand back, as if she'd just fired a bullet between his eyes.

"Say-dee." Mylène put an arm around her friend's shoulders. "Let's go home. I think you have too much to drink."

Sadie let Mylène guide her out the door. She didn't bother saying good-bye to anyone. When she awoke in her bed, ten hours later, feeling as if an axe were buried in the center of her skull, she would find herself crying, and her tears would be tears of rage.

13

For the sort of people Corky Winterset knew—that is to say, people who were generally white, educated at elite universities or so-called "little Ivies" like Craven U., and tended to have jobs in law, medicine, business, and the media—there were four distinct age groups that corresponded with the event of a first marriage. This is how Corky broke it down:

Age 21–27: The Young and the Stupid

These were the couples, fresh out of college, struggling in graduate school or striving to earn a foothold in a career, who believed they were so in love, that their love was so indestructible, they just had to get married right away. Why wait? What could possibly go wrong?

Age 28–35: The Big Roundup

Corky's guess was that about eighty percent of the sort of people she knew got married during this period. Corky turned thirty-one in April 1995 and was bracing herself for the fourth straight spring and summer in which she would, practically every other weekend, be attending, bowing out of, serving as a bridesmaid in, or reading the announcement of the wedding of another classmate from high school, law school, or Craven U. There was an unspoken consensus among the sort of people Corky knew that the period of The Big Roundup was the most sensible time of life in which to wed.

Age 36–42: Last Train Leaving the Station

This, for the sort of people Corky knew, anyway, was a desperate time. Observing older women who had, for whatever reason, not gotten hitched during The Big Roundup, Corky sensed an urgency in their search for a husband. Every blind date was pregnant with an element of fate: "Will *he* be the one?" Courtships sometimes seemed forced, engagements rushed. And, so far as Corky could tell, the men who made it to this age category without getting married were among the least desirable of the sort of men Corky knew. And these men, responding to a subtle but persistent cultural pressure rather than to the ticking of a biological clock, were often as desperate to wed as the women. These were couples chasing after a final opportunity for marital bliss or the last chance for parenthood before it disappeared into the distance.

Age 43–?: *You're* Getting Married?!

These were the people their married friends had given up on. Perhaps they had been dismissed as losers or misfits or sexual outlaws. But once the single women and men in this age group announced their intention to wed, their married friends—who, by now, were usually trapped in loveless unions—reacted with exaggerated shock followed by the smug pleasure someone who feels cheated by life takes in seeing someone else get duped, too.

Corky Winterset knew that if she ever got married at all, it would not be until she reached that final age group.

*   *   *

Back when she was in law school, Corky went to see a therapist who told her what she already knew: that she had hostile feelings toward her mother and wanted her life to be as different as possible from Nancy Winterset's. Nancy had told both her daughters that they would grow up to be hostesses. They would marry men with important jobs, and when their husbands brought home their colleagues, the grown-up Tippy and Corky would do what Nancy did for their father: serve as the perfect hostess. Whenever Corky would tell her mother what she wanted to be when she grew up—most of her childhood ambitions focused on nursing, teaching, and violin-playing—Nancy would say, "Ah, but you'll be a hostess. Your job will be to serve as a hostess for your husband." By the time she was ten, Corky regarded her mother's words as some sort of curse, a dark threat: *You'll be a hostess.*

You could be a nurse or a teacher or a violinist all by yourself, but in order to be a hostess, you had to have a husband. What, Corky wondered, was a hostess without a husband? A few years later, when Corky's father divorced her mother to marry his secretary, Corky found out. A hostess without a husband was nothing.

*   *   *

Corky Winterset liked being smart. She liked being considered smart by other smart people. She liked that most people, when she told them she was clerking for a judge, assumed she must be really smart. Judge Judith Proctor was phenomenally smart. Cruelly smart. Judge Proctor enjoyed making her smart young clerks feel stupid. Sometimes at night Corky would weep over vicious comments the judge had made about her work. Hal would get upset and tell Corky she should not remain silent in the face of unfair criticism. She should stand up for herself. Corky would then get angry at Hal and say he wasn't being supportive. Hal did not seem to understand that by making Corky feel stupid, Judge Proctor was trying to help her.

"You're so stupid." Corky, whenever she fucked up again at the courthouse, would hear her father's voice inside her head. "So stupid!" It was as if there were a tape of Chuck Winterset inside her brain. "Jesus, that's so *stupid!*" She could hear the precise way her father spat out the words, could hear the little slash of saliva on the *p*. Chuck Winterset never said the words to Corky, or to her sister, Tippy. He said them, regularly, to her mother. "Oh, for Christ's sake, Nancy, don't be so stupid!" Stepping out of the judge's chambers, after another lacerating critique of one of her drafts, Corky would quietly spit out the words as she heard her father's voice, performing a mental lip synch: "So stupid. So stupid! So *stupid!*"

For years, Corky had thought her father was being needlessly harsh with her mother. Then, after the divorce, Corky decided her father was right: Nancy really was stupid. Her mother had been stupid to link her entire fate to one man—especially to a corporate dweeb, an agribusiness executive, like Chuck Winterset. She was stupid to live in a community like Sheffield, their upscale Lincoln suburb, where a divorcée, a hostess without a husband, no longer got invited to the suppers and barbecues and bridge games populated by people who, socially, existed only as pairs classified by the name of the male spouse. The Smiths and the Cartwrights, the Dixons, the Spooners, and the McCrackens were embarrassed by fractured couples. With Chuck living in another town, "the Wintersets" no longer existed. There was only Nancy, the severed limb. They couldn't very well have Nancy—*just* Nancy—at their "couples" functions. Chuck was the one whose company they had probably wanted, anyway. Maybe, Corky thought, because Nancy had nothing to say. Nancy was stupid enough to drop out of college to marry Chuck, stupid enough never to earn her degree or work a job outside her home, and so stupid that when she did go to work, after the divorce, at the checkout desk of the Sheffield Public Library, she couldn't handle the pressure, stamping the wrong due dates on books and miscalculating overdue charges, bungling things to the point where she got fired. Corky was thrilled when, at eighteen, she was able to go "back East," to Craven University; to put three-thousand-plus miles between her and her mother. Her stupid mother.

*   *   *

Before she became part of one, Corky had assumed, when she gave the matter any thought at all, that interracial couples spent all their time talking about being interracial couples. She guessed that all their conflicts would center on race. Yet in her first year of living with Hal Hardaway, race had rarely come up at all. And when Hal and Corky fought, they fought over time, attentiveness, their emotional needs— all the same old relationship crap that she'd fought over with most of her previous boyfriends, all of whom had been white. Hal worked for a black company, but that fact in no way affected their relationship. They were both so busy—Corky often put in six- and sometimes seven-day weeks at the courthouse—that they had not had the chance to socialize much. But Corky had met some of Hal's black friends and they always seemed perfectly accepting of her. Hal had attended several weddings with Corky and had no problem getting along with her white friends. One weekend, Hal's parents came up from Philadelphia: Corky hit it off with both of them. Corky never told her father anything about her love life. She did, however, wonder how her mother, still living in Nebraska, would react to the news that she was moving in with a black guy. But after receiving a photo of Corky and Hal in January 1994, Nancy called her daughter to burble about how handsome Hal was. "He looks just like that fellow in those Hertz Rent-a-Car commercials," Nancy cooed.

Race had *sort of* come up on their first night together, when they lay in bed, naked and moist in postcoital bliss, and Corky, lazily stroking Hal's back, ran her finger across a peculiarly shaped scar near his right shoulder blade. "What's this?" she asked. She could not see the scar in the darkness of the bedroom. "Was it painful?"

"Not too," Hal said sleepily as he lay on his stomach. "It's my brand."

"Your *what?*"

"My brand. It's the Psi Delta Zed seal."

"Oh my God! They burned it into your flesh?"

"Yeah."

"I've never heard of such a thing. None of the frats I know about *brand* their members."

"It's no big deal."

"How can you say that? You're, like, permanently scarred."

"It's not all that different from a tattoo."

"But a brand. Isn't that what they used to do to slaves?"

"Yo," Hal said, his voice suddenly dropping an octave, "I'm gonna tell ya something' and I wantcha to remember it: I ain't nobody's slave."

Corky felt immediately aroused by Hal's change of speech. She kissed his sweaty-salty neck. "Yo," she growled, "neither am I."

*   *   *

Hal always expressed astonishment at what Corky did not know—or, more precisely, did not know what most people in America seemed to think—about race. Sometimes he thought her naïveté was disingenuous. Like the Sunday afternoon they spent in bed—back in her Washington apartment—playfully exploring each other's bodies, when Corky complimented Hal on the size of his penis.

"Well," Hal said, "you know what they say about black men."

"No," Corky said. "What do they say about black men?"

Hal refused to believe that Corky had never heard that black guys were supposed to have bigger dicks than white guys.

"Where would I have heard such a thing?" Corky said in exasperation after Hal kept accusing her of feigning ignorance. "You think white people in Nebraska sit around talking about black guys' dicks?"

"So you've never heard the question, What's white and ten inches long?"

"What?"

"Nothing."

They joked about Corky's innocence, as they joked about most things in those days. But sometimes Corky worried that what she did not know might hurt her. She needed advice. "I've never gone out with a black guy before," she once told Hal, "so you have to help me."

"Hey," Hal shot back, sounding annoyed, "I've never gone out with a white girl before, so *you* have to help *me.*"

Strangers on the street would look at them, Hal said, and regard her as a cultural stereotype, a horny white woman lusting after the big black stud. Well, yes, Corky thought, she did love sex, and Hal was the best lover she had ever had. But was Hal a great lover because he was black? And were all black guys as good in bed as Hal was? Did all white women involved with black men love sex as much as Corky did? Did all black men?

"Once you've had black, you never go back," Hal said. Apparently this was an old joke. Corky had never heard it.

*   *   *

Corky rarely said "I love you" to anyone and she always felt uncomfortable when anyone said it to her. Whenever someone said "I love you," it meant they expected something from you. At the very least, they expected you to say "I love you" back. Corky rarely did. After the divorce, Corky's father started saying "I love you" to her all the time. For two years, Corky would not say it back to him. Finally she said, "I love you, too." Her father responded by giving her a lot of money. The more she said "I love you, too" after one of his frequent "I love you"s, the more money he gave her. Over the years, Chuck Winterset became more stingy with his "I love you"s. But when he said it to Corky, he had come to expect that she would say it back to him. And when Corky said "I love you, too" to her father, she expected money.

Corky's mother—knowing that her daughter was unlikely to say "I love you" back—expected an extra dose of sympathy and attention when she said "I love you" to Corky. Since her mother hardly ever said the words, Corky would uncomplainingly give Nancy the little bonus of caring she expected in return.

When a man Corky had not had sex with said "I love you," it was because he expected her to have sex with him in return. Such men were always disappointed, not knowing that they had eliminated themselves from consideration the moment those three words left their lips.

Trickier to comprehend was a man Corky had already had sex with who said "I love you." Corky had never said "I love you" back to one of her lovers. She could never be certain what else they expected in return.

In their first several months of living together, Hal said "I love you" to Corky. He said it a lot. Corky never said it back to him. But she did love Hal. Corky loved Hal because, on the most intimate level, she was able to truly be herself with him.

*   *   *

By the time she graduated from Craven, Corky had stopped talking about relationships with her female friends. "Men give love to get sex," her senior housemate Simpy used to say. "Women give sex to get love." While Corky did not doubt the frequent accuracy of the first half of the hypothesis, she was iffy on the second part. Unlike seemingly all the other women she encountered, Corky enjoyed sex for its own sake, and she never made the rigid distinction between sex and love that seemingly all the women she knew made. Corky was mystified when she heard young women say they loved their boyfriends—or in later years, husbands—even though the sex "wasn't so great." Didn't these women see that sex and love were intertwined? Romantic love could not exist without sex. Someone you loved but did not relish having sex with was a friend; just a friend. And friendship, to Corky, did not constitute "love." It constituted "like."

Sometime in her mid-twenties, Corky began to realize that many of her lovers were a little bit, well, if not afraid of, then perhaps intimidated by, her in bed. It wasn't that Corky liked having lots and lots of sex. The men she was with told her she was "in the mood" no more or less than other women they had been with. What distinguished Corky seemed to be something *in the way* she had sex. *Intense* was the word that several evidently shaken lovers had used to describe her. Corky felt at once flattered and dismayed by the awestruck compliments of sweaty, sated young men. None of them could ever tell her exactly what it was she did that was so unusual. And since she no longer talked to other women about sex, she could not be certain what it was she did that other women did not, would not, or could not do. She tried not to think about it. Because she did not want to become self-conscious in bed. The only time Corky felt utterly unself-conscious was when she was having sex. Was that what scared the men? "Out of control," her hunky blond boyfriend Alec Larsen used to say after one of their bouts on the Persian rug in his London flat. "You were out of control." Corky knew that at the mind-shattering apex of an orgasm, she often had no idea where she was. Or rather, she could feel and see herself in any number of places: zooming downhill, wind whipping in her ears, at Aspen, for instance; or hang-gliding in California; or lying on the beach in Hilton Head, her skin prickling under the blazing sun. If Corky, in her ecstasy, forgot where she was, she was completely unaware of what she said at such moments. She was deaf to her genius for the well-timed, profane exhortation.

Corky felt, from their very first night together, that she could do anything she wanted with Hal in bed. And he could do anything he wanted with her. And it would be okay. Corky thought of that sense of mutual indulgence as a powerful kind of trust. Hal never flinched at her passion. And Hal knew how to let himself go without going too far. Without ever hurting her, he never acted—as so many men, with their skittish gestures, had—as if he was afraid of hurting her. And he was always so sweet and tender afterward.

Someone like Corky's old housemate Simpy would say that Corky was with Hal "only for the sex." This was why Corky no longer talked to women like Simpy about relationships. "Only for the sex," they would say, as if sex were *only* some minor element of a relationship. There were some men Corky had been involved with "only for the sex." But the involvements never lasted more than three or four nights because if the sex did not evolve quickly into love, it wasn't great sex anymore and sex that was not great was not worth having. When it came to long-term involvements, Corky knew that once the sex became "not so great," the relationship was doomed. Since Corky had the best sex of her life with Hal, it naturally followed that he was the man she had loved the most.

Of course, other things attracted Corky to Hal. He was strong and kind and funny. He seemed to get along with everyone he met. He listened to her problems and seemed genuinely concerned about her well-being. But it was through sex—of course it was through sex—that Hal and Corky expressed their deepest feeling for each other. It was in bed that she knew she was in love with him.

Corky felt it should be obvious to Hal that she loved him. She did not feel she had to say it. But every couple of weeks, Hal would say it to her, his eyes scanning her face expectantly, silently imploring her to repeat "I love you" back to him. And what else, aside from her parroting the three words, did Hal expect from Corky when he said "I love you"? Eventually Corky concluded that Hal expected her to marry him. Since they were both living in The Big Roundup age bracket, the subject of marriage, usually spurred by yet another couple's engagement or wedding, came up often, and when it did, Corky would always say:

"You don't want to marry me."

To which Hal would typically respond: "Why don't I?"

"Because you don't," Corky would usually reply. "I know you don't. Even if you don't know you don't."

Then Hal would say it again: "I love you."

Corky would either laugh, give Hal a kiss, change the subject, or snap, "Oh, stop it."

Even when they cuddled together in bed, holding each other close after an especially transcendant fuck and Hal whispered the words to her, Corky resisted responding in kind. Her fear was that once she finally did say "I love you" to Hal, she wouldn't mean it anymore.

*   *   *

Corky was haunted by the eyes of Marcia Clark. In the spring of 1995, the O.J. Simpson double-murder trial played all day and into the evening on the two televisions in the courthouse cafeteria. On her visits to the cafeteria, Corky rarely paused to watch the trial—unless Marcia Clark, the lead prosecutor, was on-screen. Marcia Clark was smart. She was really smart. Corky felt proud that a smart woman lawyer was fighting for justice in the trial of the century. If Corky won a spot in a district attorney's office, worked extremely hard, and played her cards right, she could, someday, be in the position of a Marcia Clark. Corky was mesmerized by Marcia Clark on TV. Long after she would leave the cafeteria and return to her office, Corky would still see Marcia Clark's eyes, huge eyes, eyes that seemed to be screaming in a gaunt, tired face. Marcia Clark's second ex-husband was suing her for custody of their two children, claiming that her work schedule made her an inadequate mother. Marcia Clark seemed to be losing her temper a lot that spring. Sometimes she looked scared. She was obviously exhausted, stressed out. Corky sensed a terrible vulnerability in her. She wanted to give Marcia Clark a hug. She had tremendous admiration for Marcia Clark. And watching Marcia Clark, Corky realized that she no longer wanted to be a lawyer.

Corky believed her problem was that she loved fun too much. She wanted her work to be fun. Her first three years after college— when she bounced around the world, living out of a backpack, on trips paid for by the many "I love you, too"s she had bestowed on Chuck Winterset, trying to sell freelance travel pieces—had been the most fun time of Corky's life. It was, in fact, too much fun. She wanted to be a serious person, and serious people did not write travel stories. They went to law school. They clerked for judges. They worked in the D.A.'s office. Did serious people expect their work to be fun? Was Marcia Clark having fun in that L.A. courtroom? Corky worried that the extent to which she cared about having fun was the exact measure of her inability to be a serious person. And as she had once told Hal, being a serious person was the thing she wanted most. Wasn't it?

She and Hal hardly ever had fun anymore. During their first year of living together, Corky considered their low fun quotient a sign of their maturity. Serious people working important jobs weren't supposed to have fun. Now, four months into their second year of cohabitation, Corky was becoming aware of how a lack of fun had slowly eroded the bond between them. She had been so busy at the courthouse that the erosion process had taken place without her being aware of it. Only in the spring of '95 did Corky realize that she and Hal—who had amused each other so much two years earlier, back when she was still at law school in Washington and he was living in New York—rarely shared a laugh together anymore. During their first year of living together, Corky was usually too tired to make love after a long day's work, but they often had sex first thing in the morning. Gradually the early-morning lovemaking ritual grew less frequent. Corky felt too pressed for time. At first Hal gently complained. Now, Corky realized, depressingly, Hal said nothing about it at all. They generally had sex only once a week, on Sunday morning. Corky did not know when she stopped caring about the quality of the sex. She only knew that one Sunday morning in April, she was bored in bed with Hal, that he seemed equally bored with her, and that this boredom had been seeping into their lovemaking for a long time.

Sometimes Corky wondered why she stayed with Hal, but she knew the reason: Her two-year clerkship with Judge Proctor did not end until December 29, 1995. She had no idea what she would do with her life after that date. She only knew that until that time she could not handle any major changes. In these closing months of her clerkship, what she needed most was for Hal to be supportive. There were nights when Corky, lying awake in bed, acknowledged that her relationship with Hal was dying and she wondered why she had been so quick to move in with him. She remembered that they had started living together just days before she went to work for Judge Proctor. She remembered how—despite the fact that she had traveled solo around the world—the idea of living alone in New York City had terrified her. Hal was the one person who could provide the emotional support she needed. Corky did not think this at the time. Corky, at the time, just thought she was in love.

The more nights Corky spent lying awake beside a lightly snoring Hal, puzzling over how she had fallen in and out of love with this man, the more Walker Du Pree crept into her thoughts. Walker, Corky saw now, had been a secret undertow in her relationship with Hal. Walker was the only man Corky ever regretted not having sex with. And after graduating from Craven, she would often wonder why, exactly, she had not gotten involved with Walker when she had the chance. More than any other person she knew, Walker had appreciated that she was smart. She knew during their senior year that he was in love with her. But she did not know if she was in love with him. The only way to find out was to have sex with him. So why didn't she? They kissed once and Walker came very close to saying the three words that would have doomed his chances of ever getting Corky into bed. But he did not say the words. Corky loved the way he kissed, but she did not give in to the kiss, pulled away just as she felt herself beginning to really kiss him back. What would have happened if she had kissed him back, if they had subsequently gone to bed? Would she have fallen in love with him? Had she been scared to take the risk that she might? And if so, why had she been scared? Was it because Walker was black? Yes! What other reason could there have been for her not sleeping with a guy she liked so much? Certainly, she had slept with guys she liked less, far less, than Walker. Corky must have been a closet racist. But no! It wasn't race that stopped her from having sex with Walker. It was friendship. Corky realized that no matter what happened after she fucked Walker, whether the sex was bad or was so good that she might fall in love, their friendship, as they knew it, would be over. It might be ruined. And Corky did not want sex to ruin an important friendship. Besides, Corky was not all that attracted to Walker. But *why* wasn't she all that attracted to him? Was it because he was black? Well . . . no. It was because Walker was too skinny and she had always gone for guys with big pecs. Guys like Hal.

Hal was Corky's connection to Walker. Even though she had not seen Walker since Craven, Corky, on her first night with Hal, felt, in some mysterious way, closer to Walker. Was it simply because Hal had been Walker's friend? Or was it because Hal, like Walker, was black? Was it both? Was she somehow apologizing to Walker, trying to make up for her rejection of him, by having sex with Hal? Was she trying to prove to herself that she was not a closet racist? Lying in bed beside her sleeping lover, Corky wondered if her entire two-plus years with Hal had been some sort of compensation for the love she might have had with Walker.

But that didn't make any sense, did it? How could you redeem a failure with one person by getting involved with a completely different person? Except for the fact that they were both black, Hal and Walker really had very little in common. But Hal would probably say that their both being black meant that he and Walker had more in common with each other than Corky had with either of them. And Hal had run into Walker at some sort of black men's club, which was not the sort of place Corky would have expected Walker to go. All she could think was that Walker's being black meant more to him than she realized. Walker, Hal told her after he had seen him at that meeting seven months earlier, was engaged to a black woman from their class, Sadie Broom. Corky and Sadie had lived in the same freshman dormitory, Grimm Hall. They used to say hi to each other, but they were never really friends. Like most of the black students at Craven—like Hal, for instance—Sadie socialized almost exclusively with other black students. Without knowing much about her, Corky always had the feeling Sadie was a nice person. She wished she had gotten to know her. She tried to feel happy for Walker and Sadie. She looked up Walker's number in the phone book. Several times she actually picked up the phone to call him. But she'd always wimp out before punching the number. She figured that sooner or later she would read the announcement of Walker and Sadie's wedding in the Craven alumni bulletin. Two more lassoed in The Big Roundup.

* * *

What happens to you when you don't want what everyone else wants—or seems to want? The spouse, the house, the kids, the cars. Corky was beginning to feel that there was something wrong with her. She knew if she told her old friend Simpy that she was reluctant to marry Hal, Simpy would assume it was because Hal was black. It would be beyond Simpy's powers of imagination that a woman like Corky would not want to get married and have children *at all*. Unless she was a lesbian—and lesbians were practically beyond Simpy's imagining as well.

So what would happen to Corky, she who did not want the spouse, the house, the kids, and the cars? Her clerkship would end and so, too, her relationship with Hal. Then what? Anything but domestication. Corky liked airports and anonymous hotel rooms. She liked sleeping in the woods and being surrounded by people who didn't speak English. Could such inclinations be the foundation for a life of seriousness?

Corky needed someone to tell her what to do. She hated to think it, but she knew it was true. She just wanted someone to tell her in the most wise and authoritative way possible what it was she was supposed to do. Late at night, on the edge of sleep, Corky would allow herself to think that what she really needed was an older man.

14

Amsterdam came alive in summer. Along the canals of Oudezijds Voorburgwal, the coffee shops, whorehouses, and porn parlors opened their doors and windows, filling the street with the sound of music and the pungent aroma of marijuana. People hung out on the stoops and steps of their apartment buildings; prostitutes, wearing flimsy robes over their lingerie, lingered outside their places of work, smoking cigarettes and chatting amiably. Down on the Leidseplein, the restaurants and coffee shops set up outdoor tables, and on this dazzlingly sunny afternoon in July 1995, Walker sat outside Kaffeteria with Frosty—elegant as ever in a wide-brimmed, off-white straw hat, dark green aviator-style shades, and a sunflower-yellow short-sleeved shirt—and Mbundi, the brother from Togo who favored Scandinavian women. Eva had introduced Walker and Mbundi before she left with Jean-Luc for Antibes, and they had become fast friends. Walker had met a lot of people through Mbundi—which was a relief, since he'd feared that once Eva and Jean-Luc left Amsterdam, his minimal social life might all but disappear—including Anka, a short, plump Norwegian woman with brown hair, brown eyes, and tiny, remarkably adept hands, a passionate lover who, trying to maintain a long-distance relationship with her boyfriend back in Oslo,

demanded nothing of Walker but the occasional afternoon of rhap-
sodic fornication.

Walker missed Eva terribly. He had come to believe he would
never see her again. He preferred thinking that. Anytime he felt a
flicker of hope that Eva might return, that they might make love, that
Eva might find herself feeling the same ardor for Walker that he felt
for her, he quickly extinguished it with an icy splash of probability:
Eva would probably remain in Antibes; he would probably return to
the States someday; she would probably marry Jean-Luc; and he
would probably find somebody else to fall in love with. In the three
months since Eva had left Amsterdam, Walker had received three letters from her. He had answered none of them.

"I tell you why I want to go to America," Mbundi said. "America is the only country on earth where a black man can become really
rich. Look how many black millionaires you have in America!"

Frosty took a sip of his fruit juice. "Yeah," he growled, "everybody
in America thinks they're gonna hit the big score. It's one of those core
beliefs that unites the masses: 'Someday I'm gonna hit the big score!' "

"But many black peoples in America do!" Mbundi said stub-
bornly. "In America, you work hard, you get what you deserve. Even
black peoples. My uncle visited and he tells me never had he seen so
many rich black peoples in his life as he did walking the streets of
Chicago. I'm goin', bro'! I just got to save up for my ticket!" Mbundi
was an ambitious young barber who dreamed of having his own
shop—or, better yet, a chain of barbershops. But he didn't want to do
it in Togo, or anywhere in Africa, where he felt opportunities for an
aggressive young capitalist were limited. And he didn't want to do it
in Europe, where he felt white racists would inevitably thwart any
black man who yearned for success. Mbundi's sights were set on
America. " 'Cause it's all about money there, bro'. Don't matter if
you black or white, long as you got the cash. That's what a capitalist

democracy is all about!" By now Mbundi was practically bouncing in his chair, thrilled by the promise of America. "The USA, bro'—that is where the black man will have his ultimate triumph!"

Walker had been listening to Mbundi and Frosty while struggling clumsily to roll a hash-and-marijuana-combo joint. Now, having created a crooked finger of a splief, he looked up at Frosty. He could not see the old writer's eyes behind his sunglasses, but he suspected they were, at this moment, twinkling wryly. "Yeah," Frosty said, "I've been out of the States a long, long time."

"Hey, I can appreciate that, Frosty, really," Mbundi said. "You and Walker here, you fellas are in exile. You're the American refugees."

"I beg your pardon," Walker said, genuinely irritated. "I happen to like America." He paused to light the joint and reconsider the statement. "Well, I like New York anyway."

"Then why did you run away?" Mbundi asked.

"I didn't run away. I came over on a plane, in broad daylight, and I can go back anytime I please. But at the moment I prefer Old Amsterdam to New Amsterdam."

"*I'm* in exile," Frosty said. "Walker's in grief."

Walker was startled by Frosty's comment but tried not to show it. He passed the joint to Mbundi, who said, "Grief?"

"He was in grief when he arrived in Amsterdam," Frosty said to Mbundi, talking as if Walker were not even present at the table. "He was in grief because he knew the life he'd lived up to that point was over, but he didn't know what there was to replace it. But the grief is coming to an end, and he'll soon discover what his new life is."

Walker swallowed hard. He looked out at the Leidseplein, at the hurlyburly of backpack-toting, camera-clicking tourists, the clanging trams, and rolling, weaving, gliding bicyclists. He felt vaguely embarrassed by Frosty's perspicacity.

After several drags, Mbundi offered the joint to Frosty. The writer declined. "How come you never toke up, Frosty?"

"I used to. For many years. I did it for the two reasons everyone else does it: to get sharp or to get numb. To be able to see around corners or to visit oblivion. I eventually reached an age where I no longer desired a taste of oblivion. I also learned that I could get to that zone of clarity where the herb can take you but that I could get there without the assistance of the herb. Often I used it as a pain reliever. I'm an old man now, my tolerance level for pain has increased. The herb can be strong medicine. But you have to use it intelligently."

*   *   *

By the middle of July 1995, Sadie's mood had brightened. She had passed the halfway point of her stint in the Paris office of Tanzer & Mur Consultants. In less than six months, her ordeal would be over and she could return to the United States, where, despite all the problems, you could at least get Crest toothpaste. Sadie thought that in the time she had left, she might even find something to like about Paris.

Then the bombings started. An explosion in the St. Michel metro—right in the very heart of Paris—killed seven people and left dozens wounded. Two weeks later, another bomb went off outside the metro at Charles de Gaulle Étoile, a crowded tourist area, just a few yards from the Arc de Triomphe. Riding the subway to work in the morning and back to her apartment at night, Sadie sat rigid with fear, eyes darting, scanning the crowd, looking for anyone making a false move, glancing under seats to see if some suspicious-looking bag had been left behind. Wastebaskets in every metro station were bolted shut—lest someone drop a bomb in one—with notices pasted on the lids: *Pour Votre Sécurité*. For your safety. What Sadie couldn't understand was how calm all the French seemed about this. Everybody just went about their business, no one acting nervous at all, riding the metro, reading their newspapers, wearing their usual smug and dour French expressions. "Pwuh!" Mylène exhaled with an arrogant shrug of the shoulders when Sadie asked her why she wasn't acting more scared. "What can you do? When iz time for you to die, you will die. How can you worry about ze bombs? Iz like worrying about getting strucked by lightning. Ze odds are against it." Great. Sadie was having horrific visions of being trapped in a darkened, smoke-filled subway car, buried under a pile of bloody, severed limbs, people screaming all around her, and Mylène just sat there talking laws of probability.

After the third bombing in four weeks, Sadie stopped riding the metro altogether. She took taxis everywhere. But just being out on the streets of Paris made her anxious. Members of the CRS, an elite, Gestapo-like corps of police officers who wore pointy little caps, dark blue uniforms, and shiny black boots, were on patrol everywhere. Sadie knew that the presence of the CRS was supposed to make people feel more safe, but it only made her feel more frightened. Because there were all these SWAT-team-type macho guys parading around—and still the bombings continued. Early one evening in August, Sadie went to KFC to pick up a bucket of chicken to take home, and there, standing in beady-eyed vigilance outside the restaurant, dressed in full camouflage-green combat gear, black berets atop their heads, were two young soldiers of the French army, clutching submachine guns, holding the weapons poised, their fingers on the triggers, ready to fire at the slightest provocation. Sadie was so freaked out by the sight of them—it was like something you'd expect in Sarajevo!—that she couldn't bring herself to enter the KFC. She turned around and walked quickly back to her apartment, locked all four locks on her heavy metal door, and, hands trembling, made a call to America.

"Mommy!" Sadie cried as soon as Lorraine Broom answered the phone. She immediately broke down in sobs. "Mommy—I want to come home!"

*   *   *

Walker was stretched out in the fake cowhide-upholstered window seat of the Great Dane coffee shop on a languid afternoon in the first week of September. As he drew yet another portrait of Paul Robeson—this one based on a class photo from Columbia Law School—Walker could hear the faint wail of a street musician's saxophone coming from the other side of the canal on Oudezijds Voorburgwal. He could hear the tinkling of bells on rolling bicycles and the chattering of people walking along the street, snatches of Dutch, English, German, Indonesian, and African dialects. He spat into the glass ashtray on the windowsill and stared for a moment at the bright green gob of saliva. For several weeks now Walker's spit had borne the same emerald color as the Stinky Skunk Spud he smoked. He tried not to worry about it, returning his attention to Paul Robeson, gazing at the grainy image, taking in Robeson's heavy brow, the broad nose and thick lips, the dark skin, the distinctly African majesty of the features, and thinking for the thousandth time what a beautiful man his subject was.

"Oh, Lord, won'tcha buy me a Mercedes-Benz . . ."

For a moment Walker imagined he heard Eva Thule's voice. He knew he heard *someone* out on the street sing the line from Janis Joplin, but he doubted that he'd heard the line sung in that smoky voice with the Swedish-Finnish accent, turning twangy as it always did whenever Eva imitated her favorite singer.

"Have you forgot me already, Wocker?"

There she was, standing on the cobblestone sidewalk, a gingerbread burnish to her skin that made her eyes seem more green and her hair more yellow than when Walker had last seen her, five months earlier. She was dressed in a white T-shirt and faded blue jeans; a knapsack was slung over her shoulder.

"I thought you were a figment of my imagination," Walker said.

Eva smiled. "Time to stop dreaming, Mr. Smartsy Pants. I have come to return you to reality."

The Great Dane had set up outdoor tables for the summer, and for a long time, as they sat under a crooked umbrella, Walker and Eva just stared at each other and laughed. Finally Eva told him how bored she had been in Antibes, how tired she was of bouncing from country to country, from one bar/restaurant/café/cruise ship/au pair/coffee shop job to another. "It was time for decision," she said, banging a fist lightly on the table. Eva had broken up with Jean-Luc—"at least temporary," she said—who loved tending bar in Antibes and was loathe to leave. "It is time for bold plans!" Eva declared, striking the table again. She had returned to the apartment she and Jean-Luc had shared for a year in Amsterdam. An English couple she knew, Cyril and Emily, had been subletting it; Eva had insisted that she and Jean-Luc hold on to the lease, since in the back of her mind, she knew things might not work out in Antibes. Most of her possessions were still in the apartment in Amsterdam, and as it turned out, Cyril and Emily were currently visiting England, so Eva had the old place to herself. "Now I am ready for my next move." Eva took a deep breath, then said, "I want to go to live in America."

"America!" Walker cried. "What for?"

"I want to go to university. The best are in America. Also, you know, Wocker, the U.S. is where it's *happening*." Eva began snapping fingers on both hands, a gesture Walker found jarringly uncharacteristic. "Europe is dead. America has all the action!"

"Stop snapping. I've never heard you say this, Eva. Who have you been talking to in Antibes?"

"Always I have this idea to go to America. I have never been before."

"Well, I could see your wanting to visit . . . but to *live?* To go to university?" Walker's eyes narrowed, then he said, pointedly, "Do you really think your English is good enough?"

"I will improve. You will help me. Don't you want to return to America someday?"

"I don't know. I don't know what I want to do." Walker was becoming extremely irritated with Eva, but he wasn't sure why. Why should he care where Eva lived? Just one hour earlier, he didn't think he'd ever see her again. She had reappeared like an apparition in Amsterdam. So what if, in the near future, she disappeared again? No, it wasn't the simple fact of her leaving again that annoyed Walker. It was that she wanted to go to *America.* Walker associated Eva so inextricably with Europe, with his journey into the Old World, with everything that was unfamiliar, ungrounded, *un*-American to him. Yes, Walker thought he might very well return to the States someday. But he didn't want Eva Thule living there! Once he went back to America, he would want Eva to remain always a part of the exotic Europe his memory would create. How could he, living back in New York, sustain a fantasy of his life in Amsterdam if the woman who had been so much a part of that life, of that fantasy, were living in . . . in . . . "Where," Walker asked, "would you want to live in America, anyway?"

"Seattle," Eva replied instantly.

Walker smacked a palm against his forehead. "Are you sure you just haven't been watching too much MTV?"

"What have you against Seattle?"

"Look, Eva, you can't just go to America and attend college. First

of all, you need some kind of residence status, and to get that—"
Walker stopped short. Eva said she'd split from Jean-Luc. She must
have met some rich asshole down in the South of France. "Don't tell
me you're thinking about marrying an American?"

Eva leaned forward, tilted her head to one side, and gave Walker
a long, soft look. "Maybe I am."

They spent the rest of the afternoon together at Eva's apartment,
doing the same things they'd done before, listening to the same tapes,
playing rummy, talking incessantly, drinking wine, and smoking copi-
ous amounts of marijuana. But Walker felt a new vibe between them,
a deepening of affection that came through nostalgia. Even though
they'd spent only four months hanging out together in Amsterdam
and she had been gone for another five months, Walker and Eva
shared a history. The same jokes they had cracked in January
acquired a new hilarity, thanks to the passing of time, in September.
Amusing incidents of the early winter became comic epics as Walker
and Eva recounted the details to each other in late summer. As they
headed out to dinner, Eva put an arm around Walker's waist. Walker
drew her closer to him. They walked down the street arm in arm.
Walker's heart felt full. It was a sensation he had not experienced
since his first year with Sadie, and he realized that the main reason he
had tried to blot Sadie from his thoughts was that he could not bear
to remember that feeling of full-heartedness he'd had with her. Feeling the loss of it was bad enough; he felt the loss, the absence of it,
every day. Now that the full-heartedness was back, Walker recognized what a powerful, perhaps even necessary, emotion it was. As he
walked down the street, arm in arm, with Eva, the idea, at once surprising and obvious, began to cohere: She had come back to Amsterdam for *him*.

*   *   *

"What is black man?"

Eva wrinkled her nose as she pondered the question. Walker and Eva sat across from each other in their favorite Indonesian restaurant, the remnants of their rijsttafel—the twenty tiny dishes that had been filled with individual samplings of various spicy meats and vegetables—and four empty beer bottles cluttering the table. Walker, feeling quite stoned and drunk, had been trying to explain something about the States to Eva. He knew that American racialist thinking was, to many people who had not experienced it firsthand, incomprehensible. So Walker wanted to give Eva an example of how it operated. He decided to tell her about the Amandla workshop.

"What is black man?" Eva said again, her tone changing from puzzled to derisive. "You might well as ask, 'What is man?' Because all of you mens are the same. Dick, dick, dick. That is all man is." Walker started to laugh, but Eva stopped him. "You think I say it jokatively, but I am serious. There is only one big difference in humanity: man and woman. Each woman is different. But each man is the same. It is the dick. It does something to your brains. In some way or another, it controls all your behaviors. 'What is black man?' is a fool-headed question. And to the question 'What is man?' the answer is simple: Man is dick. *Woman* is complicated."

Walker was annoyed. "I guess you'll just have to go to America to find out what I'm talking about."

"Yes, but won't you go with me?" Eva reached across the table and took Walker's hand. "Don't you want to marry with me?"

Walker squeezed Eva's hand lightly. "What about Jean-Luc? You said your breakup was 'at least temporary.' What does that mean?"

Eva stared down at the table. She said nothing. Walker squeezed her hand again, harder this time, and Eva withdrew it. "Things were bad in Antibes," she said finally. "From the first day we get there. Very bad. I say temporary but I mean permanent. The relation is over, I think."

They were both silent as the waiter cleared the table. "So what do you want to do tonight?" Walker asked.

Eva immediately cheered up. "Let's go to club! I want to have *fun!*" She threw her arms in the air. "I am free woman now! Yippeeee!" Eva laughed so hard her face turned red. "Let's go to club," she said, her voice becoming low, seductive, as she leaned across the table. "We can do the dirty dancing."

*   *   *

Walker was having an O.J. moment. As he stood on the dance floor of Chaos Theory, a monotonous and compulsive techno beat throbbing in his ears, Walker felt as if his scalp were on fire. His vision seemed to be going in and out of focus, as if he were looking at the scene before him—Eva Thule dancing with a muscular African, crushing her breasts against his chest, grinding her crotch against his—through a camera lens that someone kept adjusting. He felt as if the adrenaline churning through his system had made his entire body rigid. He had entered a hitherto unknown realm of anger. He was ready to *get physical.*

Only minutes earlier he had been in a state of erotic bliss. He and Eva had never danced together before. As they stepped onto the dance floor, Eva complained about the "stressful music" on the sound system, but she immediately threw herself into a hair-tossing, rump-shaking frenzy. After several minutes of delirious gyrations, Eva slowed the pace, though the hammering techno beat had not changed, and languorously contorted her body in serpentine undulations, moving closer to Walker, wrapping her legs around his. She grabbed Walker's shoulder with one hand and leaned her torso back, way back, and stared straight into his eyes, her mouth slightly open. She ground her pelvis rhythmically against his. As his cock grew harder, Walker saw Eva smile knowingly at him, as if to say "See what I can do to you." Walker was so horny for Eva he might have ejaculated right there had she not suddenly unlocked their thighs and spun away. Soon they were both pleasurably covered in sweat. Eva leaned against a pillar near the edge of the dance floor. Walker went to the bar to buy them a couple of beers.

With the crowd swarming around the bar, it took at least five minutes for him to get served. When he returned, a bottle of Heineken in each hand, to the place where Eva had stood, she was gone. After scanning the crowd awhile, he spotted her dancing with a white guy with a shaved head. Though she wasn't actually touching her partner, Eva danced real close and moved her body in the same brazenly sexual way she had with Walker. Finally Eva noticed Walker noticing her. He held up her bottle of beer and waggled it in the air. Eva smiled and raised her hand and Walker noticed for the first time that she was already holding a Heineken. Had the bald guy bought it for her? Walker was irritated but thirsty. Standing on the edge of the dance floor, he downed one of the beers he carried, then placed the empty bottle on a table near the wall. When he returned his attention to the dance floor, he couldn't find Eva. Eventually he spied her, lasciviously undulating again, this time with some pony-tailed loser. Walker couldn't believe it. What the fuck did Eva think she was doing? Was she trying to make him jealous? Or maybe moving her body like that meant nothing to her. But certainly it meant something to that ponytailed loser. Once again Eva noticed Walker noticing her. She gave him a casual wave and continued undulating. Walker downed the second Heineken, the one he'd bought for Eva, then placed the empty bottle on the table beside the wall. This time when he returned his attention to the dance floor, Eva was entwined with the muscular African, rubbing her body against his. Eva's partner had one hand on her ass; with the other, he clutched a hunk of her yellow hair. That was when Walker had his O.J. moment, when he felt as if flames were shooting from his head, when he felt he'd crashed through some barrier of consciousness and had entered the realm of pure wrath. It was a realm beyond words; it demanded physical action.

Eva gracefully backpedaled away from her partner. Walker strode across the dance floor as Eva continued her lewd contortions with about six inches of space between her and the muscular African. There were other dancers blocking Walker's immediate path to Eva. He leaned forward, between two strangers, stretching out his arm, taking hold of Eva's right wrist. As she turned around in surprise, Walker pulled her toward him. The African quickly grabbed Eva's left wrist and pulled her back. Walker kept pulling. So did the African. Eva's body was splayed between them, her arms fully extended in opposite directions. Walker suddenly felt as if he were in a cartoon, with Eva as Olive Oyl, caught in a slapstick tug-of-war between Popeye and Bluto. But his rage did not allow him to reflect for more than an instant on the ridiculousness of this situation. He was ready to attack. The African looked significantly stronger than him. But Walker was from Brooklyn, and he was prepared to do whatever he had to do to win the fight. At the same time, as he yanked Eva toward him, he did not think he would have to fight. Eva would realize she was out of line, that, as the old saying went, "You dance with the one who brung ya." Instead, Eva tore her wrist from Walker's grasp. "Let go of me," she said. "I want to dance!" Before Walker could say a word, the African had pulled Eva back into his arms. More dancers crowded the space between Walker and Eva. He was slowly pushed backward as he watched Eva crush and grind her body against her partner. He stood on the edge of the dance floor, his fury now replaced by a nauseating sense of humiliation.

Walker waded back into the crowd at the bar. He ordered two more beers, stood alone in an especially dark corner of the club, and drank them both. He needed to chill out. That was what he kept telling himself, that he just needed to chill out. He went to the men's room and took a piss. When he returned to the dance floor, he decided to find Eva and tell her he was leaving. She could leave with him or stay. Her decision. Of course. But Eva was nowhere to be found. Walker wandered around the dance floor, covering every foot of the space, twice. He looked for Eva in the crowded parlor upstairs, lingered for several minutes by the door of the women's room, searched the bar area, and covered the dance floor again. No Eva. His anger was returning full force now. He was getting ready to leave Chaos Theory when he saw her walk in the front door, laughing, with the muscular African and two European guys. What the *fuck* was Eva doing? Why had she left the club? Why hadn't she told him she was stepping outside? Eva waved to her three escorts and headed in the direction of the women's room. Walker stepped in her path. "I'm leaving," he said through clenched teeth. "Are you coming with me?" Before Eva could answer, Walker began striding toward the front door. He could hear Eva behind him: "Wocker, wait! Wait!" Walker pushed hard on the heavy metal door. Out on the street, in the hot night air, a small crowd was gathered, waiting to get into Chaos Theory. And there, staring inquisitively at Walker, was the presumptuous man from Mr. Happy's, with his thick glasses, trim mustache, and inscrutable little smile. The presumptuous man was opening his mouth to say hello. Walker strode furiously past him.

"Wocker!" Eva called. She was hurrying behind him. Walker couldn't remember what street he was on. But he continued his angry striding. Eva was on his shoulder now. "Please, would you slow down a little?" Eva was out of breath, and so wasted she was slurring her words.

"I'm too old for this shit!" Walker said, as much to himself as to Eva. "I'm too old for this shit! I am too old for this fucking shit!"

"But, Wocker, you are not so old. You are only thirty-one. You should have good times! Boy, am I stone or what?"

Walker had kept turning onto one block and then another, hoping he would get his bearings, but every time he turned onto a new street, he saw another stretch of seemingly identical cobblestones and canals. He had no idea where he was. "I'm not talking about having a good time. I'm talking about the shit you're putting me through." It was beginning to dawn on Walker that Eva had not been trying to make him jealous; that, in fact, she had been completely oblivious to his feelings.

"Ah, but, Wocker, I'm just a silly girl. I'm single again and I want to have fun!" Eva was breathing hard and starting to stagger. "Wocker, please wait, stop just a minute!"

Walker stopped and turned to Eva. "I thought you wanted to be with me tonight."

Eva suddenly scurried across the street and, out of Walker's line of vision, squatted between two parked cars. Walker could see only the top of Eva's head, a yellow crown in the darkness. He could hear her fiddling with her belt. "I am sorry, Wocker," she called out. "I am just a silly girl."

Walker heard Eva's urine sprinkling the cobblestones. Yes, he thought, she *was* a silly girl. And a tramp who pissed in the street. "I didn't know what happened to you at the club," he called to her. "You should have let me know you were stepping outside. I was worried about you." Walker heard the stream of urine recede to a pitter-patter of drops and realized that, even at this moment, he was overwhelmingly attracted to Eva.

"Acch, Wocker, never should you worry about me." Eva pulled back on her panties and jeans and stood up to buckle her belt. "I can take care of myself."

Realizing, at last, where he was, Walker headed in the direction of the Hotel Elyssia—it was only three blocks away. Eva had to walk rapidly just to stay two steps behind him. She was babbling about being young and free and enjoying life. Walker wanted to know why she had talked about marrying him at dinner, then started doing "the dirty dancing" with strange men at the club. Then he decided he did not want to know. He didn't even want to spend time trying to figure it out. He was sick of trying to figure things out. He just wanted to go to sleep. He wanted to be as asleep as a person could be.

They arrived at the entrance to Walker's hotel. "Can you find your way home by yourself?" Walker asked coldly. Eva said nothing. She stood on her toes, leaned forward, and kissed Walker flush on the mouth. It was a moment Walker had longed for, and now that it had arrived, all he could think of was how unpleasantly Eva's tongue tasted of stale beer and tobacco.

Everything happened very fast. They were hardly in the door before they were naked, Walker lying on his back, Eva astride him on the bed. The room was cast in blue shadows. Eva was pushing down hard on him. Walker could see that her mouth was open and her eyes closed. Soon she was tossing her head and gasping loudly. Walker came with her but wondered if Eva even knew, or cared; she seemed completely in her own world. As Walker watched her writhing above him, he wondered if Eva was even aware of who she was fucking. Maybe she thought she was with Jean-Luc, or the muscular African, or one of the other men she'd met at the club. Eva collapsed on the bed. She and Walker lay there, both of them breathing heavily, drenched in sweat. Walker wanted to say something but didn't know what. After a while, he heard Eva weeping softly.

"Baby," Walker whispered. "Are you all right, baby?" Eva twisted her body so that her back was to Walker. He put his arms around her. "Eva, baby, what's the matter?"

"It's nothing," she said. Walker could hear her sniffling in the dark. "Let's go to sleep."

Walker held her tight. "Don't be sad, honey. Please don't be sad."

"It's okay," Eva said. Soon she stopped crying.

They were both silent for a long time and Walker wondered if she was still awake. "Eva," he said finally, "I think I'm in love with you."

"I think the same," Eva said faintly.

A moment later, Walker could actually feel Eva fall asleep in his arms. And he couldn't stop puzzling over what she had said. *I think the same.* Did that mean she thought she was in love with Walker— or that she, too, believed Walker was in love with her? He was still puzzling over the line as he slipped into a deep sleep.

*   *   *

I think the same. The mysterious line was floating in Walker's head when he woke up around nine and found Eva gone. When he called her later that morning, she put on a cheery tone and thanked him for a fun night out.

"Are we gonna pretend nothing happened?" Walker asked.

There was a long pause before Eva answered. "I don't know what to say, Wocker. I have had no time to think. I just left Antibes two days ago. Not even have I finished unpacking."

"All right. . . . Well, do you wanna get together later today, tonight?"

"No, I think not. I just need one day to be alone and to think."

"Sure. Okay. Well, look, I guess—"

"Come over for dinner tomorrow night," Eva said quickly, as if she feared Walker was about to hang up the phone. They made a date for eight o'clock the following evening.

Walker was carrying a bouquet of roses when he arrived at Eva's apartment. His heart felt full again. He had done a lot of thinking, a lot of planning. He decided he would move back to the States, if that was what Eva wanted. They could get married and move to Seattle.

Eva would enroll in a college there, and Walker was sure he could find some kind of design work once his inheritance ran out. In the meantime, he would keep working on his Robeson project. Walker was sure he could be happy in America—as long as he was with Eva. She, however, might be having doubts. She might still feel something for Jean-Luc—even though Walker was encouraged by how awful their time together in Antibes sounded. Then there was the fact that the sex the other night had been awkward, rushed. But the first time with a new lover was often less than satisfactory. On the other hand, half of Walker's lovers had been one-time-only lovers, and the sex with most of them had been more than satisfactory. On the *other* other hand, when the first time was less than satisfactory, a person could be reluctant to try it a second time. Walker was certain that the second time he and Eva would get it right. He just had to do what-ever he could to make sure there would be a second time.

When Eva opened the door and Walker saw how beautiful she looked, how excited she seemed to see him, how touched she was by the roses, he felt a sudden certainty that this was the woman he would marry and spend the rest of his life with. As Eva took the flow-ers, she kissed him once on each cheek—a somewhat disappointing display of affection, but Walker didn't think much of it. As he fol-lowed Eva through her tiny foyer, Walker's heart felt fuller than ever before. Then he turned the corner and stepped into the living room, where Jean-Luc held out a hand to greet him.

*   *   *

For one excruciating hour, Eva, Walker, and Jean-Luc sat around the small dining table. Eva explained that Jean-Luc had quit his job in Antibes and returned to Amsterdam the day before. *The day before,* Walker thought. That would have been the day after he and Eva slept

together. Eva had twenty-four hours to let Walker know Jean-Luc
was back in town. But she didn't let him know. As Eva chattered
away, straining to maintain a casual tone, Walker and Jean-Luc eyed
each other menacingly. "Excuse me," Jean-Luc said, "it is been a long
time since I speak English." He then turned to Eva, took her hand in
his, and began speaking quietly in French. As Jean-Luc talked, Eva
would occasionally glance at Walker, but whenever Walker tried to
look her in the eye, she would quickly turn back to Jean-Luc or stare
at the table. She responded to Jean-Luc in French. Walker gleaned
that they were talking about Antibes, but he did not attempt to
understand everything they were saying. His senses were dulled. Eva
and Jean-Luc's voices grew faint, their faces became blurry. Walker's
entire body felt numb. He felt he could not speak. He realized he was
experiencing yet another new level of rage, a degree of anger so profound that, instead of leading him to physical action, had short-
circuited his basic faculties.

There was no food in the apartment, Walker heard Eva say. Jean-
Luc said they should order a pizza. The Frenchman rose and fairly
swaggered to the phone. When he placed the order, he did so in a self-
consciously authoritative voice. Jean-Luc, Walker sensed, was playing lord of the manor, trying to take charge, to show that *he* was the
one who ordered the pizza around here! While Jean-Luc manfully
demanded extra green peppers, Walker glared at Eva and Eva stared
down at the table. Why hadn't she just picked up the phone and told
him Jean-Luc was back in town? That was all she had to do. Yes, he
would have been disappointed. But he would have been spared the
shock of seeing Jean-Luc standing in the living room and the indig-
nity of having to be the audience for this frog's pathetic display of
domestic authority. Why hadn't Eva called him? That was all she had
to do. But she hadn't. And now she could not even look him in the
eye. Walker wondered how Eva had managed to do what she had

done to him. In the past forty-eight hours, Walker had experienced not one but two veritable seizures of rage. The first had led him to furiously grab Eva on the dance floor; it had him primed for violence in a way he had never been before. The second had left him stupefied. How was it that Eva triggered this anger? Was her ability to do this to Walker the ultimate sign of his love for her?

Jean-Luc, finished with the phone call, returned to the table and, standing over Eva, assured her that the pizza was on its way. He leaned down and, taking Eva's chin in his hand, kissed her gently on the lips. Eva tried to turn her head, but Jean-Luc kept hold of her chin and kissed her again.

"I hope you all will excuse me," Walker said, "but I've lost my appetite." He rose and, without saying good-bye, left the apartment. Outside, the sun was just beginning to set. He walked along a canal, still feeling dazed. Now he knew why Eva had not called him. She wanted Walker to see for himself how in love she and Jean-Luc were. She *wanted* him to feel hurt, rejected, embarrassed. Eva had planned it this way. And as he continued along the canal, Walker thought of Marion Barry, the black mayor of Washington, D.C. He remembered watching grainy footage, shot by a hidden video camera, of Marion Barry and a woman smoking crack in a cheap motel room. The woman had lured Barry there and offered him the drugs as part of an FBI sting. As agents burst into the room and handcuffed the mayor, Marion Barry suddenly realized the woman's role in the entrapment and the words he mumbled, dumbfounded, over and over, were the same words that came to Walker as he pondered what had just happened in Eva's apartment: "Bitch set me up. Bitch set me up."

After a lonesome meal at Mr. Happy's, Walker went to Slow Hand Easy and smoked several bowls of dope. As he trudged back to his hotel, he felt a leaden fatigue. He was so stoned, exhausted, and emotionally benumbed that he wondered for a moment if he was hallucinating when he saw Sadie Broom standing on the steps of the

Hotel Elyssia. Even standing face-to-face with Sadie, staring into her
soft, sad eyes, listening to her speak—"I just left you a note at the
desk. I got into town this afternoon. I was afraid you'd gone out for
the night. But here you are and, hey, you're alone"—he still could not
believe this was happening. Then he fell into her arms and exploded
in tears and he knew Sadie was as real as a person could be.

*   *   *

Walker and Sadie spent most of the next thirty-six hours in Sadie's
bed in an elegant hotel near the Van Gogh Museum. They made love
and cried, bathed together, called for room service, made love and
cried some more, and sometimes they slept. "I had to come and get
you," Sadie whispered tenderly. "You couldn't run away from yourself any longer. We belong together." Walker held Sadie tight and
rocked back and forth. "It's time to go home, baby," Sadie whispered. "We belong together. Back home."

It rained buckets on Walker's last full day in Amsterdam. He was
glad about that. He would want to remember the town for its delicious gloom. When Walker and Sadie went to the Hotel Elyssia to
collect his things, there were three messages from Eva waiting for
him. Sadie did not ask who Eva was and Walker offered no information. In his vaguely urine-scented room, Sadie stared—the expression
on her face seemed at once impressed and appalled—at the drawings
of Paul Robeson that covered nearly every inch of wall space: Robeson in Moscow, Robeson in London, Robeson in Provincetown,
Robeson smiling, singing, shouting, glowering. Sadie said nothing
about the work, but she handled the drawings with care as she helped
Walker take them down from the walls and pack them with the rest
of his stuff. Walker checked out of the Elyssia and moved his gear to
Sadie's hotel. He did not return Eva's calls.

That afternoon, Walker went to see Frosty at Kaffeteria. He told the old writer he was returning to America the next day. He told Frosty all about his relationship with Sadie.

"So she came all the way from the States to get you back?" Frosty said.

"Actually," Walker explained, "she's been in Paris since January. Sadie's a management consultant. She was supposed to stay in her company's Paris office till the end of this year, but she cut her stint short. I think all the terrorist bombings in Paris this summer scared her."

Frosty let out one of his hacking cough laughs. "Tell Sadie she could get blown up by terrorists in Oklahoma City, too!"

Walker smiled. "Yee-hah," he said flatly.

Frosty took a sip of his fruit juice, then said quietly, "You're in love with Sadie?"

"Yeah. I guess I am."

"Love. It's the most important thing in life. People have said it so much, they've banalized the idea to such an extent, that nobody really believes it anymore. But it's true."

Walker knew that Frosty was twice a widower. His first wife, the German Ilse, had been killed in a car accident while visiting Munich in 1956. Frosty's second wife was a Nigerian named Chinyelu. She died in 1989, after a harrowing struggle with ovarian cancer.

"I've lived without love for a long time," Frosty said. "If you're in love with Sadie, you should be with her. Wherever you have love, that's where you should be. It's too difficult to live without it."

Walker wanted to thank Frosty. He felt that over the nine months he had known him, the writer had given him something, but he didn't know what it was. He wanted somehow to return the favor, to give Frosty something. But he didn't know what.

After leaving Kaffeteria, Walker dropped a postcard in the corner mailbox. "Dear Eva—I'm outta here," the message read. "If you're ever in New York, look me up." Walker had scribbled down his Greenwich Village address and phone number. "Good luck with Jean-Luc. Love, 'Wocker.' " He knew that Eva would not receive the postcard until the following afternoon, when he and Sadie would be on a plane to New York.

*   *   *

"How can you possibly think that?" Walker asked Sadie.

They were flying over the Atlantic Ocean, somewhere between Amsterdam and New York. In the three days since Sadie showed up at the Hotel Elyssia, she and Walker had not had a single argument. Walker knew they were bound to start disagreeing sooner or later. And he didn't mind. In a way, he had come to enjoy arguing with Sadie, because she was such a worthy opponent in debate. Sadie was one of the most scrupulously logical people Walker had ever known. Even when he objected to her opinion, Sadie's point of view always made sense. That was why on the flight back to America, Walker found what Sadie had just said to him incomprehensible. It made no sense at all. This was something that only a completely irrational person could believe. Sadie had just told Walker she thought O.J. Simpson was innocent.

"I don't think he did it," Sadie said again.

"But, Sadie, that's crazy!" Walker was beside himself. He and Sadie had been together in New York the summer of the murders. That fall, before Walker left for Amsterdam, they often discussed the case. Walker could not remember a single occasion when Sadie had questioned O.J.'s guilt. How could she? His guilt was so obvious. But here they were, ten months later, in September 1995, and Walker felt almost as if he were speaking to an impostor, or someone who had been brainwashed, had her mind taken over by aliens. Sadie believed that O.J. Simpson was innocent. Sadie, a shrewd judge of people, a woman with few illusions about human nature, a sister who said she had trouble trusting black men—yet she now trusted, of all the black men in the world, O.J. Simpson, believing his claim of innocence.

"But, but, but," Walker spluttered, "what about the Bronco chase?" Walker and Sadie had watched it together on television—along with roughly half the population of the United States—less than a week after the murders: the white Ford Bronco, rolling down the freeway, O.J.'s homeboy Al Cowlings behind the wheel, O.J. in the back, holding a gun to his head, a fleet of police cars pursuing them at a respectful distance. Walker was furious that night because NBC had interrupted the pro basketball championships to show live footage of the chase. "Let O.J. blow his brains out!" Walker had yelled at the TV screen. "The Knicks are in the finals! Get back to the fucking game!"

"O.J. was just flipped out," Sadie said aboard the KLM flight bound for New York. "A lot of people would be suicidal in those circumstances."

"But he was fleeing! He had his passport and thousands of dollars in cash! What about his suicide note? He said, 'Forget this lost person.' He knew he had gone out of his mind and killed those people!"

"Hold up, Walker. First you say he was fleeing, then you say he was going to commit suicide. Which is it?"

"He hadn't made up his mind."

"That still doesn't prove his guilt. And besides, in the so-called suicide note, he said he had nothing to do with the murders."

"What about the dog? Nicole was walking her Akita. If a stranger had tried to attack her, the dog would have ripped him apart. Or the killer would have had to kill the dog, too. But the dog didn't attack. Why? Because it recognized O.J."

"All I've heard about the dog is that it was howling in distress. I'm not at all convinced it would have attacked a stranger. I've met plenty of big, timid dogs. They aren't all Rin Tin Tin." The more flustered Walker became, the calmer Sadie got. She spoke in the same rational tone she always used when arguing with him. "Why are *you* so convinced he did it?" Sadie asked.

"Aw, come on, Sadie. Who else had a motive? Who else would hack somebody up like that? It's a classic crime of passion."

"Not necessarily."

"What, you think Colombian drug dealers drove to exclusive Brentwood on a Sunday night to chop up a white lady on her doorstep? Have you ever heard of such a thing?"

"Yes," Sadie said matter-of-factly. "Walker, don't be naive."

"Naive! Why wouldn't they just *shoot* her? And what about the bloody footprints near the bodies? You think Colombian hit men were wearing size-twelve Bruno Magli shoes, just like O.J.'s?"

"I think there are a lot of dubious things about the evidence. They say O.J. cut his finger wrestling with Ron Goldman, but then how come there's no split finger on the glove *they say* O.J. was wearing at the time? How come O.J. could barely even fit into the gloves when they made him try them on in court? And what about the racist detective? Didn't you hear what he said on tape, bragging about setting up black people?"

"Okay, okay, Mark Fuhrman is a racist, of course—"

"A racist who planted evidence!"

Walker squirmed in his cramped little seat. "Actually, you know what I think? I think two things that most people seem to consider mutually exclusive *both* happened. I think, yes, O.J. killed those people and, yes, the police tried to frame him. It's precisely because I think O.J. committed the murders that I believe Fuhrman planted the bloody glove. If O.J. had the presence of mind to get rid of the murder weapon, why would he then be so careless as to bring a bloody glove back to his house? It doesn't make any sense."

"Hah!" Sadie fairly shouted. "So if you believe evidence was planted, how could you possibly vote to convict him? Planting evidence is against the law. It raises reasonable doubt. It—"

"Whoa, whoa, whoa, slow down. Look—if I were a member of the jury, I could not vote to convict him. Because I believe evidence was planted. Because of Mark Fuhrman, the case should probably never even have gone to trial. This is the great irony. A racist cop is so eager to nail a black man—especially a rich black man who was married to a white woman—that he ends up fucking up the whole case against him."

"So we agree," Sadie said victoriously.

"No! Because while I could not vote to convict O.J., I still *know* that he's guilty. You're saying that you truly believe he did not commit these murders."

"That's what I'm saying."

"And this, to me, is madness. In fact, I don't even think you really think it. You just don't want to *believe* O.J. is guilty. You can't stand the idea that someone like him could practically decapitate an innocent woman and—"

"Innocent woman! Who are you talking about? That tawdry blond slut?"

"She was a human being and she never killed anyone. Whatever she was like, she didn't deserve to be murdered. Are you saying she did?"

Sadie's words were coming out fast and hot now. "I'm just sick of people talking about Saint Nicole. People die, people are killed, all the time, everywhere. Anonymous black people are murdered every day in L.A. and nobody gives a shit! But this tawdry blond slut gets killed and everybody is ready to string up O.J. Do you know how many black men have been lynched or executed or sent to prison because they were accused of harming precious white women? Think of Emmett Till. Think of the Scottsboro boys. Yussef Hawkins."

"This is a completely different situation."

"Is it? I think to most of white America, O.J. is just Bigger Thomas in an Armani suit."

"You think Nicole Brown Simpson deserved to die."

"I think people should respect the lives of black people as much as they respect the lives of people like Nicole Brown Simpson. But America is so obsessed with these Barbie Doll women, these blond-haired, blue-eyed—"

"Nicole's eyes were brown."

"Oh, excuse *me*, I haven't examined photos of her as closely as you have, obviously."

"You're just going with the stereotype, blond hair, hence blue eyes. You're dehumanizing her by turning her into a cliché."

"Well, that's the ideal, Walker! Women like her. That's what's thrown up in your face every day in America. How do you think that makes women like me feel? I mean, couldn't O.J. have just married a sister who *looks* white? That's what most black celebrities do. That's what my father did after he dropped my mother. Did O.J. have to go whole hog?"

"So would it have been better if O.J. had mutilated a black woman?"

"If the victim were black, America wouldn't care."

"If the victim were black, you, Sadie, would believe O.J. was guilty. But because she's white and blond—"

"The ideal."

Walker paused, then said, "You're glad he killed her. Aren't you?"

"I'm not glad."

"Yes you are. I can see it."

"Walker, if you think that about me—"

"Well, maybe not glad. But you don't *mind* that she's dead. That somebody like her got slaughtered."

"Let's just drop it, Walker. Obviously, you and I are going to have different feelings about this, given our different . . . backgrounds."

"What's that supposed to mean?"

"I'm going to sleep." Sadie pulled her night mask from the seat pocket in front of her, strapped it around her head.

"Are you gonna answer my question?"

"I'm going to go to sleep," Sadie said, her eyes concealed. "And you should do the same."

3

Verdicts

15

Life was better on automatic pilot. For most of 1995, Hal Hard-away cruised along, deciding it was wiser not to try to take control of his career or his relationship. "Fake it till you make it," he heard someone say on TV. He took this to mean that if you pretended to be a happy and successful person, eventually you would become one. Hal threw himself into his fakery with gusto. He decided that the miserable year he had in '94 was the result of his own negative atti-tude. In '95, instead of fretting about Godfrey Burnish freezing him out, Hal spent more time at the office, avidly sucking up to the founder. In '94, Hal felt that his friends had withdrawn from him. In '95, Hal realized it was he who had retreated. It wasn't his friends who made him feel self-conscious about moving in with Corky Win-terset. His self-consciousness was his own fault. Hal did not start socializing more, but he did become more thoughtful about keeping in touch with his old friends by phone or E-mail. And Hal made a daily effort to put on a happy face with Corky. No longer would he agonize or analyze. He stopped trying to figure Corky out, stopped worrying about whether she loved him as much as he loved her or what the future held for them.

"I think we need to be nicer to each other," Corky said to Hal as they lay in bed together, their naked bodies entwined, on a Saturday afternoon in June. That morning Hal had been in the kitchen making coffee when Corky walked in wearing nothing but a T-shirt and panties. She said she was due at the courthouse in an hour. She yawned and raised her hands to her face, then, balling up her fingers, rubbed both her eyes. There was something ineffably sweet in the gesture. Hal laughed and told Corky she looked like a little kid. Corky smiled. Minutes later they were back in bed, making love more passionately than they had in a year. Corky decided not to go to the courthouse. Hal thanked her for choosing to spend the day in bed with him. "I think we've just fallen into some bad habits," Corky said. "We've started to take each other for granted. Let's start being nicer to each other." Corky reminded Hal how grueling her clerkship was. She said that she hadn't felt like herself in the year and a half she had been working for Judge Judith Proctor. But on December 29, 1995, her two-year stint with Judge Proctor would be over. Corky knew she did not want to practice law after her clerkship. But she did not know what she wanted to do instead. She only knew she had to make it to the end of the clerkship. "If you could just be patient with me until the end of the year," Corky said to Hal as they cuddled in bed. "That's all I ask of you. I know I'm stressed out these days. I know we don't get to see that much of each other. But after December twenty-ninth, I'll be free. Then I'll be able to concentrate on our relationship. Can you just be patient with me until then?"

"You know I can, baby," Hal said. "Hey, maybe when you're done with the clerkship, we should go on a trip."

The very mention of travel was enough to brighten Corky's mood. "Yeah," she cooed, "a long, long trip."

Lying in bed, they came up with the plan: In January, after the end of Corky's stint, Hal would take a three-month leave of absence from Burnish Enterprises. Together they would travel to Kenya,

Ghana, South Africa, Egypt, Morocco, and India. Hal and Corky would have three full months to explore the Third World and rediscover each other. Hal suggested they call a travel agent soon.

"The only hitch," Corky said, "is if the judge wants me to work another year."

"What? I thought your clerkship was *two* years!"

"Clerks are *required* to work two years. But sometimes if you want to and the judge really likes you, you can stay a third year."

"Don't tell me you're considering that," Hal said, trying not to sound too angry. All Corky did was complain about her job. The clerkship had become an ordeal that must be endured. Hal could not imagine why Corky would want to go through another year of low pay and long hours working for a sadistic tyrant like Judge Proctor.

"Are you kidding?" Corky said. "I can't wait to get out of there. But I know the judge would like me to stay on. She thinks I'm really smart."

"Well, it's great that she recognizes your talent, but—"

"She has until the beginning of October to decide on next year's lineup. Until then she might try to pressure me to stay. But I've already told her I'm leaving."

"Good."

"I mean, if I really didn't know what I wanted to do, I might, maybe consider staying another year. But now that I know we're going to India and Africa, I have some sort of plan."

"I'm really looking forward to our trip. I think three months alone together is just what we need. You're not gonna let the judge spoil that for us—are you?"

"No way."

Hal was determined to be patient with Corky. If he could just stay on emotional autopilot until the end of the year, he was sure their relationship could survive. The fact was that he and Corky still did not know each other very well. They simply hadn't had enough quality time together. But once the clerkship was over, they would have the time at last. Only then would Hal be able to fully integrate Corky into his life. He was sure that once his friends got to know Corky, really know her, they would like her. And if they didn't, well then, to hell with them.

One night Hal and Tiny Jenks went out to shoot pool. Tiny kept asking about Dahlia Burnish. How was she doing in Los Angeles? Did Hal speak to her often? Didn't he miss her? Hadn't the breakup been somewhat traumatic for him? Without mentioning Corky at all, Tiny began to imply that Hal had only started seeing her because he was on the rebound from Dahlia. "She must have been a hard woman to get over," Tiny said.

"Yo, Tiny," Hal said. "Dahlia's a great woman. But so is Corky. Corky is the woman I'm in love with now. And you have to respect that."

Tiny seemed surprised by the edge in Hal's voice. Hal was surprised by it himself. "Sorry, bro'," Tiny said, patting his friend on the shoulder. "No disrespect intended."

Fake it till you make it. For months, Hal repeated the line like a mantra. When unpleasant thoughts crept into his mind, he would remind himself not to think them. Eventually the weirdness in his head subsided. He no longer heard scraps of Negro spirituals in his dreams at night and stopped seeing violent images in his mind's eye during the day. Hal was just cruising along. He was on autopilot and he liked it. He just didn't know how long he could keep it up.

*   *   *

Emmett talks at you like a white person, in the way that white people have always talked at you—like you're stupid.

"There's no such thing as demons," Emmett lectures. "That's just ignorant religious garbage. Negro folklore that we have to let go of. We can appreciate it, celebrate it as cultural myth, but it has no material component. It is not reality-based. There are no demons. Only in those dumbass exorcist–devil child, Stephen King movies. Have you been watching too many of those movies, LaTonya?"

He is dripping condescension as he talks at you. At first, in September 1994, he was sympathetic. He mentioned the name Hal Hardaway and sent LaTonya plummeting off a cliff. Only the demon saved her from hitting the ground and shattering in a thousand pieces. The demon saved the woman called LaTonya in the way it had not saved the girl called Tony.

Though she did not shatter or disappear into the world of shadow, the woman called LaTonya did have a "slight breakdown." That was what Emmett called it, those three days she spent in bed, sweating and shivering as memories exploded in her brain. LaTonya, during those days in September, told her husband what she remembered. She told him about Uncle Daddy, about the aspiring hoodlums who hung out in front of Grandy's liquor store in Slackerton, Michigan. She told him about Craven University, about the white boy Duane Kordo and what happened at Smegma House twelve years earlier.

"He raped you?" Emmett asked.

"Yes," the woman called LaTonya answered.

She told him of the white boys who stood by watching, all the names coming back to her: Steve Loomis, Arnold Wilson, Dave Carmichael, Richie McBride. And the black boy: Hal Hardaway.

"But Hal," Emmett said, "didn't *do* anything, did he?"

"No," LaTonya said. "He didn't do anything."

LaTonya described the way Tony shattered. She tried to explain the world of shadow, the world of clarity. She told Emmett about the demon, about how Uncle Daddy had put the demon in her, how the demon had once protected her, then went into a deep, comalike sleep

for many years but was now back and raging in pain. She could feel
it, feel the demon roaring inside her face, feel its porcupine needles
prickling the inside of her skin. The demon wanted to save her. The
woman called LaTonya told Emmett this.

"You're an incest survivor," Emmett said. "You're a victim of terrible sexual abuse. I always suspected it."

He was very sympathetic, LaTonya's husband, during the three
days of her "slight breakdown." He listened. He did not judge. He
asked questions, one of the most frequent being "Did Hal Hardaway
do anything to you?"

"No," LaTonya would say. But that didn't explain it. You know
that didn't explain it.

After her three-day slight breakdown, the woman called LaTonya
gets out of bed. Her husband, Dr. Emmett Mercy, tells her he is proud
of her. She has successfully recovered painful repressed memories. He
talks about the need for healing. He talks about forgiveness and transcendence. He stares hard into LaTonya's eyes, asks if he is getting
through to her. She tells him she hears him, but the demon has taken
control. The demon is wide awake now. And its nature has changed.
The demon possesses clarity. The demon will see that justice is done.

Emmett wants to know what she means by "justice."

"The girl called Tony was destroyed," the woman called LaTonya
says, explaining it again and again to her husband. "She shattered in
a thousand pieces. Uncle Daddy was punished for what he did to
Tony. Duane Kordo was punished for what he did to Tony. They paid
with their lives. Hal Hardaway has never paid for what he did."

"But you said Hal didn't *do* anything!" Emmett cries.

"Tony Dawson died at Smegma House. Yet from that night
onward, Hal Hardaway prospered. He flourished. That is not justice.
The demon demands that justice be done!"

Emmett starts preaching again. Healing. Forgiveness. Transcendence. He seems desperate to defend Hal Hardaway. Even though

Hal stood by and watched as Tony Dawson was abused by Duane Kordo, Emmett implores LaTonya to absolve the brother. "Hal could be very important to our future."

"I would like to forgive and forget," you hear LaTonya say, "but the demon won't allow it."

Soon, whenever the subject comes up, Emmett talks at LaTonya—at *you*, you, this body, this lump of flesh and ectoplasmic consciousness that contains the woman called LaTonya and the demon—like a white person, sneering at her, acting like she's stupid, telling her there is no such thing as demons. But you know better. You are the one who feels the demon's power.

You feel the demon every day in LaTonya's writing room. Your fingers move across the keyboard, but it is the demon writing this book. You feel its power in your fingertips. You feel its power burning in your brain. At the end of each writing day, you scroll through the words on the computer screen and feel a mixture of awe and dismay. You think, Look what just fell out of my head. LaTonya is supposed to be writing Emmett's second book, *The Destiny of Our People*. But each morning, in the writing room, she is in thrall to the strange energies of the demon. She is no longer listening to Emmett Mercy's rambling, tape-recorded thoughts. The demon is writing something altogether different. This is the book of LaTonya. All the raging pain is being turned into language. And LaTonya is being constructed sentence by sentence. Between September 1994 and September 1995, as the demon writes in a fever, you feel more connected to the girl called Tony, the woman called LaTonya. You are no longer just a body, an unanchored consciousness, an internal hidden camera. You are becoming fused with the girl who was, the woman who is. The demon is guiding it all. In the fever of writing, the true LaTonya is taking shape. When the demon's work is done, you will finally know who you are.

Emmett is scared of you now. Yes, he gets mad and talks at you

like a white person—but he is scared. He could handle LaTonya, the
poor victim, the homeless girl alone in the world. But the power of
the demon is more than he can handle. He was kind during the three-
day slight breakdown, but when he saw, months afterward, that
LaTonya was incandescent with the demon's fury, Emmett freaked
out. It was just as well he spent most of 1995 away from home, lec-
turing at colleges, bookstores, and men's groups around the country.
When Emmett was in Hallisbury, LaTonya spent even more time
locked behind the door of her writing room.

"So, um, how's the book coming?" Emmett would ask when they
lay in bed together.

"Fine," you answer.

"Well, er, am I gonna get to read some of it one of these days?"
Emmett asks, forcing a laugh.

"Yes."

"When?"

"Dunno."

Emmett didn't worry when LaTonya was at work on the first
book, when he believed she was simply transcribing his tapes. But
this time around, when he could only hear the furious clacking of
keys on LaTonya's computer through the locked door of the study on
the second floor of the big house in Hallisbury, he got panicky.
Because now he realizes he is married to a writer, and he doesn't
know what to expect.

"Come on, LaTonya," Emmett says, his voice sounding whiny in
the darkness of the bedroom. "It's my book, too."

You just laugh, softly, demonically. The demon is having fun,
fucking with Emmett. By the summer of '95, the demon has taught
you to look differently at LaTonya's husband. The demon makes you
see that Emmett doesn't care what happened to Tony at Smegma
House. Emmett defends Hal Hardaway. "He could be a very impor-

tant person for us," Emmett says. "An important contact. He can
help us get our message out. So you need to get over whatever bit-
terness you feel toward the brother. You hear me, LaTonya. Get over
it." The demon shows you that Emmett cares only about his career—
a career that wouldn't even exist without LaTonya! Emmett believes,
has managed to convince himself, that *he* wrote *Blactualization*. But
Emmett Mercy is no writer. He just wants to travel around the country listening to himself talk. He just wants to be famous. He just
wants money. It was Emmett who insisted they buy the big new house
in Hallisbury's most exclusive enclave. LaTonya had been perfectly
happy in their modest apartment in the old town section of Hallisbury, where Chester Beer was their neighbor. But Emmett doesn't
care what LaTonya wants. The demon makes you see that. In the year
after LaTonya's slight breakdown, Emmett rarely has sex with his
wife. You don't care. The demon has no need of Emmett's loving. The
demon needs only to finish the book of LaTonya, and to see that justice is done.

*   *   *

"Tell me," Ludvilla said in her Transylvanian accent, "do you dream
of O.J.?"

Corky, sitting in the courthouse cafeteria as the sun went down
behind the grimy windows, sipping a cup of room-temperature coffee as she watched Marcia Clark on TV roll her huge, haunting eyes
in frustration at yet another ridiculous decision by Judge Lance Ito,
pretended not to hear the question. Ludvilla, one of Corky's fellow
clerks in Judge Judith Proctor's office, had arrived in New York from
Romania in 1990. Ludvilla was devastatingly smart, and—with her
lank, jet-black hair, sallow complexion, bruised-looking eyes, all-
black wardrobe, spindly fingers, and Bela Lugosian accent—kinda

spooky. Seeing that Corky was ignoring her, Ludvilla, spindly fingers wrapped around Styrofoam cup, leaned forward and, in her ghoulish drawl, said again: "Tell me, do you dream of O.J.?"

"No," Corky said.

"*I* do," Ludvilla said in a confessional tone. "I see him, this beautiful black man, on telly every time I come into this place. He is always there on telly, this always-silent, beautiful black man, sitting in the courtroom, saying not a syllable. And at night I dream of him. I dream O.J. is coming to get me. He is trying to break into my apartment. And I know when he does . . . he will rape me. And perhaps . . . he will *beat* me. So I pray he does not break in. And I pray that he does. Always I wake up a little damp."

"This is getting too personal for me, Ludvilla," Corky said. She rose from the table. "I have to get back to the office."

Ludvilla grinned. Her teeth were jagged and yellow. "Surely I am not the only one."

*   *   *

By the summer of '95, O.J. was like the weather. On a typical morning, Corky would run into an acquaintance at the courthouse. "Gonna be another scorcher today," they would say. "I hear it might break a hundred degrees." Then, in the next breath: "So did you see the DNA testimony yesterday? Pretty convincing." To Corky and her colleagues at the courthouse, the O.J. Simpson case was like a combination of the best criminal law seminar you ever took and the sleaziest murder mystery you ever read. They talked about evidence and judicial procedure, about time lines and courtroom strategy and tactics. The question of guilt or innocence was beside the point. What mattered was which team—the prosecution or the defense—was winning.

Corky and Hal, during the half hour they saw each other on most mornings and the half hour they saw each other most nights, sometimes talked about the Simpson case. But not very often. Hal would get extremely agitated when the subject came up. He would talk about how racist the L.A. cops were.

"Sure," Corky said once, "but race doesn't have anything to do with this case. I mean, I don't care if O.J.'s black. It doesn't matter to me whether he's purple, orange, or green."

"I can't stand that!" Hal barked.

"What?" Corky said, taken aback.

"What you just said. White people always say that." Hal put on an exaggerated white-man accent that sounded like a cross between George Bush and Forrest Gump: " 'I don't care if you're black—or purple, orange, or green.' " He returned to his normal voice, fuming: "As if being an African American is like being a Martian. Or a Smurf."

"I'm just talking about color," Corky protested.

"Well, when you're talking about black people, you're *not* just talking about color! You're talking about ethnicity. We're not just *painted*. And being black is not some bizarre anomaly like being purple, orange, or green!"

"Okay, okay, you don't have to get abusive about it."

"Who's being abusive? I'm just making a point!"

"But you're yelling at me!" Corky yelled.

Hal took a deep breath. "I'm sorry. I didn't mean to raise my voice."

"Well, you did. And it's not very pleasant. I feel like a battered woman."

Hal threw up his hands and walked out of the room.

Corky could understand why Hal would be upset about O.J. Simpson. O.J. had been one of his childhood heroes. And Hal—as

Nancy Winterset observed—even looked a little bit like O.J., though younger and leaner. Given Hal's history of family violence, it would not be surprising if the case had an unsettling resonance for him. What bothered Corky was that Hal seemed so eager to give O.J. the benefit of the doubt. Whenever someone asked Hal whether or not he thought O.J. had committed the murders, he gave the same answer, a response that Corky considered both reasonable and a cop-out: "I don't know. I wasn't there."

*   *   *

"I think Brother O.J. might have been trying to help those people. Or maybe he stumbled upon the scene of the crime afterward and that's why you have his footprints there. Either way, I think O.J. *knows* who committed these heinous murders. But he can't talk. These are dangerous people from the drug underworld. If O.J. exposes them, they might go after his children. So Brother O.J. is forced to keep his mouth shut. To save the lives of his kids."

Hal had just clicked on his office radio—which was always tuned to WBUR—and caught the closing minutes of *The Nadra Prince Hour,* the station's most popular talk show. Nadra's guest on the afternoon of Tuesday, September 26, 1995, was, Hal believed, talking nonsense. But it was compelling nonsense. And it was spoken in a sonorous, preacherly, and definitely familiar voice. Where had Hal heard it before?

"Well, that's certainly an intriguing theory," Nadra Prince said in that tone of hers that managed to be at once respectful and sarcastic. "We've been talking with Dr. Emmett Mercy, author of *Blactualiza-tion . . .*"

Hal laughed and clapped his hands. Mercy, mercy, mercy. One year had passed since the Amandla workshop. What a bizarre night that had been. Seeing Walker Du Pree again. Listening to that crazy motherfucker Jojo. Hal impulsively picked up the phone and called the WBUR studio, which was located two floors below him. He talked to Nadra's producer, asked her to send Dr. Mercy up to his office.

Ole Doc Mercy still looked like an undertaker in his black three-piece suit and starched white shirt. When he first arrived at Hal's office, he seemed a bit diffident. He apologized for the collapse of the workshop a year earlier. Once he realized that Hal was unfazed by what had happened, Mercy relaxed. He started blathering pompously about the book he was writing. He said how grateful he was for the opportunity to appear on *The Nadra Prince Hour* and called Nadra a genius. He talked about the greatness of Burnish Enterprises and complimented Hal on the size of his office and the prestige of his title. He said he had an idea for a TV show, a weekly one-hour program about all the most pressing "psycho-spiritual" issues in the African American community, a show that could be very cheaply produced, would be a perfect fit for Burnish Arts and Information Television, and would star Dr. Emmett Mercy. Hal leaned back in his leather swivel chair, tickled by the audacity of Dr. Mercy and thinking that this grave-looking but energetic self-promoter might actually come across well on TV.

"Tell you what," Hal said. "You send me a videotape of one of your lectures and any TV appearances you've had. We'll take a look, see how you come across on camera, then maybe get together for lunch with Godfrey Burnish."

"Brother Hal," Dr. Mercy said, "I am humbled that you would even consider me for your network." He then proceeded to babble about how he needed the broadest possible forum for his message. After much thanking of Hal and praising of God, Dr. Mercy finally left, promising to deliver his videotape within a week.

*   *   *

"Are you trying to destroy us? Is that what you want to do?" Emmett
is lying beside you, propped up on one elbow. It is Tuesday night. You
can barely make out his features in the darkness of the bedroom. You
can hear the desperation in his voice. "Are you just trying to fuck up
our lives?" You do not answer. You know how much your silence
unnerves him. The demon enjoys fucking with Emmett. Emmett is
just one more person who has denied, diminished, your pain. Like
Grandy, like Uncle Daddy, the aspiring hoodlums, Duane Kordo, Hal
Hardaway. "You have to let go of this obsession, LaTonya. Okay?"
You do not answer. "I met with Hal Hardaway today. He's interested
in putting me on television. My own show."

"You saw him?"

LaTonya speaks in such a low, growly, unfamiliar voice that
Emmett wonders for a second if she really is possessed by a demon.
"Yes. I saw him. Today. He wants me to give him a videocassette of
myself so they can get an idea of how I come across on camera. Sort
of a screen test. So I'm gonna be dealing with that."

"You saw him."

"Yes. You have to understand, LaTonya. Hal Hardaway is going
to be my—our—business partner. Are you listening to me? I don't
understand what's happening to you."

"Bring him to me."

"What?"

"Bring him to me."

"Bring Hal to you?" Emmett sighs heavily. "I would like for y'all
to meet, but, LaTonya, what would you do to him?"

"The demon knows what to do with him. The demon showed it
in a dream."

"Showed what?"

"I'm gonna cut his dick off and shove it down his throat."

"God*damn,* LaTonya!" Emmett squeals. "You are fucking insane! What the fuck is going on with you? Do you need more medication? When's the last time you saw your psychiatrist?"

"I don't need no doctor. I need Hal. Bring him to me."

"Stop it, LaTonya! Stop talkin' this crazy shit!"

The demon laughs its soft, hollow laugh. Fucking with Emmett.

"Don't you fuck with me, LaTonya!" Emmett is out of the bed now, screaming in his pajamas. "Don't you laugh at me, you crazy bitch! Remember where your ass was when I saved you! Do you remember? You wanna find your ugly black ass out in the street again? Huh? Do ya? You keep fuckin' with me, LaTonya! You just keep it up!"

Emmett stomps out of the bedroom. He sleeps on the couch in the TV room downstairs, as he has done before. Over the past year, ever since LaTonya's "slight breakdown," the TV room has become Emmett's private little corner of the house. He rarely informs LaTonya of his speaking schedule. She does not know which city he is in on any given day. When he spends the night at home—which he hardly does at all anymore—he often sleeps on the couch in the TV room. You don't care. You are working longer and longer hours now, locked behind the door of LaTonya's writing room, deliriously banging out the final chapters of the book.

*   *   *

It is late Thursday night—or, rather, early Friday morning. You wake up in the darkened bedroom, go pee, then head downstairs for a glass of milk. As you pass the TV room, you hear Emmett's voice. "I want to talk to you today about the three E's," you hear Emmett say stiffly, his voice amplified through speakers. You realize he is watching his screen test videocassette. "Emancipation, Esteem, Empowerment..." Emmett intones.

"Try it with your glasses off, baby."

Through the closed door of the TV room, you hear the second amplified voice, the woman's voice. You hear the tape stop, hear the whir of the tape winding in the VCR. Then there is Emmett's voice again, self-consciously stentorian: "Emancipation, Esteem, Empowerment..."

Then the woman's voice again: "Try it with your glasses off, baby."

"Are you sure?"

"Trust me."

Pause. "I want to talk to you today about the three E's. Emancipation, Esteem, Empowerment."

"Much better. Much sexier."

Suddenly you hear the tape stop. There is silence behind the closed door of the TV room. It is alert, wary silence; the silence of someone listening. Does Emmett sense your presence in the hall? You return to the bedroom upstairs, try to sleep. The demon seethes.

*   *   *

Hal was cooking dinner that Friday night—a rare occurrence. When he and Corky ate dinner together, which they did one or two nights a week, they almost always called out for a delivery or went to a restaurant. But Hal and Corky had decided to make tonight a special occasion. Corky was scheduled to meet with Judge Judith Proctor in her chambers at six o'clock that evening. Corky knew the judge was going to make one last effort to get her to extend her clerkship another year. But Corky was not going to give in to Judge Proctor: December 29 would be her final day. Then she and Hal would leave for their three-month trip to Africa and India. Corky knew that the judge desperately wanted her to stay: All of the other second-year clerks already had jobs waiting; the judge, meanwhile, was particularly unimpressed by her current first-year clerks and didn't trust any of them to help her break in the next crop of rookies in January. In recent weeks, Judge Proctor had started flattering Corky on everything from her competence to her shoes. She seemed to take an inordinate interest in Corky's plans for the future. Corky was too embarrassed to tell the judge she was going to travel. She knew the judge would consider that frivolous. Still, Corky was determined not to let Judge Proctor talk her into staying a third year. At the six o'clock meeting, she would give her final no. Judge Proctor had to commit to next year's lineup the following Monday, October 2. On Friday, September 29, Corky would tell the judge once and for all that she would not be a member of her 1996 staff. Then she would go home to her loving boyfriend, who was preparing a small feast for them: gazpacho, broiled salmon steaks with a special cream sauce, and Häagen-Dazs chocolate-chocolate-chip ice cream—Corky's favorite flavor—for dessert. Hal had also bought a bottle of Dom Perignon so they could toast Corky's personal proclamation of emancipation and look forward to her freedom in three months' time. Hal got home at six o'clock that Friday so he could start fixing dinner. Corky told him her meeting with Judge Proctor would last no more than half an hour. "I should be home by seven," Corky told Hal that morning. "Seven-thirty at the very latest."

When, at eight o'clock, Corky still had not come home, Hal began to worry. He called the courthouse. Someone who sounded like Count Dracula answered the phone, said Corky had left "some time ago." By nine o'clock, Hal was seething. He consumed half the gazpacho, both salmon steaks, and three quarters of the ice cream, washing it all down with the bottle of Dom Perignon. When Corky walked in the door at ten, Hal was sitting at the kitchen table, working on a bottle of Jack Daniels. "Do you know what time it is?" he growled.

"I'm sorry I'm so late, sweetheart," Corky said breezily. Her face was flush, her manner exhilarated. "I just had a really intense evening with the judge. We started talking at six, then she invited me out for a drink and we just kept talking and talking. She really opened up to me. Judith has had *such* an interesting life! I had no idea."

"I thought you were gonna be home by seven. Seven-thirty . . . at the latest."

"So did I." Corky was fluttering around the kitchen, peering into the refrigerator, pouring herself a glass of milk, talking excitedly. "But there was no way I could leave. Judith and I really bonded tonight."

"Have you eaten?" Hal sat perfectly still at the kitchen table, clutching his glass of bourbon, smoldering.

"Judith took me out to dinner. Hal, it's just incredible. You would never know what this woman has been through. Do you know she was raped by her father when she was thirteen? Can you imagine?"

"You could have called me."

"I'm sorry, honey, there was just no good time to step away to a phone."

"I've been telling you for months you should buy a mobile phone," Hal said, his voice low and steely. He felt as if he were concentrating very hard, focusing all his energies on not blowing up.

"Hal, I said I was sorry."

"I made dinner."

"I know, honey, thank you so much. Though I'm not that hungry."

"You know, Corky, if I did this to you, you would have a fucking shit fit."

"Please don't swear at me, Hal."

"I'm just sick of you and your double standards! If I showed up three hours late without calling, you would throw a tantrum!"

"I would not! If you told me you had an important business meeting, I would understand."

"If I waltzed in the door three hours late without calling and you had made a special dinner—"

"If it was an important meeting like I had with Judith, I wouldn't be upset."

"You are so full of shit! Jesus, Corky, if I wanna watch a football game, you think I'm some kinda macho brute, and now you're gonna tell me—"

"Stop yelling at me!"

"Oh, yeah! It's all right for you to yell at me, but if I yell at you, I'm being abusive, right?"

"Okay, okay, okay, okay." Corky held up both palms. "Shhhhh . . . Shhhhh . . . Let's just lower the volume here." Corky sat across from Hal at the table. "I'm sorry I didn't call."

"I made dinner," Hal muttered.

"Yeah, I saw the gazpacho. I think I'll have a bowl."

Corky sipped her cold soup. Hal sipped his bourbon. For a long time, neither of them said a word. Finally Corky tried to make small talk. "So, anything interesting happen at work today?"

"No," Hal said evenly. "Did you tell the judge you're quitting in December?"

Corky stared into her bowl, fiddled with her spoon. "I tried to."

"You *tried* to?"

"Well, you know, Hal . . . Judith really needs me. She thinks I'm really smart. Anyway . . . I told her I'd think about it some more this weekend. I have until six o'clock Monday to give her a definitive answer."

"What about our trip?"

"I don't know. Maybe we could put it off a year. I don't know."

"You mean you don't care."

"Well, Jesus, Hal, I'm sorry I'm a talented attorney."

"I'm not faulting you for being a talented attorney!" Hal buried his face in his hands. "Aaaaaaaarrrrrrrgghh!"

"Shhhhh. Shhhhh. We can talk about this later."

They were silent again. Soon the silence began to fester. Corky groped for something to say, anything to lighten the mood in the kitchen. She and Hal just needed to talk to each other like human beings. They needed to chat about something innocuous. Something like the weather. "So," Corky said brightly, as if she were speaking to a colleague at the courthouse, "did you see that the O.J. case has gone to the jury?"

"They don't start deliberations till Monday," Hal said tonelessly.

"Yeah, but just think, soon this will all be over."

"No it won't. It's gonna be a hung jury and then we'll have to go through the whole thing all over again. Another criminal trial. Another circus." Hal poured himself a fresh glass of bourbon. "It's just a TV show now. People don't even realize that a man's life is hanging in the balance."

"Yeah, poor O.J.," Corky said sarcastically.

"Innocent until proven guilty. Ain't that the American way, Corky?"

"I know how you must feel, Hal." Corky rose and walked over to the sink. "It's a personal thing for you. Because black men are violent."

"What?"

Corky began washing her bowl and spoon. "I mean, generally speaking, black men tend to be violent."

"How can you say that?" Hal was out of his chair now. At first he thought Corky might be joking. Then he thought she was just try-ing to be provocative. He now realized that she was saying exactly what she believed.

"Hal, I'm sorry, but I work in a courthouse. I see how many black men are charged with violent crimes every day."

"So you think black men are inherently violent?"

Corky whirled around to face Hal. "Don't yell at me!"

"I can't believe what you're saying!"

"That's because you're just like O.J.!"

"And you're a racist!"

"I am not!" Corky lunged forward and punched Hal in the shoulder. "You stupid jerk!"

At that moment, something happened to Hal. It was as if the entire kitchen had suddenly been whited out. He was blinded, his eyes seared by a sunburst of rage. He felt as if his arm was about to fly out of his body, as if his fist would fly off his wrist and crush Corky's face. He could not stop it, could not even see it.

But Hal did not strike Corky. He did not know what stopped him. Some sort of internal, fail-safe mechanism. His arm did not fly from his body. Rather than moving toward Corky, he fell back in his chair, shaking all over.

"What's the matter with you?" Corky shrieked. "You're scaring me!"

"Just back off!" Hal shouted, clutching his own shoulders, trying to keep his body from springing out of the chair.

"You're just like O.J.!"

"I AM NOT O.J. SIMPSON!" Hal bolted upright, howling uncontrollably. "I AM NOT O.J. SIMPSON! I AM NOT O.J. SIMPSON! I AM NOT O.J. SIMPSON!"

Corky ran from the kitchen, then ran out of the apartment, slamming the door behind her.

Hal stumbled into the living room. For a moment, he almost chased after his girlfriend. Instead, he flung himself on the couch. "I am not O.J. Simpson!" he sobbed, his face mashed in a cushion. "I am not O.J. Simpson. I am not O.J. Simpson. I'm not O.J. Simpson. I'm not O.J. I'm not O.J. I'm not . . ."

*   *   *

Hal was lying awake in bed when Corky returned to the apartment at one in the morning. She undressed in the dark, then slipped into bed beside him. "Are you all right, honey?" she whispered.

"Yes," Hal said. "Are you all right?"

"I think so."

"I'm sorry, Corky. I was very upset."

"I'm sorry to have upset you."

"You shouldn't hit me. And you shouldn't call me names. I don't do that to you. Don't do it to me."

"I won't. But you have to control your temper."

"I won't lose my temper again, Corky. I'll just leave. That's what you have to understand. I won't get mad again. I'll just *walk.*"

Corky was crying now. She wrapped her body around Hal's. "Don't leave me. Please don't leave me. Please don't leave me."

"Don't worry," Hal said. He knew that even if he continued to live with Corky until the end of the year, the rest was free fall.

After a while, Corky stopped crying. She pressed her body more tightly against Hal's. "I love you," Corky said.

16

Chester Beer is crying. The tenderhearted man tries to stop his tears as he sits at the kitchen table in the big house LaTonya never wanted. Chester has hardly touched his coffee. It is Monday morning, October 2. The day before, the demon finished writing the book of LaTonya. The demon's work is almost over. Once the demon sees that justice is done, it will be able to rest in peace forever.

You want to put your arms around Chester, but you are afraid it might embarrass him. After all, it is LaTonya who should need consoling. But she sits dry-eyed at the kitchen table. The demon will allow no tears. Chester Beer has just told LaTonya that Emmett is having an affair, that he has been carrying on with a woman in town for almost a year, that this woman has accompanied him on many of his speaking engagements. The woman is probably with Emmett right now, in whatever city he is visiting. You can see how much it hurts Chester to tell LaTonya this. You feel so bad for Chester. But information is needed.

"Who is she?" the demon asks Chester.

The woman called LaTonya has considered this possibility before. And she remembers well the woman's voice on Emmett's screen test videocassette. She always thought that if Emmett was going to cheat on her with somebody they both knew, it would be Rhonda Roos, who, with her amber skin and ironed light brown hair, looked just like old photos of Emmett's mama, Lady Mercy. So it is a surprise to learn that Emmett's lover is, in fact, Gladys Gable, a single mother and singer in the choir at the church where Chester Beer is head deacon. A full-figured, dark-skinned gal, Gladys looked more like LaTonya than anyone else in Hallisbury.

Chester wipes away his tears. "I'm so sorry, LaTonya. I didn't want to be the one to tell you. Emmett has no idea I was gonna do this. But I just couldn't stand it anymore. I am so sorry."

"Don't be," the demon replies. "This will only make everything I have to do easier."

*   *   *

Sadie Broom's mother, Lorraine, often said that life was full of necessary mistakes. There were certain blunders, errors in judgment, foolish miscalculations that one simply had to make. You lived through them, learned from them; but you should never think they were avoidable. Three weeks after her return, Sadie was thrilled to be back in New York, back to old friends and things familiar. The eight months she'd spent in Paris had changed her not at all. Her Upper West Side apartment was exactly as she had left it. Her job in the New York office of Tanzer & Mur was as satisfying as she remembered. But Sadie was beginning to think that going to Amsterdam, retrieving Walker, and bringing him home to America to resume their relationship constituted a major but necessary mistake.

It had been necessary for Sadie to go to Amsterdam. She knew that Walker was just wasting his life there—she had to rescue him from himself. It was necessary to try to salvage their relationship. Because they had been good together. Walker was crazy to have left her. Sadie was more convinced of that than ever. It was necessary that they be back in New York together, that they try to regain what they had. Ultimately, though, it was a mistake. While the rest of Sadie's New York life snapped neatly back into place, Walker no longer fit into it. Walker had changed. Or, rather, all his most detrimental qualities had, as far as Sadie could see, grown worse. Walker was back in his Greenwich Village apartment, smoking dope and drawing all day. He seemed even more distracted, more removed from the real world than he had before his ten—obviously drugged-out—months in Amsterdam. He refused to tell Sadie how much of his inheritance he'd spent or how he planned to preserve what was left of it. In fact, since they had returned to New York, he resisted having any kind of serious conversation with Sadie. When she asked reasonable questions about his plans for the future, he responded with lame jokes. Sadie would, in turn, become irritable, snappish, with him. After three weeks, it was time for Sadie to acknowledge her mistake—and to cut her losses.

"So," Walker said, "did you hear about this thing Louis Farrakhan is organizing?" It was the first Monday in October. Walker sat in the breakfast nook of Sadie's kitchen, flipping through the newspaper. He was still wearing his bathrobe. Sadie, fully dressed, ready for work, stood at the sink, sipping a cup of coffee.

"Of course I've heard about it," Sadie said.

"A million black men marching on Washington."

"Sounds more like a million looters to me. I hope Clinton's gonna have the National Guard standing by. I don't want those niggas trashin' my hometown."

"A day of atonement, he calls it. Atone for what, I wonder. Hmm. It's two weeks from today. Maybe I'll go."

"You? Walker, you're too lazy to revise your résumé. Where are you gonna get the energy to go down to Washington?"

"Jeez, Sadie, you don't have to be so nasty."

"Well, I'm just getting exasperated with you, Walk. You're just, like, totally feckless."

"That's not true. I have lots of feck. I just don't like to flaunt it." Walker was trying to get Sadie to smile. It didn't work.

Sadie buttoned her suit jacket, picked up her briefcase. "When you go this morning," she said sternly, "please leave the keys to my apartment on the coffee table."

Walker was taken by surprise. "Wow," he whispered. "I guess you don't wanna see me tonight, huh?"

"Not tonight."

"Okay . . . um . . . when?"

Sadie sighed. "I'll call you tomorrow morning. At your place."

"All right," Walker said faintly.

"I'm sorry," Sadie said. Then she left for work.

*   *   *

"Hello, Mr. Hardaway, this is LaTonya Mercy, the wife of Dr. Emmett Mercy," the demon says sweetly. "How are you today?"

It is eleven o'clock Monday morning. You are sitting on the couch in the TV room. As the demon talks into the phone, you stare at the videocassette that has been ostentatiously left lying on the coffee table, labeled DR. EMMETT MERCY SCREEN TEST. You have looked through Emmett's desk calendar, so you know he will not return from Philadelphia until late tonight. He has left the tape behind for LaTonya to watch. But she does not watch the tape.

"Fine, thanks. Please call me Hal. What can I do for you, Mrs. Mercy?"

Yes, the voice is just as smooth as you remember. "Well, Emmett has made this little audition tape for you. Unfortunately, he's out of town on an important speaking engagement right now. But he wanted me to get this tape to you as soon as possible."

"Okay, well, why don't you just put it in the mail and—"

"Oh, no, Emmett wants this hand-delivered. Unfortunately, I live all the way up in Hallisbury and—"

"I can send a messenger up there if you like, Mrs. Mercy."

"That's so sweet of you," the demon says in its syrupy, artificial voice. "You must be a very kind and thoughtful man. Please, call me LaTonya. Actually, I was planning to come into the city later."

"All right. Do you have my office address?"

"Yes, I do."

"What time is good for you, LaTonya?"

"Six o'clock."

"Six o'clock it is."

"I don't want to inconvenience you, Hal, but Emmett insisted I get this to you, and if he comes home and finds out I was lax in my duties . . ."

"Oh, it's no inconvenience at all."

"I'll try not to be late. For all I know, you might have a wife waiting at home with dinner on the table."

Hal laughed. "Don't worry about that. My girlfriend rarely gets home before ten."

"All right, then." The demon pauses, then says, "You know something? We've met before."

"Have we?"

"You don't remember me?"

"LaTonya? Well, you have a beautiful name." Now Hal is flirting. "I would think I'd remember."

"Hmmmmm," the demon purrs. "Tonight I'll have to refresh your memory. See you at six."

But you have no intention of going to Hal's office at six. You will go to his home, later. You've been through Emmett's files, so you know exactly where Hal Hardaway lives.

At five o'clock you make a final check. The luggage is packed and waiting by the front door. You should wait till you return from Brooklyn to load it all in the station wagon. The house is well stocked with lighter fluid. That, too, will be for later. You walk out to the station wagon. The briefcase sits in the passenger seat. You snap it open, take one last look to make sure you have everything you need for your visit to Hal Hardaway: the handcuffs, a souvenir from all those nights you worked as a security guard at Hallisbury General Hospital; the vials of chloroform, smuggled from the hospital, along with other strange substances that caught LaTonya's fancy back when she worked there; the sturdy length of rope, secured from Emmett's toolshed; the duct tape, for gagging; the bandana; the vial of ammonia; the meat cleaver; the frying pan; the jumbo bottle of Crisco cooking oil. You only hope that Hal has a working stove.

*   *   *

Everything happened for a reason. Sadie Broom was in no conventional sense a religious person. She liked to believe that God existed but she rarely prayed. She went to church on holidays but tended to regard the services as performance art—especially if there was a gospel choir present. She gave no thought at all to heaven and hell. But she believed, absolutely, that everything happened for a reason. If she had ever had cause to doubt it, the events of Monday, October 2, 1995, would confirm her faith forever.

That morning, she asked Walker to return the keys to her apartment. When she got to the office, her girlfriend Pauline—the very person who had hooked her up with Walker—called to invite Sadie to lunch. They were to meet at twelve-thirty at Ancestors, the new hip restaurant of the bupoisie. Ancestors had opened while Sadie was in

Paris. She passed through the restaurant's revolving door at twelve-thirty sharp. Ancestors seemed as large as an airplane hangar, with high ceilings and vast wall space covered with full-color poster-style portraits of African American heroes, grouped by field of endeavor. There was Jackie Robinson, Arthur Ashe, Wilma Rudolph, and a host of others in the Sports Legends section. Martin Luther King Jr., Malcolm X, Sojourner Truth, et al. stared down from the Freedom Fighters area. Zora Neale Hurston, Langston Hughes, Richard Wright, and a dozen other scribes filled the Literary Giants space. Beneath the benevolent gazes of the black pantheon dined its progeny. Ancestors was filled almost to capacity with a clientele made up exclusively of African American professionals. Sadie felt a powerful rush of affection for her people: smart, sharply dressed brothers and sisters, makin' moves and gettin' paid, taking time out from their busy schedules to do lunch and network over barbecued spare ribs and black-eyed peas, chitlins, fried chicken, collard greens, and cornbread. And on the walls surrounding them was the history of their indomitable tribe. Sadie was about to go misty-eyed with pride when the hostess came up to her, asked her name, and said there was a call for her. Pauline was on the line, sounding freaked out by some sudden crisis in the layout department at the *Downtown Clarion*. She wouldn't be able to make it for lunch. Sadie couldn't stand eating in a restaurant alone, especially when she hadn't brought along something to read. And she didn't recognize a single face in the crowd, no one whose table she could ask to join. She was sad to leave Ancestors, but there was no way she would dine alone in a public place. Pushing on the revolving door, Sadie realized the fateful, overarching reason why Pauline had invited her to Ancestors and then canceled. As she was revolving out of the restaurant, she caught the eye of a young brother, through the glass panel, revolving his way in. It was Hal Hardaway. Sadie spun her way back into Ancestors.

For a long time they stood in the foyer of the restaurant, laughing, hugging, standing apart to get a good look at each other, then laughing and hugging again. Nine and a half years had passed since they had last seen each other, nine and a half years since that night when they made out, so clumsily and self-consciously, in Sadie's off-campus apartment in Craven, Delaware. Hal told Sadie his boss had just canceled their lunch date. Fortunately, Hal had reserved an intimate corner table.

*   *   *

"I shoulda been in Congress by now," Hal said. He was on his fourth bottle of beer, having devoured his gumbo, spare ribs, and pecan pie. It was two-thirty. Ancestors was clearing out. "That was what I used to think, back when we were at Craven. That I'd get elected in 'ninety-four. Can you imagine? Right now I'd be voting for the Contract with America."

"No way," Sadie said. "You'd be fighting it. Congress needs people like you. People like us." Sadie was on her third beer and feeling wonderfully stuffed and tipsy after her lunch of fried shrimp, catfish, and ambrosia. "I'd vote for you, Hal."

"Yeah," Hal said glumly. He downed the last of his brew. "Then I thought I'd be an actor. Do you remember?" He laughed. "Dreams of glory."

"Don't you still wanna be rich and famous?"

"I'll settle for just rich. I wanna be famous for being rich."

Hal and Sadie smiled. The old rapport, the subtle communion, was still there. Over the past two hours, Sadie and Hal had discussed their careers, their families, old acquaintances, life in New York, and, briefly, the O.J. trial. But they had carefully avoided talking about their current lovers.

"Craven U.," Sadie sighed. "Can you believe our tenth reunion is next May?"

"No."

"You thought you'd be a politician or an actor and I thought that by now I'd be married. Or at least engaged." Sadie paused before taking the plunge. "Walker told me he saw you at that meeting last year. Emmett Mercy's workshop."

"I figured he did." Hal looked down at the table as he spoke. "So you know I was involved with Corky Winterset."

"Yes," Sadie said. "Am I mistaken or did you just use the past tense?"

"We're in the final stages."

"Corky and I lived in the same dorm freshman year. I didn't know her very well. But I always kinda liked her."

"What about you and Walker? Last time I saw him, he said he was leaving the country."

"He did. He went and lived in Amsterdam for, oh, just about ten months. Now he's back in New York. I've seen him. But we broke up a year ago."

"Good."

"You probably have to be getting back to your office."

"Not really. Nobody's keeping tabs on me. What about you?"

"Pwuh!" Sadie made the odd little French noise she used to hate. "I have no appointments this afternoon. I was thinking about taking the rest of the day off."

"Word," Hal said with a smile. "Well, maybe you'd like to join me for an after-lunch cocktail at another place I know?"

"Maybe I would."

*   *   *

It had been many years since Sadie had thought of her life as a movie, but the afternoon of Monday, October 2, 1995, unfolded with a cinematic fluidity and unrealness. As soon as Sadie and Hal stepped out of Ancestors, they were all over each other, kissing hungrily in broad daylight, in the middle of Fifty-seventh Street. The next thing Sadie knew, they were groping in a taxi. Then they were in her apartment. Their clothes seemed to fall magically from their bodies. They were naked, tumbling in the sheets in Sadie's sun-drenched bedroom.

Suddenly, but only for a moment, reality intruded. Just as Sadie reached into the drawer of her bedside table and pulled out a condom for Hal, she remembered that she was menstruating. Sadie never liked having sex during her period. It always made her self-conscious, her fear that the man would be repulsed by her blood. "We better not," Sadie said as she handed Hal the condom. "It's that time of the month for me."

"I don't care," Hal said. "Do you?"

"No."

It had taken ten years for Sadie to be proved right. A decade earlier, back at Craven U., she knew that if she and Hal Hardaway had sex, he would be hers forever. She knew—she just *knew*—that they would be as compatible physically as they were emotionally. When she looked into his eyes after they made love that Monday afternoon, she saw the devotion she felt inside reflected back at her. She knew—and she knew Hal knew—that they were going to spend the rest of their lives together.

At five o'clock, Hal got dressed and prepared to go back to his office. He said he would call Sadie the next day, and she knew he was telling the truth. Wearing nothing but a towel, Sadie walked Hal to the door and gave him a lustful kiss good-bye. When she returned to the bedroom, she saw that the sheets were smeared with blood. Sadie lay down in the bed, curled up in the sheets. She felt closer to Hal than she had ever felt to anyone. She felt, oddly, profoundly, that blood bonded them.

*   *   *

Hal was sure that Godfrey Burnish must have died suddenly. When he got back to his office at five-thirty Monday afternoon, a funereal quiet filled the halls of Burnish Enterprises. Hal's colleagues passed him in the corridors and gave grim nods or sad little half-smiles. There was a silent acknowledgment that Hal must have heard the bad news—thus, no need to say anything. But Hal had spent the afternoon with Sadie Broom, having the most sublime sex of his life. As he walked past his secretary, she shook her head dolefully and said, "Lotsa messages for you *today.*"

As soon as Hal sat at his desk, his deputy, Yolanda Yancy, called. "I've been trying to reach you all afternoon," she said. "The kids at BAIT need to know how we're gonna cover this."

"Yolanda, I'm sorry," Hal said. "I've been out of the office since lunch. What happened?"

"There's been a verdict in L.A."

"Already? The jury just began deliberations this morning!"

"That's right. It took them four hours to reach a unanimous decision."

"Fuck. Is he guilty?"

"The jury has only announced that they've reached a verdict. We won't know what it is until one o'clock tomorrow—New York time."

"Only four hours of deliberation?"

"It doesn't look very good for Juice. All the legal experts are saying that a quick verdict is almost always a guilty verdict."

"Damn. I better call the founder."

"Youngblood!" Godfrey Burnish boomed when he heard Hal's voice on the phone. "I've been callin' you all afternoon. Get your ass up to my office—pronto!"

When Hal entered Godfrey Burnish's all-white lair, the founder
was pacing excitedly, his smooth, spherical baby head bouncing on
his shoulders. "Sit, sit!" As Hal sat down, Godfrey Burnish continued to pace. "Youngblood, we are entering the seventeenth month of
the Simpson saga. And as you know, the whole time, I have steadfastly refused to cover the story in *Esteem* magazine. Against the urg-
ings of some very sharp people, yourself foremost among them, of
course." The founder abruptly stopped pacing and leaned back, resting his butt against the front of his desk. "Well, youngblood, I've
changed my mind. I have an idea for our special year-end issue of
Esteem." The founder looked heavenward and held up his hands as
if he were receiving divine inspiration. "Johnnie Cochran," the
founder said rapturously, "Man of the Year."

*   *   *

No matter what the actual hour, it always felt like the middle of the
night in Judge Judith Proctor's chambers, where the heavy, floor-
length, wine-red curtains were always closed and the only light came
from the tiny lamps scattered about the wood-paneled office. The
amber lamplight flickered on the round lenses of Judge Proctor's
wire-rimmed spectacles. The reflected light made it impossible for
Corky Winterset to see the judge's eyes as she sat on the other side of
her boss's vast oak desk. Corky glanced at the shadowy face of the
grandfather clock in the corner. It was five-thirty. The judge cocked
her head in an owlish gesture. Corky could see little sparks of gray in
Judge Proctor's sandy, close-cropped hair. After nearly two years of
working for the judge, Corky still had no idea how old Judith Proctor was. Taut-skinned and athletically trim, the judge could have
been anywhere between forty-five and sixty.

"You don't seem very pleased with your decision, Eleanor," the judge said, addressing Corky by her middle name, the name she went by at the courthouse, the name that appeared on her business cards.

"I know it's the right thing to do," Corky said. She had just told the judge that, yes, she would extend her clerkship another year. "I just don't know what to do about my living situation." Corky had also told the judge about her troubles with Hal. "Since Friday night, I'm scared to stay in the apartment."

"Do you think he would do you physical harm?" the judge asked.

"I already feel like a battered woman."

Judge Proctor gasped. "Has he hit you?"

"No."

"Has he ever threatened to hit you?"

"No."

"Raised a hand to you?"

"No. I mean, I feel *emotionally* battered."

"Does he yell at you?"

"Yes."

"Do you yell at him?"

"Sometimes."

"Does he curse at you?"

"He said I was full of shit."

Judge Proctor paused, then said, "Is that all?"

"He's said it a few times."

"Does he call you a bitch?"

"No."

"A whore? A slut? A cunt?"

"God, no."

"Have you ever called him a name? The N-word?"

"Never."

Corky had forgotten that she'd punched Hal and called him a

stupid jerk. She had forgotten it one second after it happened and would never remember it.

Judge Proctor removed her glasses and rubbed her eyes. "So— what exactly has Hal done?"

"He's yelled at me and said mean things. He called me a racist."

Judge Proctor slowly put her glasses back on. "And you say you feel like a battered woman?"

"Yes."

"Eleanor—I spent the first seventeen years of my life in the same house with a battered woman: my mother. Every Friday night, my father would come home from the factory and . . . let off steam, as he called it. And every Saturday morning, my mother would have fresh bruises on her face and body. Eleanor—my mother was a battered woman. For you to compare yourself to her is to completely trivialize the plight of women who are subjected to real physical abuse."

Corky bowed her head. "I didn't mean to do that."

The judge sighed heavily. "Eleanor—you are from a generation of crybabies! You're all so desperate to be victims that you've completely lost sight of what real suffering is. *Emotional battery.*" The judge snorted. "If you only knew what a joke that is in the face of actual violence, you would be as disgusted with yourself as I am with you."

"I'm sorry."

"But I understand your current domestic dilemma. You're welcome to stay at my house for the next few nights. My partner and I have a comfortable guest room. And I'm sure Janet won't mind if you want to camp out at our place for a while."

"Thank you, Judge."

"Call me Judith."

"Thanks, Judith."

After a long pause, Judith said, "Nicole Brown Simpson. Now, there's a victim for you. But at least that scumbag is going to pay for what he did to her."

"You think it's a guilty verdict?"

"Of course it's a guilty verdict! Did you see Marcia Clark's summation? Brilliant! Calm, dispassionate, rational. She appealed to the intelligence of the jury."

"But what about all the black jurors?"

"Most of them are black *women*," the judge pointed out. "They know a thing or two about male aggression and violence. That's why they only needed four hours to decide. They know what that bastard was capable of."

*   *   *

Johnnie Cochran was the sort of black man who always reminded Hal of his dad: a slick, silver-tongued brother in his fifties, self-invented, oozing confidence, effortlessly charming, and unmistakably a race man—definitely down for the community—who could manage to look cool, even dignified, while wearing a green suit and an orange tie. Hal worshiped his dad, and he couldn't help but like Johnnie Cochran, the supernova of O.J. Simpson's all-star legal defense team. During his theatrical summation, Johnnie owned that courtroom—Hal could feel it. Cochran relentlessly hammered the racist cop Fuhrman—who took the Fifth Amendment against self-incrimination when asked if he had planted evidence on the night of the murders—and used the gloves that his client could barely squeeze into in court as a metaphor for the prosecution's case. "If it doesn't fit," Johnnie Cochran told the jury again and again in a Jesse Jacksonesque refrain, "you must acquit." Hal was proud of the brother. But Johnnie Cochran as *Esteem*'s Man of the Year, an honor that until now had been designated for Colin Powell?

"Gee, youngblood," Godfrey Burnish said, his voice laced with disappointment. "I thought you'd be excited."

Hal sat in the founder's office, puzzling over the suggestion. Yes, Johnnie Cochran had performed admirably given the impossible task that confronted him. Hal had been sure that most if not all of the black jurors would vote to acquit. But with the nonblack jurors voting guilty, there would inevitably be a mistrial. That was why the quick unanimous verdict had been such a shock. How could Johnnie have lost every one of the black jurors? Unless . . . "You don't think the verdict is not guilty?" Hal asked. "Do you?"

"Of course the verdict is not guilty!" Godfrey Burnish erupted. "Doesn't everybody know that? Rise and shine, youngblood! This is a milestone in the struggle. For maybe the first time in American legal history, the police tried to frame a black man and failed! And it's all thanks to Johnnie Cochran. The trial of the century has been won by a black lawyer! Sing hallelujah, youngblood! The system works! Any rich white man in O.J.'s shoes woulda *walked.* And now O.J.'s gonna walk! Is this a great country or what the fuck? Johnnie Cochran is the greatest lawyer in a society of laws. And we, youngblood, African Americans, are the greatest people in the greatest nation on the face of the earth!"

*   *   *

Ordinarily, the first time Hal had sex with a new lover, he experienced a triumphant rush, a feeling akin to blasting into the end zone and ferociously spiking the football into the turf: *YES! Scooooooore!* But as he returned to his apartment in Park Slope Monday evening, just a few hours after making love with Sadie Broom for the first time, Hal felt no thrill of victory. Nor did he feel that lightning bolt of infatuation that usually struck him after the first time. Instead he felt a serenity washing over him. For a moment, in Sadie's apartment that afternoon, Hal had a twinge of the dread that had come over him when he was making out with Sadie in Craven, Delaware, in 1986. He feared, as he had that night, that Mr. Bone would not be up to the task. But the twinge of dread passed and Hal gave in to the tenderness he felt for Sadie, the same tenderness that had scared him when he was a younger man. The intimacy he had found unbearable then soothed him now. That Monday evening, he knew his life had reached a turning point. I can stop looking now, Hal thought to himself. He had finally found what he thought he'd had with Dahlia, what he wanted so badly to have with Corky. And staring into her eyes after they had made love, Hal thought Sadie was the most beautiful woman he had ever seen.

He entered the apartment he had shared with Corky for the past twenty-one months, took off his work clothes, slipped into a pair of gym shorts, opened a cold bottle of beer, and reflected on his extraordinary good fortune with women. It *was* extraordinary, wasn't it, the way each of his relationships had segued fluidly into the next? His relationship with Corky had gone into free fall on Friday night. On Monday afternoon, a chance meeting with Sadie Broom heralded the beginning of a new romance, the romance that he knew would be his last. Hal was so ready. Ready to be somebody's husband. Somebody's father. He had begun the day depressed about his relationship with Corky. But now, as he settled back in a cushy armchair, he felt warmed by his love for Sadie. What's more, Godfrey Burnish had convinced him that the O.J. verdict to be announced on Tuesday would be "not guilty." It had turned out to be a magnificent day.

The downstairs buzzer sounded. He glanced at his watch: seven-thirty. Who the hell would be dropping by unannounced? Rising grudgingly from his cushy armchair, Hal suddenly remembered his appointment with Dr. Mercy's wife. With everything that had hap-

pened that afternoon, he'd completely forgotten about it. But he
hadn't left his office until almost seven. And Mrs. Mercy hadn't
shown up or called to cancel.

"Yes?" Hal said into the intercom.

"It's LaTonya Mercy," a soft, virtually expressionless voice
answered. "I missed you at your office."

Hal was taken aback. He could hardly believe that Emmett
Mercy's wife had gone through the trouble of tracking him down at
home.

"Oh, I'm very sorry, LaTonya, I—"

"Can I bring this tape up to you?" LaTonya asked tonelessly.

Hal thought about offering to come downstairs to get it. But he
was dressed only in gym shorts. "Well, I—"

"Please."

Hal sighed. "I'm on the third floor," he said, pressing the button
to let LaTonya Mercy into his building. As Hal put his shirt and pants
back on, a runaway train of thought came barreling down the tracks
of his mind.

"We've met before," LaTonya had said on the phone that morning. Hal had noted that Dr. Mercy's wife had a lovely telephone voice,
pleasant and animated, just a tad flirtatious. Her voice on the intercom, however, was bland, uninflected, and cringingly familiar.

"You don't remember me?" LaTonya had said on the phone that
morning.

"Do you ever think of Tony Dawson?" Walker had asked Hal
after the Amandla workshop a year earlier. Hal had pretended not to
hear the name as his taxi pulled away. The fact was, he almost never
thought of her. Every once in a while, over the past thirteen years, he
would see her in a dream or hear that sound that came out of her as
she slumped on the moist grass of the Smegma House lawn, that
sound that was neither cry nor sob nor scream—that long, anguished
moan. But such dreams were rare.

"Tonight I'll have to refresh your memory," Dr. Emmett Mercy's wife had said on the phone.

So by the time Hal Hardaway opened the door to his apartment to greet LaTonya Mercy as she walked toward him down the corridor, securely buttoned up in a beige trenchcoat, black leather gloves on her hands, hauling a boxy, black briefcase, he was not at all surprised to see that she and Tony Dawson were the same person. He only wondered what exactly it was she wanted from him.

Hal quickly decided there was only one way to play this match and that was casual. He shook LaTonya's glove-covered hand and beckoned his guest into the living room, inviting her to sit on the couch. LaTonya, still clutching her briefcase, sat down. Her demeanor was as polite as Hal's. As he returned to his armchair, nonchalant, casual as could be, Hal thought that while LaTonya Mercy looked almost exactly the same as the Tony Dawson he had known briefly in the fall of 1982—the same short, curly Afro, the same broad features, the same hard, rather masculine jawline, the same crazy absence in the eyes—the overall effect was far more attractive. Back in the Craven football locker room—before the incident at Smegma House—Titus Boggs had called Tony "a brown-paper-bag bitch," meaning it would be fine to fuck her—what with that ass, those tits, all that cash butter—so long as you covered her face in a grocery sack. Thirteen years later, LaTonya Mercy remained bundled in her trenchcoat as she sat on Hal's couch, but Hal could tell she hadn't let her cash butter turn to lard. Looking into her face, though, Hal thought how stupid, how narrow-minded, how blind he and the other football players had been. LaTonya was actually a good-looking woman. Or maybe, Hal wondered, the apparent change in her personality made her seem more attractive. While Tony Dawson had been withdrawn, self-conscious, LaTonya Mercy—in the first minutes she spent in Hal's apartment—gave off an air of social ease and self-possession. Yet she still had that unnerving stare, even as she smiled at Hal and launched into the kind of long-time-no-see chitchat—speaking now in her pleasant telephone voice—that any other old college classmate might initiate. Hal played along. "Well, LaTonya," he said, "I have to say you're really looking well."

"A whole lot better than last time you saw me, huh?" LaTonya said, smiling, staring crazily. "But I was a completely different person then."

"Congratulations on your marriage. Emmett's a good man."

"Well, it takes one to know one."

Now Hal was nervous. This was a fucked-up situation, and all he wanted was to get out of it—to get Tony, LaTonya, whatever the fuck she wanted to call herself, out of his apartment. "So—you've brought a videotape for me."

"Yes. Emmett is very impressed with you. He says you're a very important person."

"Well," Hal said, trying to make a joke, "it takes one to know one."

"A senior vice-president. At the age of thirty-one."

"I've been very lucky."

"Lucky? You've prospered, Hal. You've flourished."

Hal cleared his throat, stared at the floor. What did this woman want from him? What could he do to get her to leave? "Not so," he said.

"Oh, yes, you have." LaTonya maintained her polite tone. "Ever since the last night we saw each other, everything has gone your way."

"Um, look, Tony—"

"Tony is dead. You're speaking to LaTonya."

"Okay, LaTonya—"

"Aren't you going to offer me a drink?" She pointed to Hal's half-empty bottle of beer on the coffee table.

Shit, thought Hal, what can I say to get her to leave? He decided to keep playing it casual. "Excuse me, LaTonya. I guess I was so surprised to see you, I didn't think to offer. What can I get for you?"

"How about a cup of tea? Please."

Hal rose and walked into the kitchen. "I'm not a big tea drinker myself, but I'll see what my girlfriend has in here." He raised his voice slightly so LaTonya could hear him in the living room. As he opened a cupboard, he heard LaTonya snap open her briefcase. Good. Maybe she would just give him the tape and get the hell out after she finished her tea. "You just make yourself at home," he called out. "Feel free to take off your coat and gloves." Standing over the sink, Hal began to fill a kettle with water. He sensed LaTonya walking up behind him.

"I'll keep 'em on, thanks," he heard her say, slipping back into her toneless voice.

Hal continued filling the kettle. Though he could feel LaTonya coming up on his shoulder, he did not want to turn around suddenly. He did not want to seem scared. Turning off the tap, he smelled something strange, a harsh, medicinal odor, jarring his olfactory nerves. He was just about to say, "What's that smell?" when he felt LaTonya's arm around his neck, felt her hand, still covered in a leather glove, now clutching a red-and-white bandana, slam into his face. The bandana was soaked in chloroform. Hal struggled to fight back as the stench and the taste of the chloroform filled his mouth and nostrils. He felt himself tumbling backward into LaTonya as he lost consciousness.

*   *   *

Hal smelled home: the aroma of something frying in his mom's kitchen in Philadelphia; the gristly scent of grease crackling in an iron pan. He could not open his eyes—or, rather, he did not want to. He was lying down on his back, barely conscious, enjoying the smell of home. Suddenly a blast of ammonia burned his nasal cavity. Leather knuckles rapped his cheeks. His eyes opened and he was distressed to learn that he was not in his boyhood home but in the shadowy bedroom of his Park Slope apartment. He tried to open his mouth but found his lips sealed with duct tape. His arms were above his head, his wrists locked in handcuffs that had been looped around two of the eight smooth oak bars that composed the headboard of the bed Hal had shared with Corky for twenty-one months. Hal looked down and saw his ankles bound by heavy lengths of rope. The ropes were tied to the two oak posts at the foot of the bed. Hal noticed, grimly, that he was completely naked.

The only light in the bedroom came from the street lamp outside the half-open blinds of the window. He turned his head and saw LaTonya sitting in a chair beside the bed. His eyes adjusting to the room's dim blue shadows, he could see that LaTonya still wore her trenchcoat and gloves. The big black briefcase lay open on the floor, but Hal, wriggling in the handcuffs, could not tilt his head enough to see what might be inside. Craning his neck some more, he saw another chair beside LaTonya. And he saw the edge of a large, rectangular metal plate that Corky used to place hot pots and pans atop on those extremely rare occasions when she cooked dinner. The metal plate sat on top of the chair beside LaTonya, and sitting on top of the heavy metal plate was a very heavy-looking black iron frying pan filled to the brim with Crisco cooking oil, spewing clouds of greasy smoke, crackling madly.

"How you like it, Hal?" LaTonya growled.

"Mgmfpfffmghhhfff," Hal heard himself say through the duct tape. He was trying to talk nice to LaTonya. What else could he do?

"How you like it?" LaTonya said. "Helpless. Can't get away. How you like it, Uncle Daddy?"

"Mmmfffghhff."

"Why you watch Tony die like that, Hal? You remember that night? Don't lie now. 'Cause I *know* you remember. Did you enjoy yourself? I coulda nailed your ass, you know that? Tony shattered and died. I lost my youth. But you. Look at you! Mistuh Big Executive. Got the nice apartment. Got the fancy clothes. Got the white girlfriend. You stood there and watched Tony die. And ever since, you prospered. You flourished!"

Finally Hal stopped struggling, stopped twisting his rope-bound ankles, stopped wriggling his wrists in the handcuffs, stopped mumbling against the duct tape. He simply lay still, stared at LaTonya's silhouette, and listened. He could see, in his mind's eye, Tony Dawson slumping to the grass at Smegma House, letting go that sound, the pure agony in her moan. He felt the compassion he should have felt that night. And he felt sick with shame.

"You never paid for what happened to Tony," LaTonya said. "When I think about what happened to her, I just hate you so much. When I think of the pain you caused me and how you never felt it, I just wanna make you suffer. I wanna make you suffer so bad."

The grease crackled furiously in the iron frying pan. Hal was consumed by shame. He felt tears sting his eyes—but he didn't know if they were the result of his shame or the smoke from the crackling Crisco.

"So tonight I'm gonna make you suffer. I'm gonna burn the shit outta you. I brought my best skillet, specially for the occasion. You know how hot this grease is? You gonna be one extra-crispy nigga before this night is through. How you like me now, Uncle Daddy?"

Uncle Daddy? That was the second time she had said that. What the fuck was she talking about?

"Then I'm gonna cut your dick off and shove it down your throat." LaTonya reached into her briefcase and held up something for Hal to see. He could just make out the shape in the shadows, the blade of the meat cleaver. LaTonya held the meat cleaver in her right hand, poised directly over Hal's flaccid penis. Hal did not move a muscle. "I'm gonna Bobbitize you, motherfucker. Then I'm gonna ram that dick down your throat. And you know what? That's too good for you!"

Hal was praying now, praying that this was some weird nightmare he was having. He whimpered through the duct tape. "Mmmgghhffmm."

LaTonya smiled malevolently. She placed the meat cleaver on the floor. With her left hand, she took hold of a corner of the duct tape that covered Hal's mouth. "I'm gonna take off this gag now. I'm gonna give you a chance to say something for yourself. But don't you try to scream for help or I'll just start choppin'! You dig? I'm gonna let you speak your last words. Just don't tell me you're innocent."

Hal nodded. LaTonya ripped the tape from his mouth. He felt a tear roll down his face. "LaTonya," he whispered, "I . . . I . . . didn't . . . do . . . anything."

"Don't you tell me you didn't do anything!" LaTonya hissed. In one swift, fluid motion, she grabbed the frying pan filled with crackling hot grease with both gloved hands and leapt from her chair, screaming, "Don't you tell me you didn't do anything!"

"That's my sin!" Hal shouted. "That's my sin! I should have done something!"

LaTonya had fully risen from the chair now, clutching the frying pan in both hands. She was in mid-swing, in the midst of the gesture of tossing the pan full of scalding Crisco all over Hal's naked body, when, hearing his cry, she abruptly stopped—but not before one large, tear-shaped globule of grease flew from the skillet. LaTonya froze, leaning forward slightly, the frying pan suspended over the edge of the bed, held aloft in her glove-clad hands. The single sizzling globule of grease landed dead center in Hal's solar plexus. Writhing and violently grinding his teeth to keep from screaming, Hal felt as if the globule were burning a little hole straight through him.

"That's my sin," Hal said again, through clenched teeth. "I should have done something! And I didn't!" The pain began to subside. Hal stopped writhing. LaTonya stood over him, frying pan suspended in her hands. Hal spoke as calmly as he could. "I should have . . . intervened. But I didn't. It was terrible what happened to you, Tony. I should have tried to stop it. But I was drunk. And I was stupid. And I was eighteen years old. Maybe that's no excuse. But I am so sorry . . . I am really . . . really . . . sorry."

At that moment the demon died. There was no shattering, no pain. The demon simply dissolved, evaporated, passed away. And LaTonya found herself standing in this strange room, holding this heavy frying pan, feeling as if she had just emerged from a trance and, at the same time, feeling more whole, more real than she had ever felt before. Staring down at this naked, frightened man, she could see little Tony, trapped in her bed with Uncle Daddy atop her, she could see Tony tied to that tree at Smegma House, the white boy pounding into her, she could see Grandy, beating her. And she knew she did not want to be, could not make herself be, like her attackers. Staring down at this pathetic man, this helpless, naked person begging her forgiveness, filled with the abject spirit of atonement, saying something that no one had ever, in thirty-one years, said to her, LaTonya finally felt free. The demon was dead—but LaTonya lived! And this man beneath her might be a coward, he might be a fool, but he was no longer her enemy.

For a long time, LaTonya continued to stand above him, swaying slightly, the pan of grease still crackling. Then, very slowly, carefully, LaTonya lowered the frying pan, placing it back on top of the metal plate on the chair. She placed another strip of duct tape over Hal's mouth. Then LaTonya leaned down, putting her face close to Hal's, and said, tonelessly, "Apology accepted." She stood upright, turned as if to leave, then whirled around again, thrusting a glove-clad finger in Hal's face and yelling: "BUT DON'T FUCK UP AGAIN!"

The next thing Hal knew, the chloroform-soaked bandana was back in his face. He awoke many hours later, the sun streaming through the half-open blinds. He was still naked on top of the bed. But there were no handcuffs on his wrists, no duct tape on his mouth, no ropes around his ankles; no chairs, no frying pan, no meat cleaver; no sign of LaTonya Mercy at all. Were it not for the smell of Crisco hanging in the air, the entire incident might have been a gruesome hallucination.

*   *   *

Driving home late Monday night, guiding his car down the winding roads of this neighborhood he loved, this enclave of Hallisbury's black elite, Dr. Emmett Mercy was thinking, even more obsessively than usual, about his future. He knew he was going to have to get rid of LaTonya. Gladys Gable was his woman now. But he would have to let LaTonya down easy. He could see what a dangerously unstable person she was. For a while, he had thought he might stay with her until she was finished with *The Destiny of Our People*. Now Emmett wondered if his wife was really working on the book at all or simply banging down crazily on the keys of the computer in the writing room. Emmett would have to insist that she turn the manuscript over to him so he could find a publisher. He would still allow her to have the "as told to" credit on the jacket. He could afford to be that magnanimous. But he was keeping the house. Other assets he would consider splitting more or less evenly—but the house was *his*.

Emmett smelled the smoke before he saw it. Once he spotted the black clouds billowing above the trees, spreading across the midnight sky, he immediately told himself it could not be *his* house on fire. Even as he bolted from his car, running madly around his house—which was now one giant ball of orange flames—screaming his lungs out, helplessly, flailing his arms, Emmett could not believe this was happening. He did not think of LaTonya until he saw her standing at the far end of the driveway, leaning against the hood of the station wagon—their second car—her arms folded against her chest. Emmett ran toward her, shrieking, "What happened? What happened?"

LaTonya just stood there, in her beige trenchcoat, staring impassively at the burning house. Then she said, barely loud enough for Emmett to hear, "This is just my way of asking for a divorce."

Emmett dropped to his knees, howling. "You crazy bitch! You crazy fucking bitch!"

"Don't worry," LaTonya said. "I rescued the manuscript."

"You crazy fucking bitch! You crazy fucking bitch!"

As Emmett screamed and pounded his fists on the gravel driveway, LaTonya calmly got into the station wagon and took off.

*   *   *

Walker knew when Sadie called Tuesday morning and suggested they get together for lunch that their relationship was over. A public place in the middle of the day. Perfect for a breakup conversation. One couldn't get too angry or tearful in a restaurant. And afterward there would be no temptation to sleep together since Sadie would have to get back to the office. Walker was relieved. By the time their plane had touched down in New York three weeks earlier, he sensed that the renaissance of their love was doomed. But the relationship wouldn't be over until Sadie decided it was over. Obviously she had made up her mind.

As he prepared for lunch that Tuesday, Walker wondered where he would live next. He felt out of sync with the United States and he still had oodles of money to burn. London? Paris? The Caribbean? Or back to the land of windmills and legal marijuana? He missed Amsterdam. But if he went back, Eva would probably still be there. And he did not want to see her. It would be too painful. It would make him too angry. What about Prague? He'd never been there before. Or maybe he would stay in America. Walker was actually feeling fairly optimistic about the country that morning. In a few hours, the O.J. Simpson jury would announce its verdict and Walker assumed it would be "guilty." He found this reassuring. It meant that despite the possibility that the police had planted evidence, the jurors realized O.J. was the only person who would have, could have, and in fact did kill his ex-wife and her friend. That a predominantly black jury would convict a black celebrity like O.J. seemed, to Walker, an encouraging harbinger of racial reconciliation.

When Walker arrived at Ancestors at twelve forty-five, the restaurant was packed. Clusters of well-dressed buppies gathered around every television in the joint, waiting for the verdict. Sadie apologized when Walker finally made his way through the crowd to her table. "I thought we'd have more privacy," Sadie said. "I must be the only person in the country who forgot what was happening today."

"Nice place," Walker said. "However"—he pointed to the large portrait on the wall behind Sadie—"my worst Robeson is better than that one." Sadie's eyes looked sadder than Walker had ever seen them. He tried to make a joke. "What's the matter? You depressed about O.J.?"

Sadie smiled wanly. "I'm depressed about *us*. As for O.J., well, let's wait and see."

"Okay, but I promise not to gloat when they convict his ass." Walker grinned. Sadie shook her head reproachfully and picked up her menu. Walker noticed that since he had sat down at the table, Sadie had avoided eye contact with him. They gave the waiter their orders, then sat in silence as the crowd around them buzzed. Finally Walker said, "I know what you're thinking."

Now Sadie looked directly at Walker. Her eyes were filled with tears. "Do you?" she said plaintively.

"Here we go, everybody!" someone yelled.

The crowd suddenly went quiet as the volume on every television in the place was cranked up. Walker and Sadie stared at a TV that hung from the ceiling in the corner nearest to them. There on the screen was O.J., standing in the Los Angeles courtroom, facing the jury. Walker heard the voice of the court official who was about to read the verdict. He tried to suppress a smile, thinking how coura- geous it was for the black members of this jury to resist the ties of blood and skin for the sake of justice. Then he heard the court offi- cial say the word "Not . . ."

Walker was lost in an explosion of sound and movement: ecsta- tic screams, leaping bodies, joyous whoof-whoof-whoofs, arm- twirling, palm-smacking high fives, piercing cries, couples reeling as they embraced. Walker remained in his seat, stunned. He looked up at Sadie, who was standing, both fists thrust in the air, wailing in exultation. Walker noticed a woman through the swirling crowd—a dark-skinned woman who wore a kente-patterned outfit and African headdress—sitting across the room, looking as baffled as he must have looked. He and the woman locked eyes. She shook her head sadly and shrugged. Walker did the same. Next thing he knew, Sadie was shaking his shoulders, yelling in his face, beaming. With the cheers of four hundred other people ringing in his head, he didn't hear a word Sadie screamed at him. Soon the pandemonium sub- sided, but Ancestors was still in a New Year's Eve party mode. Friends of Sadie's converged on their table, babbling excitedly. Peo-

ple were ordering champagne. "We won!" Walker heard several people shout. "We won!"

Walker knew that he and Sadie would not be having their
breakup conversation now. Sadie was surrounded by friends, and
friends of friends, celebrating. Walker left a fifty-dollar bill on the
table for their lunch, then slipped away without Sadie noticing.

Two hours later, he lay on the couch in his apartment, wondering
why he felt so sickened. If he had been on the jury, he would have
voted to acquit. That was what he believed. But the reality of O.J.'s
acquittal was a shock. Because he was sure O.J. had killed those people. He was glad that the racist cop had been unable to get away with
framing O.J. But he certainly didn't feel like celebrating the vindica-
tion of a man who was, at the very least, a wife-beater. At the same
time, he did not feel outraged by the verdict. Right now he just felt
like throwing up.

The downstairs buzzer sounded, giving Walker a start. He wondered if, perhaps, Sadie had come by for their breakup conversation.
"Hello," he said into the intercom.

"Oh, Lord, won'tcha buy me a col-ore tee-vee . . ."

He recognized it immediately, that raspy Scandinavian accent
twanging awkwardly as it imitated Janis Joplin. Eva Thule was in the
lobby of his building.

17

4 May 1997

Dear Frosty,

Well, it's been twenty months since I returned to the evil empire, and I have to say, it ain't so bad if you don't watch TV. Seattle is a good place for me to be workwise: plenty of opportunities for freelancers who know something about computer graphics. I'm still working on my Robeson project, only now I'm doing it as a CD-ROM. I miss Amsterdam a lot. Sometimes I miss New York. But Seattle is where Eva wants to be, and as far as I'm concerned, home is wherever Eva is. She loves it here, loves America in general. "Truly, this is the New World," she says. "New, new, new! Everything new! The people even like to say the word *new!*" Eva's going to college part-time but devotes most of her energy to fixing up our new house and being pregnant. That's right. The baby is due in another six weeks. I'm still a bit freaked out by the whole concept of fatherhood. On the other hand, marriage has been a hell of a lot more fun than I ever anticipated, so maybe I'll be pleasantly surprised again. If I love the child half as much as I love Eva, everything should be all right. Right?

Walker set down his pen and took a sip of his cappuccino. He still couldn't get used to sitting in a coffee shop and *not* smoking marijuana. This section of Seattle had at least one coffee shop on every block, each of them serving innumerable varieties of latte but not one offering a drug menu or a slice of chocolate hash cake. Just as well, he told himself. Eva had not inhaled grass or tobacco since she learned of her pregnancy, and she persuaded Walker to drastically scale back his pot consumption. Sometimes he teased Eva that he would move to California, where you could now legally purchase dope so long as you had a doctor's prescription. "I'm sure I could find an M.D. who would hook me up," Walker joked. Eva was not amused. Walker doubted she would ever go back to smoking. Maybe, he thought, it was time for him to give it up, too. Then again, maybe not.

Through the window of the coffee shop, Walker saw his wife waddling merrily down the sidewalk, carrying a bag packed with fresh vegetables from the farmer's market. Eva was immense with child. The pregnancy had changed her face, too. Much of the old radiance, the conventional beauty, was gone. She seemed much more pale than she had in Amsterdam. To Walker's eyes, Eva looked a bit, well, doughy. "I'm losing my looks," Eva said, staring into the bathroom mirror one morning. Her voice sounded almost giddy. She turned to Walker, beaming. "I'm losing my looks!" she trilled, as if she had been granted her fondest wish. Eva threw her arms around her husband, giggling uncontrollably. "Yippee! I'm losing my looks!"

Walker folded up his unfinished letter, tucked it in his jacket pocket, and went out to the street to meet Eva. As they walked to the nearby parking lot, Eva prattled gleefully about decorations for the baby's room. They climbed into the jeep and Walker helped Eva strap the seat belt across her massive girth. He gently rested his palm on the warm mound of her belly and smiled. Eva continued to babble about all the stores they needed to visit, all the things they needed to buy. Finally she stopped and noticed the curious grin on her husband's face. "What do you think of, Wocker?"

"I was just thinking how much I love you."

"Acch! You were thinking, Eva has become a Nice American Girl. Weren't you?"

"I just want to make you happy." Walker looked into his wife's eyes. "That's what I want to ask you. Are you happy?"

Eva, smiling serenely at her husband, replied, "I have what I want."

* * *

"Kill your master!" LaTonya cried, and the women in the bookstore cheered. "Kill your master!" she shouted exultantly, loving the sound of her own voice. There were no other voices in her head anymore. Only her own. Because she knew who she was. And the women in the audience loved her for who she was. They cherished her voice. She could see the love in their eyes as they gazed at her, standing proud and tall at the lectern, beside a long table stacked high with copies of her manifesto, currently in its eighth printing, with 400,000 units sold: *The Book of LaTonya: One Black Woman's Journey from Enslavement to Empowerment.* She no longer had any use for last names, diminutives, protective demons, antipsychotic medication, or fragmented consciousness. She was simply LaTonya. And people loved her for it.

"Maybe your master is a man," LaTonya said, "who exploits and humiliates you." The audience began to applaud, but LaTonya held up her hand to stop them. "Or maybe your master is a woman. A woman who wants you to feel worthless—who wants to make you feel like you're a piece of garbage! Or maybe your master is an idea.

Some idea that's been imposed on you. Maybe your master is beauty—some twisted notion of what you're supposed to look like. Ideas can be the cruelest masters of all. But you cannot allow yourself to be enslaved. Kill your master—and burn that plantation down!"

The audience was on its feet now, clapping ecstatically. The bookstore crowd was mostly made up of sisters, but there was a healthy portion of white women present as well. LaTonya had seen this everywhere on her nationwide book tour: white women who were as attracted to her message as black women were. "Burn it down!" LaTonya wailed. "Burn it down to the ground!"

There was only one man in the audience at this Manhattan bookstore. He stood clapping and smiling, a look of inexpressible pride and affection on his face. It was LaTonya's husband, Chester Beer.

As the ovation died down, LaTonya continued, in a calmer tone. "Now, y'all know—at least I *hope* you know—that I'm not urging you to actually kill anybody. I ain't talkin' about settin' no real fires. I do not advocate physical violence. But I want you to be violent in your conviction. You gots to be fierce and ruthless and brutal in your faith—your faith in *you!*"

LaTonya autographed so many books that night, her hand ached. Standing discreetly behind his wife, Chester watched as women came up to LaTonya, hugging her, praising her, thanking her for writing this book. Some women had tears in their eyes. Others said they felt that LaTonya had been able to read their minds. After the signing, Chester drove them back to the cozy apartment they shared in the old town section of Hallisbury. As they cuddled in bed, Chester said, "They must wonder why you're with me."

"What?" LaTonya asked. "Who?"

"Your fans. You're famous, honey. You write best-selling books. You appear on television. Hillary Clinton invites you to the White

House to ask your advice on big issues. You're a glamorous figure. People must wonder why a beautiful woman like you is with an old man like me."

LaTonya smacked Chester, in playful admonishment, on the chest. "Don't be silly."

"I'm not being silly. I'm serious. People must wonder why you would choose me."

"You're talking about strangers, Chester. They don't know what exists between us."

"Yes, but on a purely cosmetic level, people must consider us a mismatch."

"Then those people are fools," LaTonya said. "Because they don't understand the first law of attraction."

"Which is?"

"There's no accounting for taste."

*   *   *

Tiny Jenks felt sorry for Dr. Emmett Mercy. It had been at least two years since he'd talked to the author of *Blactualization,* but Tiny had heard that Dr. Mercy had fallen on hard times. The brother's house had burned down, his wife had divorced him, and he had yet to publish his second book. Tiny could hear a certain desperation in Dr. Mercy's voice when he called one night in May 1997, pleading with Tiny to come to an Amandla workshop. Dr. Mercy explained that he'd had to suspend the workshops for a while—"It was just a brief hiatus of about twenty-four months"—but he was ready to resume. Several times during their phone conversation, Tiny said he wouldn't be able to make it. He and Deirdre had a three-month-old baby boy, and all Tiny's "free" time was consumed by taking care of his son. Dr. Mercy, however, would not take no for an answer. "Please,

Brother Tiny, can't you come to just one meeting?" Finally, out of
pity, Tiny gave in.

The new Amandla workshop did not take place in Manhattan
but in a church basement in a remote, nondescript section of Queens.
And Tiny was the sole participant. "I was expecting ten or twelve
brothers," Dr. Mercy said unconvincingly. "Who knows? Maybe they
got lost. This place is kinda hard to find." Dr. Mercy seemed jittery,
distracted. He talked vaguely about new projects he was working on.
He told Tiny that royalties on *Blactualization* had dried up. Dr.
Mercy was now living in Queens, struggling to make ends meet. He
also seemed lonely, desperate to find another mate. "If you could
introduce me to any young sisters you know, Brother Tiny, I'd surely
appreciate it." The conversation meandered awhile, Dr. Mercy telling
of his blues, Tiny responding with sympathetic words of encourage-
ment. "You know what I would really like to do?" Dr. Mercy said.
"I'd love to organize another Million Man March."

"Were you at the first?" Tiny asked.

"Naw, man. That was just two weeks after my house got all
burnt up. I was tied up with Jew lawyers and insurance agents. I
couldn't make it. I was scheduled to give a speech there, too. Did
you go?"

"Oh, yeah," Tiny said in his soft but sharp voice. Dr. Mercy
noticed a dreamy look in Tiny's crossed eyes. "It was really something. Being surrounded by so many brothers like that. The spirit that
day, the sense of mutual respect, the simple gestures of courtesy—it
was beautiful. One man had brought his baby son, in a stroller. You
should have seen the way the crowd parted to let that man push his
way through. At one point two brothers lit up a joint and, immediately, all the men around them started complaining. So the brothers
apologized and stubbed it out. And you know something? After the
march, I was certain that white folks—I mean, strangers, shopkeep-

ers, service people, pedestrians—they were more polite to me. I mean, noticeably more polite. It was like we—black men—had shown so much respect for ourselves that they had to respect us now, too."

"Wow," Dr. Mercy sighed. "And what about the speeches? What did you think about what Jesse Jackson had to say? Or Minister Farrakhan?"

"You know, it's a funny thing. I was at the march all day. I remember how great it felt. I remember conversations I had with brothers I met there. But I can't remember a single word from any of the speeches. I don't think anybody was really listening to the rhetoric. I guess *I* wasn't, anyway. Somehow that wasn't the point."

The Amandla workshop was scheduled to last until eight o'clock, but Tiny Jenks, explaining that he had to get back home to his wife and kid, rose to leave fifteen minutes early. As he walked Tiny to the door, Dr. Mercy asked, "Are you still in touch with Brother Hardaway?"

"Of course," Tiny said. "I'll be seeing him this weekend. Hal got married, you know."

"To the white girl?"

"Naw. He married a sister. Actually, his wife was the former girlfriend of . . . well, it's too complicated to get into."

"And he's still working at Burnish Enterprises?"

"Oh, yeah. He's doing great. Godfrey Burnish is going to retire when he turns eighty in a couple of years. Hal might very well take over the company."

"You don't say." Dr. Emmett Mercy began to stroke his sideburns. "Maybe I should give Brother Hal a call. He and I discussed a project together back in 'ninety-five. But then my house got all burnt up and I got divorced and whatnot. I never got back in touch with him. . . . I was too embarrassed."

Tiny looked puzzled. "Embarrassed. What for?"

"Never mind."

Dr. Mercy seemed worried. Tiny gave him a reassuring smile and a pat on the back. "Call him," he said in his Boy Jesus voice. "I'm sure he'd love to talk to you about any of your projects. Brothers gotta stick together. Right?"

*   *   *

It was a glorious May afternoon in Amsterdam, with the sun shimmering on the waters of the canals. Corky Winterset—dressed in a T-shirt, ratty old sweater, blue jeans, and sneakers, knapsack slung over her shoulder—was in such an outrageously good mood, she practically skipped along the cobblestones. A curious thought occurred to Corky: the idea that, in just the past four months, she had finally become herself. On December 31, 1996, she ended the third and final year of her clerkship with Judge Judith Proctor. On January 2, 1997, she donated all her lawyer clothes to the Salvation Army, and the following day, she flew to Paris. Then she made her way to Sarajevo, where she wrote an article on how the city was recovering from its state of siege. Corky was thrilled when a British magazine bought the piece. Sure, one might dismiss what she had written as a travel piece—but it was a *serious* travel piece, for serious readers. Corky's new career was off to a promising start.

Corky had been in Amsterdam for three weeks. It was Walker Du Pree who had recommended the city to her—one she had never visited before. She had phoned Walker back in January of '96. They met one Sunday afternoon for coffee in Greenwich Village. Corky was nervous but hopeful that day. Hal Hardaway had dumped her and Sadie Broom had dumped Walker. Somehow it made sense to Corky that she and Walker should get together. The symmetry of it would be perfect. First she would apologize for not having had the sense to go out with him back at Craven U. She was certain Walker would invite her back to his apartment, where they would, at long last, make love. When she arrived at the café, Walker seemed ecstatic. Corky assumed he had been even more eager to meet than she. Then Walker told her he had just gotten married and was planning to move to Seattle in the spring. His wife was a Finn he'd met in Amsterdam. Walker was so obviously thrilled, Corky thought it would be rude to show her disappointment. Still, it was good to see her old friend. The easy rapport between them had not changed. Corky told Walker that she planned to travel when her clerkship ended in a year's time. Walker said she *had* to go to Amsterdam. And when she did, she *had* to look up his friend Martin Frost.

"Hello, my sweet," Frosty said to Corky. He was sitting at one of Kaffeteria's outdoor tables. Corky had seen him smile when he spotted her coming across the Leidseplein. Corky gave Frosty a long, sensuous kiss, then sat across from him at the table. They had only slept together three times, but Corky was already falling in love.

"Isn't it a beautiful day?" Corky said.

"Ah, yes," Frosty said. "Sunny Amsterdam."

"This could be a nice place to settle down. Don't you think?"

Frosty frowned. "I don't really think that way. I've been in Amsterdam a few years now. Maybe it's time to move on." Frosty could see the sudden disappointment in his young lover's eyes. "I told you, baby, I'm a travelin' man."

Corky smiled. "All right," she said. "So where are we going?"

*   *   *

Sadie Broom made her deadline. In May 1996, she showed up at her Craven University tenth class reunion with a fiancé on her arm and a huge-ass rock on the third finger of her left hand. That the fiancé was

Hal Hardaway, the prettiest nigger in the Class of '86, made her situation all the sweeter. Sadie was cool about it, though. She did not
gloat—at least not visibly. Yet she could not help but take a certain
cruel pleasure in the fates of the serious divas: Miranda, still single,
desperately man-hungry; Cassandra, divorced with a bratty five-year-
old and a deadbeat ex-husband who constantly stiffed her on child-
support payments; Diandra, unhappily married to a fat, boring loser;
and Alexandra, still single, desperately man-hungry. Both Walker Du
Pree and Corky Winterset were conspicuously absent from the
reunion.

The wedding took place in Washington, D.C., in October 1996,
close to one year from the day Hal and Sadie ran into each other at
Ancestors restaurant. Sadie's older sister, Victoria, the gorgeous,
charismatic one, who, at thirty-six, was lonely and unmarried, served
as the maid of honor. Tiny Jenks was the best man. Sadie and Hal
honeymooned in Paris, and for the first time, Sadie had been able to
recognize the awesome beauty of the city.

By May of 1997, Sadie and Hal were settling into the grand
apartment they had bought on Prospect Park West, the Gold Coast
of Park Slope. One lovely Sunday afternoon, they entertained Tiny,
his wife, Deirdre, and their three-month-old baby boy for brunch.
Deirdre went on, as she usually did, about astrology. "Uranus and
Neptune are still in orb of each other," she said importantly, though
no one, except maybe Tiny, knew what the hell she was talking
about. "They won't be more than ten degrees apart until about this
time next year. So the conjunction is still having an effect on us all.
Of course, things are calmer than they were at the height of the conjunction. But just wait till 1999 and the year 2000. We've got some
amazing planetary activity in store then. So hold on to your hats."

Sadie, Hal, and Tiny barely listened to Deirdre. They were all
staring, mesmerized, at the baby as he gurgled and squirmed con-

tentedly on the couch. "It's wild," Tiny said. "They don't do much at this age, yet you can't take your eyes off them." He looked up at Hal and Sadie and smiled. "Y'all should get yourselves one of these."

"We're working on it," Hal said, giving his wife an affectionate wink. Sadie had not yet told her husband that her period was already two weeks late.

*   *   *

Tiny, Deirdre, and child left Hal and Sadie's apartment at four o'clock that Sunday afternoon. Deirdre suggested they take the subway back to their place in Fort Greene, but Tiny insisted they catch a cab.

"But we're so close to home already," Deirdre said.

"Exactly," Tiny replied. "So a taxi won't cost us too much."

Before Deirdre could protest, Tiny flagged a taxi and they climbed into the backseat. Tiny recognized the driver immediately. He wore the same darkly tinted glasses, the same leather jacket. His head was just as clean-shaven as it had been more than two and a half years ago—as smooth as a humongous brown egg. And his neutral expression as he sat behind the wheel of his taxi was a menacing scowl. Tiny leaned forward to catch a glimpse of the driver's ID card, which hung on the dashboard. Yep. It was Jojo Harrison. Tiny slid down in his seat, hoping the madman of the Amandla workshop would not recognize him. He certainly didn't want this lunatic railing about niggas and bitches and having his asshole licked in front of Deirdre and their son. Fortunately, they did not have far to drive. But Tiny could see Jojo peering into the wide rearview mirror. Finally Jojo's face split into a jack-o'-lantern grin. "Yo," he exclaimed, "little man!"

"Hi," Tiny said.

"Don't you remember me?"

"Yes, I do."

"Well, how y'all doin'?"

"Fine, thanks. This is my wife, Deirdre. Deirdre, meet Jojo Harrison."

"Hello," Deirdre said warily.

"Good afternoon, ma'am. I see you got a li'l baby in your lap."

"That's right," Tiny and Deirdre said in unison.

"What's the name?"

"Orlando," Tiny said.

"That's a big name for such a li'l person!" Jojo let out a booming laugh. But it was a laugh full of generosity, of goodwill. "I just hope he grows up to be a proud, strong black man like his daddy."

Tiny, taken aback, said, "Thank you."

"You got yourself a fine husband, ma'am," Jojo said to Deirdre. "It just makes me so happy to see a young black family just startin' out in the world. I can't tell you how happy that makes me!"

Tiny wondered for a moment if Jojo was mocking them, but he quickly dismissed the notion. Jojo's joy was obviously genuine.

The taxi pulled up to Tiny and Deirdre's building. Tiny reached for his wallet, but Jojo cleared the meter before he could pay. "Hey," Jojo said, still grinning joyfully, "it's on me."

"Are you sure?"

"Y'all have a nice Sunday. You're beautiful. Just beautiful. God bless you. And God bless your family."

As the cab pulled away from the curb, Deirdre said to Tiny, "Is that who I think it was? From Amandla?"

"Yes," Tiny said, staring at the taxi as it disappeared down the street.

Once they got upstairs, Deirdre took a nap. Tiny, meanwhile, paced around the living room, cradling Orlando in his arms. And he wondered: How could that taxi driver be the same man who blew up at the Amandla workshop? Surely this made no sense. Had Jojo Harrison undergone some life-altering transformation? Or maybe he had just been putting on a show at the workshop back in September '94? Or maybe he had just been putting on a show in his taxi? Or maybe both personalities existed in the man? Was such a thing possible? Utter contempt and unabashed affection—at such extreme levels. Was Jojo Harrison just totally schizoid? Slowly the recognition of Tiny's own duality crept up on him. He knew how people perceived him: nice, cheerful Tiny, everybody's friend. But did anybody see his rage?

Orlando squirmed and gurgled in his father's arms. Tiny smiled at his son. "Someday you'll be a man," he said softly. "A black man . . . But there's just one thing I want you to be." Staring into the baby's eyes, Tiny imagined that on some level Orlando could understand him as he said: "Your *own* man."